CW01024432

# T
# BOX HILL
# KILLER

An absolutely gripping mystery and suspense thriller

# BIBA PEARCE

*Detective Rob Miller Mysteries Book 4*

JOFFE
BOOKS

Joffe Books, London
www.joffebooks.com

First published in Great Britain in 2021

This paperback edition was first published
in Great Britain in 2022

Cover art by Nebojša Zorić

ISBN: 978-1-80405-325-6

*For Jack*

# PROLOGUE

It was the perfect place to dump a body.

The woody terrain and dense bush made it impossible to see further than a few hundred metres along the road in daylight, let alone in pitch darkness. It was out of the way, accessible only by a series of dirt tracks. Popular with cyclists, but at this time of night, nobody was out for a scenic ride.

There were no houses nearby. Box Hill was in an Area of Outstanding Natural Beauty and therefore protected.

The killer stood in the clearing and inhaled. Earth, leaves, moss. An ideal canvas. Fitting, given the nature of the ritual.

The body was heavy, but then he was a fully grown man. Even heavier now the life had drained out of him. The killer positioned the body in the centre of the clearing. It required precision. He had to be laid out just right. Like the others.

Carefully, so as not to get it wrong, they spray-painted a white circle around the corpse. Protection and unity. It wasn't quite perfect, not with tufts of grass getting in the way, but it was close enough.

Next step, the pièce de résistance.

The killer took out a long kitchen knife, the kind used for cutting meat. They had sharpened the blade until it sang. Now it was ready to do its deadly work.

1

Straddling the body, the killer carved a five-pointed star into the victim's naked torso. It was slow, painstaking work. The open cuts glistened in the moonlight.

There was a lot of controversy about the inverted pentagram. Popular culture attributed it to devil worship and the occult, but it was never meant to be evil, and it didn't represent Satan. To early civilisations, it had represented the five elements: earth, air, fire, water and spirit. Since then, other esoteric groups had adopted the symbol and given it their own meaning. Balance and harmony. Male and female. Mercy and justice. It was believed to be most powerful in midsummer when the sun was at its highest.

The killer snorted. How ironic. This man was anything but powerful now.

In life, he'd been rich and successful. He'd given the illusion of having the perfect life, the perfect career, the perfect family — but it had all been a lie. He was rotten to the core.

The killer hated liars. He deserved to be punished.

Now his dark side had been extinguished. Offered back to the earth. Cleansed. Killing him was freedom — for them both.

The killer wiped the knife on a rag and stood back and surveyed their handiwork. *Perfect.*

The scriptures were right. It was grounding. Stabilizing. A form of rebirth. The killer hadn't felt this good in years.

Time for the final touches. Five candles positioned at each point. A guiding light, if you will. They were long, tapered dinner candles and would stay lit for hours.

The killer lit them using a box of matches from the glove compartment.

*There.* The scene was set. It was mesmerising — beautiful, even. Although not everyone would appreciate it.

The killer stared at the mutilated corpse for a moment longer, then turned away. A small creature rustled in the bushes. Shadowy trees stabbed the night sky. Somewhere in the distance, a fox cried out.

It was time to go.

# CHAPTER 1

*Twelve years ago*

Suzie Palmer peeled herself off the couch. She glanced at her phone. Nearly midnight. Noah had been gone for hours. It was time to start worrying.

"I'm doing fifty kilometres this evening," he'd told her when he'd left, a determined smile on his handsome, sun-tanned face. "Last big session before the race."

Fifty kilometres would take him two hours. Noah was fit. He trained regularly, usually doing shorter stints during the week and saving the longer rides for the weekend, but tonight was different. It was a flawless summer evening with not a breath of wind. The race was on Saturday, three days away, and he wanted to get in one last training ride.

It was dark now. The sun had eventually disappeared behind the red-brick houses and bushy treetops, enveloping everything in a thick, dark blanket.

She tried his mobile phone again, but it diverted straight to voicemail. The battery may have died by now.

She checked on the children. They were all sleeping soundly. Matthew was spread out like a starfish, Rebecca curled up in the foetal position and little Joey on his stomach, his dummy discarded on the mattress beside him.

Three kids under the age of seven. She often wondered how different her life would have been if she hadn't married Noah. An actress, her star on the rise. She'd gone from bit parts in local productions to walk-ons in bigger budget productions, and then a supporting role. She still remembered her utter joy when she'd got the call. The heart-thumping excitement of having actual lines to rehearse, of playing an active role. A professional actress.

She'd met Noah at a party in London. Charming, successful, handsome. He was everything she'd wanted in a man. Ticked all the right boxes. Soon, they were going out. He proposed and before she knew it, Matthew was born. Acting had taken a back seat. There were more important things in life, like being a mum.

Two years later, Rebecca came along, and then Joey two years after that. Perfectly timed. But then she was a planner. It was one of the things Noah loved about her.

"I can always count on you to remember things," he would tell her.

She ran their lives like clockwork. Nothing was left to chance. Even now, as she debated what to do. The children's school lunches were prepared, packed in Tupperware boxes, waiting to be placed into rucksacks for school in the morning. Except for Joey, of course. He was still too young for school.

Suzie stared out of the window into the pitch darkness. He'd been gone long enough. It was time to call the police. No, not the police. Sam. He'd know what to do.

She picked up her phone again and realised her hands were shaking. Once she made this call, she was admitting Noah was missing.

She scrolled through her contact list looking for Sam Lawrence's number. He was a police detective with the London Met. He had the sway to put things in motion.

"Hi, Sam. It's Suzie. I'm sorry to call so late . . . No, actually it's not. I'm worried about Noah. He hasn't come home yet. He went for a bike ride hours ago. He's training for this race on Saturday . . . He left just after five, I think . . . Okay, thanks."

Sam was there twenty minutes later.

Suzie opened the door and sagged in relief. "Oh, Sam. I'm so glad you're here. He's still not back. I'm getting frantic. I just know something's happened."

Sam put an arm around her. "Come on, let's sit down."

They went into the lounge, a spacious room with high ceilings, plush carpeting and walls painted in 'skimming stone' grey. A giant L-shaped sofa dominated one corner, while a matching armchair lent balance in the other. It was elegant and contemporary, and her favourite room in the house. She'd designed it herself after completing her interior design course several years ago.

On the wall was a huge flat-screen television that was permanently tuned to CBBC. It was off now, however, and instead, the calming tones of Classic FM played in the background.

Sam led her to the sofa. "How long has he been missing?" he asked. "You said he left at five?"

"Yes." Her eyes filled with tears. "That's over seven hours ago. Oh my God, Sam. Something's definitely happened to him. He must have had an accident or something."

Sam's forehead was furrowed. "It's possible. Have you tried ringing him?"

"Of course."

"Sorry, stupid question. Is it going straight to voicemail or ringing off?"

She gulped. "Straight to voicemail."

"Okay, we'll see if we can trace it anyway. I'm going to get a squad car to look for him. Do you know which way he went?"

"Sort of," she said. "He's training for the Ride London cycle race on Saturday. I think he was going through Kingston towards Esher and out toward the Surrey Hills, but I can't be sure."

"That's a fair distance."

"He wanted to do fifty kilometres tonight. He said it was the last big push before the race."

Sam raised a bushy eyebrow. "I didn't realise he was so dedicated. Okay, let me call this in. I won't be a moment. Perhaps you could make us a cup of tea?"

She nodded and got up.

From the kitchen she heard him ring 999 and report Noah Palmer missing. Sam had the kind of booming voice that carried. She hoped he wouldn't wake the children.

"I'm a personal friend of the family, I'd appreciate you getting somebody on this right away."

What would she do without Sam?

He came into the kitchen a short while later. "They've dispatched several squad cars to look for him."

"Thanks, Sam." She handed him a cup of tea. A little milk, no sugar. She knew how he liked it. They'd been friends ever since she'd met his wife, Diana, at the Chelsea Design Centre three years earlier. Even though there was at least ten years between them, they'd clicked straight away.

Sam and Noah had taken longer to warm to each other. Sam was a hardened police detective, rough around the edges and naturally suspicious, while Noah was a young, smooth-talking, champagne-swilling investment banker. Worlds apart. Yet Noah had managed to charm the gruff inspector and while they were never going to be best mates, they had a mutual respect for each other.

"We're also triangulating his mobile phone signal."

"I hope he's all right." She wrapped her hands around the mug. "And isn't lying by the roadside somewhere . . ."

"Don't think like that," he told her. "Noah is a fit, able cyclist. He'll be fine."

"Then why isn't he picking up?" Her voice wobbled.

"I don't know, Suzie, but try not to panic. It won't do any good."

"I know." She wrung her hands. "I can't help it. I keep thinking something awful has happened. This isn't like him at all."

An hour later and there was still no sign of Noah. His phone hadn't picked up any signal.

"I'll ring the hospitals," Sam murmured.

Suzie stifled a sob.

There were several large hospitals in the area where he could have been taken in the event of a road accident. Charing Cross or Chelsea and Westminster were the closest to home.

"He's not at either of those," Sam said. "I'll try Kingston since he was headed out that way."

Noah wasn't at any of the hospitals. The police officers hadn't spotted him along the route. "Would he have gone off-road at all?" Sam asked.

She could tell he was running out of ideas. "I don't think so. His bike isn't made for it."

Sam shook his head. "I'm sorry, Suzie. I don't know what to tell you. We'll keep looking. I'll let you know as soon as we find something."

She tried to put on a brave face. "Okay, Sam. Thanks for your help."

He hugged her. "Try to get some sleep."

She sniffed. "I'm not sure I'll be able to."

He gave a sympathetic grin. "You don't want to be a zombie tomorrow for the kids."

Suzie shut the door after him and sank back down on the sofa. She was too wired to sleep, still buzzing with nervous energy. She put the television on and watched a mindless documentary on predators in the wild. Eventually, she dozed off, her phone beside her, waiting for news.

* * *

Suzie woke to a loud ringing.

Her alarm?

No, it was the doorbell. She rolled off the couch and went to answer it.

"Hello?" Her voice was croaky from lack of sleep and she had to squint against the bright sunlight. A familiar figure stood silhouetted against the glare. "Sam, what are you doing here? Have they found something?"

"I think you'd better sit down, Suzie."

She froze. That was never good. She clutched his arm. "What is it? Tell me now."

"They've found Noah."

"Oh, thank God. Is he okay?"

"No, I'm sorry, Suzie. We found his body this morning on Box Hill. He's been murdered."

Suzie stared at him as the words registered.

Then she started screaming.

# CHAPTER 2

*Present day*

Rachel Norton entered the plush five-storey Harrods building and sighed. She loved it here. The shiny marble floors, the ambient lighting, the elaborate décor, and the warmth. It was freezing outside.

*COLDEST JANUARY IN A DECADE,* shouted the newspaper headlines in the *Metro*. She'd picked up a discarded copy on the Tube. She always read the newspaper. The *Metro* in the morning and the *Evening Standard* in the afternoon. Her teacher, Miss Hayes had told her knowing what was going on in the world was essential for those who wanted to be a part of it. And she did.

One day, she too would be able to shop here among the rich and famous. Her driver would drop her outside the front entrance and wait while she picked up dinner at the food hall on the ground floor, or a trinket from the fine jewellery room, or a sexy dress for a cocktail party that evening.

A woman in her thirties wafted past on a cloud of Chanel. Rachel closed her eyes and inhaled, then followed her through the luxurious Egyptian-themed room to the escalators. Wide-eyed pharaohs stared down at shoppers as they headed up and pillars stretched to the elaborate arched ceilings.

The woman took the escalator to the womenswear department. Rachel followed, lost in her fantasy world. She was a successful businesswoman, her clothing all designer brands. A chiffon Stella McCartney dress, Jimmy Choo stilettos, glittering Tiffany earrings and a Gucci bag slung over her shoulder.

The lady picked a tailored wool jacket off the Burberry rack and held it up against her gym-honed body. It went well with her glossy dark hair and red lipstick. She tried it on, parading up and down and doing a little spin. She smiled and took it to the till. Not once had she looked at the price.

The woman's mobile phone rang and she answered it with one hand, while she flashed her gold card with the other. "Hi, darling. I'll meet you in the Oyster Bar in fifteen."

Rachel was green with envy. *That* was the life she wanted. *One day*, she promised herself. *One day*.

She browsed the clothing for a while longer, then moved on to the accessories — scarves, hats and gloves in a dazzling array of colours and fabrics. She flexed her fingers, still rigid from the cold. A glance told her the sales assistant was at the other end of the department, so she slipped her mottled fingers into the soft, fur-lined leather and sighed. They were so fluffy.

Footsteps alerted her to the sales lady's return. Reluctantly, she took off the gloves and put them back on the rack.

"Do you want to try that on, dear?"

Rachel realised she was still holding a black T-shirt that she'd picked up in the clothing section. It was very rock chic with a silver skull on the front. It was the kind she'd seen celebs wear in *OK!*.

Why not? She may as well pretend . . .

"Yes, please."

"Follow me."

The lady led the way to a changing room that was bigger than Rachel's bedroom. It had a bench at the back and was surrounded by spotless mirrors. Not a smudge marred her shabby reflection.

The T-shirt fell to just above her knees. It was meant to be worn with tiny shorts or black leggings, but it didn't look too bad with her ripped jeans and trainers. The holes were from wear and tear, not because she'd bought them that way. But here, no one knew the difference. Rich people could wear anything and get away with it.

She wrapped a silk Hermès scarf that someone had left in the changing room around her neck and gazed at herself. A different person stared back at her. *That* girl was going places. *That* was the girl of her future.

She changed back into her own clothes, pulling on her ancient jacket. It really wasn't warm enough for this weather. Her mother had been promising to get her a new one for months, but it had yet to materialise. Rachel wasn't holding her breath. There were more important things to spend her benefit money on. Like gin. One thing Rachel knew with utmost certainty was that she would never turn out like her mother.

She fingered the soft scarf. What would it be like to own it, to feel the silky softness against her throat as she walked down the street? She took it off and folded it up in her hands. It was so thin, nobody would even know she had it. The security tag was on the label, so she gently ripped it off. Heart hammering, she stuffed it into the bottom of her rucksack. Eighty pounds for something that took up no space at all.

After exploring a few more floors, Rachel decided it was time to go home. She had work to do. Her GCSEs were coming up and she had to study if she wanted to go to sixth-form college. No way was she staying in that shithole of a flat with her mother for any longer than necessary.

She paid a pound to use the luxury toilets and after washing her hands, covered them with moisturiser, then spritzed herself with enough eau de toilette to make the other guests gasp.

She walked out of the building, a smile on her face. She'd done it. The scarf was buried inside her rucksack and nobody was the wiser. Piece of cake.

She crossed the road and had walked as far as the corner when four men on mopeds screeched to a halt beside her. She watched, bewildered as they rushed past her into a jewellery shop, still wearing their helmets and carrying metal rods in their hands.

Screams. Breaking glass. Men shouting.

Bloody hell! They were robbing the place. Right here in front of her, in broad daylight. Rachel stood frozen to the spot. What should she do?

With shaking hands, she pulled out her phone.

"No, you don't!" yelled a voice and an arm pulled her roughly into the store. She fell to her knees, wincing as the shattered glass tore into her skin.

"Ow! Let me go!"

The man grabbed her phone and pushed her into a corner. "Stay there!" He tossed the phone behind the counter, out of reach.

The four helmeted men were systematically crashing their way through the cabinets, scraping up rings, watches and necklaces and throwing them into bags.

Rachel drew her knees up and tried to make herself as inconspicuous as possible. A female customer whimpered beside her, while a fat man with a beard — who she assumed was the owner — cowered in the back corner.

A woman's voice from outside yelled. "It's a robbery. Someone call the police!"

Rachel wanted to move, to run, but the fourth man, the one who'd grabbed her off the pavement, was watching them. He also kept an eye on the door. Outside, a crowd had gathered.

Someone managed to flag down the police and two officers ran into the store, batons drawn. The fourth man let out a yell and stabbed one of the police officers in the gut.

Rachel screamed. The officer bent over, then toppled to the floor. She crawled towards him and pressed her hands against the wound.

"Why the fuck did you have to stab him?" she shouted at the knife-wielding thief.

He ignored her.

The other cop, realising he was outnumbered, retreated to wait for backup.

"Let's go!" yelled the fourth man.

The three others zipped up their rucksacks and scrambled over the broken glass and out into the street. Rachel thought perhaps she ought to do the same. Soon, the place would be crawling with cops, and she had a stolen scarf in her rucksack.

She got to her feet and ran out after them, only to find herself surrounded by armed police officers all pointing rifles at her. The only consolation was that the four robbers were in the circle with her.

The police shouted for them to get down on the ground. She didn't move. Time seemed to slow down. They couldn't mean her, could they?

A hand shoved her down onto the tarmac and pulled her arms behind her back. Before she could utter a sound, she was in handcuffs.

"This is a mistake," she tried to tell them, but nobody heard her among the chaos.

Tears sprung into her eyes. Her nice day ruined, just because this lousy lot decided to rob a jewellery store on Brompton Road. What were the chances? Now she'd be late home and wouldn't get a chance to study.

She was bundled into a waiting police car. There was a policewoman in the driver's seat wearing a bullet-proof vest. It smelled of stale hamburgers and greasy chips. The radio crackled and urgent voices gave updates.

Rachel peered out of the steamed-up windows at the crowds on the pavement. Most were rushing towards the Tube station, eager to get out of the cold. Some stopped to watch, to point at the glass on the street and the convoy of police vehicles.

It was warm in here. Too warm. She was breaking a sweat, and her knees hurt from the glass. She glanced down and saw her hands were covered with blood. The policeman's blood. Would he be okay?

"Where are we going?" she asked.

"Police station, love," said the woman, glancing in the rear-view mirror. "You've been nicked."

# CHAPTER 3

"How many times do I have to tell you, I had nothing to do with it."

Rachel sank onto the stained bench in the holding cell and fought back the tears. Why wouldn't they believe her? Why didn't they say anything? She had no idea what was going on.

She'd been interviewed by a police detective, a solemn man with an ugly moustache, who'd asked her a ton of questions but gave no response to her answers.

*I don't know those men.*

*I was phoning the police when he grabbed me.*

*I tried to help him.*

*I swear, I had nothing to do with it.*

Eventually, she was allowed to wash and change into a badly fitting tracksuit they'd given her. They'd taken her other clothes, which were covered in blood, and sealed them in a plastic bag. She hoped she'd get them back. That was her only warm jacket.

A first-aider came and inspected her knees, dabbed them with antiseptic and put a large plaster over each one. At least they didn't sting anymore. She'd asked Rachel for a DNA swab. Rachel hadn't known what that was, but she'd rubbed a cotton bud on the side of her mouth and put that in a plastic tube too.

"Can I go now?" she'd asked.

"Not quite yet."

A niggling feeling in her stomach told her something wasn't right. Surely they believed her, didn't they?

A lump formed in her throat as she glanced around the small, concrete room. It was stuffy and it smelled like the subway behind her block of flats. This was a place for real criminals. Burglars, thieves, murderers. Not her. She stifled a sob.

"Never talk to the police," her mate Flick had told her. "They're out to get ya. Just say 'No comment' to everything."

But she hadn't done anything. One tiny scarf didn't count.

Was that what this was about? Was that why they weren't releasing her?

She wrapped her arms around herself. She wanted to go home. Suddenly, the squalid flat she shared with her mother on the Hounslow estate didn't seem so bad. At least it was warm, and she could go into her bedroom and close the door.

She'd never got her phone back. It was still behind the counter in the jewellery store. Her requests to phone her mum had been ignored.

The hours passed, but Rachel had no idea what time it was. The light eventually dimmed, and she began to panic. She had to get home. She had work to do.

She banged on the door.

The metal peephole slid back. "What's the problem?"

"Why am I still here? Where's my mother?"

"You're being held in custody until the morning, love. We tried to ring your mum on that number you gave us, but she's not answering. We'll keep trying. Try to get some sleep."

Sleep? In this place?

Eventually, she lay down on the makeshift bed and closed her eyes.

She could last until tomorrow. Tomorrow her mother would come, and all this would be cleared up. Tomorrow, she could go home. Tomorrow.

* * *

Rachel woke to the sound of the heavy metal door being opened. She squinted against the dim overhead light. Was it morning? She had no way of knowing. There were no windows in the little cell.

She sat up and waited.

An officer poked his head around the door. "All right?"

She nodded.

"One of the detectives wants to have a chat with you."

She didn't move.

"Now. Come on."

Rachel got off the bench and moved stiffly towards the door. "What does a detective want with me?" she asked.

All she got was a disinterested shrug. Guess she'd find out soon enough.

She followed the officer down a cold corridor and into an even colder interrogation room. She shivered and wrapped her arms around herself.

"Take a seat. He'll be here shortly."

Rachel looked around her. Everything was bolted to the floor, the table and the four chairs. Up in the corner, a camera was angled at the table. There was another one diagonally opposite. Was someone watching her now?

Her heart pounded and her mouth went dry. Suddenly, she felt afraid. Were they out to get her, like Flick had said?

A few moments later the door opened, and a tall man strode in. He didn't look like a detective in those faded jeans and a black puffa jacket. His hair was messy, like it had been blown about by the wind, and when he sat down, she noticed he was wearing Nike Air Max trainers like her friend Mikey. They even had the same red air cushions and rubber soles.

"You police?" she asked, just to be sure.

"Yeah. DCI Rob Miller." He sat down, his long legs stretching under the table.

She sniffed. "You don't look like a detective."

He chuckled. "How is a detective supposed to look?"

"I dunno. Smarter, maybe."

He glanced down at his attire and shrugged. "My job is to catch criminals, not win any style awards."

A woman followed him in. Rachel recognised her as the social worker who sometimes surprised them with a visit.

"Hello, Rachel," she said. "I'm acting as the appropriate adult in this interview."

"Where's my mum?"

"We can't get hold of her," said the detective. "Ms Stevens is going to sit in."

Rachel studied him warily. "I'm not a criminal."

He glanced at a document in a folder in front of him. "You have, in fact, been reprimanded for shoplifting. Two years ago. Topshop in Hounslow."

"That was a stupid mistake. I don't do stuff like that anymore."

"I'm glad to hear it." He closed the file. "A witness in the jewellery store confirmed your story. You're not under arrest."

She scowled. "Then why am I here?"

"We had to wait for your DNA results to come back."

Rachel remembered the swab. "What did they say?"

"We'll get to that in a minute. I've got to let you know that, from now on, everything said in this room will be audio and video recorded."

She blinked, holding back tears.

"Let's start with your name.

"Rachel."

"Rachel who?"

She sniffed. "It's on the form."

"I want you to tell me."

"Rachel Norton."

"How old are you, Rachel?"

"Sixteen."

"And where do you live?"

"In Hounslow."

"With your mum?"

"Yes."

"What about your father? Where's he?"

"Dunno."

She glanced at her hands. She'd never had a father. It wasn't unusual in her neighbourhood. Lots of her friends were missing one parent or the other. It was just the way things were.

The detective opened the folder again and took out a photograph. He slid it across the table to her. "Do you know this man?"

She stared at it. The man was a complete stranger. "No."

"Are you sure? Look again."

She picked up the photograph. He was about her mum's age, handsome, sandy-blonde hair, very white teeth.

"I don't know him. Was he one of the robbers?"

The detective smiled at her. "I doubt it. His name is Noah Palmer. That ring any bells?"

"Like Noah's Ark?"

He nodded.

She shook her head. "What's this got to do with the robbery?"

"Nothing."

Now she was really confused. She glanced at the social worker. "I don't understand what's going on."

She sighed. "Neither do I. Detective, is there a point to this line of questioning?"

"Yes, there is," he said. "This man, Noah Palmer, died twelve years ago."

Rachel raised an eyebrow. "What's that got to do with me?"

"We found some unidentified DNA on his body."

A shiver went down her spine. "It can't be mine. Twelve years ago, I was four."

He smiled. "No, not yours, but a familial match."

She glanced at the social worker. "What does that mean?"

Ms Stevens leaned over to her. "What it means, love, is that someone in your family left it there."

# CHAPTER 4

Rob studied the grubby teenager sitting in front of him. She was slender, undernourished by the looks of things, with a pale complexion. Her hair was a dirty blonde, tangled mess, and she stared back at him with hazel eyes battered by dark shadows. She would have been pretty if not for the pasty skin and acne.

After the incident in Knightsbridge, the police had rounded up everyone involved and brought them here, to Kensington Police Station for processing. As soon as her DNA had flagged the alert on the system, one of the detectives had given him a call.

"Are you saying someone in my family killed this dude?" She nodded to the photograph.

She was a quick study.

"What makes you think he was killed?"

"Why else would you be looking at DNA?"

Very quick. He narrowed his eyes. "Noah Palmer died in . . . unusual circumstances. We can't be sure of anything yet."

That was putting it mildly. The Pentagram Killer, as the press had dubbed the person — or persons — had committed four ritualistic murders in the space of one year.

The general consensus was he'd been arrested on a different charge or moved overseas. Perhaps the police had got too close, and the killer had decided it was time to run. For all they knew, he could be sipping piña coladas on a Mexican beach right now.

Rachel folded her arms across her chest and stuck out her stubborn chin. "I still don't understand what this has got to do with me."

"We want to find out whose DNA was on his body and what it was doing there," Rob explained.

Her eyes bore into his, then she looked away. "You'll have to ask my mother. I've got no idea who he is."

"Where is your mother, Rachel?"

A little shrug. "I don't know."

"We've checked at your house. She isn't there. Is there somewhere else she likes to go?"

"You could try her dickhead boyfriend's place."

The mouth turned sulky, and the girl's shoulders drooped. Not a fan, then.

"Does this dickhead boyfriend have a name?"

"Some loser called Bruno."

Rob glanced at the social worker, who shrugged.

"Do you know where Bruno lives?" Rob asked Rachel, expecting another shrug.

To his surprise, she said, "Yeah, on the estate next to ours. Number twenty-seven. I can't remember the name of the block, but it's the third one."

"Thank you, Rachel. That's very helpful."

"Can I go now?"

"Not just yet. Would you like a drink or something to eat? You must be hungry." He'd heard they'd kept her in overnight, but apart from the few biscuits and bottled water they'd given her, she hadn't eaten a thing.

She nodded eagerly.

"I'll be right back."

Rob got up and left the room. He found his way to the canteen, then called his sergeant, DS Will Freemont, back at the Metropolitan Police's Homicide and Serious Crime Command in Putney, where he was based.

"I've got an address for the mother. Her daughter thinks she might be at her boyfriend's place. His name is Bruno. Next estate along, third block — she can't remember the name — and flat number twenty-seven."

"Got that. We'll send a patrol car to see if she's there."

"Keep me posted. I'll be back once I'm finished with the kid."

He grabbed a chicken sandwich, a packet of crisps and a Coke from the canteen and took them back to the interrogation room.

"Here."

She shot him a suspicious look, as if she wasn't quite sure whether to go for it or not. He nodded encouragingly, and she fell on the food like a ravenous dog.

He let her eat, pretending to read from his folder while the social worker sat in silence.

"Do you have any siblings?" he asked when the sandwich had been reduced to crusts and she was licking crisp remnants off her fingers.

"No, just me."

"What about friends? Have you got some good friends?"

She gave a little shrug, then a nod. "Yeah, I guess so. Why do you want to know about them?"

"I'm just trying to understand you a little better," he said. There was no point in beating around the bush with this one.

She didn't seem to know what to say to that, so she picked up her can of Coke and took a long glug.

"What were you doing at Harrods?"

The suspicious look flew back into her eyes. "Browsing."

"Browsing, huh?" He raised his eyebrows. "My ex-wife used to work there."

Rachel's eyes widened. "She did? Which department?"

"Lingerie. Do you know it?"

She nodded. "I go there often. Not to that department, but to the store. I love it there."

"It's very expensive," he remarked.

"Too expensive for the likes of me, you mean?" came the quick retort. There was a definite chip on her shoulder.

"Too expensive for me too," he added. "Even with the discount my ex could get me."

She snorted. "It's top quality, that's why. Mostly designer brands. Only the rich shop there."

"Is that why you go there? You want to be rich one day?"

She sat up straighter in the hard-backed metal chair. "I *will* be rich one day. That's why I'm studying hard. I've got GCSEs coming up."

"When are they?" Her determination was palpable. The Coke can crunched as she tightened her hold.

"June, although we've just had our mocks."

"And how did you do?" he asked.

"I got 9s for most of my subjects except French." She grimaced. "I'm not very good with languages."

He smiled. "That makes two of us." Even though he'd had a French wife, he'd never managed to master more than the basics. He could get by at a push, but it wasn't something he'd ever excel at.

She began to relax.

"Why don't you get some extra help with your French?"

She snorted. "Seriously? Have you seen the estate where I live? Most people can't speak proper English, let alone French."

He chuckled. He was beginning to like this kid. "I haven't. Hounslow, you say?"

"Yeah, it's a shithole. I can't wait to leave."

"I'm sorry to hear that. What will you do after your GCSEs?"

"I'm going to sixth-form college. I don't know where yet, but I'm definitely going."

In order to go to a sixth-form college to study A levels, she ought to have applied by now. He looked at the social worker. "Perhaps that's something you could help Miss Norton with?"

She nodded. "Of course."

Rachel narrowed her eyes. "You didn't offer before."

"No, because my job is to make sure you're receiving appropriate care and access to education and health services, which you are. Your mother is doing much better now, so I don't come round as often."

Rachel sniffed. "I haven't seen you in at least a year."

She cleared her throat. "But if I'd known you were so motivated, we could have discussed your educational needs in more detail."

"Now you know." Rob shot her a pointed look.

She nodded and made a note. "I'll get in touch, Rachel, and we can have a chat."

"Okay."

"How is your mother?" asked Rob.

"Same old," she replied without emotion.

He'd get the details from her social worker later.

"Do you get on?" he enquired.

"Not really." She glanced at the social worker, then back at the table. Rob got the feeling she'd have opened up more if she wasn't worried about the consequences. One thing was clear to him. This girl wanted to go places and she wouldn't let anything stop that from happening, even if it meant living with an alcoholic mother who was hardly ever home. It was preferable to an unknown foster family or social care. Better the devil you know.

Besides, she was sixteen — old enough to take care of herself. He gave her the once-over. Her nails were clean, her teeth white, and she didn't appear to be sickly or anything. Her hair was a mess, but that was from the incident at Knightsbridge, and she wasn't eating enough, judging by the way she'd wolfed down the snack and the sallow tone to her pimple-prone skin.

"I'm sorry to hear that," he said again.

She shrugged as if it hardly mattered.

"And you have no idea who your father is?"

The slender shoulders stiffened. "No, I've got no idea. He could be anyone."

Rob frowned. "What do you mean?"

The social worker shifted in her chair.

Rachel's eyes burned into his. "Didn't you know? My mother used to fuck people for money."

# CHAPTER 5

"Is it true?" Rob asked the social worker once the interview was over and Rachel had been offered a lift home in a squad car. She'd refused, of course.

"Don't want my mates to see me in that. They'll think I'm a grass."

She'd tossed her matted blonde hair over her shoulder and stalked off to the bus stop without so much as a backwards glance. He didn't ask what they thought she'd be grassing on.

"Sadly, yes. Bella Norton was a sex worker for several years before she had Rachel, and a chronic drug user. That's why we got involved. At one point, we were going to take Rachel away and put her in foster care, but then Bella cleaned up her act. She stopped the prostitution and the drugs and got a proper job. So, we left Rachel where she was." She shrugged. "We try to keep the family unit together if at all possible."

Rob knew that. "Did you check on her?"

"Of course." A frown of indignation followed by a shadow of guilt. "We conducted monthly checks at first, but everything seemed to be okay. Bella was clean and Rachel was always fed and warm. A neighbour looked after her while Bella was at work, but there was no reason to worry."

"And after that?" He couldn't explain it, but he felt for the sixteen-year-old. There was something about her that he recognised. The will to succeed, even though life had dealt you such a shit hand.

Perhaps she reminded him a little of himself at that age. Desperate to leave home, to get away from his drunk, heavy-handed father. If his uncle hadn't suggested he join the police force, God knows where he might have ended up. He didn't often think about it, but he highly suspected it would have been on the wrong side of the law. He'd been heading that way fast, before he'd signed up.

A twist of fate, that was all it took.

"Once we knew she was stable, we didn't follow up as often. When we did, they were surprise visits and things appeared normal. Bella had some dependency issues — she liked a drink or two in the evenings and smoked like a chimney, but she was off the drugs and never so far gone that she couldn't look after her child."

Rob wasn't sure the checks were as frequent as he would have liked. "Rachel seems like a bright girl."

"She is. Always did well at school. Her teachers said she could excel if she put in the effort."

"Well, she seems to be putting in the effort now."

Her face had lit up when she'd spoken about her GCSEs. All except the French.

"I'm very glad to see it," the social worker said. "She'll go far if she keeps on this track. She has a lot of potential and we don't have many success stories in my job." She smiled wearily.

Rob noticed she had tired eyes and lines etched into her forehead, no doubt from years of dealing with dysfunctional families, hardship and pain. It couldn't be easy doing what she did.

"Thanks for coming in." He held out his hand. "You will follow up with her about the sixth-form college, won't you?"

She shook it. "Of course. I'll give her a call tomorrow and set up a meeting."

\* \* \*

"Is it really the Pentagram Killer?" blurted out Will as Rob walked into the Putney office where the Major Investigation Team was based. The drive from central London had taken forty minutes and he was gasping for a coffee.

Heads across the squad room bobbed up. It seemed everybody was interested in the answer.

"It could be related," he said carefully. "We have a lead on the DNA."

An excited murmur fed through the office. The Pentagram Killer was a confounding case that had remained unsolved for over a decade. It had happened before his time, and before most of the detectives in this office's time, except for Galbraith, who was in his early forties.

"Never did catch the bastard," the newly promoted DCI said in his Scottish brogue.

"How come?" asked DS Harry Bryson, one of the newer sergeants who worked on Galbraith's team. Nicknamed Bollywood because of his Indian heritage and movie-star good looks, he was confident and chirpy and enviably popular with the women in the department.

"No evidence." Galbraith shrugged. "I was a young DC back then. Sam Lawrence was the SIO. We investigated several suspects but couldn't link them to the murders."

Detective Chief Superintendent Sam Lawrence — Rob's former mentor and boss. Now it made sense why Kensington had called him about the DNA partial.

Lawrence had retired last year after the serial killer known as the Shepherd had been apprehended. It had been his last big case.

"At least I'm going out with a bang," he'd told Rob before he'd left. After thirty years in the police service, the man deserved no less.

His replacement, Superintendent Hodge, was still getting to grips with her new position. A striking black woman in her mid-forties with scraped-back hair and a penchant for navy trouser suits, she'd kept to her office and hadn't mingled with anyone. According to Will, who googled everyone, she'd come from the fraud division. She'd been fast-tracked up the ranks, and Rob suspected the busy west London murder squad was way out of her comfort zone.

"How many murders were there?" asked DS Evan Burns, another sergeant on Galbraith's team.

"Four, if I remember correctly. All wealthy, powerful men. CEOs and the like. Each body was displayed inside a circle with a pentagram engraved on the chest. That's how he got his name. It was bloody weird."

DC Celeste Parker, the youngest member of the team, shivered. "Sounds like something to do with witchcraft or devil worship."

"Aye. We looked into all the local nutters, couldn't find a connection to any of them. Eventually, the case went cold."

"What about the DNA on the victim's body?" said Rob. "Do you know what it was? Hair? Body fluids?"

"Sorry, mate. Cannae remember. I do know that it didn't match the victim's or any of the suspects, though."

"Well, that could be about to change." Rob turned to his sergeant. "Did you manage to find Bella Norton?"

Will nodded. "Yeah, she was at the boyfriend's place. A squad car is bringing her in."

"Are we reopening the case?" asked DS Jenny Bird, an experienced sergeant and an invaluable member of his team. Quietly spoken and more than competent, she'd proven herself many times over the last few years.

"Possibly. I'll have to run it by Superintendent Hodge." A murmur of enthusiasm flitted across the room. "But first, I need a coffee."

"I'll get you one." Celeste took the giant coffee mug off his desk and made her way to the coffee machine out in the waiting area. The mug had *Non, je ne regrette rien* written on the front. Ironically, it was the last thing his ex-wife Yvette had ever given him. The only reason he kept it around was because it was the biggest mug he could find. He didn't have time for those flimsy plastic cups that were empty in two gulps.

"Okay, back to work, everyone. I'll let you know what Hodge says and there'll be a briefing if we're reopening the case."

The Putney murder team had gained something of a reputation over the years as experts in serial killings. With Rob's good friend, the nationally renowned criminal profiler Tony Sanderson, affiliated with the squad, other major investigation teams were now consulting them or passing serial cases along to them.

Tricky at the best of times, serial cases often came with a lot of pressure from the media and the public, which translated into pressure from above. The National Crime Agency had even been known to get involved, which is how he sometimes ended up working alongside his current girlfriend, Jo.

Consequently, other murder squads were cautious about taking such cases on. They didn't want to blot their copybooks, whereas the Putney team had already done that, multiple times. Luckily, in most of the cases they'd taken on, they'd secured a conviction, even if the road had been a bit bumpy along the way.

"Thanks, Celeste," he said as she handed him the steaming mug. It was going to be a long day, but for the first time in ages, there was a buzz of excitement in the office.

Recently, their caseload had consisted of gang stabbings and domestic homicides, the two most common forms of murder in the capital, and apart from those, they'd been preoccupied with trial preparation and stale investigations with no new leads. The whiff of a new possible serial killer case had raised everybody's spirits. He smiled. They were an unusual bunch. He wondered if Superintendent Hodge knew what she was in for.

Rob finished his coffee and knocked on her door.

"Come," she called.

He entered the igloo. They'd renamed it as such because Hodge always kept it at sub-zero temperatures. Whereas Lawrence used to like the blinds up and the door open — it had made him feel like part of the team — Hodge preferred everything closed and the air conditioner at full tilt.

"What is it, DCI Miller?"

He took a seat opposite her and suppressed a shiver. It was midwinter, for Christ's sake. Everywhere else in the building, the heating was on. He half-expected steam to come out of his mouth when he spoke.

"We've had an interesting development in an old case." He chose his words carefully.

"Oh?" She sat back and gave him her full attention.

"It's a case from twelve years ago. You might remember it? A serial offender nicknamed the Pentagram Killer murdered four men and posed their bodies inside circles?"

She frowned. "No, I don't think I do."

Mid-forties — she was old enough, but then he remembered her background in fraud. The serial murders had probably passed her by.

"Anyway, the case was never solved, but there was some unidentified female DNA found on the fourth victim's body. A saliva sample." He'd looked it up. "We've now found a partial match to that DNA."

Her eyebrows shot up. "How?"

"It was a fluke, really. A young girl was arrested in connection with another crime and her DNA showed a familial match. Kensington nick called me, since it was retired Chief Superintendent Lawrence who was SIO on the original case twelve years ago."

"I see." She thought for a moment. "And you want to reopen the case? Is that why you're here?"

"No, ma'am," he said.

She pursed her lips. "What then?"

"I'm just letting you know I'm interviewing the girl's mother this afternoon. I hope she'll provide a DNA sample for us. If it is her DNA on the fourth victim, we have to consider that she might be connected to the other three."

"And then you'll reopen the case?"

He nodded. "Yes, ma'am."

"Okay, DCI Miller. I'm going to allow you some leeway with this one. If it's her DNA, you've got my permission to reopen the original investigation. It will be good if we can solve a twelve-year-old case."

It'll look good on her record, she meant. The new DNA evidence was a definite lead, but Rob was experienced enough to know that nothing was black and white. It might point to the killer, but it might not. The mystery DNA had only been found on the fourth victim and might be completely unrelated to the serial murders.

"Thank you, ma'am."

She nodded. The meeting was over. Rob was glad to escape the igloo and get back into the warmth of the outer office.

# CHAPTER 6

Bella Norton was almost as thin as her daughter, with a proud face that had been knocked into submission years ago. The drugs, booze and cigarettes had taken their toll. Once she may have been beautiful, but she now looked washed-up and haggard.

Her hooded eyes stared back at him. "I ain't done nothing wrong."

That remained to be seen. Rob took a seat and checked the recording was on. Will sat beside him, taking notes, but she'd waived her right to a solicitor. Rob suspected it was because she didn't know one and was under the mistaken impression that if she asked for one, she'd have to pay for it.

"That's not why you're here, Mrs Norton." He attempted to put her at ease.

She frowned. "It's *Miss*. Why'd you bring me in, then?"

"We want to ask you some questions about someone you might have known a long time ago."

"Who?" Her eyes narrowed. Rob suspected she'd known many dodgy characters in her life. He'd looked up her file. She'd been arrested twice for soliciting, but that had been nearly twenty years ago. The only other mention was when she'd been caught using crack cocaine, but she'd got away with a caution. It hadn't been enough to be considered dealing.

When Rachel was little, however, she appeared to have cleaned up her act. There were no more arrests or cautions. There was nothing drug-related and she'd even got a proper job. Rob didn't know what it was, but records from HMRC showed she'd been paying tax.

That was also when the serial killings had stopped.

"A man called Noah Palmer. Do you know him?"

She frowned, then shook her head. "No, sorry. Name doesn't ring a bell."

"He was an investment banker. Worked in the city."

She snorted. "Sounds fancy. I wouldn't know anybody like that."

"This was twelve years ago, Miss Norton." He took a photograph out of his pocket. "Here, this might help."

She stared long and hard at the photograph. "Yeah, I knew this guy. He was one of my regulars. But his name wasn't Noah. It was Nick."

Rob's pulse ticked up a notch. "Nick? Do you remember his surname?"

"Sweetheart, I barely remember their first names. Most of them don't give their real ones, anyway." She nodded at the photograph. "I remember this guy because we had a good time together."

Did she have a good time with the other victims before she bludgeoned them to death?

"Did you see him often?"

"Yeah, every few weeks, usually on a Friday or Saturday night. We had a blast, him and me."

"In what way?"

"He was always up for a party. He had this boring wife. Little Miss Perfect, he used to call her." She chortled. "Perfect mother. Perfect wife. On the school PTA. You know the type." She raised a plucked eyebrow.

Rob nodded. He didn't, but he could guess.

"Poor old Nick just wanted to let his hair down. That's why he came to see me. We used to go clubbing, knock back a few, have a good laugh." She smiled. "He was great fun. Sometimes he'd spend the night, sometimes he'd go home. Once or twice, my friend joined us. He had a thing for blondes."

"Friend?"

"Yeah. He liked to dial it up a bit. Definitely wasn't shy, was Nicky."

"What happened?"

She shrugged. "All good things come to an end, don't they? One day, he just stopped ringing. I figured he'd moved away, or the wife had got wind of it and put a stop to it."

Rob took out a picture. It wasn't a flattering one. It had been taken at the crime scene and showed Noah, stark naked, lying in the middle of a white circle. His arms and legs were splayed apart and there was a five-pointed star carved into the centre of his chest.

"This is what happened." Rob handed her the photograph. "He was murdered."

Her hand flew to her mouth. "Jesus H. Christ. Is that Nicky?"

She stared at the picture, her eyes the size of handcuffs. The colour drained from her face.

"I always wondered," she murmured, in something of a daze. "I mean, it seemed strange not to have said anything. Not even a goodbye, you know?" Her eyes wandered back to the image. "And all that time he was dead. Poor Nicky."

Poor Nicky indeed. The fourth victim of a deranged serial killer.

"When did you last see him?"

She blinked, coming out of her trance. "You're kidding? It was years ago. Decades, even."

"It was twelve years ago," Rob clarified.

"Exactly." She threw up her arms.

"Try to think," he urged. "It's important. You may have been the last person to see him alive."

Will glanced at him. In the original case file, Noah Palmer had left work early, gone home and then gone out for a cycle. There was no mention of the escort. But his sergeant knew better than to question his methods.

Bella rubbed her forehead. "Oh, God. I put Nicky out of my mind because he let us down. I thought he wasn't interested anymore."

"Us?" Rob jumped on the word.

"I meant me," she said.

"Your daughter Rachel was about four years old then, wasn't she?"

Bella glanced up. "Yeah, so?"

"Is that who you meant when you said 'us'?"

She sighed. "Noah liked Rachel. He was good with her. But when I went out with him, Rachel stayed over at my mum's. I never mixed business and pleasure."

It seemed like Noah had been both business and pleasure, but he let it slide. "Let's focus on Noah. You said he just stopped coming. Can you remember when that was? Did he leave yours in the morning and go home, or did he come and see you on his bike, before he went cycling?"

She shook her head. "I don't know. It was too long ago."

She dropped her head into her hands. Rob gave her time. Was she really trying to recall what happened or was she desperately trying to come up with an alibi for the time of his death?

She laid her hands on the table and smiled. "I've got it."

Both Rob and Will stared at her. "Yes?" prompted Rob.

"The last time I saw Nicky was on a weeknight. We went to a work function. I remember now. It was one of those posh affairs at some rooftop bar with views over London." She smiled. "Nicky often took me to work dos. He said it was more fun than having his hoity-toity wife with him. Besides, she had to stay home with the kids. They had three young ones, one still in nappies." She rolled her eyes.

Rob kept a straight face. What did Noah Palmer's work colleagues think when he arrived with an escort on his arm? Or did that sort of thing happen often in banking circles?

"That was a fun night." She gave a sad smile. "It was always fun with Nicky. Anyway, he stayed over and went straight to work the next morning. It was nice. It felt like we were a real couple. We had breakfast together and then he left. I wasn't expecting to see him again that week because there was a big cycling race on that weekend. Nicky was really into his cycling."

*Bingo.*

Or was she providing a logical, well-thought-out explanation as to how her saliva had ended up on his body? He couldn't be sure.

"Shit, I can't believe I remembered that."

He couldn't either. It seemed a lot of detail for an ex-druggie with a hangover.

"Miss Norton, would you mind giving us a DNA sample?"

"Why?" She immediately went on the defensive.

"Because DNA that's a familial match to your daughter's was found on his body. We think it might be yours."

She frowned. "What if it is?"

"Then we know he was with you." He forced a smile. "It doesn't mean you had anything to do with his death."

The frown turned into a scowl. "You're trying to pin this on me, aren't you?" She tapped the photograph still lying on the table. "Bloody typical. I didn't have anything to do with this. This is sick shit. I'm not like that."

"We're not pinning this on you, Miss Norton. But it would make sense that your saliva was on his body, if he was with you that morning. It would help us get a clearer picture of his last movements."

She thought for a moment. "Okay, if it'll help."

Rob gave a curt nod. "Great, thanks for your cooperation."

"Do you wanna do it now?"

"Yes, but I'll get a forensic technician to come and do it in a moment. There are just a few more things I need to ask you."

She sighed. "What?"

He nodded to Will, who arranged three more photographs on the table in front of her. These were head shots of the other men who'd been murdered in the same fashion as Noah Palmer. Splayed out. A white circle sprayed around them. A pentagram carved into their torsos.

Except these were the 'before' photos. The kind found on company websites and in glossy financial reports. Work shots. Corporate smiles. Blissful ignorance.

Bella stared at them. "Who are these guys?"

"Were they 'clients' of yours too?" asked Rob.

She frowned and leaned closer, studying their faces. "I don't think so. I don't recognise any of them." She shrugged. "But I suppose they could have been. I don't recall everyone I . . . worked for back then."

"None of them look familiar?"

"No."

Rob studied her. She could have been lying, of course, but he didn't think so. There was no dilation of her pupils, no tightening of her lips, no tension in her body. She appeared to be telling the truth.

"Okay, we'll leave it there for now. If you don't mind waiting, Miss Norton, a forensic technician will be with you shortly to do the DNA swab."

She grunted a reply.

Will gathered up the photographs and put them back in the folder.

Rob handed her his card. "In case you remember anything else."

He made his way back upstairs to the squad room with Will. "What do you think?"

"I'm not sure. It looked like she was being honest, but you never know. She could be lying."

"It would make sense that her DNA was on his body if she saw him that morning," Rob rationalised. "She probably kissed him goodbye."

"That is the most likely scenario," Will agreed.

Rob frowned. "Let's wait for the results to come back, then we'll know for sure if it was her. In the meantime, we'll look into her background and see if we can find a link between her and the other victims."

"So, we're not ruling her out just yet?" Will asked.

Rob grinned at him. "Oh no, DS Freemont. We're just getting started."

# CHAPTER 7

"We're officially reopening the case," announced Rob when they got back.

A cheer went up.

"Briefing, five minutes."

Just enough time for him to grab a coffee and update the Superintendent. He didn't mention that their only suspect might not have had anything to do with the pentagram killings, and that her only connection was likely to be to Noah Palmer.

Five minutes later, they were all crammed into the largest of their three glass-panelled incident rooms. Rob had asked Galbraith to include his team. There was a lot to get through with four victims.

The big Scot had jumped at the chance. "The team needs something to get fired up about."

"You all know why we're investigating this case," Rob began, glancing at the rapt faces of his fellow officers. "This morning, sixteen-year-old Rachel Norton's DNA flagged on the system. It showed a familial match to DNA found on one of the four victims of the gruesome pentagram killings twelve years ago."

There were a few nods. Most people knew that much.

"Our old guvnor, Chief Superintendent Lawrence, was SIO on the pentagram case," Rob continued. There were a few raised eyebrows. "That's why Kensington police got hold of me. The original case was never solved. DCI Galbraith was also part of the original investigation, so I'm going to ask him to give us an overview."

Galbraith, who'd been reading up on the old case files, nodded. Rob stood aside.

"It was a long time ago, but I've had a look at the files and refreshed my memory," he began. "All four murders took place within the space of a year. It was very strange, because after the fourth victim, Noah Palmer, they suddenly stopped. We think the killer got spooked and fled the country."

"Tell us about his MO," said Rob.

"The victims were middle-aged men in their forties, wealthy and successful. They were all abducted while alone. McKenzie, the first victim, was taken while jogging. His wife said he went out for a run and never came back." He glanced up. "It's a similar pattern for all of them. Langton was abducted en route to one of his company suppliers. We found his car in a bush — it had been run off the road. Sutton, in a bold move, was taken from right outside his house late one evening. When we got there, the motor in his car was still running." There was a soft murmur of surprise. "And finally, the fourth victim, Palmer, was taken while he was out cycling. His bike was found discarded a mile from the crime scene."

"The killer was brazen," remarked Evan, in his soft American drawl. Having come over to the United Kingdom with his parents while still at school, Evan had met and married a Brit and, as far as Rob knew, had no plans of returning to the States, but the accent remained. He was an efficient, hard-working detective and they were lucky to have him.

"Yes, especially since all of the victims except for Sutton were taken while the sun was still up. Unfortunately, there were no witnesses. Nobody saw a goddamn thing."

"They were all abducted in isolated spots," pointed out Rob. "Wilderness, mostly."

Galbraith nodded. "Aye, except Sutton. He was taken outside his house, but it was close to midnight. He'd just got back from a business trip. The neighbours dinnae hear a thing."

"Were they found close to where they were taken?" asked Jenny.

"Apart from the first victim, the other three were all found in the general vicinity of Box Hill," he confirmed. "Heavily wooded areas, secluded spots. The closest inhabitants were a gypsy encampment. Travellers, I mean. Transient folk."

"Could one of them have been the killer?" asked Harry.

Galbraith shook his head. "We looked into them. I remember going to their camp myself, but you know what they're like. Jittery at the best of times. Clammed up faster than you do when it's your round at the pub."

There were a few sniggers.

"We got naught out of them, even though one of them had a police record. He'd done time for GBH. We hauled him in, but he no commented his way through the entire interview. It was a waste of time." Galbraith rolled his eyes. "We dismissed them in the end, because they dinnae have any links to the victims. A week later, the whole lot of them buggered off, never to be seen again."

Rob gave a sympathetic nod. Dealing with transient communities was tough. They were impossible to trace, and they were a law unto themselves.

"Any other suspects?" he asked.

"There was this one crazy woman who lived in Esher, near to where the third victim was taken. Nutty as a fruitcake, believed in all that Wicca stuff. She had chimes in her garden and crystals hanging from trees." He shook his head. "We thought maybe she was involved somehow, but she didn't have any links to the victims. None that we could find, anyway."

"Would she have been able to abduct four fully grown men?" asked Jenny, always the pragmatist.

"It's doubtful," admitted Galbraith. "However, the victims all died of blunt force trauma to the head, so if she'd knocked them out when they weren't expecting it, she might have been able to do it."

"She could have had an accomplice," suggested Will.

Galbraith shrugged. "Aye, that was the most likely scenario, but we couldn't find one. She was a loner, kept to herself. Even the locals said she was a wee bit strange and stayed away."

Rob was beginning to see why the case had remained unsolved.

"But there was a third suspect." They all sat up again and took note. "A postie called Alfred Whitaker. He also worked in Esher. He came to our attention because he knew one of the victims. He voluntarily came forward and offered up the information. Sutton's house was on this guy's postal round. When we looked into him, it turned out he'd used to be a bigwig himself, before he'd had a mental breakdown."

"Sounds promising," said Rob.

"Well, we thought so at first, but he didn't know the other three. He'd lived in Esher all his life, didn't own a vehicle and seemed a simple sort of fella. Said he wasn't cut out to run a company. The stress got to him."

"So you ruled him out," Rob finished.

Galbraith nodded.

"How come Lawrence got the case when the bodies were found outside of London?" asked Will. It was a good point. Usually that would fall under the Surrey and Sussex major crime team.

"The first victim was discovered on Wimbledon Common, which meant we got the call-out. Since we were already familiar with the case, the chief constable at the time ruled we should keep it. I wish we hadn't. It was one of those dead-end investigations that stuck around like a bad smell. Made us look bad."

Rob couldn't remember Lawrence ever mentioning it, but perhaps that was why.

"Okay, thanks for that." Rob took over the meeting. "Your homework for the weekend is to familiarise yourself with the original investigation. All the case files are on HOLMES and we have access, although feel free to print them out if it's easier. On Monday, we'll look into whether Bella Norton knew any of the other victims. DCI Galbraith's team can take the first two, McKenzie and Langton, and my team will take Sutton. It's possible they may have used her services in the past."

Nods all round. The ball was rolling.

Rob tied up the meeting and went back to his desk. There was just one more thing he had to do before he called it a week and that was telephone Sam Lawrence, his old boss. It was time he got his view on the case.

## CHAPTER 8

"Why the hell do you want to know about that?" growled Lawrence, cradling a Guinness.

Retired Detective Chief Superintendent Lawrence had mentored Rob when he'd first arrived at the major crime team almost five years ago now. He'd been stern but fair, and Rob had him to thank for his stubborn streak. He'd never known Lawrence to give up on a case, no matter how long it took or how over budget it went.

They'd met at the Roebuck, a small pub on the top of Richmond Hill. On a summer's day, the punters took their drinks outside and sat on the benches at the top of the terraced gardens overlooking the meandering Thames. It was one of the best views in London, in Rob's opinion.

Tonight, however, it was bucketing down. Huge droplets pummelled the streets and filled the gutters until they were roaring torrents, turning away everyone but locals.

Inside the pub, it was warm and cosy. Jo, Rob's partner, had met them there and the three of them were at a table by the window. Jo worked at the National Crime Agency, though she was now on leave — and six months pregnant. They still weren't living together, something Rob hoped to change in the near future, certainly before the baby was born, but they saw each other every weekend.

Most coppers didn't talk about their work with their spouses or partners, but Jo was different. They'd been through a lot together over the last few years and being in law enforcement herself, she wasn't about to be left out of anything.

Rob filled Lawrence and Jo in on their latest case, starting with Rachel Norton and the DNA match. When he got to the bit about Bella being Noah Palmer's paid escort, Lawrence erupted.

"No way! Noah Palmer paying an escort? You've got to be shitting me."

"Why is that so surprising?" asked Jo.

"He was a happily married man," spluttered Lawrence. "My wife and I knew them well. We used to go round to theirs for dinner. I can't believe he was playing away from home."

"I interviewed Bella Norton myself," confirmed Rob. "By the sounds of things, they had a hell of a time. He even used to take her to the odd work function."

"Jesus Christ," muttered Lawrence. "Poor Suzie."

"I take it she didn't know?"

"God, no. She was devoted to Noah, and to their kids. She was the perfect wife and mother. Never put a foot wrong. The house was always immaculate, the kids were polite and well-mannered. Put our lot to shame."

Jo smiled. "Sounds too good to be true."

"Exactly," said Rob.

Lawrence was shaking his head. "I can't believe it. You think you know someone . . ."

"Do you think this escort murdered all those men?" Jo asked.

Rob shrugged. "I don't know. That's what we're trying to find out. It's possible they were clients of hers. Perhaps she had a grudge against them, who knows?" He'd worked on a similar case before.

Lawrence frowned. "We didn't find any links to prostitutes when we looked at them the first time round. We dug into every aspect of those men's lives. One had some soft porn on his computer, but none of them frequented sex workers."

"Except Noah Palmer," said Rob.

Lawrence snorted. "He kept that well-hidden."

"Well, you would, wouldn't you?" said Jo. "Especially if you didn't want your wife finding out."

"Which means the others might have too."

Lawrence pursed his lips and shook his head. "We checked their call records, their computers, their bank accounts. Nothing suggested any illicit activity. All of them were stand-up guys." He glanced at Rob. "Except Noah, obviously."

"Can you take me through what you remember?" asked Rob.

Lawrence rubbed his forehead. "It was a long time ago, Rob. I'm not ashamed to admit that was one case that I was glad to put behind me. I'll never forget the crime scenes, though. The way their bodies were laid out like something out of a horror film."

"Describe it to me," said Rob.

The retired Chief Super's gaze flickered, but he didn't refuse. "They were left naked, posed and mutilated in white painted circles in secluded wilderness areas around the Surrey Hills — except for the first one, McKenzie, who was found on Wimbledon Common."

Rob was impressed he could remember the victim's name, but then when a case like this haunted you, it became ingrained in your consciousness. He remembered every one of the Surrey Stalker's victims, as well as the victims of the other serial offenders they'd caught over the years. A macabre database of dead people that he carried in his head.

"Why do you think that one was different?" asked Jo.

Lawrence shook his head. "I don't know. We pondered it for months, but there was no logical link between the victims. They didn't know one another, they had no friends or colleagues in common, hadn't been to school together, they didn't even frequent the same places."

Rob winced in sympathy.

"We drove ourselves mad," Lawrence said, "until we got told to dump the case. It was taking up too many resources and had gone way over budget. We couldn't justify it anymore."

No wonder it had left such a bad taste.

"We managed to trace the brand of spray paint to a handful of shops in the Leatherhead area," Lawrence continued, "but none of them had CCTV installed, so there was no way of knowing who had purchased it."

"Galbraith told us about the suspects," said Rob.

"Ah, yes. The shifty travellers. But at the end of the day, we didn't think they or any of their clan were responsible. They weren't even around for the first two murders."

"He also mentioned a woman in the woods?"

"Mrs Marlow. She was a character. Harmless, but completely batty. No, I don't think she had anything to do with it. There was this other chap, though."

"The postie?"

"Yeah, that's right. He came forward of his own accord to help with the investigation."

"That in itself can be suspicious," said Jo.

Lawrence nodded. "Except he didn't appear to know any of them. We looked into him thoroughly. There was no connection, apart from one of the victims living on his postal route. We had nothing on him."

Rob made a mental note to get the team to look into the third suspect in more detail. Things that had been hidden then may have come to light in the last twelve years.

"And if it was him, why's he been inactive all this time?" Lawrence continued. "A serial killer lives for the thrill, as you well know, Rob. How many years have we been doing this? He wouldn't have committed four murders, then miraculously been cured of his affliction."

He did have a point.

"Our theory was whoever it was had left the country."

"What about prison?" asked Jo.

"We checked new inmates in the months after the last murder, but there were none that stood out. All nasty bastards, but no one mad enough to have done that."

"So that was that," said Rob.

Lawrence took a long pull on his Guinness, as if getting rid of the bad taste. "Yep. Good luck to you if you plan on reopening it. I can't see you having any more luck than we did, unless your mysterious DNA has anything to do with it. That was only found on the last body, by the way."

"We know," said Rob. "It's tenuous, I'll admit, especially since it probably belongs to the escort. We'll get the results in a day or two."

"Twelve years is a long time. Leads have gone cold, memories fade. If I were you, Rob, I'd steer well clear of this one."

"Too late." He grinned. "My team has already got their teeth into it."

Jo laughed. "Things must be dull at the murder squad."

Rob rolled his eyes. "You have no idea."

Lawrence finished his drink. "Another round?"

"I'll get it," said Rob. He ordered at the bar and came back carrying another Guinness, a lager for himself and a tonic water for Jo.

"One of the downsides of being pregnant," she moaned. "I miss my glass of red in the evening."

"How are your girls?" Rob asked Lawrence, trying to lighten the conversation. The retired chief still had lines etched into his forehead and a haunted look in his eye.

"Oh, they're good," he said, the lines clearing. "They're both at university now. Zoe's at Southampton and Brittney's at Bristol. Why they couldn't go to the same institution, I don't know."

Rob chuckled. "Lots of driving for you."

"I've got nothing better to do." He glanced up and a smile tickled the corners of his mouth. "Now, why don't you tell me all about this new superintendent of yours. What's she like? Any good?"

Rob grimaced. "Where to begin?"

# CHAPTER 9

"Any news from Bella Norton's DNA results?" Rob asked when he got in on Monday morning.

"I'll check," said Jenny. "Sorry, we've been a bit distracted."

The department had received a 999 call during the night from a man saying he'd just murdered his wife. The on-call team had been dispatched and were at the scene along with Forensics. It would be up to the major crime squad to piece together a timeline of the husband's movements and figure out what happened.

"Apparently he stabbed her repeatedly in the kid's bedroom," said Jenny. "Celeste said it's a right mess."

"Jesus," whispered Rob.

"That is why I'll never get married," said Will. "Six years and then he knifes her."

"More likely to be the other way round with you," quipped Harry, who happened to be passing.

Will gave him the finger.

"Okay, I've got the DNA results here," said DS Jenny Bird. "They've just come in."

Rob raised his eyebrows. "Let's have it."

She clicked her mouse and then grinned. "It's a match! The DNA on Noah Palmer's body is a match to one Isabella Norton."

"Yes!" Rob punched the air. "We're in business."

"There's more." Jenny stared at the screen. She'd gone quite still.

Rob frowned. "What is it?"

"The daughter's DNA is also a partial match to Noah Palmer's."

Rob stared at her. "Rachel Norton is Noah Palmer's daughter?"

"Yeah, it looks like it." Jenny scrutinised the on-screen report. "I don't know why it didn't flag before, but the forensic tech says they're definitely related."

"Call them and find out, won't you? We should have known about this the moment Rachel's DNA was entered onto the system."

"Will do, guv."

Rob went to inform Superintendent Hodge.

"What is it, DCI Miller?" She looked up from her laptop.

"An update, ma'am. Bella Norton's DNA results came back. It's a match with that found on the fourth victim, Noah Palmer's body. It proves she was in contact with him before he died."

"Excellent news. I take it you'll be bringing her in for questioning?"

"We've already done that, ma'am," he said. "This backs up what she's already told us, that she was Palmer's lover."

There was a brief pause. Hodge's eyes narrowed. "So this might have no bearing on the serial case?"

"It's possible that it's unrelated, yes, although we're looking for connections to the other victims. She was a sex worker at the time, so there's that angle."

"You think the four men may have been . . . clients?"

Rob nodded. "It's a line of enquiry. We're also going to dig a little deeper into the victims' backgrounds and see if we can find a link between them. It's possible something was missed the first time round."

"Okay, but this was a real white elephant twelve years ago. We don't have the time or the money to dedicate to it now. If this prostitute's DNA is another dead end, then I want the case dropped. We're not going to find anything new over a decade later."

"Except we already have, ma'am," said Rob, his voice terse. "Noah Palmer was seeing an escort. That wasn't picked up in the preliminary investigation. He also had a child with that escort."

Another pause.

"That gives the escort a possible motive to kill Noah Palmer, but what's the link with the other victims? Did she give birth to their children too?"

"No, ma'am. We haven't established a link yet. Like I said, we're still working on it."

She sighed. "Don't take this the wrong way, Detective, but I'm here to cut costs and make the department more efficient, not throw money away. Tie this woman in with the cold case or let it go. We've got a new domestic violence homicide to work on and the Henderson case is going to trial this week. There is a lot of paperwork that hasn't been filed, and I understand your team *still* hasn't been on the ethics course."

Rob grimaced. He'd been putting off the ethics course for weeks. "Yes, ma'am."

"That'll be all." Her eyes were already back on her screen.

* * *

"I haven't been here in ages," remarked Will as they crossed the river into Chiswick. "There used to be a fantastic Indian restaurant on the High Road. I forget what it's called now. Best tikka masala you've ever tasted."

They passed rows of neat, terraced houses in wide, tree-lined streets. A refuse lorry was blocking one of them as it loaded blue boxes of recycled waste into the back. Rob diverted and took the next road.

"That's her." He turned into a short, paved driveway and parked behind a white Mercedes SLK.

Suzie Palmer lived in a beautifully restored Edwardian townhouse set back from the road. Golden bricks glowed in the weak winter sunshine, while the mock-Tudor cladding and timbers at the top of the house created an impressive facade.

Will whistled softly under his breath. "Not short of a few bob, is she?"

"Noah was an investment banker," Rob acknowledged, although it was clear Suzie had done fairly well for herself in the years since his death. She was an interior designer of some repute, apparently. Jenny had researched her online and found several articles about her in local magazines, such as *Surrey Life*.

Pulling their jackets around them, they made for the porch covered by shiny wooden frames. The front door was solid and painted a glossy black. A brass knocker gleamed at them, daring them to knock. There was no bell.

Rob thumped the thing and stood back.

A young woman with long dark hair opened the door. She couldn't have been more than sixteen.

"Hello. Can I help you?" she said with a hesitant smile. She was wearing leggings and a big, knitted jumper that reached her knees. Her feet were in socks although it was warm in the house. Rob could feel the heat coming at him from the doorway.

"I'm DCI Miller and this is DS Freemont. We'd like to speak to Suzie Palmer, if she's in?" said Rob.

"Are you the police?" Her face wrinkled with concern.

"Yes, but it's nothing serious. Just a routine visit."

"Oh, okay then. Wait here and I'll go and get her."

They watched as she pranced up the stairs two at a time.

"Mum, the police are here. They want to talk to you."

A woman's voice replied but it was too muffled to hear properly.

"I don't know," the girl responded. "Hurry up, they're waiting downstairs."

A short time later, an expensively coiffed woman floated down the stairs, wearing a cream trouser suit and a string of pearls around her neck. Hardly your usual working-from-home attire.

"Mrs Palmer?" Rob asked.

She nodded. "Yes, how can I help you, gentlemen?"

"We'd like to ask you a couple of questions regarding your late husband's death."

The blue eyes turned chilly. "Noah died twelve years ago. Why do you want to talk to me now?"

"Shall we sit down and then I'll explain," said Rob.

She nodded stiffly and showed them into a double reception room, stylishly decorated, with the biggest vase of lilies Rob had ever seen on a low coffee table. He sat opposite her but couldn't see her through the flowers.

"I'll just move these, shall I?" Will picked them up and put them on the dining room table. Suzie watched him without comment until he sat down again.

"Now, what's this about?" she asked. She didn't offer them tea or coffee, but then this wasn't a social call.

"I don't know how familiar you are with the details of the case, Mrs Palmer, but there was some unidentified DNA found on your husband's body that the police couldn't account for."

She frowned, then gave a curt nod. "I seem to recall something to that effect, yes."

"We've now found the source of that DNA."

She raised a perfectly plucked eyebrow. "Really?"

He noticed she didn't ask whose it was. "It belongs to a woman called Isabella Norton." He watched her for a reaction, but her pale blue eyes barely wavered.

"Is that name supposed to mean something to me?"

"Do you recognise it?" asked Rob.

"No, and I'm pretty good with names."

Rob dropped that line of questioning. For now. He wanted to get the basics out of the way first. If he went into who Bella Norton was now, she might kick them out.

He hesitated. "Mrs Palmer, would you mind taking us through the events of that day, up to when your husband went cycling?"

"I went through all this with the authorities at the time," she said. "It's been twelve years, I'm not sure if I'll remember everything now."

Rob smiled. "I've got the original report, but I'd like to hear it from your perspective, if you don't mind."

She sighed, then glanced at her wristwatch. "If you insist, although I don't have all day."

He nodded and Will attempted a smile.

"Whenever you're ready," said Rob.

"I remember it was a weekday — a Wednesday, I think. Noah had come back from work earlier than usual. There was a big cycling race on at the weekend, and he wanted to fit in one last training session. Fifty kilometres, if memory serves."

"That's a fair distance," remarked Rob.

She nodded. "He was used to it. He'd been training for months."

"Did he go with a group of cyclists or alone?" Rob asked.

"Alone, unfortunately. They only trained together at weekends."

Will made a note on his iPad.

Rob missed Mallory. His old sergeant had had such a brilliant memory, he didn't need to write anything down. He kept it all in his head until he got back to the station and wrote up the reports. They were incredibly detailed too. Mallory was now running his own show at Woking CID, and deservedly so. He'd been transferred there after their last case.

"What time did he set out?"

"He left just after five o'clock. I remember because I was about to make tea for the children. They were all under seven back then. My youngest, Joey, was only two."

"Quite a handful," Rob remarked. He thought about Jo, pregnant with their first, and wondered if this was just the beginning. Having never thought about kids before, he couldn't believe he was about to be a dad.

She smiled serenely as if it was nothing she couldn't handle. "Anyway, Noah left and I had a quick chat to Mrs Jenkins next door, then went back inside to finish supper."

Mrs Jenkins was the neighbour. Rob remembered seeing her name in the report. She'd given Mrs Palmer the all-important alibi.

"And you didn't go out that evening?"

"No. I could hardly leave three kids alone by themselves, could I?"

Rob nodded. Fair enough. "When did you call the police?"

"I didn't," she said. "I called Detective Inspector Sam Lawrence, a family friend, and told him Noah hadn't come home and I was worried. He called the police."

Rob frowned. "Lawrence was here, at the house?"

"Yes, he came straight over. He was a great help. I was frantic, I didn't know what to do. He took care of everything. Then, when they found Noah—" She took a steadying breath. "When they found his body the next morning, Sam went to see where it had happened."

"Box Hill, wasn't it?" asked Rob, knowing full well it was.

"Yes, that's right. I didn't go to the crime scene myself. Sam advised me not to. Apparently, it was pretty horrific. There had been a string of other murders, all following a pattern. I'd read about them in the newspaper, so I knew what to expect." She shivered. "It was awful to think of Noah like that."

"It must have been a very traumatic time for you."

She nodded. "I still have nightmares when I think about it."

There was a brief pause as Rob collected his thoughts. "How do you know Sam Lawrence?"

"Oh, I met his wife, Diana, at the Chelsea Design Centre years ago. Gosh, it must have been a few years before Noah died. We hit it off straight away."

Rob recalled Lawrence's wife was also an interior designer.

"You have a lovely home. Is this your work?" he asked, even though he knew it was.

She glowed. "Yes, thank you for noticing, Detective. I consult nowadays, which gives me more time at home with the children. The teenage years are particularly trying."

Rob swallowed. He still had all that to look forward to.

"How old are they now?" he asked.

"My eldest is eighteen. He's in his first year at Oxford. Rebecca is sixteen — you met her at the door — and my youngest, Joey, is fourteen."

"Two years between them," he remarked. "Did you plan it that way?" It didn't hurt to know these things. Not that he and Jo were planning a vast family, but he was keeping his options open.

She nodded. "I plan everything. It's just the way I am."

So much for spontaneity.

Little Miss Perfect, Bella had said. Looking at the pristine lounge, the elegant sofas, the magnificent lilies, and the luxurious stylishness of the house, he could see what she meant. There wasn't a scatter cushion out of place.

The same went for the woman herself. Rich brown hair coiffed into a French twist, perfectly manicured fingernails and a smattering of lip gloss on her thin, rather unforgiving lips. She was every inch the professional interior designer. When he worked from home, he wore tracksuit pants and a T-shirt.

Her mobile phone rang, and she got up to answer it. "Excuse me. I'll be right back."

Rob studied her as she took the call out in the hall. A confident, well-spoken woman. He couldn't imagine her taking Noah's extracurricular activities particularly well.

"I think the silk sheers would work best, David," she was saying. "But I can bring you some samples of the linen, if you'd like."

He wondered if Jenny had managed to track the neighbour down yet. They needed to confirm Suzie's alibi. He only hoped Mrs Jenkins was still alive.

Suzie returned, tapping the mobile phone against the palm of her hand. "Is that all, detectives? I really must get back to work."

"Just a few more questions, Mrs Palmer, if you don't mind. Then we'll get out of your hair."

She sighed and sank back onto the sofa.

"What was your relationship like with your husband?"

She scowled. "Fine, not that it's any of your business. He was great with the kids. We made a great team."

He noticed she didn't mention the L-word. "How did you two meet?"

"I really can't see what that has to do with anything."

"Humour me." He smiled.

She inhaled. "We met through a mutual friend. It was a blind date, of sorts." Her eyes softened. "I knew immediately he was the one for me."

"Love at first sight?"

"Something like that." Her phone beeped and she glanced down, the link to the past broken.

"Mrs Palmer, I hope you won't mind me asking this, but did you ever suspect your husband of being unfaithful?"

"What?" Her eyes blazed. "No, never. Why on earth would you ask me that?"

He hesitated. "The woman whose DNA was found on your husband's body was . . . an escort."

Suzie's eyes widened. "An escort? You mean like a prostitute?"

He nodded, watching as she stumbled over her words. "I–I'm sorry. I don't know what I'm supposed to say. Are you sure?"

"Yes, ma'am."

She clutched her phone in her lap. "Well, that doesn't mean he was seeing her, does it? I mean, he could have bumped into her on the street. Perhaps she was standing next to him on the train. There could be any number of reasons why her DNA was on his body."

She was grasping, trying to make sense of it.

"There was saliva on his neck," he said softly.

She shook her head. "No. I can't explain it, but I can tell you that there is no way my husband was sleeping with a prostitute. He wasn't like that. He was a decent man. He worked hard and came home to his family. I would have known if he was paying for sex. I would have known." She repeated the last sentence almost like she was convincing herself.

Rob felt sorry for her. It must be awful finding out your spouse had been having an affair twelve years after their death. It would make you look at your whole relationship differently. If he hadn't said anything, she could have carried on grieving him and missing him and never knowing the truth about him. But unfortunately, that wasn't his job. He was a pursuer of the truth, no matter what the cost.

"I'm sorry," he said. "I have to ask these questions, even if they're uncomfortable."

She'd gone white. Her eyes were focused on the dark screen of her phone, in an unseeing stare.

It was going to get worse. "Mrs Palmer, we have reason to believe your husband had a child with this woman."

"What?" She stared at him, shock all over her face.

"There's a daughter. She's sixteen."

Suzie dropped her head into her hands. "Stop. I don't want to hear any more. I can't."

"I'm sorry, but I have to ask if you knew?"

She shook her head, then looked up. "No. How could I have? Are you sure it's his?"

60

"Yes, the DNA matches. It's conclusive."

"Oh, God." She dropped her head back down and covered her face with her hands. She was shaking.

"I think I'd like you to leave now." Suzie got slowly to her feet. She wavered and for a moment, Rob thought she might be about to pass out.

"Yes, of course." There was no point in continuing now. She walked to the door in a trance.

"Thank you for talking to us," Rob said. "I'm sorry for the shock. Is there someone you can call to be with you? A friend, perhaps?"

"I'm fine," she croaked, clutching the door handle.

"Okay, if you're sure."

She didn't reply, just closed the door.

* * *

They got back into the car. "I feel bad about that," Will muttered.

"Yeah, that wasn't pleasant." Rob started the engine and reversed out of the driveway. "She fell apart when she heard about the kid."

"No way she knew," said Will. "I'm sorry, but no one's that good an actress."

"No," agreed Rob. "And if she didn't know about the mistress or the child, then she's got no motive."

"It's amazing how two people can live together, have kids together and yet not know each other at all."

Rob grunted.

"I'm not surprised he had an affair, though," said Will.

Rob arched a brow. "What makes you say that?"

"You've seen her house," said Will. "Her husband was probably too scared to put a foot wrong. Everything is perfectly in its place. Can you imagine? I'd be afraid of bringing mud into the house every time I walked through the door. It's no wonder he looked for a little freedom elsewhere."

His sergeant did have a point.

"Most people hang out with their friends to let off a little steam," Rob said. "They don't hire escorts."

"Perhaps he didn't have any friends." Will snorted. "He was an investment banker."

Or maybe there was no one he could trust not to tell his wife.

## CHAPTER 10

"How are we doing linking Bella Norton to the other three victims?" asked Rob, when he and Will were back in the office. He'd called for an impromptu update.

Galbraith spoke first. "We haven't had much luck. Neither McKenzie or Langton appear to have any connection to Bella Norton, the escort agency she worked for, or any other agency, for that matter."

"I analysed their call logs in the months leading up to their deaths," said Evan. "But there wasn't so much as an 0800 number. Of course, we can't know whether they contacted an escort via a website, since we don't have access to their computers."

"You could probably get access," said Will, who was something of a tech whizz. "There's no reason why they won't still work. The batteries will be dead, but they'll still power up when plugged in."

Galbraith scratched his chin. "Okay, we'll see if we can get our hands on them. Let's send them to the forensic tech. What's his name again?"

"Joe," said Harry, who knew everyone.

"Harry, will you handle that? See what he can pull off?"

The sergeant nodded and made a note on his phone.

"We also looked at their bank accounts," continued Evan. "No miscellaneous payments, nothing dodgy. A couple of cash withdrawals, but that's normal. Again, we can't know if that was for escorts, or spending money. I'd guess the latter. The amounts weren't high enough."

Harry raised an eyebrow but resisted a quip.

"We'll keep at it, but nothing so far," finished up Galbraith.

Rob nodded. "Okay, and what about you, Jenny?"

"I'll start with Sutton," she said, her eyes glittering. Rob got the feeling she had something but was holding it back. "Sutton was a big spender, but he didn't have many vices. He didn't gamble, no suspicious payments, no mention of the escort agency, and no massive bar bills either. He liked fancy restaurants, but most of his disposable income went on education for his kids, travel and his wife's trips to the spa." Her hands fluttered in the air as she spoke. "Again, like the other two, there are some cash withdrawals, but nothing to suggest he was spending the money on sex."

"It's beginning to look like it was only Noah who was seeing an escort," sighed Rob.

"More than seeing," clarified Will. "She had his kid. He was spending time with them as a family."

"That's right," agreed Jenny. "There are no suspicious payments from Palmer's account to the escort agency either, which would suggest he was no longer paying her for sex."

"You're right, they were in a relationship by then," agreed Rob. "Rachel would have been four years old at the time of Noah Palmer's death."

"But he was sending her monthly maintenance payments," said Jenny, with a flourish.

Rob stared at her. "Are you sure?"

"Absolutely. The reason it wasn't picked up before was because the payments came from his business account and were referenced a Stonewall Storage Co. Ltd, which I checked. And there is no such company, but the account number matches Bella Norton's."

Galbraith whistled under his breath.

"Nice work, Jenny." Rob clapped her on the shoulder. "Well, well. Bella Norton lied to us, Will. She claimed not to know Noah's real name, but he was sending her payments every month."

"Shall I bring her in?" asked Will.

"Oh, yes," Rob replied. "Miss Norton has some explaining to do."

* * *

Bella Norton looked up as Rob and Will marched in. She certainly brightened up the dull interrogation room with her electric-blue faux-fur coat and blonde hair. A sweet, floral aroma drifted about the room. It was a pleasant alternative to the usual smelly lowlifes they had in here.

"That's the second time you've hauled me in a police car like a common criminal," she complained, as he took a seat and started the recording. "People are starting to talk."

"Hello, Bella," Rob said congenially. "You remember Detective Sergeant Freemont? We need to ask you a few more questions. You've been cautioned, and you've decided not to have a solicitor present."

"What for? I ain't done nothing."

Rob wasn't going to argue with her. He opened the file on his desk. "You lied to me, Miss Norton." He fixed his gaze on her, giving her nowhere to look.

Her mouth turned into a fuchsia sulk.

"You did know Nicky's real name, didn't you?"

She stared at him, unresponsive.

"I know you did, because he was sending you money. A thousand pounds a month." He leaned forward. "Tell me, what were you doing for him that cost a grand a month?"

"Use your imagination," she snapped.

"It wasn't for services rendered, was it?"

"No comment."

He studied her. Wary eyes, tense shoulders, petulant pout. "It doesn't take a genius to work out that he began paying you around about the time Rachel was born." They'd cross-checked her daughter's birth certificate with the dates on the bank statements. "Rachel is Noah's daughter, isn't she?"

She sniffed. "Don't be ridiculous."

"We have DNA proof, Miss Norton."

"Then why did you ask?" She scowled at him.

He exhaled. "Why didn't you tell me? What were you trying to hide?"

"I didn't want you to think I had anything to do with his murder," she said. "If you knew he'd knocked me up, then I'd have had a motive, wouldn't I? I know how you guys operate."

Rob relaxed. "Firstly, we don't operate anything like what you think you know. Most of what we do is dull police work, like going through bank statements."

She avoided his gaze.

"And secondly, why would that have given you a motive? He was paying you maintenance. If anything, that would work in your favour."

"He stopped paying," she mumbled. "I thought his wife had cottoned on to it or something."

"Stopped when? From your bank statements, it looks like he paid you right up until the month before he died."

"Yeah, but I didn't know that he'd died, did I? I thought he'd stopped paying. I tried to call him, but he didn't pick up. His phone went to voicemail. When that got full, I gave up. I thought about going to the courts, but I couldn't afford to hire anyone to look into it. Family solicitors cost a fortune."

She wasn't wrong there. He'd spent a packet divorcing Yvette and that had been amicable. She couldn't wait to get rid of him.

"Okay, so the money was for your daughter. Is that why he was at your house so often? Was all that stuff about having a good time a lie too?"

She sighed. "No, it wasn't. That's how it started. He was great fun, old Nicky. We had a blast together. Then I got

66

pregnant. I didn't tell him straight away, but when it became obvious, I had to. At first, he didn't believe it was his, but when Rachel was born, and she had his sandy-blonde hair and hazel eyes . . . Well, it was obvious."

"Did he ask for a paternity test?"

"No. He just knew. Anyway, he wanted to pay, and I wasn't going to argue. He carried on for four years, until . . . until he didn't."

"How did you cope when the money stopped coming in?" said Rob.

"Not very well." She stared at her fingernails. "We'd come to rely on it. He never gave me his address, you see, so I couldn't go and look for him. I didn't know where he worked. All I had was a phone number. I had to get a job. I couldn't carry on doing what I was doing before with a kid at home, so I got work as a cleaner at a hotel and got off the drugs."

Rob nodded. That tallied with what the social worker had said.

"The pay was crap, but it put food on the table."

"Did you claim benefits?" asked Rob.

She nodded. "Yeah, that helped. I was getting a bit past it, anyway. You don't see many escorts over thirty, do you?"

He'd take her word for it. "Let's go back to the last time you saw Noah. In your previous statement, you said he'd stayed over the Tuesday night and left for work on Wednesday morning. Is that still true?"

"I don't remember the actual days, but yeah, it's true. He liked spending time with us. He loved Rachel and it was more relaxed at our place than at his. 'I can't breathe in that house, Bella,' he used to tell me. 'It's like being in a fucking prison.'" She gave a smug grin. "He'd never have left his stuck-up wife, but he preferred being with us."

"What did he tell his wife when he was with you?" Rob said.

She smirked. "He told her he was out with his best mate. I can't remember the guy's name, but he used to cover for Nicky all the time."

At least one of his friends was in on it, then. Will made a note. They'd have to look into the best friend and get his side of the story.

"You know," Rob began, "now that you have proof that Rachel is Noah's biological daughter, you might be able to claim compensation from his trust."

Will glanced at him in surprise.

Rob bit his lip. He probably shouldn't have said that, but then Rachel deserved better. She was a bright kid. A little money would go a long way, and now she might be able to get it.

Bella stopped fidgeting. "Really? You think we could get some of his money? For Rachel, I mean?"

He shrugged. "It's possible. I'll post you a copy of the test so you've got proof, but you'd have to contact a solicitor and get legal advice. I can't advise you on that matter."

"But you just said . . ."

"I know and I shouldn't have. I'm sorry. Please contact a solicitor and ask them. That's it for now." He stood up. Will did the same.

As they were about to leave, a thought struck him. "Rachel doesn't know, does she?"

Bella shook her head.

"Maybe it's time you told her," he suggested. Again, it was none of his business, but he felt like she deserved the truth. "I think she has a right to know who her father was."

He exited the room, leaving Bella staring after him.

"Do you think it was wise to let her go?" Will said when they got outside.

"We've got nothing to hold her on."

"Her DNA was on the victim's body and he was the father of her child."

"Yes, but as Hodge goes to great pains to point out, that's circumstantial," Rob replied. "Besides, she doesn't have a motive. Why would she kill her daughter's father, a man who was giving her money? It doesn't make sense. No, Noah Palmer was of more use to Bella Norton alive."

## CHAPTER 11

After he left the station, Rob swung by the lab where Home Office pathologist Liz Kramer worked. The Montgomery Centre was a wide, squat building that covered a whole block in Wandsworth. There were no river views, no landscaped green spaces, and the windows looked out onto the drab car park at the front and a sprawling cityscape at the back.

Inside, however, was a different story. Rob walked into a modern foyer with tiled floors, subtle lighting and a shiny reception desk. He signed in, walked through a security door and down a plush corridor, almost like in a hotel.

He passed spacious, functional laboratories with glass windows, which he knew contained the latest forensic equipment, and ergonomically designed offices and conference rooms. At the back of the complex were the new, state-of-the-art storage and disposal facilities.

He found Liz in her office, typing up reports. "Rob, this is a surprise. What are you doing here?"

"Do I need a reason to visit you?"

She raised an eyebrow but couldn't hide the twinkle in her eye. Dr Kramer was a fiercely bright, no-nonsense woman who didn't suffer fools gladly. Rob had learned this the hard way. But they had developed a mutually respectful relationship, as long as he didn't bother her too often.

"I hope this isn't about another dead body," she said. "I haven't recovered from your last case yet."

The grisly mass burial site in Bisley Wood had been a mammoth undertaking for a team who were, at the time, very short-staffed and under-resourced. She'd done a marvellous job.

"Actually, it's four bodies," he said, to which both eyebrows shot up. "But before you say anything, hear me out. The victims died twelve years ago. I don't know if you remember the Pentagram Killer case, as it was known in the press?"

"Pentagram? Hmm . . . Yes, that does ring a bell. I wasn't in London then, but I do remember reading something about it in the papers. Carved pentagrams in the torsos?"

"That's it. Well, we've reopened the case."

"Ah." She studied him, her interest piqued. "Do take a seat and tell me about it. Shall I make us some tea, or would you prefer something stronger?"

"Tea is fine, thanks."

While the kettle boiled, Rob told her about Rachel Norton and the partial DNA match, Bella Norton and a possible link to the other victims.

"You think these other men might have been johns?" Liz asked.

He smiled at the American terminology. "Yes, it's a possibility. My team hasn't been able to find any links, but it's early days yet."

"What do you want me to do?"

"I was wondering if you could take a look at the old post-mortem reports and let me know if anything strikes you as odd."

"They were killed, mutilated and posed," she exclaimed. "They're all bloody odd."

"You know what I mean," said Rob. "It's been twelve years. You might spot something that was missed back then."

"I doubt it," she said. "Twelve years wasn't that long ago, forensically speaking. But if it will make you happy, I'll have a look. Can you send them to me?"

"I'll email you a copy first thing tomorrow morning. Thanks, Liz. I owe you."

She surveyed him over her tea. "Yes, you do."

* * *

Rob was almost home when his phone buzzed. He answered it using his hands-free kit.

"Will, what's up? You still at work?"

"Yeah." He sounded distracted. "I was looking into Noah Palmer's background. He worked for Global Standard, the big investment bank."

"I've heard of it," Rob said.

"Well, he worked on the Asia desk."

Rob slowed as two swans waddled across the road. The traffic began to build up behind him. "Is this going anywhere, Will?"

"Sorry, yes. It's nothing concrete, but the year Noah died, his colleague, Raza Ashraf was suspended pending a money laundering allegation. It seems he inadvertently — or advertently, who knows — moved money belonging to some drug traffickers. The bank's compliance department flagged it as suspicious and there was an internal inquiry."

"What was the outcome?" Rob asked. A pedestrian was now shooing the swans back into Barnes Pond.

"No action was taken. The inquiry cleared Ashraf of any wrongdoing, owing partially to the testimony of his colleague, Noah Palmer."

Rob blinked. "Noah got him off the hook?"

"It looks that way. I don't know the particulars, there isn't much online. It was buried pretty sharpish."

Rob frowned. "Raza Ashraf? Why does that name ring a bell?"

Will took a deep breath. "Because he's running for mayor in the upcoming London elections."

Rob let out a low whistle.

"We're going to have to tread carefully with this one, guv."

"You can say that again," Rob replied. The birds had made it safely across the street. He waved a thank-you to the helpful pedestrian and put his foot on the accelerator. This case had just got a whole lot more interesting.

# CHAPTER 12

Rob's alarm went off at the same time as a hyperactive Trigger slobbered all over his face.

"Okay, boy. Hang on." He rolled out of bed, pulled on a pair of tracksuit pants and a T-shirt, and went downstairs, squinting against the daylight.

He opened the sliding doors and stiffened against the biting cold. It was a crisp, winter morning, but the sky made up for it. It was a magnificent cobalt blue. Frost glistened at the edges of the grass, but the golden Labrador didn't seem to mind. He pranced around like a mad thing, his tongue lolling to the side and his tail a blur.

Rob had got the dog for his ex-wife because she didn't like being alone. He couldn't blame her — his first serial killer case with the major crime squad had almost cost her her life. But she hadn't taken to him. When they'd split up, she'd made it clear Trigger was his responsibility. Now, almost a year later, Rob had become attached to the crazy mutt.

Luckily, his neighbour had too. Mrs Winterbottom had started taking Trigger while Rob was at work, so he didn't get lonely. Rob paid her dog-sitting fees, even though she insisted she didn't need it. "I'm only too happy to have the company," she'd told him. "Trigger's an absolute darling."

Rob wasn't sure about that, but it was the perfect arrangement and one of the reasons why he'd never move.

He left the sliding door open and went to make a coffee. Jo had recently given him a fancy Nespresso machine and he was still figuring out how to work it. It had this built-in memory where it remembered your last cup of coffee, except Jo had managed to confuse the hell out of it and he hadn't got round to reading the instruction manual on how to read-just the settings, so he had to be content with a foamy cappuccino instead of his preferred espresso. Still, it wasn't bad coffee and it hit the spot.

He dropped Trigger off next door and drove into work, taking the river road. The Thames dazzled in the early morning sunlight. Not surprisingly, there were a couple of eight-man rowing boats taking advantage of the pristine conditions, probably from a local school or boat club. They looked young, around seventeen or eighteen, their toned shoulders pulling in unison as they sliced through the water. They were going fast, almost keeping up with his car. In the end, diesel won out over brute strength and he left them behind.

He got a text just as he was pulling into the car park. He cut the engine and checked his phone. It was from Jo.

*He's kicking like crazy!*

She'd included a photograph of her hand on her belly. Her bump was getting bigger by the day.

Jo was set on a boy, although as yet, they didn't know the sex of the baby. They could have found out at their twenty-week appointment, but they had still been assimilating, getting their heads around the fact that they were going to be parents. They'd decided to let it be a surprise.

Rob called her back.

"Does it hurt?" he asked.

"No, they're light, feathery kicks, that's all. Maybe he'll be a football player."

Rob chuckled. "You never know. How are you feeling?"

She'd had terrible morning sickness the first few months but that had subsided now.

"Great, actually. I'm going for a walk in a bit. It's a lovely morning."

"Well, be careful. It's still pretty frosty. Make sure you don't slip."

"I won't." He heard her laugh into the phone. "Don't worry so much. I'll be fine."

"Enjoy. I'll call you later."

"Okay, bye." She hung up.

Rob smiled. Things were moving along. They had to sit down and have a talk about moving in together. Jo was fiercely independent, and they'd only been seriously seeing each other for a short while, which was why he hadn't brought it up before now. He wasn't sure how she'd react. But with the birth only three months away, he'd have to broach the subject soon. He didn't want to be an absent father.

* * *

As soon as Rob got to work, he asked for an update on Raza Ashraf.

Will had done some digging. "It seems that compliance officers at the bank had noticed millions of dollars flowing into an account in Hong Kong controlled by a dodgy shelf company linked to black market activity. It was at least the third in a series of so-called suspicious activity reports that the bank's internal watchdogs had lodged over the previous few months."

Rob put his rucksack down and took off his jacket. "Drug money?"

Will shrugged. "Probably, except nothing was done about it. The warnings were buried, and the bank continued to handle the company's flow of dirty money into — and out of — its accounts at the bank."

Rob sat at his desk and powered up his laptop. "They were profiting from the money laundering scheme," muttered Rob.

"The person in charge of the flow of money through the Hong Kong subsidiary was Raza Ashraf."

Rob glanced up. Will nodded. "Yep. Noah was also on the Asia desk. Together, they provided banking services to a host of shell companies, many of whom were linked to drug dealers, arms dealers and questionable government agencies from third world countries."

Rob whistled. "What happened?"

"Compliance decided not to indict them, mainly because Global Standard declared it was improving its vetting procedures and internal processes. Noah Palmer testified that Ashraf was not aware of the nature of the transactions. Ashraf was put on probation for three months but was allowed to continue working."

"How did you get this information?" Rob asked.

He grinned. "It's out there if you know where to look."

At Rob's questioning gaze, he elaborated. "I contacted a financial journalist who worked on the original story. A lot of what he told me was never published, but he said the bank continued to process dirty money from alleged criminal activity despite the warning. Leaked documents show billions of funds processed from Panama-based organisations linked to drug cartels."

"Christ."

"My contact said it's a global problem. The benefits of doing business with these shell companies outweighs the penalties."

"The question is, how much did Noah Palmer know? His testimony saved Raza Ashraf his job, but at what cost? Noah Palmer could have had knowledge that Ashraf didn't want to come out, particularly in light of his future political ambitions."

"That might be, but how does it link to the other victims?"

Rob shrugged. "I don't know. Did the other victims have anything to do with money laundering?"

"I don't think so. Galbraith is waiting to give you an update. They may have found a potential link between two of the victims."

Rob perked up. "Really?"

"Yes, but I don't know any more than that. Do you want to bring Ashraf in for questioning?"

"Not yet," said Rob. "We need to be careful with this one. We don't want to ruffle too many feathers unless we have to. Perhaps an informal chat is better at this stage."

"I'll get his home address," said Will, and went back to his desk.

"I hear you have an update?" Rob approached Galbraith. His team sat in the half of the office closest to Hodge's igloo. Was it his imagination or did the ambient temperature dip when he crossed to this side of the room?

The burly Scot, who had his shirtsleeves rolled up, didn't seem to notice. "Aye, we might have found a link between two of the victims."

"Yeah?"

"Kyle McKenzie, the first victim, owned a property development firm. At the time of his death, he had fifty properties in south-west London on his portfolio, including a shopping centre."

"Impressive, but where's the link?"

Galbraith held up a hand to indicate he wasn't finished. "Paul Sutton was a solicitor who dealt in property law. We think he might have done some work for McKenzie."

Rob raised his eyebrows. "If he did, that's a definite link between the two of them. Are any of the others involved in property development?"

"Not that we can see. Langton's company sold heavy equipment to the construction and agricultural industries. There could be a link there, but we haven't found it yet."

"What about Noah Palmer?"

Galbraith shook his head. "Nothing we've found ties him in with the construction or property industries. But we'll keep looking."

"Okay, great." Rob exhaled slowly. Was this the beginning? Had they found the connection? A surge of adrenalin shot through his system as he went back to his desk. First Ashraf, now this property angle. Maybe things were starting to turn around.

# CHAPTER 13

The phones didn't stop ringing. The team working on the domestic homicide needed more hands on deck to prepare for trial. Rob loaned them Jeff and Celeste, who was eager to get as much experience as she could.

Rob had a few leads to follow up himself. Apart from Raza Ashraf, who Will was still looking into, they needed to track down Noah Palmer's best friend. He figured a well-placed call to Suzie Palmer might be the easiest way to get that information.

She wasn't especially pleased to hear from him.

"What can I do for you, Detective?" she said, her voice brittle. She hadn't forgiven him for dropping that bombshell on her last time. He couldn't really blame her. He still felt bad about that.

"I apologise for bothering you," he began. "But I'm trying to trace a friend of Noah's. His best friend, in fact. Would you happen to know who that was?"

There was a slight hesitation. "Noah had lots of friends. How am I supposed to know which one you mean?"

"Who was his best friend? The person he spent the most time with?"

"I suppose that would be Greg Fairchild. They met at university."

"You don't happen to have a number for him, do you?"

"Sorry, no. I didn't keep in touch with Greg after Noah passed away. The last time I saw him was at the funeral."

"Okay, thank you, Mrs Palmer."

"What university did Noah go to?" asked Will.

"Oxford, like Matthew."

It took his sergeant all of two minutes to find an address and telephone number for Greg Fairchild. "According to his LinkedIn profile, he's an IT project manager. Get this, he works for the Home Office."

"The Home Office? Shit. They're not going to want us sniffing around. Still, we need to talk to him. He's the person that knew Palmer best."

"Shall I call him and set up a meeting?"

"No, let's pay him an informal visit. We've got his address."

"Sure thing, guv."

* * *

They waited until eight o'clock in the evening before they paid Greg Fairchild a visit. Not only would it give him time to get home from work, but they'd also miss the traffic. Most of west London quietened down around seven.

Greg Fairchild lived in a pretty Victorian terraced house in Fulham. It was situated in a quiet cul-de-sac with a large park at the end. Evenly spaced street lamps shone pools of light onto the empty pavement.

"Nice area," murmured Will.

The front door was painted sunflower yellow with two vertical stained-glass panels in it. A security light flicked on as they approached.

Rob rang the buzzer. They heard footsteps on the wooden floorboards. The door was opened by a middle-aged man in a suit with a quizzical expression on his face. "Can I help you?"

"Greg Fairchild?" enquired Rob.

"Yes, who wants to know?"

"I'm DCI Miller and this is DS Freemont from Putney Major Investigation Team. We'd like to ask you some questions about Noah Palmer."

His eyebrows shot skyward in surprise. "Noah? Christ, there's a name I haven't heard for a while."

"I understand you were friends?"

Greg nodded. "Yes. Yes, we were. Come in." He stood back to let them enter. "Let's go into the living room. It's on your right."

Rob walked into a warm, comfortable lounge with beige carpeting, lots of well-used furniture and a giant television mounted to the wall. It was tuned to a muted football match. A half-drunk bottle of beer was on the side pedestal.

"Please, sit down."

They did so, perching on the sofa. Greg took the armchair.

"I can't believe you want to talk about Noah. He's been dead for over ten years."

"Twelve," said Rob, with what he hoped was a reassuring smile. "Mrs Palmer told us you were Noah's best friend."

"Yes, we were at uni together. Different courses, but we were both in the dramatic society."

Rob nodded. "I see. And you saw a lot of him before he passed away?"

"We went out from time to time. He had a young family that kept him busy while I was still footloose and fancy free, so to speak." His eyes crinkled at the sides.

"He had two young families," corrected Rob.

Greg's smile vanished. "What makes you say that?"

"He had a baby with a woman called Bella Norton, who I suspect you knew about?"

Greg swallowed. "I swore I wouldn't say anything."

"We believe that you covered for Noah. He told his wife he was with you when in fact he was with Miss Norton and their baby girl."

"I don't know what he told his wife," Greg murmured.

"But you were on standby, so that if she called, you'd be able to vouch for your friend. Isn't that right?"

He gave a slight nod.

"Would you say Noah and his wife had a happy relationship?"

Greg sniffed. "What do you think?"

"I'm asking you."

"On the face of it, yes. They led everyone to believe they were this perfect family. Three great kids, a loving relationship, successful careers. Even I was jealous of them."

"But that wasn't the truth?"

Greg shook his head. "Noah was going crazy inside. He wanted out but he knew that it wasn't an option. He couldn't do that to his kids."

"So he sought out escorts?"

Greg sighed. "It's not as bad as it sounds. We met Bella at a bar and they hit it off. She was a stunner, and great fun. She had some crazy friends, access to drugs, knew all the bouncers at the best nightclubs. She was wild and exciting. So different to the life he had at home."

Rob didn't comment.

"We went out with her and her friends a few times, then Noah started staying over. I warned him to be careful, that if Suzie found out, his marriage would be over."

"He didn't listen?"

"No, he was having too much fun. Whenever Suzie rang, I said Greg had crashed out on the couch. He saw Bella once or twice a month, I think. It went on for years. Suzie blamed me and my wicked ways for him being out so much. Because I was single and liked to party, I was the perfect scapegoat."

"And she never found out?"

He paused.

Rob jumped on him. "What?"

He chewed his lip as if he wasn't sure whether to continue or not.

"Mr Fairchild, if Suzie found out about Noah and Bella, you have to tell me."

He frowned. "Why are you looking into Noah after all these years?"

"It's to do with his death."

"What? Those awful murders?"

"Yes, we're following up some new leads."

Greg's eyes widened. "I see."

"Now, did Suzie find out?" Rob pressed.

He ran a hand through his hair. "I don't know, but she came over one night. It was about two in the morning. She was in a terrible state. I've never seen her like that before. She was usually so controlled, but that night she was like a crazy person. When she discovered Noah wasn't with me, she went ballistic."

Rob exhaled. She bloody knew. All this time she'd been lying to them. "What did you do?"

"I tried to calm her down. I said I'd left him at the bar with some other guys. I don't know if she believed me. She demanded to know which bar, so I gave her the name of our local. We hadn't been there, of course. I'd had a few drinks with mates at the rugby club. She stormed out, and that's the last we ever spoke of it."

"When was this?" Rob's voice was low.

"It was a couple of months before he died."

## CHAPTER 14

"What am I doing here, Detective?" Suzie asked the moment he walked into the interrogation room. Will followed close on his heels.

Next to Suzie was a petite woman with auburn hair and a severe expression on her face. Her solicitor.

"This session is going to be recorded," he stated, ignoring Suzie's question. If he made it as official as possible, he might intimidate her into telling the truth. "Can everybody state their names, please?"

"DS Will Freemont."

"Harriet Donaldson," said the solicitor.

Rob glanced at Suzie.

"Susan Palmer," she muttered.

"DCI Rob Miller from the Major Investigation Team," he barked. "Right, let's get to it. Mrs Palmer, when we last spoke, you denied having any knowledge of your husband being unfaithful, is that correct?"

She nodded.

"Could you verbalise your reply for the recording?" he asked.

"Yes." She gave him an annoyed look. "That's right."

"Your husband was making monthly payments to Miss Norton. Did you not question him as to what these payments were for?"

She frowned. "I didn't know he was making monthly payments."

Rob studied her. Hair twirled in a French bun, expertly applied make-up, back ramrod straight. She was prepared for battle.

"We spoke to Greg Fairchild, who as you know was Noah's closest friend. He told us that he used to cover for your husband when he was with Miss Norton. One night, you arrived at his house demanding to know where Noah was. Do you remember?"

"No. It was a long time ago."

"Let me refresh your memory. It was two in the morning. According to Mr Fairchild, you were in quite a state."

Her clear gaze flickered. "Oh, yes. I remember now. I was expecting Noah back and when he didn't come home, I went to Greg's to find him. I was furious because we had something on the next morning. I can't remember what, but I needed him there. Usually, when he stayed over at Greg's he didn't come back until at least mid-morning."

It sounded plausible. Any wife would be annoyed if they'd planned something and their husband had stayed out the night before.

"Are you sure you didn't go round there because you wanted to check up on your husband? You suspected him of having an affair and you wanted to make sure he was where he'd said he was?"

"I went to Greg's to bring him home," she clarified.

"What did you do when you discovered your husband wasn't there?"

"I was furious. Greg said he'd left him at the bar, so I went to the bar, but I couldn't find him."

"Because he was at his mistress's house?"

"I don't know where he was." She fastened her arctic blue eyes on him. "But when I eventually got home, he was there. We had a row. He said he'd left the bar and come home. I believed him. He smelled like a brewery."

They only had her word for it.

"And you say you didn't know about the monthly payments your husband was making to Miss Norton?" Rob said.

Tears sprang into her eyes. "If he was paying her, it wasn't coming from our joint account. I didn't have access to his personal accounts."

"A thousand pounds a month," Rob supplied.

She gaped at him. "How much?"

Rob softened his tone. "What about after he died? Did you have access then?"

She shook her head. "Our solicitor handled everything. When Noah's accounts were closed, I got a cheque from the bank. I didn't see any bank statements from his personal accounts."

"Who was your solicitor?" he asked.

She sniffed and dabbed her eyes. "I don't remember. It will be in my files."

"Could you check for us please, Mrs Palmer? We'd like to substantiate that."

She nodded, then sniffed and straightened her back. "Is that it? I have things to do."

He couldn't keep her for any longer. "Yes, that's it," he said. "Interview terminated at eleven twenty-three a.m."

* * *

"I can't decide if she's a brilliant actor or if she really didn't know about the affair and the secret child," said Rob, as they made their way back to the squad room.

Will fell into step beside him. "If she's acting, it's an Oscar-winning performance."

Superintendent Hodge marched past. "DCI Miller, I hope you and DS Freemont have attended the ethics training course?"

"It's on my list of things to do, ma'am," he replied.

She shot him an annoyed look. "Book yourselves in, please. Today."

"Yes, ma'am."

Will rolled his eyes. "I'll book us in for this afternoon. It's all online so you just have to listen and then do the test at the end."

"Test, bloody hell. What are we? Twelve?"

Will shrugged and walked away.

\* \* \*

Ethics training got postponed again as Rob insisted Will come with him to talk to Raza Ashraf. The politician had agreed to an informal interview, although he didn't know what it was about. Rob had been purposefully vague on the telephone.

The mayoral candidate lived in a Victorian terrace not unlike Greg Fairchild's, but whereas Greg's was bright and pretty, Ashraf's was the complete opposite. The stark brown-brick facade, shuttered windows and heavy front door seemed designed to keep visitors away.

It was dusk and the street lights had only just come on. It was especially cold this evening, probably due to the lack of cloud cover, and they both rubbed their hands together and stamped their feet as they waited for the door to open.

A woman in a headscarf, who Rob took to be Ashraf's wife, welcomed them in. They followed her into a dimly lit hallway with an austere sideboard and shoe rack.

"If you don't mind," she said, nodding towards it.

Rob grunted and they took off their shoes. Thank goodness he'd worn matching socks that morning. The same couldn't be said for Will, whose left sock had *Tuesday* and right had *Friday* embroidered across the toes. At least he'd got one day right. Will flushed and shuffled ahead so he wouldn't have to see Rob's grin.

The lounge was more welcoming. Beige carpeting softened the stark edges, and a Persian rug added a flash of colour. A chandelier emitted a soft half-light, as if it was set on a dimmer, but with the blinds drawn, the room was still on the dark side.

"My husband will be with you shortly," the woman said and disappeared into the hallway.

They sat down.

"Good afternoon, gentlemen." Ashraf strode into the room, a practised smile on his handsome face. He was smaller than average, but what he lacked in stature, he more than made up for in character. He walked with a purposeful gait and exuded confidence. "What can I help you with?"

"Thank you for seeing us," began Rob. He wanted to stay on the man's good side.

"Always. I'm a great fan of the police force, as I'm sure you're aware. In fact, at the moment, I'm campaigning to reopen the many smaller police stations that have shut, leading to an increase in crime in those areas."

"I've heard. That's much appreciated, sir," said Rob. He meant it. The recent cutbacks had been brutal on the police force.

Ashraf perched on the sofa opposite them. "What was it you wanted to talk to me about?"

"Well, it's a delicate issue involving a man you used to work with at Global Standard. Noah Palmer."

The mayoral candidate's eyes narrowed. "He died, didn't he? Got caught up in those witchcraft killings. I remember reading about it in the paper."

"Yes, that's right," said Rob.

"It was very sad. What a way to go."

"Did you attend the funeral?" asked Rob.

"No, unfortunately not. I wasn't able to get away." He didn't say from what.

"Were you friends?"

"Colleagues, Detective. We worked in the same department, but we weren't close."

"That would have been the Asia desk?"

Ashraf looked surprised, then nodded. "You've done your homework."

"I wouldn't be doing my job if I hadn't." He took a breath. "Mr Ashraf, I know this is a bit sensitive, but could you explain to us what happened with the money laundering investigation that you were involved in?"

Ashraf's gaze hardened. "What's this really about?"

"We're looking into Noah Palmer's death," Rob supplied. "There are some aspects of it that don't make sense, so we're interviewing everyone who knew him around that time."

"I see. And what bearing does the investigation at Global Standard have on the case?" Ashraf's dark eyes fixed on Rob.

"We're looking for reasons someone might have wanted him dead." Rob held his gaze. If the smooth-talking politician thought he could intimidate him, he was sorely mistaken.

Ashraf looked away first. "I thought it was that deranged serial killer who murdered him. Weren't there several bodies? You can't think I had anything to do with that, surely?"

"No, of course not, but we have to check every line of enquiry. The money laundering allegation was serious enough to warrant further investigation, as I'm sure you will agree. The sooner we can rule it out the sooner we can move on with other avenues."

"Well, let me put your mind at rest. I was cleared of all wrongdoing in the compliance matter at Global Standard. In fact, Noah supported me. There were no charges brought against me or the bank."

Rob suspected he wasn't going to get anywhere on that front, and he didn't want to ruffle the man's feathers more than he already had. Ashraf was in a position to make life extremely uncomfortable for the department.

"Okay, thank you, sir. I apologise for disturbing you at home." They got up to leave.

Ashraf walked them to the front door.

"Oh, one last thing," said Rob, as an afterthought. "I don't suppose you can remember where you were on the day of Noah Palmer's death?"

The politician laughed. "After all these years? I don't think so."

"It was Wednesday the fifth of August 2009, if that helps."

Ashraf thought for a moment. "If it was a weekday, then I would have been at the office. I used to work long hours at the bank, usually leaving late in the evening." He smiled. "I wasn't married back then."

"Did you use a security pass to gain entrance to the building?" Rob asked.

"I believe so, yes."

Rob nodded. "Great, then we can check. They may have records."

Ashraf kept smiling, although it didn't meet his eyes. "I hope I've answered your questions sufficiently."

*Nowhere close.* "Yes, that's it for now." Rob forced an equally fake smile. He didn't like the banker-turned-politician. He was far too smarmy. "Thanks again for your time."

He couldn't resist a shiver as he left the dark house and emerged onto the well-lit street.

# CHAPTER 15

"DCI Miller, a word in my office, please."

Rob hadn't been in long. Word had obviously got out that they'd gone to see Raza Ashraf yesterday and the Superintendent wasn't happy about it. Actually, that was an understatement.

She was furious.

"What were you thinking?" she fumed, pacing up and down her frigid office. Despite the cold, her cheeks glowed pink. "Raza Ashraf called the Deputy Commissioner, who happens to be a friend, and lodged a formal complaint. He said you insinuated he was a suspect in Noah Palmer's murder."

"I merely asked him about his relationship with Noah Palmer," Rob said. He'd known this was going to be sticky. Politicians always were. They seemed to think they were above reproach. It pissed him off.

"I thought this was about the serial murders. Why on earth are you questioning the future mayor?"

"Potential future mayor," Rob corrected. *God help us.*

She shot him a dark look.

"He had a motive to want Noah Palmer dead, so we had to look into it. Ashraf should be treated like any other suspect."

"But he's not a serial killer, he's a politician! Obviously, he didn't murder those other people."

Just because he's a politician doesn't mean he isn't also a serial killer, Rob wanted to point out, but he didn't think now was the time to provoke her. She was worked up enough.

She spun on her heel. "Raza Ashraf is a big supporter of law enforcement. We need his backing. I would have thought you'd have had more sense than that."

Rob wasn't going to apologise for doing his job. "We were polite and respectful," he said. "But the guy is shifty. He sidestepped the question about the money laundering at the bank, and he was purposely vague about his relationship with Noah Palmer."

"He's a politician. That's what they do."

"Well, this is a murder inquiry. No one is above the law, ma'am."

She paused to catch her breath. "If he was a legitimate suspect, I would give you some leeway, but don't go looking for suspects where none exist. Raza Ashraf had nothing to do with those pentagon murders."

"Pentagram, ma'am."

"What?" she snapped.

"Nothing."

"Your job is to follow the evidence and there is nothing linking Raza Ashraf to the crimes. No DNA, no witnesses, no CCTV."

She wasn't wrong there.

"Except Noah Palmer was involved in the money laundering cover-up at the bank," Rob pointed out. "He could have been killed to stop the truth coming out."

"And the other victims?" snapped Hodge. "Were they involved in this cover-up too?"

"We're still in the preliminary stages of the investigation, ma'am. There is no hard evidence yet, but I would like your permission to check up on Ashraf's alibi for the days of the murders. All four victims were killed during the week, so that should be easy enough to check. If that's the case, then we'll have ruled him out from our inquiries. There'll be no need to contact him again."

Hodge gave an exaggerated sigh. "This is the last straw, DCI Miller. Run the checks, then leave the man alone. I don't want you to go near him again. Is that understood?"

"If he checks out, you have my word."

She gave a curt nod.

* * *

"How'd it go?" asked Will when he emerged from her office.

"She wasn't happy," said Rob. "Warned us off Ashraf."

Will nodded as if he'd expected as much. "What do you want to do?"

"Let's check out his alibi for the days the men were taken, and if that's in order, we'll strike him off the list of possible suspects."

"I've already put in a request," Will said. "But we're not likely to hear back from Global Standard's HR department until Monday morning."

Rob grunted. "That'll have to do, then."

"You got a minute?" Galbraith was striding towards him.

"Yeah, you got something?"

"Maybe — fancy some fresh air?"

Did he ever?

They went outside and Galbraith lit up a smoke.

"I thought you'd quit," said Rob.

"I did, but I started again. Not as bad as before, though, and I don't smoke at home. I'll pack it in after this case."

"That bad?" Rob asked.

Galbraith shrugged. "Nah, not really. It's the second time I've battled with this and reviewing the case files has brought it all back."

Rob had forgotten he'd actually been there, at the crime scenes, twelve years ago.

"I'm sorry, mate."

"I wanna get the bastard this time, ya ken?"

Rob did ken. He wanted to get the bastard too. "So, what you got?"

"We were right. Sutton did work for McKenzie, but only once. There was a case where the bank foreclosed on a house that McKenzie subsequently bought at auction. The only problem was, the couple living there refused to move out. They had to get a court order to evict them. It got messy and they had to be forcibly removed."

Rob frowned. "Who was the couple?"

"A Mr and Mrs Simms. We're trying to trace them."

Rob nodded. "You haven't found a link to the other guy, Langton, have you?"

"Not yet."

"Anything to do with money laundering, banking, financials?" It was a long shot.

Galbraith shook his head. "Why d'you ask?"

Rob sighed. "It's a lead we're following up. Noah Palmer was involved in a money laundering scam at the bank he was working for at the time. His colleague was in on it too. I was just wondering if there was something there, but . . ." He shrugged. "I guess not."

"No, I'll let you know if we find anything like that."

"Thanks." There was a pause as Galbraith dragged on his cigarette. Rob inhaled the secondary smoke and a long-forgotten craving resurfaced, but he ignored it. He wasn't about to go there, not with a baby on the way.

"What about the other suspects? Have you managed to track them down?"

Galbraith smirked. "That old witch still lives at the same address. Can you believe it? Evan is going to head out there this afternoon, if you'd like to tag along?"

Rob grunted. "Yeah, why not? I could use a change of scene. Anything beats doing that ethics course."

Galbraith laughed. "Okay, I'll let him know you're riding shotgun."

* * *

Amber Knowles lived on the edge of Esher Common, some way back from the road. The only access was from the common car park and across the heath via a worn gravel path.

"What's that place?" asked Rob. Evan was holding his phone in his hand, following the GPS to the cottage. Glimpses of a majestic stone building with palladium-style pillars could be seen through the trees.

"That's Claremont Fan Court School," said Evan, who'd done his research. "It's a private secondary school. Its extensive property backs onto the common."

"Wow." Rob gazed at it. He couldn't imagine going to a school like that. His comprehensive had consisted of a rectangular building and some prefabs around a concrete playground.

"Yeah, apparently all the Chelsea footballers send their kids there. The training ground is close by."

Rob raised his eyebrows.

"That's it," said Evan, as they followed the path round a copse of trees and the house came into view.

"You're kidding?" said Rob.

"I know. It's like something out of a fairy tale. The boss did warn me."

As they got nearer, the gravel path they'd been following turned to uneven brick and led right up to the diminutive front door. On either side of the path was a rambling, wild garden, which would be spectacular in summer, but now looked creepy and bare.

Ancient oaks whispered overhead, and Rob could hear the hollow sound of bamboo chimes rattling somewhere in the distance.

"She doesn't have a telephone, so we couldn't arrange an appointment," said Evan. "I just hope she's home."

Rob did too. It was a long way to have come for a walk.

The front of the cottage was a tangled mess of rambling, dormant rose stems. They gave the cottage a desolate, edgy feel. As if it wasn't eerie enough.

Evan knocked on the door. There was no buzzer.

"Does she even have electricity out here?" Rob asked.

Evan shrugged.

There were certainly no telephone lines overhead. They waited, but it was silent inside.

"She could be dead for all we know," muttered Rob.

The door swung open.

"I'm not dead, Detective. Not yet, anyway. Would you like to come in?"

Rob glanced at Evan, then at the old woman. She was at least eighty, with a weathered face and long white hair that flowed around her shoulders. She wore a paisley tunic with leggings and an assortment of beaded necklaces around her neck. On her feet was a pair of thick socks.

"How did you know we were with the police?" Evan asked.

"Intuition," she said smiling. "And nobody else comes to visit me."

Rob couldn't resist a grin.

"Please come in. Standing here with the door open is letting out all the heat."

They entered the gingerbread cottage and followed Mrs Knowles into a surprisingly neat lounge. Rob glanced around them. Wooden beams held up the house, but the walls were fresh and white, and the terracotta stone floor was covered with an assortment of rugs, all with esoteric patterns on them.

Two armchairs were positioned on either side of a fireplace with a wood-burning stove in it. There didn't appear to be any central heating. An ornate wooden coffee table stood between the two armchairs. Rob admired the intricate design.

"You do this?" he asked.

She nodded. "I used to whittle a bit, although I don't do it so much anymore. Arthritis, you know."

The entire room was encased in a rosy glow from the fire and a tall floor lamp in the corner. It was both quaint and cosy. Rob quite liked it. He couldn't imagine himself living here, but it had a definite charm.

"Please, do sit down," Mrs Knowles said. "I suppose you want to talk about those murders again?"

Rob's eyes widened. How on earth had she known they'd reopened the case?

"What makes you say that, Mrs Knowles?" asked Evan, equally surprised.

She spread her hands. "Why else would you be here? Has there been a fifth murder? Or has new evidence come to light?"

Okay, that was uncanny. "New evidence," Rob said.

She nodded. "I thought as much. Well, whatever it is, I had nothing to do with it."

"We've reopened the case, Mrs Knowles," said Rob. "It's a new team of detectives, so we're retracing old ground. That's why we're here."

"That's understandable," she said. "But like I told that lovely man who was in charge before . . . What's his name now?"

"DCI Lawrence," Rob provided.

She snapped her long, gnarled fingers. "That's it. Well, like I told him, I didn't know any of the victims of those horrible crimes."

"You're familiar with the Wiccan movement?" asked Rob.

Her forest-green eyes glittered. "I think you know I am."

The corners of Rob's mouth turned up. There were no flies on this one. "The victims had Wiccan symbols carved on their chests," he said. "An inverted pentagram. Symbolises devil worship, doesn't it?"

"Ah, the infamous inverted pentagram."

Rob waited for her to continue.

"They have such a bad reputation." She shook her head. "I blame Hollywood. All those low-budget horror movies. Gives everyone the wrong impression. No, my dear, the pentagram, inverted or otherwise, is indeed a pagan symbol but it's not evil. Far from it."

They both stared at her.

96

"What is it, then?" asked Evan.

"It symbolises the interconnection between the elements," she said. "Balance, if you like. In Wicca, we believe it signifies the male energies. The woods, the forests, the trees — all fuelled by the sun, so strongest in the summer months."

The murders had all occurred between May and August.

"So, by carving the pentagram on their chests, the killer was making a statement," said Rob. "He was attempting to balance out something. Get even. Or perhaps it was a woman who wanted to subdue male energy?"

He wasn't sure if he was asking her or telling her, but she gave a knowing smile. "I think you're getting closer to the truth, Detective."

"And you're certain you didn't know these men?" he said.

"No, I still don't know their names. I read about it, obviously, but I didn't take note."

"Do you have any other thoughts on the murders?" Rob asked, just as Evan got up. "I know it's been a while, but you said you'd read about it at the time."

"I think the killer was angry," she said. The sparkle had gone from her eyes now. Evan hovered and then sat down again. "I think they were righting a wrong, striving to correct an injustice."

Rob let her carry on, although he watched her warily.

"I thought that the moment I saw the newspaper article on the first victim," she said. "Wimbledon Common, wasn't it?"

Evan nodded.

"So much rage . . ." She blinked. "But I think they'd got it out of their system by the fourth one."

"What makes you think that?" asked Rob.

"Well, there were no more killings, for one," she said with a thin smile. "But I sensed the anger had petered out by the last one. It didn't strike me as being quite so violent as the others."

"What makes you think that?" he asked.

"Oh, it's nothing specific. Just a feeling. It lacked the same energy."

That was something to think about. Rob wondered if Liz Kramer had had time to look over the post-mortem reports. He'd be interested to see if she had come to the same conclusion.

"You could sense this from a newspaper article?" Rob said.

"It was on the news too. I have a small telly upstairs in my bedroom."

"So you do have electricity here?"

She laughed, although it was more of a cackle. "Of course. I know it's isolated, but it's hardly the Outer Hebrides. I get Amazon deliveries, the postman delivers my mail and if I have to go anywhere, my Uber driver comes right up to this side of the car park."

He had to smile. "I'm sorry, I meant no offence."

"None taken. I just like nature and my privacy, that's all. You don't find a lot of either nowadays. The locals know me, but newcomers are suspicious, I think." She shrugged. "People are often fearful of what they don't understand."

She wasn't wrong there.

Rob thanked her and they walked to the front door. As they said goodbye, Evan nudged Rob and glanced down.

To the left of the door was a rug with a pentagram on it.

CHAPTER 16

"She's definitely suspicious," said Evan, the next morning in the briefing room. Both Rob and Galbraith's team were squeezed in and the smell of freshly brewed coffee permeated the air. Celeste and Jenny had gone across the road to Caffè Nero and bought them all drinks. "I don't know how Lawrence ruled her out the first time round. She even whittles wood, for Christ's sake. She'd know how to carve those pentagrams into the victims' chests, no problem."

Galbraith frowned. "She had no motive. She rarely left the cottage, she had no vehicle and didn't know any of the victims. Just because she looks like a witch, and probably is a witch, that doesn't make her a murderer."

Evan shivered. "She gives me the creeps."

Despite having liked the old woman, Rob tended to agree with Evan. "I don't think we can rule her out. There might be a link we haven't found yet. She mentioned hiring Ubers. Do you think we can find out where she goes?"

"Uber wasn't around twelve years ago," supplied Harry.

"I meant in the last few months. It might give us some idea of her movements. She may be more active than we think."

Harry coloured and glanced at Galbraith, who nodded. "It's not a bad idea. We may as well dot every i."

"Yes, guv."

"Anything on the postie?" Rob asked.

Galbraith shook his head. "Nothing new. He's retired now. Lives in East Molesey. He's part of the local sailing club, but other than that, keeps a low profile. Harry and I went to visit him yesterday."

"Anything strike you as odd?" asked Rob.

"No, in fact, he was very helpful. He remembered the old case."

"Sutton was the one abducted from right outside his house, wasn't he?" Rob frowned, remembering the case notes.

"Aye. Nobody saw a thing. We did a door-to-door at the time, but it was too late for most folk. They were already in bed or asleep."

"How did the killer know Sutton would be back late?" Rob mused. "He must have had access to his schedule."

"Or Sutton knew him and told him," put in Jenny. "Like on a postal round?"

Galbraith put a question mark beside Alfred Whitaker's name on the white board. "That's worth looking into in more detail. We've only got the old postie's word that he didn't speak to Sutton."

"What about Sutton's wife?" asked Rob. "Have you spoken to her?"

"Not recently," Galbraith said. "She was asleep when it happened. She alerted the police around two in the morning when she woke up and realised her husband wasn't home. She rang his mobile but got no reply. When she went outside, his car was still running. He hadn't turned off the engine. His phone was in the car, along with his briefcase and travel bag."

"Why was he home so late?" asked Jenny.

"He'd been away on a short business trip. His flight landed at Heathrow around ten o'clock that evening, if I remember correctly."

"Well, the killer knew exactly when to expect him," said Rob. "That's where we should start."

"I'll bring the wife in. See if she remembers anything," said Galbraith with a curt nod.

* * *

Sutton's wife was a tall, statuesque woman who reminded Rob of Jerry Hall, the eighties model and fashion icon. Despite being in her mid-fifties, she'd aged well and would still turn heads if she walked into a bar. Rob was watching from the viewing room as Galbraith and his sergeant, Evan, began the interview.

Mrs Sutton — "Please, call me Brigit" — sat with her long legs crossed in front of her, her arms loosely folded and a smile on her delicately made-up face.

Galbraith smiled back. "Thank you for coming in on such short notice. We appreciate your time."

"It's not a problem, but what is this about? Have you learned something new about my late husband's death?" She hugged herself a little tighter as she said the words.

"Not as such." He gave her a sympathetic smile. "We were just wondering who knew your husband was going away on a work trip that week? Did either of you mention it to anyone?"

She blinked and pursed her lips. "I think quite a few people knew. It wasn't a secret. His work colleagues, of course, and maybe one or two of our friends."

"Could you make me a list?" Galbraith asked.

She exhaled. "I can try, but it's been twelve years. I can't remember everyone we might have had round or talked to before he left."

"I understand it's difficult, but it might be important."

She gave a little nod.

"Also," Galbraith continued, "you didn't happen to mention it to the postman, by any chance?"

She gawked at him. "The postman?"

"Yes, a man by the name of Alfred Whitaker? He delivered the post to your area."

She stared at him as if he was mad. Rob had to admit, it was a bit left field.

"Um . . . I don't know. I don't recall talking to the postman."

"Okay, not to worry. Thank you for your time, Mrs Sutton. I mean, Brigit. If you wouldn't mind making me that list, that would be very helpful. Then you can go."

Rob left the viewing room deep in thought. It had been a long shot. Perhaps the well-meaning Whitaker was just that and, like Hodge had said, they were looking for suspects where none existed.

* * *

That evening, Rob met his old friend, Tony Sanderson at the Cricketers for a pint. The criminal profiler had helped them on previous cases, his insights often contributing towards their major breakthroughs. Rob had been wanting to pick his brain for some time. However, his esteemed friend had been in America, giving a talk at the FBI Behavioral Analysis Unit.

"Hitting the big time now, eh?" Rob joked, when he saw him.

Tony grinned and pumped his hand. "Hardly. The FBI have been streaks ahead of us in the profiling game for years. We're only just catching up."

They found a high table at the back, where it wasn't so busy that they couldn't hear each other talk. Rob got the first round.

"So, what is it this time?" asked Tony, when Rob returned with two lagers.

He grinned. They hardly ever met up other than for work these days. "Remember those pentagram killings back in 2009?"

Tony thought for a moment, sorting through his encyclopaedic knowledge of serial killers. As a university lecturer, he studied all the recent cases and presented them to his criminology honours students. His latest book, *The Evil Mind*, delved into the psyche of these individuals and what made them kill. Rob had read it a couple of months back in one sitting.

"Ritualistic killings, weren't they? The bodies were found dotted around the Surrey Hills. I seem to recall some connection to witchcraft or the occult."

"That's right. Four men killed by blows to the head, then arranged like Da Vinci's Vitruvian Man in a white circle with a pentagram carved into their torsos. There were candles positioned around the body."

"Yes, it's coming back to me now. Interesting case. The authorities never did find out who the murderer was."

"Not even close," said Rob. "When the leads dried up, the case was shelved."

"What is this new evidence you've found?"

Rob spent the next ten minutes filling Tony in on everything they'd uncovered. The DNA, the escort, the property development angle, the witchy woman in the woods, and the possible link to money laundering. When he was finished, Tony had reached the bottom of his glass. He hadn't interrupted once.

"The problem is, we can't find any consistent link between the four victims. There's no obvious connection."

"There might not be one," Tony said casually.

Rob frowned. "What do you mean? Of course there's a connection. Why else were they targeted?"

"I've seen a few cases like this one, mostly in the States," he said. "And mostly involving shootings, but the goal is the same. Where there doesn't appear to be a link between the victims, it's often because there isn't one. The victims have been chosen at random, to mask one particular murder."

Rob stared at his friend.

"Think about it. You have four apparently random murders, after which the killing stopped. Why would he suddenly stop? If he was a real serial killer, stopping wouldn't be an option. He'd have done the opposite — escalate over time. The killings would get more frequent, bolder as he got a taste for it. But your guy killed four people then called it a day."

Rob was listening intently.

"That tells me this was a one-off killing spree. But they chose to kill four people—"

"To make it look like a serial killer was at work," finished Rob.

Tony nodded. "Exactly. The definition of a serial killer is three or more murders with the same MO. The killer wanted to draw attention away from the one person who they really wanted dead. The one person, who if he'd died in isolation, would have led back to the murderer."

It was a cunning but sick plan. "The killer took three innocent lives just to disguise one true murder," Rob muttered. "He must be a messed-up bastard."

"And devious," said Tony. "If I had to profile someone like that, I'd say you're looking for someone who is meticulous and organised. Well educated, probably to degree or diploma level, with a creative flair. This person won't be obvious, they'll prefer to fly under the radar. The showy nature of the crimes is just that, a show, designed to detract from the obvious. It's not because they like to show off. Just the opposite. They'll be quiet and unassuming. Probably quite normal. Well integrated into society."

"Do you think this could be a woman's work?" asked Rob, thinking of the old woman in the woods.

"Statistically, it's more likely to be a man," said Tony. "And the nature of the abductions and the physical blows to the head are typically male. I'd say you're most likely looking for a male killer."

Mrs Knowles was looking less likely, while Ashraf was still a big question mark. "Okay, thanks." Rob exhaled noisily. His head was spinning. "You've given us a lot to think about."

"You're welcome." He grinned, then grew serious. "Listen, this is only my best educated guess based on the information you've given me. I don't know the full details of the case. There might be other factors at play that would throw this theory off."

"It makes sense, though. Each of the victims was a wealthy, successful man. They'd have stepped on toes to get there. Made enemies along the way. We need to look at the individual victims to see who wanted them dead, rather than the case as a whole."

"That's what I'd do." Tony drained the last of his drink. "Then, I'd look at *how* the killer found the other three, not *why*. Did he pick them out of *Who's Who?* The newspaper? A radio bulletin?"

Rob ran a hand through his hair. "Location must have something to do with it. Three of the four bodies were found in the Box Hill area. Only the first was found in Wimbledon."

"I'd start with that one," Tony said. "It's the odd one out. But conversely, the killer may have been seeking variety, to prevent the police from looking too close to home."

Rob sighed. "You're not making this easy."

"It never is." Tony stood up and took his coat off the back of his chair. "Good luck. Let me know how you get on. I've got to get back, my eldest, Lexi, is bringing her new boyfriend round for supper." He sighed. "It's always a fraught affair. She keeps telling me not to look at everyone like they're a serial killer."

Rob laughed. "Occupational hazard."

"Unfortunately. By the way, Kim asked me to invite you and Jo over for dinner one evening." He grinned. "Preferably before the baby's born."

"Sounds great, I'll get Jo to give Kim a ring and set something up. Thanks, mate. I mean it. Once again, you've been extremely helpful."

"Glad to be of service. See you soon."

He pulled on his long, black coat, strode to the pub door and disappeared out into the rain.

# CHAPTER 17

It was gone eight thirty by the time Rob got home. He spent the next few hours cleaning the house, because Jo was coming round tomorrow for the weekend.

Family time.

He was going to be a dad. A shiver of anticipation mingled with dread shot down his spine. The world he lived in was so ugly. How was he going to protect his child from that?

Trigger, who was curled up at his feet, glanced up as if to say, "I'm there for you, buddy."

He stroked the dog's ears, then got up to take him for a walk. It was too bloody cold to stay out long. They went once around the block, then retreated back to the warmth.

Rob lay on the couch and watched a comedy show before going to bed. It was a lame attempt to lighten his mood. It didn't work. His thoughts automatically returned to the case.

If what Tony had surmised was true, who was the original victim — the one the killer wanted dead? He sat up and took the folder out of his rucksack. He picked up the in-depth report on each victim.

Was it Kyle McKenzie, the property developer? Did someone blame him for kicking them out? For taking their house away from them? McKenzie often bought repossessed houses at auction. There was that couple that had refused to move. Had the killer been one of them? Or both?

What about Nathan Langton from RBM Machinery? His company had grown into a behemoth in the decade before his death. Surely, he must have had a few enemies?

Then there was Paul Sutton specialising in family law. Had he pissed off one of his clients? There was never a winner in divorce cases, he knew that first hand. But was someone angry enough to have murdered him and three others in cold blood just to get even?

And finally, Noah Palmer. Investment banker, possible money launderer or part of a cover-up. A cheating husband who'd had a secret child with a prostitute behind his wife's back. There were any number of suspects there, but right now, Rob's money was on Raza Ashraf.

* * *

"Ashraf's hiding something," said Rob over his seafood linguine the next evening. He and Jo were having dinner at an Italian restaurant in Richmond. Jo had a hankering for creamy pasta, and he wasn't going to refuse a pregnant woman.

"I agree, it does sound suspicious, but Global Standard is not an anomaly. The role of big banks in facilitating money laundering has been a hot topic for a few years now. In fact, the National Crime Agency set up the National Economic Crime Centre to coordinate the UK's response to that very thing, for all the good it's doing."

"It's not working?" Rob asked, twirling pasta around his fork.

"The problem is, the major banks have been brought in to help design the economic crime policy. So instead of holding them accountable, the government has partnered with them to tackle the problem."

"I see what you mean," said Rob. It was a lot more complex than he'd thought.

Jo nodded. "The banks continue to process their proceeds of corruption and are never held to account. There is a dire need for corporate liability reform, but nothing's happened as yet."

"That's why the case against Raza Ashraf was dropped," mused Rob. "Even after the bank's internal watchdog had brought it to the attention of the powers that be."

"Global Standard wouldn't have wanted the negative publicity either," pointed out Jo. "If there wasn't enough evidence, or as in your case, a colleague testified that Ashraf wasn't responsible, then that would have been enough to brush it all under the carpet."

Rob speared a prawn. "That's exactly what happened."

"It is what it is," said Jo. "But why is this important now? Ashraf's been out of the banking sector for years."

"It gives him a motive. Noah Palmer could have had proof of his illegal dealings, something he didn't want to come out."

Jo pursed her lips. "Have you spoken to anyone else at Global Standard? Anyone who worked with them back in the day?"

"No. I went to see Ashraf at his house and the Super had a shit fit. Apparently, he called the Deputy Commissioner and complained. They're friends."

Jo rolled her eyes. "Of course they are."

"I've been told to back off Ashraf. It wouldn't do to keep pestering his old work colleagues. It's bound to get back to him."

"I could look into it," Jo suggested.

Rob frowned, but her eyes were sparkling. "On the QT, obviously. I could look into who they worked with back in the day. If they're still around, I might even be able to contact them and have an off-the-record chat."

"Is that wise? You're on leave."

"Exactly, I haven't been given the sack. I still have access to the system, and the building for that matter, not that I'm planning on going in."

Jo hadn't been back to the office since her sister's attacker had been apprehended last summer. Shortly after that, she'd discovered she was pregnant, and had decided to take extended leave followed by maternity leave.

Her boss had been surprisingly okay with it, but after her refusal to let go of the investigation around her sister's killer, he'd been looking for an excuse to get rid of her. She'd given him the perfect opportunity.

"I don't want you getting into trouble," Rob said.

"I'll be careful, I promise. Pearson will never know. Besides, it will give me something to do."

They took Trigger for a walk in Old Deer Park after dinner. It was freezing outside, and the grass crunched underfoot.

"I'm sure it's going to snow," Jo remarked, looking up into the night sky.

"It's certainly cold enough." Rob took her hand.

Trigger bounced around oblivious to the temperature, his tongue hanging out. He darted to the end of the field and then back again, steam billowing out of his mouth.

"Come on," called Rob, when he could no longer feel his fingertips. "Time to go home."

They walked back and got comfortable on the couch. He sat with his legs up while Jo curled up next to him, her head on his shoulder.

"This is nice." Rob stroked her hair. He was still getting used to the new dynamic in their relationship. The pregnancy had been a massive surprise, but not an unpleasant one. He loved Jo, he knew that now, even if he hadn't told her. A baby was the natural next step, albeit that it was happening a bit sooner than he would have liked, but then some things were out of their control. "I could get used to this."

She smiled up at him. "Are you saying you'd like us to move in together?"

He grinned back. He'd been dropping a few hints lately, but she'd brushed over them with her usual nonchalance. They'd never really talked about it. "I would, yes. What do you think?"

"I'm not sure. I love being with you, but there's nothing romantic about midnight feeds and dirty nappies. I don't want it to ruin what we have."

"I want to be a part of it," he told her. "You can't cope with all that by yourself."

"But then I'm moving in out of obligation, and I don't want that either."

"It wouldn't be like that," he insisted. "I want us to be a family. I want to be a part of our baby's life. All the time. Not just on the weekends."

The last thing he wanted was to be a good-time dad.

"What about work?" she said. "You know how stressful the cases can be."

"I'll manage," he said. "Other working parents do. Besides, the same thing could be said for you, when you go back to work."

She bit her lip. "I don't know if I am going back to work."

"What?" He turned to look at her. "Are you serious?"

"Yes." She stroked her stomach. "I don't want to put our child in childcare so I can go back to chasing organised criminals. I don't enjoy working for Pearson and now that my sister's killer is behind bars, I don't feel the urgency I used to anymore. It's like something's changed inside me. I'm not sure it's what I want anymore."

Rob hesitated. "It could be the pregnancy hormones talking. Your mothering instincts kicking in. Maybe when the baby's born, you'll feel differently."

"Maybe . . ." she mused, although he could tell by her voice that she wasn't convinced.

"What will you do if you don't go back to the NCA?" The National Crime Agency had been her life. She'd been so ambitious, rising to the rank of DCI in under ten years. She was a good detective too. One of the best he'd worked with. He couldn't see her giving all that up.

"Be a mum. Maybe take on some consulting work part-time."

"I see you've been giving this some thought." He was both hurt and surprised that she hadn't confided in him.

"I have," she acknowledged. "This break has made me look at things differently. Besides, one of us should be available to look after the baby, at least for the first few years."

She had a point there.

"Well, just so you know, I'll support you whatever you decide to do."

She leaned over and kissed him. "Thank you, Rob. That means a lot to me." He sensed some of the tension she'd been carrying dissipate.

Of course, that meant that his job was even more important. "I'd better not rock the boat too much with Ashraf, then." He gave a low chuckle. "We can't both be without a job."

She squeezed his hand. "Normally, I'd say chase down every lead, but in light of our current situation, I agree, caution is called for. You might have to let this one go, Rob."

He knew that she knew that would never happen.

## CHAPTER 18

Rachel stood outside the massive house, her heart pounding. She wasn't at all sure this was a good idea, but she had to try.

After her mother's tearful confession, she'd been struck by an overwhelming urge to find out what her biological father had really been like. She'd never had the chance to get to know him, but it helped that he'd wanted to be a part of her life. He hadn't run away like so many of her friend's fathers. They didn't want to know. But her dad had paid money every month for her. He'd cared.

No one knew she was here. A Google search had helped her locate Noah Palmer's home address. Compared to her council flat on the Hounslow estate, this was a mansion. It had a paved driveway, pot plants in urns on either side of a glossy front door and shuttered windows that sparkled in the weak winter sun. It was the kind of house she'd always dreamed of.

Now it really existed. She couldn't wait to meet her three half-siblings. And her father's wife seemed nice. In the newspaper clippings she'd read, she'd been devastated by her husband's death. A woman who felt that much pain couldn't be mean, surely?

Anyway, she was about to find out.

She didn't expect a warm welcome, but she hoped the lady would talk to her about her father. Tell her some of the things she desperately wanted to know.

What was he like? Was he sporty? He must have been if he rode bikes. Was he smart, like her? Good at maths? She'd heard he worked in a bank, so perhaps she took after him in that respect. She had so many unanswered questions. If only the lady would help her answer them.

She walked up to the front door and thumped the knocker. It reverberated around the house. She held her breath as she heard footsteps, and then the door was flung open.

"Yes?" asked the woman she'd seen in the newspaper, except she didn't look heartbroken or kind. Her hair was pulled back in a tight up-do, her face was made up and she was dressed like she was about to go out somewhere fancy.

Rachel hesitated.

"Can I help you?" asked the woman.

She had cold blue eyes. Suspicious eyes. Rachel had second thoughts. She took a step backwards. "Um . . . Actually, this was a mistake. I'm sorry."

"Who are you?" barked the woman, taking a step forward. In the sunlight, her features were even harder. Meaner.

Rachel swallowed. "I'm Noah Palmer's daughter."

The woman's face drained of colour. She put a hand on the wall to steady herself. "Good Lord."

Her eyes raked over Rachel, starting at her hair and moving down over her face and body and then back up again. "What are you doing here?" she croaked.

"I came to say hello," she said. "But if it's a bad time . . ."

"A bad time?" The woman made a strangled laughing sound. "A bad time? Is it ever a good time to meet your husband's whore's child?"

Rachel gasped.

"Go away," snarled the woman, swatting at her like she was an irritating fly. "Get out of here. You're not welcome."

That much was clear.

"Mum, who's that?" came a voice over the woman's shoulder.

"No one, dear."

A teenage girl her own age appeared next to her mother. She was pretty, much prettier than Rachel, with long, shiny brown hair, huge blue eyes and a healthy blush to her cheeks. She gazed at Rachel with open curiosity.

Rachel ran a hand through her tangled blonde hair, aware of her cheap clothing, her pasty complexion and her pimples.

"I'm Rachel Norton," she said.

"I don't care who you are," said the woman, one arm pushing her daughter back into the house. "Leave now."

"I just came to ask about my father." She figured she may as well get it out.

"He's not your father," came the hissed response. "You were a mistake. An error of judgement that should never have happened. You have no right to come here. Now bugger off."

"Mum!" said the girl inside. "You can't speak to her like that."

"She's no one, dear. Just a delinquent trying to scam us. I should call the police."

Heat crept into her face. "I'm going," she spat. "I'm sorry I came to see you. I thought . . . Well, it doesn't matter now. You're just a mean bitch. No wonder he slept with my mother."

The woman marched out the door and slapped her. "Get off my property right now, you little slut."

Rachel's cheek burned. Tears sprang to her eyes. The teenager had gone back inside and hadn't seen what her mother had done.

Her sister.

Nobody cared.

She turned and ran.

Behind her, the door slammed shut. Rachel kept running until she reached the end of the road. Gasping, her eyes stinging with tears, she stopped and caught her breath.

*What a fucking bitch.* How dare she talk to her like that? Like she was filth.

She might be poor, but she was a much nicer human being than that woman. She stomped back towards the bus stop. She'd had to take two trains and a bus to get here. What a waste of time and money.

She passed a house under construction. A pile of bricks lay on the pavement outside, waiting to be used. On a whim, she picked two of them up and ran back down the road to the Palmers' house.

"Take this, you rude cow!"

She hurled the bricks at the window. The first flew right through the lounge window, shattering it completely.

*Good.*

She threw the second brick and it hit the next window, smashing that into a million pieces. There was a scream from inside.

Rachel didn't wait for a response. She took off down the road, sprinting as fast as her legs would carry her. Soon she was back at the bus stop.

*That'll teach them.*

Her breath came in loud gasps and she exhaled slowly trying to get it under control. The bus arrived and the doors opened with a soft wheeze. She climbed in and took a seat. Her pulse was racing from the adrenalin, but she didn't regret it. Not one little bit.

If that's the type of family he came from, no wonder he'd sought out her mother. Hopefully he had found a little happiness with them. He certainly wouldn't have found any with *her*.

As the bus trundled down the lane towards the station, she saw a police car, siren blaring, racing past in the opposite direction.

She touched her cheek. If that woman was going to call the police, she'd lay an assault charge. She took out her phone and snapped a selfie of her face. The handprint was vividly outlined. She was no fool.

That bitch was going to get what was coming to her.

No one messed with Rachel Norton and got away with it.

## CHAPTER 19

Rob had just opened a beer and sat down to watch the rugby when he got the call from Chiswick Police Station.

"Shit," he muttered.

"What is it?" Jo came into the lounge.

"Rachel Norton just threw a brick through Suzie Palmer's window," he said. "They've brought her in and she's asking for me. I'm sorry, I'm going to have to go."

Jo nodded. "Okay. I'll see you later."

First, Rob went to Suzie Palmer's house to survey the damage and find out exactly what had happened. The officer he'd spoken to had said Rachel was threatening to lay an assault charge. Something bad had obviously gone down. Rachel could stew a bit. It wouldn't do her any harm. He'd told the Chiswick Police to keep her in custody until he got there.

A police vehicle was parked in the driveway when he arrived and a uniformed officer stood outside the window taking photographs with his mobile device.

Inside, he found Suzie talking to another officer, surrounded by broken glass. "It's lucky nobody was hurt," she was saying.

"Right, thanks for your statement, Mrs Palmer. We'll be in touch."

Suzie nodded.

"Good afternoon." Rob came into the room. He glanced around. It was a mess. The cream carpet glistened with shards of glass. "How do you know it was Rachel Norton?"

Suze sighed in exasperation. "Because I saw her. She came to the house. Said she wanted to find out about her father. Can you imagine the cheek of the girl?"

So, Bella had told Rachel about her dad. Now she was on the hunt for more information.

"And did you help her?" he asked, knowing the answer.

"Of course not," huffed Suzie. "Why on earth would I want to talk to my husband's illegitimate daughter? It's insane. She ought to have known better than to come here."

"What *did* you say to her?" asked Rob.

"I told her to get lost. Not in those exact words, obviously, but I don't want her to think she can arrive unannounced and harass us like this."

"I'm sure she had no intention of harassing you," explained Rob. "I expect she just wanted some info on her father, like she said. She's only just found out about him."

"That's not my problem." Suzie inspected her white-tipped nails. "Don't expect me to be nice to my husband's brat."

Rob raised an eyebrow. This was a side to Suzie he hadn't seen before. "Was she upset when you told her to leave?"

"I don't know. I didn't wait to find out. I went inside and shut the door. My daughter is home studying for her exams. I can't have her distracted by some crazy person. She probably just wants money, anyway."

"Did she ask for money?"

"No, but I know her type."

Rob didn't comment.

"She could have hurt someone," Suzie repeated. "It was a blatant act of vandalism and I will be pressing charges."

"Did you actually see her throw the bricks?" Rob narrowed his gaze.

Suzie hesitated. "No, but I sent her packing less than five minutes before that. It was obviously her."

"They may not think so in a courtroom," said Rob, an edge to his voice. "Whereas Rachel Norton has a photograph of her cheek after you slapped her."

Suzie gasped. "I did no such thing."

"Again, a court may disagree."

"She could have slapped herself and taken the photograph."

Rob bowed his head. That was true, although a magistrate might not see it that way. "Do you mind if I give you some advice, Mrs Palmer?"

She pouted but gave a terse nod.

"You have every right to press charges, but if you do, I think you'll find Rachel Norton will do the same. Do you really want to go to court on an assault charge? In addition, Rachel is your husband's biological daughter, and as such, has certain legal rights. You might want to think twice before you antagonise her."

"Antagonise her!" She snorted. "*She's* the one who antagonised me." But the fire had gone out of her eyes.

"I'm just saying, think about it," he urged. "You don't want this to escalate."

Suzie's lips clamped together.

"I must be off," Rob said. "But thank you for your time." He flashed her a polite smile and got back into his car.

\* \* \*

"What were you thinking?"

Rob sat opposite Rachel Norton in a private interrogation room at Chiswick Police Station.

"She made me so mad," Rachel ground out. "What a bitch!"

Rob shook his head. "Why did you go there in the first place? How did you even get her address?"

"My mum told me about Noah Palmer, so I googled him. It wasn't hard to find his wife's name and address. Everything is online nowadays."

Rob cringed. "Okay, fair enough. And you thought you'd go and have a cosy chat with your late father's wife, did you?"

"I wanted to find out more about him," she sulked. "The newspaper article I read had a picture of her in it. She looked devastated, so I thought she couldn't be too bad." She sniffed. "Man, was I wrong."

"What did she say to you?" asked Rob.

"She was rude from the get-go," huffed Rachel. "She spoke to me like I was some homeless beggar or something." She tossed her unbrushed golden hair over her shoulder. "I explained who I was and that's when she lost it."

Rob didn't miss the tears that sprang to her eyes or the hurried attempt to blink them away. "And that's why you tossed two bricks through her window?"

"I thought she deserved it. Stupid cow."

"You know she threatened to press charges?"

Rachel scoffed. "Let her try. She slapped me across the face. I've got a photograph to prove it."

Rob sighed. "Look, I've spoken to Mrs Palmer. She's agreed not to press charges if you don't."

"You have? When?" She looked visibly hurt he'd gone to see Suzie Palmer first.

"Earlier. I had to assess the damage and find out what had happened before I spoke to you. You should be glad I did — I managed to talk her down."

"Thank you," Rachel mumbled. Her face reminded Rob of a basset hound's. All soulful eyes and mournful expression. His heart went out to her. She was just a lost kid, looking for information on her father. What kid wouldn't want that?

He softened his tone. "If you want to get a proper job one day, you're going to have to clean up your act. No more brushes with the law. Stay out of trouble, concentrate on your exams and work hard. Then you'll go places. This path you're on now, this will only lead to more trouble. Trust me, I know."

She gave him a sideways look. "How?"

"I wasn't always a cop. There was a time when my path could have taken a very different route."

She thought about this. "Okay. I'll be as good as gold from now on."

He grinned.

"Do *you* know anything about my father?" she asked.

"I know he worked in a bank and that he was good at his job. I know he cycled a lot and was training for a long-distance race. I know he enjoyed spending time with you and your mother." Bella had told him that much. "I also know he was supporting you financially, even if he couldn't be there physically."

She gave a sad smile. "It's so strange. For years my father was this shadowy figure in my mind, some loser my mother had slept with. A nobody. And now I find out that he wasn't like that at all. He actually seems like a decent guy."

"I think he was."

"I wish I could have known him."

Rob nodded. An instinct he could only describe as paternal kicked in. He had to finalise things with Jo. Their child deserved to have both parents on hand. He didn't want to be a stranger like Noah had been to Rachel.

He stood up. "Okay, we're done here. But stay away from the Palmers' house from now on."

"Are they going to keep me here?" she asked.

"No, there are no charges being brought, so you're free to go." Rob called the custody sergeant, who filled out the necessary paperwork. But before Rachel left, he had one more thing to put to her.

"If you still want some help with your French, I know someone who might be able to tutor you."

Her eyes widened. "Really?"

"Yes, my ex-wife's sister. She's not a teacher, but she is French, and I know she wouldn't mind helping you practise. She's a mum herself. Three kids. You'll like her."

Naomi was completely different from Yvette. Stable, settled and maternal, Rob was sure she'd be happy to help Rachel.

"Okay, but you know I can't pay her anything?"

"I know," said Rob. "I'll ask her and get back to you."

"Thanks, DCI Miller." Rachel gave a shy smile.

"You can call me Rob."

* * *

"You've got a soft spot for that girl," said Jo, once he'd got home and told her what had transpired.

Rob grimaced. "I know. I can't help feeling that if she can just get through school without getting into any more trouble, she's got a shot at a decent life, you know?"

Jo smiled and squeezed his hand.

That's all anyone could ask for, really. A shot. He only hoped Rachel wouldn't screw it up.

# CHAPTER 20

Rob's mobile phone buzzed. He'd just said goodbye to an excited Trigger, who hadn't spared him so much as a backwards glance before darting into the neighbour's house in expectation of his morning treat.

"Cupboard love," murmured Rob, as he got into his car and picked up the call.

"Guv, have you seen the *Mail* this morning?" said Will.

"No, what's up?"

"There's an article about Rachel Norton being Noah Palmer's secret daughter. It seems a journalist got wind of the story. Suzie Palmer is fuming. She's already been on the phone to the Superintendent, who is out for blood. Thought I should give you a heads-up."

He slammed his hand down on the steering wheel. "Fuck, how did they find out?"

"I think it had something to do with the brick incident. Rachel is quoted in the piece, so she's obviously spoken to them."

Rob sighed. Rachel hadn't mentioned talking to a journalist. They must have ambushed her over the weekend and offered her money. Rachel would have spilled the beans for a hundred quid. This was going to get messy.

"Okay, I'm on my way in."

No superintendent minded the occasional well-placed article singing the praises of their department, but this sort of unplanned, negative publicity was out of their control and therefore much feared. Desperate to make a good impression, Hodge would be looking for someone to blame.

Three guesses who that would be.

Rob hadn't even taken off his jacket before he was summoned into her office. She was prancing around, clearly agitated. With her was the cool-as-cucumber press liaison officer, Vicky Bainbridge.

"Hello, Rob," Vicky said breezily.

"Morning, Vicky." Rob shot her a thin smile. He turned to Hodge. "I've heard about the article, ma'am, but I haven't seen it yet."

She picked a newspaper up off her desk and slapped it into his chest.

He frowned and glanced down.

*DEAD BANKER'S POOR LOVE CHILD*, read the headline.

Catchy.

It went on to explain about Noah and Bella's relationship, and how after the banker's death, Rachel Norton had been cut off and lived in poverty. Rachel was described as bright, articulate and ambitious, hampered only by her council estate upbringing.

Rachel was all of those things, and nothing the article said was untrue, however, he could imagine Suzie Palmer having a meltdown over it. God forbid the PTA should find out her husband had slept around, and with a prostitute too.

"I've had Mrs Palmer on the phone," Hodge said, hands on her hips. "She's blaming us for the leak."

"It had nothing to do with us," said Rob. "Rachel brought this on herself when she threw those bricks through Suzie Palmer's window. It got attention. This reporter—" he glanced down at the article — "Hanna Whitby, obviously got the whole story out of Rachel, who would have delighted in making life uncomfortable for Suzie Palmer. The woman wasn't very nice to her."

"Can't say I blame her," ranted the Super. "Rachel is the product of her husband's illicit affair. The daughter of a sex worker, no less."

"Ex-sex worker," pointed out Rob. "Isabella Norton cleaned up her act after she had Rachel. She hasn't been on the streets in at least twelve years."

"You know what I mean," huffed Hodge. "Mrs Palmer is threatening to sue us for defamation of character and God knows what else."

"She'll have to sue the paper if she feels that strongly about it. Not us," cut in Vicky. Thank goodness he had her cool head backing him up.

"Mrs Palmer assaulted Rachel Norton prior to the brick incident," Rob divulged. "I managed to convince both of them not to press charges."

Vicky whistled. "I'm sure she won't want that coming out."

Rob nodded. "Exactly."

Hodge mumbled something under her breath. "Where are we on this case anyway, DCI Miller?"

Rob told her about his talk with Tony Sanderson. "I've still got to confirm with DCI Galbraith, ma'am, but we're going to change our focus to the individual victims and look at possible suspects who wanted them dead. It might be that three of the murders were random attacks to disguise the one true murder."

"For fuck's sake," she muttered. "Why couldn't this be a simple DNA case? I'd heard things about this department, but I thought people were overexaggerating. I take it back. It's all true. You guys attract trouble. Serial cases, deranged murderers, revenge killings. Nothing's black and white with you lot, is it?"

Vicky shot him a sideways grin. "I'm going to leave you to it. Unless there's anything else, ma'am?"

"No, that's all, Vicky. I trust you'll divert any attempts by Suzie Palmer to sue us towards the offending newspaper."

"Of course."

Vicky left the room, closing the igloo door behind her. Rob shivered. If anything, the temperature in the room was frostier than usual. Or perhaps that was the atmosphere.

"Where does that leave us with Raza Ashraf?" Hodge asked.

Rob gave her a straight answer. "We're looking into his alibi for the days of the killings. Jenny — DS Bird, rather — is on the phone with the HR department at Global Standard as we speak. Hopefully, it will be a quick process and we can eliminate the mayoral candidate from our inquiries."

She gave a curt nod. "Be sure that you do, and for God's sake, keep this under wraps."

Rob left the Super's office and went straight to Jenny's desk. She was typing up a report. "Jen, did you speak to the HR team?"

"Yes. They're going to look into it and get back to me. I stressed the urgency."

"Great, let me know as soon as you hear anything."

"Will do, guv."

A ruckus on Galbraith's side of the office caught his attention. Evan and Harry were whooping and high-fiving, while their DCI looked on, a huge grin on his ruddy face.

"Good news?" Rob stalked over. They needed a breakthrough. So far, none of their inquiries had panned out.

"We've found a definite link between Sutton, McKenzie and Langton," said Evan, a little breathlessly. "And one of the original suspects."

"Not the weird old lady in the woods?"

Galbraith shook his head. "The postie."

"Whitaker?" Rob raked through his hair. "The postman? Really?"

"Aye. The bastard had ties to all three of them, and a motive."

"What was it?" asked Will, who'd caught the tail end of the conversation and scooted over on his wheelie chair.

"Get this," said Evan. "Whitaker was evicted from the family home for defaulting on the mortgage. When he had his breakdown, he lost his job and couldn't make the payments. The mortgage company didn't want to know. Neither did the new owner, who hired a lawyer to kick him and his wife out."

"Let me guess. Sutton?" said Rob.

"You got it. McKenzie hired Sutton to evict Whitaker and his wife. They took it very badly."

"Why didn't they pick this up before?" asked Rob. "Wasn't the couple's name in the original case files?"

"Yes, but the house was in Whitaker's wife's name, Simms. Lawrence and his team never made the connection."

Rob exhaled. "What about Langton? How does he fit into it?"

"He's the wife's new husband," said Harry with relish. "After she left Whitaker, she met and married Langton. It was love at first sight, apparently. He was everything Whitaker wasn't. Stable, solvent, attentive." He grinned. "I spoke to her this morning."

Rob was stunned. Tony had been wrong. It wasn't four murders to disguise one, it was four murders to disguise three. Unless . . .

"What about Palmer?" he asked. "Any ties there?"

"Not that we've found. We thought maybe Whitaker had worked or invested at the bank, but he worked for a big pharmaceutical company before his breakdown. We've sent uniform to pick him up. Maybe he'll have something to say about the fourth victim, if we can get him talking."

Rob slapped Galbraith on the back. "Great work, guys! I suggest you go and update Hodge. She could use some good news."

Galbraith grinned. They'd all felt the icy wind blowing from her direction of late. "Allow me."

* * *

The Whitaker interrogation took place at three o'clock that afternoon. Present were DCI Galbraith, DS Evan Burns, Whitaker's solicitor (a greying man in a pinstripe suit) and the suspect himself. Whitaker leaned back in his chair, aloof but calm.

Rob gazed through the one-way mirror, watching for signs of nervousness or tension, but there were none. Whitaker wasn't smug or overconfident, but he didn't seem worried either.

Rob frowned. Did he know that all they had were a sequence of events connecting him to three of the four victims? That his role in the killings would be hard, if not impossible to prove? The only way they were likely to get a conviction at this rate was if Whitaker confessed. It would take all of Galbraith's experience and cunning to break him.

Galbraith started by establishing the facts. "You used to work for Inverna Pharmaceuticals, is that right?"

A nod.

"Please respond out loud for the recording," said Evan.

"Yes, that's correct." Easy stance, relaxed shoulders, hands resting in his lap. No sign of anxiety.

"It was while you were working there that you had your nervous breakdown."

A flicker. So small it was hardly noticeable.

"Yes."

"Could you tell us what brought it on?"

A shrug. Eyes cold and reserved. "I was head of research and development. I'd spent years working my way up the ropes. I thought it was what I wanted, but when I got there, it wasn't at all. I couldn't handle the pressure. I wasn't any good at budgeting, at making decisions that affected the entire company. It was too much for me. I began dropping the ball and got given a warning. That made things even worse. I tried to carry on, but I couldn't."

"What happened?"

"I started having panic attacks, waking up filled with dread. I didn't want to go to work. I began making excuses, calling in sick. It got so bad I took voluntary sick leave. When that ran out, I left the company."

Evan was making notes, while Galbraith sat casually opposite Whitaker, his hefty presence both reassuring and intimidating.

"Stress is a killer," Galbraith murmured.

Whitaker nodded. "It can be. Luckily, I got out in time."

"But not in time to save your marriage."

A slight stiffness in the shoulders, his jaw jutting out more than before. Barely observable, but there. Galbraith was getting to him, slowly chipping away at the composed exterior. But there was still a way to go.

"My marriage fell apart after I lost my job," Whitaker said.

"Because you couldn't pay your bills, including your mortgage," said Galbraith. "The bank foreclosed on your property. Sold it out from under you."

Whitaker's gaze turned to granite.

"He's cracking him," whispered Will, who was also watching. Jenny had come down too, as had Harry. The little viewing room was filled to capacity.

"It was sold to a property developer called Paul Sutton," continued Galbraith, chiselling away. "Does that name ring any bells?"

Whitaker didn't respond.

"Let me refresh your memory," said Galbraith. "Paul Sutton lived at 14 Bramble Crescent, Esher. That was on your route when you worked for the Royal Mail, wasn't it?"

No answer.

"Could you answer for the recording?" said Evan.

"Yes."

"Good, now we're getting somewhere." Galbraith broke into a smile. "I know you knew him because you told the police as much after he died. You voluntarily came forward and told them he was on your postal round. You wanted to help with their inquiries. Do you remember that?"

A sulky, "Yes."

"According to your statement back then, Sutton's car wasn't outside his house on the morning of his death." Galbraith glanced at the sheet of paper in front of him. "You passed his house on your round at roughly nine thirty."

"Yes, that's right." A stubborn glint was back. Whitaker had managed to compose himself again.

"When you were asked where you were on the night of the twenty-third of July 2009, you said, 'At home, asleep.'"

"It's the truth."

Galbraith nodded. "Did you blame Sutton for kicking you out of your home?"

"No, why would I?"

The change in tack had caught Whitaker off guard. He splayed his hands briefly over his thighs and then closed them again in his lap. Galbraith and Evan may not have seen the gesture, being on the opposite side of the table, but Rob did. So did the others in the viewing room.

"What about Kyle McKenzie? Did you blame him for purchasing your house from the auction? The auction that happened without your consent."

"No. What are you talking about? I don't know a Kyle McKenzie."

He had a good poker face. Rob gave him that much.

"McKenzie was the man who bought your house and then demolished it to build a luxury apartment block. He met you repeatedly when he asked you to move out of the house before it was demolished. After you refused, he got the solicitor, Sutton, to get a court order to have you forcibly removed. You and your wife."

The hands clenched a little harder together.

"I don't remember," Whitaker said.

"I think you do," corrected Galbraith. "You see, McKenzie was very thorough. A good businessman. He recorded every instance he met you. Every time he knocked on your door and asked you to leave. Every time he knocked on your door and you didn't answer. His solicitor supplied us with the documents earlier today."

Whitaker sat sullenly, his gaze on the table.

"Was that why your wife left?" Galbraith asked. "She'd had enough of scrimping and saving, of never knowing when the wrecking ball was going to knock the bricks and mortar down around you. It must have been terrible living like that."

Whitaker shot him a malicious look.

"With no income, she had to go out and find work, didn't she?" said Galbraith, chipping off bigger and bigger pieces now. "She managed to get a job with a construction supplies company. RBM Machinery, wasn't it?"

Whitaker kept staring.

"She was the executive assistant for the CEO, a Mr Nathan Langton." Galbraith looked up. "That's a good position, EA to the top dog. You must have been so proud of her."

The muscles in Whitaker's jaw tensed.

"But then she fell in love, didn't she? I suppose it happens a lot in the workplace. Langton had recently lost his wife and Maggie was stressed out over you and the house . . ." He shrugged. "Somehow, they ended up falling for each other. 'Love at first sight' was how Maggie described it."

Whitaker's face turned a mottled purple.

"Gotcha," whispered Rob.

"Rubbish," hissed Whitaker. "Langton seduced her. Filled her head with nonsense. She'd never have walked out on me, on our marriage, if it wasn't for him."

"Is that why you killed him?" asked Galbraith.

Everyone in the viewing room held their breath.

The moment stretched out. It was like the air had been sucked from the room.

"I haven't killed anyone," Whitaker said. "And I can prove it."

"Fuck," muttered Will, echoing what they were all thinking.

"What can you prove?" Galbraith asked.

"Let me see the days those murders were committed on." He nodded to the folder in front of the DCI.

Galbraith frowned but pulled out a piece of paper with the dates of the pentagram killings on it.

*Kyle McKenzie — 12 May 2009*

*Nathan Langton — 17 June 2009*

*Paul Sutton — 23 July 2009*

*Noah Palmer — 5 August 2009*

Whitaker smiled. "I was hospitalised for depression in the last week of July 2009. I spent three months trying to get my head straight. The NHS will have a copy of my file."

# CHAPTER 21

"It checks out," Galbraith fumed when he got back to the squad room. "He was in bloody Kingston Hospital for three months, like he said. Suicide attempt."

"Jesus," muttered Rob.

"That means it wasn't him?" Evan looked crestfallen.

"It has to be him," cried Harry. "I could see it in his eyes."

"That's why he was so calm," Rob said. "He knew we couldn't pin the murders on him."

"I'm going to have to let him go," Galbraith grumbled. "Got nothing to hold him on. We did a search of his house in East Molesey. Nothing."

"It has been twelve years," pointed out Jenny.

"I was hoping we'd find a souvenir or something from the crime scenes." Galbraith's broad shoulders sagged. "Fuck!"

"What about the hospital?" said Rob. "Is there any way he could have snuck out and committed the fourth murder without them knowing?"

Galbraith perked up. "Good point. Evan, Harry, go and check it out. He was an inpatient for three months. They'll have his records on the system."

"Will do, boss," said Evan. They grabbed their coats and left.

"I'm going to hold him overnight," said Galbraith. "Just in case I want to have another crack at him."

Rob nodded. "Wise move." He turned to his team. "This isn't over yet. In the meantime, let's try to find a link between Noah Palmer and Whitaker, or his wife, for that matter. He obviously blames McKenzie, Sutton and Langton for destroying his marriage and ruining his life. Perhaps Noah Palmer played a hand in that somehow."

"I'll look into the finance angle," said Jenny, who was the most financially savvy of the three.

"I'll look into the wife. What was her name again?"

"Maggie," said Rob. "Harry interviewed her this morning. Her statement will be on the system. She's reverted back to her given name, Simms. I'll take Whitaker. See if I can trace him back to Noah Palmer."

"Do you want me to chase up Ashraf?" said Jenny.

Rob thought for a moment. "No, leave him on the back burner for now, Jen. Let's rule out Whitaker properly, before we make more work for ourselves."

"Okay, guv."

They got back to work. The digital clock in the squad room announced every hour that passed with a neon blue click. The sky blackened outside, and officers began knocking off for the night.

At six o'clock, Rob decided to go downstairs and get some air.

He was checking emails on his phone when the door to the building opened and Hodge walked out. Not wanting to have to be nice, Rob darted around the corner. It was cowardly, he knew, but he'd had just about enough of the Superintendent for one day.

A car pulled up and the window opened.

Hodge bent down. "What the fuck are you doing here?"

Rob froze.

"Denise, we need to talk."

Rob pursed his lips. He hadn't known her first name was Denise. Hadn't taken the time to notice.

The engine stopped and a well-built black man got out of the car. He was dressed casually in jeans and a hooded top. A gold watch flickered on his wrist. "Come on, babe. Don't be like this. I ain't done nothing wrong. Giving me the silent treatment is only making things worse."

How many times had Rob heard those words? The man was lying, he could tell from a mile away. Or rather ten metres. Hodge would know it too.

Except she hesitated. "I'll talk to you when you start telling the truth," she said.

Rob felt bad for listening to her private business, but if he moved or walked away, she'd hear him. There was nowhere for him to go.

"I am, babe, I swear. There's nothing going on."

"Then where were you the other night? And why did you get home at four in the morning smelling of some other woman's perfume?"

"I went clubbing with Lenny and Patch. You know what those places are like."

Hodge tapped her fingers on the open window. "You're full of shit, Clive."

"Honestly, that's the truth. Come on, let me take you to Reggie's for dinner. We'll have some wine, relax. We need a date night."

She paused, then relented. "Okay, fine, but you'll have to drop me at work tomorrow. My car's here."

"Deal."

Her heels clacked on the tarmac as she walked round and climbed into the BMW. The car took off, easing out of the car park into Putney high street.

Trouble in paradise? No wonder Hodge had been so grouchy lately. He was about to go upstairs when his phone beeped. It was a message from Liz Kramer.

*Rob, I've found an anomaly in those reports you sent me. I'm busy tonight but come by the office tomorrow and we'll talk. Liz.*

* * *

134

Rob woke up late. The rollercoaster of the day before had taken it out of him. He glanced at his phone lying beside the bed.

*Shit.* If he didn't get a move on, he'd miss the morning briefing.

He got dressed, dropped Trigger next door and ran to the car. Driving as fast as he dared, he made it into work just as the team were piling into the incident room, a stony-faced Galbraith at the helm.

Not good news, he took it.

"The hospital confirmed Whitaker was there from the twenty-seventh of July to the sixteenth of October 2009. He'd tried to hang himself from the banister and dislocated his back. He was in a wheelchair for the first month, on heavy antidepressants and antipsychotics. There's no way he could have escaped and murdered Noah Palmer."

Silence descended on the room like a heavy blanket.

"That's it then," said Harry. "He's in the clear."

"Looks like it," muttered Evan.

Galbraith looked thunderous. "I'm going to have to release him."

Rob didn't hang around to watch Whitaker waltz out of the building. He told Will he had an appointment and went to see Liz.

"Ah, you're a star," she said, as he handed her a takeaway coffee. Strong and black, just how she liked it.

"Take a seat, Rob."

"What did you find?"

She took a sip and sighed. "Bliss. Beats the shit out of the stuff in our canteen, I can tell you."

Rob couldn't help smiling. It was good coffee. He'd taken a special detour to get it.

"Okay, so I had a look at those post-mortem reports you sent me and there is indeed something odd, as you put it."

"There is?" He leaned forward in his chair.

She opened a folder on her desk. In it were the reports he'd emailed her, photographs of the crime scenes, and a page of handwritten notes.

"The post-mortems all said the same thing. Cause of death was blunt force trauma to the back of the head. A brick or a stone, maybe even a hammer, although the indents aren't conclusive. Pentagram carved on the torso, made by a knife of some sort, hard to say what size or make, since only the tip of the blade was used."

They knew all that. Rob waited. Liz wouldn't have called him in if she hadn't found something new.

"It's the crime scene photographs that I found so remarkable," she said. She reached into the folder and pulled them out, arranging them upside down on her desk so Rob could see. "If you look closely, you can see the fourth circle is neater than the other three."

Rob stared at the clear, full-colour photographs. All four were taken from the same angle, in front of the body. The fourth circle did appear to be rounder than the others. "Is that significant?"

"Not on its own," she said. "The killer may have become more confident — after all, he'd done it three times already. But if you take the carving into account, it suddenly becomes more important."

"What about the carving?" Rob leaned over the photographs, peering at the mutilated torsos of the victims. The pentagrams inscribed on their chests looked raw and painful, glistening in the forensic teams' artificial lighting.

"Look carefully." She handed him a magnifying glass. "The first three are deep and wet. The killer has used an even pressure to make the incisions."

Rob looked. Sure enough, the first three all looked the same.

"Now take a look at the fourth victim."

Rob moved the magnifying glass over Noah Palmer's body. He saw immediately what Liz meant. "It's not as deep," he said.

She nodded. "The incisions are not as deep and the pressure varies. If you look at the start—" she pointed to the top of the pentagram — "it's deeper there, but becomes lighter and less certain as the diagram progresses. The sides of the triangles are deeper than the bottom."

"What does that mean?" asked Rob, but he thought he knew. A surge of adrenalin hit his system and he found he was holding his breath.

Liz's eyes were sparkling. "It means that you may have a copycat killer on your hands."

# CHAPTER 22

"A copycat?" Galbraith blurted out, nearly spilling his tea.

Rob nodded. "The indentation of the carvings was different on the fourth victim, as was the circle around the body."

Tony hadn't been entirely wrong. It was one killing made to look like the other three. That's why there was no connection between the first three victims and Noah Palmer.

"But I don't understand. The paint used at all four crime scenes was identical. Exactly the same composition. How would the copycat have known where to get it?"

"I can't answer that," said Rob. "But I trust Liz Kramer. If she says the fourth victim was murdered by someone else, then it's worth considering."

"If that's true, Whitaker could have murdered the other three," cut in Evan. "His alibi is only valid for the fourth murder."

"Fuck, I've let the bastard go!" Galbraith jumped up. He turned to Evan. "Get uniform to bring him back here. Right now."

"Where does that leave us, guv?" asked Will, once Rob had brought them up to speed. He could see by their wide-eyed stares and confused frowns that both Will and Jenny had been caught off guard by the sudden U-turn in the case.

It was like they'd been hurtling down one road after a target, and now the target had moved and they suddenly found themselves in another, unfamiliar road having to start all over again.

"From now on, we're treating Noah Palmer's death as separate to the others. Galbraith's team will continue with the pentagram killings while we tackle this one."

"So, they're not connected?" said Will. "Just so we're clear."

"It doesn't look like it," said Rob. "It makes sense when you think about it. There were a couple of things that didn't add up. Noah Palmer was at least ten years younger than the others. He wasn't connected to Whitaker's wife, Maggie, and he had no ties to the other victims. Plus, he lived in Chiswick and his body was found on Box Hill."

"Langton and Sutton were also found on Box Hill," pointed out Will.

"Yes, but they lived in the general vicinity. Langton was from Oxshott and Sutton from Esher. McKenzie lived in Wimbledon and was found on Wimbledon Common."

"If it was the same killer, his MO would have changed with the fourth victim," finished Jenny. "Everyone else was found near to where they lived, except Noah Palmer."

"Correct." Rob smiled at her.

"And then there's Whitaker's alibi," she continued. "He was in hospital in August. He murdered the three men he held responsible for the collapse of his marriage and then tried to hang himself."

"Sounds about right," said Rob. A tragic hypothesis.

"How did Noah Palmer's killer know what to do?" said Will. "I mean, the details . . ."

"Most of it would have been in the paper," cut in Rob. "There were graphic images of the crime scene, particulars of the carvings, the circle, the candles."

"Not the paint," said Will.

"No, I confirmed that with Lawrence. The type of paint definitely wasn't mentioned in the press," said Rob.

"Which means Palmer's killer had inside knowledge?" surmised Jenny.

"Possibly." It was a conundrum. "Could be someone leaked that information," said Rob. "We'll never know for sure. It was too long ago."

"Okay, I'll get back on to Global Standard's HR team. They should have an answer for me by now. I suppose the dates of the first three murders don't matter anymore. It's Noah Palmer's we need to focus on."

"That's right," agreed Rob. At least it made things simpler.

Several hours and cups of coffee later, Jenny came rushing over. "The HR team just got back to me. On Wednesday the fifth of August, the day Noah Palmer died, Raza Ashraf left work early."

Rob's eyebrows shot up.

Jenny continued, her eyes flashing, "He left the building at three forty-five and didn't return until nine o'clock the next morning."

Rob's pulse went into overdrive. He slapped his hand on the desk. "Well done, Jenny. You know what this means, don't you?"

She nodded. "Rasa Ashraf doesn't have an alibi for Noah Palmer's death."

"We're going to have to speak to him again," said Rob. He was pacing circles around his desk.

"We can't. He's already complained once," replied Jenny.

"And you're in enough shit already," Will pointed out.

Rob frowned. "Just because he's a politician, it doesn't mean he can get away without being questioned by the police. He's a person of interest in this case."

"It could be completely innocent," argued Jenny. "It was a long time ago, after all. I don't remember what I did on a specific day twelve years ago. Do you?"

"It depends which day." Rob worked his jaw. But she did have a point. "Still, we need to find out why he left work early. If he's innocent, he won't remember, but if he's guilty, he'll be lying — and I'll know."

"He'll never agree to come in voluntarily," said Jenny. "And you don't have enough evidence to arrest him."

Will shook his head.

"Let me speak to Hodge." Rob took a deep breath. "Maybe once she hears what's happened with the investigation, she'll give us the go-ahead to bring him in."

* * *

"Absolutely not," fumed Hodge, twenty minutes later.

So much for that idea.

"But, ma'am, he doesn't have an alibi. If he were any other suspect, we'd haul him in here and question him, probably under caution."

"We have nothing linking him to the case," the Superintendent insisted. "So what if he left work early on the day of Palmer's murder? We don't have any camera footage placing him at the scene. We don't have his fingerprints or DNA on the bike or the body. We have nothing. Based on that, I'm not prepared to 'haul him in here', as you so delicately put it."

"How are we going to question him about his alibi, then?" asked Rob.

"It's simple. You're not." She stood up behind her desk. "Find something concrete that puts him in the frame and then we can think about interviewing him. Until then, I'm not going to antagonise the future mayor of London any more than we already have."

Rob rubbed his forehead. "Okay, fine. But just for the record, I don't think we should be treating politicians any differently from our other suspects."

"Your concern is noted, DCI Miller," she snapped. "Now if you'll excuse me, I have work to do."

* * *

The day got progressively worse.

As it happened, the newspaper article had attracted the attention of an ambitious young solicitor keen to make a name for herself, and she'd contacted Bella Norton and convinced her that her daughter had a claim to a portion of Noah Palmer's trust fund. As his biological daughter, she was entitled to the same benefits his other children enjoyed.

It was Bella who called Rob to give him the good news. "Apparently, I need a court-approved DNA test," she said, breathlessly. "You said you'd post it to me."

"I did indeed," Rob muttered, making a mental note to get that off to her as soon as possible. The police DNA test would stand up in court.

"I also need a copy of the will," she added. "But my solicitor says that won't be a problem. Apparently, it's easy enough to get a copy from some registry or another. It's only going to cost me six quid. That's a fair deal for Rachel getting the money her father would have wanted her to have."

In a way, Rob was glad things were looking up for Rachel, but he knew what a shock this would be to the Palmer family. Suzie wasn't the type of woman to take the claim lying down. He envisioned a long and bitter court case and hoped Bella's solicitor knew what she was doing.

## CHAPTER 23

"I think we should talk to Noah Palmer's former boss," Rob said to his sergeant as he waited for the agonisingly slow coffee machine to fill his mammoth mug.

"At Global Standard?" asked Will.

"Yeah. They might know more about Noah's relationship with Ashraf."

"We're not meant to be investigating Ashraf." Will cast a worried look at the igloo.

"We're not. We're enquiring about Noah's work relationships." He sighed. "Look, we've got nothing else to go on. We need a lead."

Jenny came to join them. "I finally got an address for Mrs Jenkins," she said. "I've been trying to track her down for days. She lives in a care home in Twickenham. I thought I'd pop over there now and confirm Suzie Palmer's alibi."

"Good idea." The machine finally gurgled to a stop. "Keep me posted."

Jenny nodded. "I'll take Celeste with me."

* * *

Rob and Will walked into the tall glass-and-chrome building just before midday. It was a typical corporate high-rise in the city. The lift whisked them up to the sixteenth floor, which housed the department where Noah Palmer once worked.

They'd called ahead and arranged an appointment. When they emerged from the elevator, a sleek blonde woman was waiting to meet them.

"Good morning, officers," she said with a practised smile. "Mr Hedley is expecting you. Come this way, please."

They followed her across a marble lobby, down a plush, carpeted corridor and into a lofty waiting area with leather chairs positioned around a glass coffee table. In the centre was a huge vase of assorted flowers, predominantly lilies. It reminded Rob of the arrangement on Suzie Palmer's table. Soft classical music played in the background, designed to relax anxious clients.

"Can I get you some tea or coffee?" she asked.

"Coffee would be good," said Rob, never one to miss an opportunity.

"Same." Will smiled.

She nodded and disappeared through a side door.

Several suited bankers marched past them and through a door to their left. The boardroom.

Through the glass panels, Rob could see that it was much larger than their briefing rooms back at the station. This one could seat about thirty people around a huge wooden table. A smartly dressed woman was setting the tech up for a presentation. The room was filling up.

The receptionist returned with a silver tray, on which were two steaming cups of coffee. They smelled good.

"Thank you," said Rob with a grin as they both took a cup. Good coffee made waiting much more bearable.

The boardroom was almost full to capacity when a middle-aged man with thinning hair and shrewd eyes behind thick spectacles loped over to where Rob and Will were sitting.

"Sorry to keep you waiting." He held out his hand. "I'm Scott Hedley."

"DCI Miller," said Rob. "This is DS Freemont. Putney Major Investigation Team."

Hedley nodded. "I believe you wanted to talk about Noah Palmer?"

"Yes, that's right. It won't take long," said Rob.

Hedley looked to the boardroom where the meeting was about to start. "Right. Let's go to my office."

They followed him down another short passage and through a door on the right.

*Not bad.* Rob admired the light, spacious office. Wide floor-to-ceiling windows offered a panoramic view over most of London. He also noticed the director's desk was positioned so his back was to it. How often did the director look out of the window, or was it a view he'd seen so many times before it had become invisible?

"Please, take a seat," said Hedley. "I must say, I was surprised to get your call. I worked with Noah a long time ago, before his tragic passing. I'm not sure how much help I'll be."

Rob drew his gaze away from the view. "We're looking for some background information on him — what kind of person was he, what was he like to work with? That sort of thing."

"Noah was a great guy." There was real warmth there. "He was confident and friendly and had a way with the clients. They all loved him."

That easy-going charm, thought Rob.

"Did he get on with his co-workers?"

"Oh, yes. Noah got on with almost everybody."

"*Almost?*" Rob eyed Hedley.

The director shifted uncomfortably. "There was only one person he didn't see eye to eye with and that was Raza Ashraf."

Rob frowned, pretending to think. "Wasn't there some investigation into money laundering?"

Hedley flushed. "Yes, but it was handled internally. No charges were brought. We've since updated our vetting processes and have a much firmer grip on compliance."

"That's good to hear," said Rob, not that he gave a crap. "Could you fill us in on what happened? I thought Noah Palmer testified in Ashraf's favour at the hearing."

"He did, but the relationship between the two of them was strained. It got to the point where they were unable to work together. To be honest, if Noah hadn't died, we would probably have moved him to a different department. Infighting like that unsettles the investors."

"I can imagine," mused Rob.

They couldn't tolerate each other. Noah may have testified in Ashraf's favour, but he can't have been happy about it.

"Do you know why they were at loggerheads?" Rob asked. "Was it just the compliance issue?"

"Sorry, Detective. I was their boss, not their friend. Neither of them confided in me."

"Is there anyone still working here who was friendly with them?" It was a long shot, admittedly. Twelve years was a long time by today's standards.

"Not that I can recall," he said, but then he pursed his lips. "Actually, Heather might be able to help you. She used to work in the back office and handled the admin for the Asia desk. She was pretty close to both Noah and Raza. They were something of a team."

That sounded promising. "Where can we find her?" he asked.

Hedley stood up. "She's in front of office now," he said with a proud smile. "Follow me, I'll take you to her."

Heather was a chic, middle-aged woman with lustrous dark hair greying at the temples and sharp, very blue eyes. She smiled when she saw Hedley.

"Hello, Scott. This is a pleasant surprise. What can I do for you?"

"I've got two police officers here who'd like to ask you some questions about Noah Palmer. You don't mind, do you?"

"Noah? Of course not."

She smiled at Rob and Will. "Come and take a seat."

"Thank you," said Rob.

Heather's office wasn't as big as Hedley's, but it wasn't bad. She had a smaller view, but equally as majestic, facing the opposite direction. Here, the Thames rambled up towards his neck of the woods, Putney. Mounted on the wall was a flat-screen monitor with share prices flashing across it. Bloomberg. Up-to-the-minute information on the markets as they opened across the world. It permeated the office with a sense of urgency. Time was money.

Her computer beeped an alert and she glanced down.

"We're sorry to disturb you," began Rob. She was obviously a busy lady.

"I'm always happy to help the police," she said. "What can I tell you about Noah? I was devastated to hear how he died. Absolutely terrible. And he was such a nice man."

"Did you know him well?"

"Yes, pretty well. I did the administration for their trades."

"What about Raza Ashraf? Did you know him too?"

"Oh, yes. They were as thick as thieves, those two."

Interesting choice of words. "I believe they had a falling out?" Rob said. "Do you know what that was about?"

She took a deep breath. "That was unfortunate. It was the money laundering debacle. I suppose you've heard about that?"

Rob nodded.

"Nothing was ever proven, but it was thought they had links to organised crime."

"You mean drug money?"

She nodded. "That and trafficking. All sorts of shifty activity. But like I said, nothing was ever proven."

"What was the argument about?"

"There was a rumour — and this is completely unfounded, by the way — that Raza was benefitting from the trades. Noah picked up on it and came to talk to me. He was worried there was something untoward going on. I couldn't see it, myself, but it soured the relationship between them. I don't think Noah trusted Raza after that."

"Did Noah tell you this?" enquired Will.

"Yes, we were friends. He came to me for advice."

Rob frowned. "I thought Noah testified in favour of Raza."

"He did, but that was to protect the bank. Had he voiced his concerns, the internal watchdog would have come down hard on us. There was talk of an investigation by the Financial Conduct Authority."

"So Noah protected the bank's reputation by backing up Ashraf's story?"

"Yes, but like I said, there was no hard evidence. Nothing was ever proven. The investigations committee found no wrongdoing and that was that. Back to work as usual."

"Except it wasn't, was it?" said Rob. "Relations between Noah and Ashraf were strained."

"Yes." She smiled sadly. "Noah was going to put in for a transfer, but he died before he could."

"And now Raza Ashraf is running for mayor," said Rob.

Her blue eyes sparkled. "Yes, isn't it funny how things change? He left the bank shortly after the scandal and went into local politics. It suited him better."

*And his banking reputation was sullied*, thought Rob.

"Of course," said Heather, after a beat, "there was also that thing with his wife."

# CHAPTER 24

"What thing with whose wife?" Rob asked.

"Noah's wife. Susan, I think her name was. Very elegant, petite woman."

Rob glanced at Will, and then back to Heather. "What happened?"

"It was about the same time as that money laundering scandal." She glanced past them towards the window, remembering. "At the summer party. It was so strange. Up until then, Noah and Raza had been great mates. The next thing you know, Noah punched Raza across the dance floor. I remember because he barrelled into me and sent me flying."

"Do you know what the fight was about?" asked Rob.

"Not really," she confided. "I just remember Raza yelling something like, 'Well, what did you expect with the way you carry on?'"

"He said that?" Will was furiously taking notes.

"Something like that," confirmed Heather. "Now, I'm not one to gossip, but Noah was a bit of a charmer, if you get my drift. All the ladies in the office adored him, myself included." Her eyes brightened. "And he knew how to party. These traders like to burn the candle at both ends."

Rob remembered what Bella Norton had said about Noah taking her to corporate functions. "Did he ever attend an event with a woman that wasn't his wife?"

Heather shook her head. "I didn't see him with anyone other than Susan, but there were rumours. Noah and Raza were always being invited to clients' parties. Anyway, Noah didn't like what Raza was implying and they got into a bit of a fight. Susan pulled Noah out of there and they left. I helped Raza find some ice for his black eye." She chuckled. "He was furious. Kept saying that a woman like Susan didn't deserve a man like Noah."

"Do you think they had an affair?" whispered Will. "Raza and Suzie?"

"Heavens, no," said Heather. "Raza wouldn't do that, but he was fond of her. The three of them had been out to dinner a few times. I even accompanied them once or twice to make up a fourth. That was before I was married. It was all very friendly. I think I would have known if they were having an affair."

Raza Ashraf wouldn't sleep with his colleague's wife, but he'd launder billions for organised crime gangs.

"I miss those days." Heather sighed softly. "Before Noah and Raza fell out. We had fun, the three of us."

"I'm sure," said Rob, his mind working overtime. Had Raza been sleeping with Suzie Palmer? Is that why Noah had punched him across the room? Then, the money laundering scandal had hit and, despite his obvious animosity, Noah Palmer had backed up his colleague. And suddenly, he was murdered on Box Hill.

Were they connected? Had Ashraf been involved? If the banker had been sleeping with Suzie, he had even more of a motive to want Noah out of the way.

Except, they hadn't ended up together. Perhaps Rob was barking up the wrong tree and there was, as Heather said, nothing between them.

* * *

"What do you make of that?" Rob asked Will. They were outside the sandwich shop waiting for their chicken mayo baguettes to go. The clouds had parted, and a burst of sunlight beamed down onto the steaming pavement.

"It's a damn shame we can't interview Ashraf again," said Will. "I'd love to hear his explanation for that fight at the summer party."

"Suzie Palmer would know," said Rob. Whether she'd tell them, he was less certain.

"Do you think they were having an affair?" asked Will, whose thoughts had run in the same direction as Rob's. "What else could Ashraf have meant when he'd said, 'What did you expect with the way you carry on?' He could only have been referring to Noah's liaisons with Bella Norton."

Rob nodded. "It's all very suspicious. We need some clarification. Let's stop at Suzie Palmer's on the way back and see if she's home."

* * *

Suzie answered the door in a smart navy skirt suit with a crisp white blouse. Around her neck hung a silver pendant that matched her bracelet. She looked as stylish and elegant as always.

"Come in, detectives. I was just taking a coffee break. Won't you join me?"

Rob gave a surprised nod. Suzie Palmer must be in a good mood. They'd never been offered anything before. "Thank you," he said.

They followed her into a pathologically neat kitchen. Granite countertops gleamed with shiny appliances and the wonderful smell of roasted coffee beans filled the room. He would hazard a guess that Suzie's coffee was better than Global Standard's, which hadn't been bad.

"What can I help you with today?" She poured the coffee into three white china mugs. They were scarcely bigger than a child's mug, but Rob accepted it willingly anyway.

He was right. It was sublime.

He took a moment to savour the taste. "Mrs Palmer, I'm sorry if this is a bit delicate, but could you tell us about an argument Noah had with Raza Ashraf at the Global Standard summer party?"

She stared at them blankly for a few moments. "Gosh, that's going back a bit."

"We spoke to a colleague of theirs who remembers your husband punching Raza. Do you remember what that fight was about?"

She put her cup down on the counter. "It was about me," she said softly.

Both Rob and Will stared at her, unmoving.

"The children were very young back then — our youngest wasn't even two — and they were quite a handful. Noah was out a lot and I was struggling to cope. I called Raza and asked if he would have a word with Noah about it. I knew they were close. I thought maybe he could talk some sense into him. Those early years were very difficult," she admitted, looking away.

Three kids under seven with a husband who was partying and seeing escorts . . . No wonder Suzie was bitter.

"Did it help?" Rob asked.

She shook her head. "No, it didn't. If anything, it made matters worse. Noah and Raza fell out over it. Noah told him to mind his own business and Raza told him that was no way to treat your wife. It escalated into a fight."

"You weren't having an affair with Raza Ashraf?" asked Rob.

"God, no!"

She looked so stricken that Rob held out his hands. "Sorry, I had to ask."

She grabbed the counter for support. "I never once thought about being unfaithful to Noah. He was my world. Him and the kids. I dedicated my life to them."

Rob nodded.

"Before I met Noah, I worked in the film industry." She brushed an imaginary speck off the counter. "But the children put paid to that, which is why I went into interior design. I began studying while I was pregnant with my second, and slowly built up a business."

"You've done very well for yourself." Rob glanced around at the expensive furnishings. "It can't have been easy with three children."

"It wasn't," she admitted. "But working for myself meant I could be flexible. That helped a lot."

Rob clenched his jaw. Neither he nor Jo had that advantage. They were both hands-on detectives and spent long hours on the job. Sometimes nights, even. How were they going to manage with a baby? Suddenly what Jo had said about taking some time off made sense.

"I loved him, you know," Suzie whispered. "I knew what he was like before we got married. That he could be . . . wild. I had hoped marriage and children would calm him down, but it didn't. If anything, it made him feel more trapped." She glanced at her hands. "I guess people don't change."

# CHAPTER 25

It was late afternoon by the time Rob and Will got back to the station. The Superintendent was still out, so they'd avoided any awkward questions about where they'd been.

"How'd you get on with Mrs Jenkins?" Rob asked Jenny.

She shook her head. "Didn't happen. The care home said she's in hospital at the moment having a hip replacement. They expect her back next week."

"Bugger," muttered Rob.

"I'll keep tabs on her," said Jenny with a rueful smile. "When she's back, I'll go and have a chat."

"Let's hope she makes it," said Will.

Jenny shot him a look.

"What? You said she's ninety. That's a risky age for a big op like that. I know, my nan had one last year. Took her ages to recover."

Rob didn't want to think about that. He didn't want to suspect Suzie Palmer, but now the serial killer theory had gone out the window, the only thing ruling her out from their inquiries was that alibi.

"Thanks for trying," he said to Jenny.

\* \* \*

Rob updated the files on what they'd discovered and went to speak to Galbraith. He was fuming because Whitaker had disappeared.

"Fucker's done a runner," he ranted, and told Rob how they had teams out searching for him.

"He'll pop up somewhere," Rob said with more enthusiasm than he felt. "I take it you've alerted Border Control?"

"Yeah, they're watching the airports and the ports, he can't get far."

It was close to knocking off time when Rob's phone buzzed. He didn't recognise the number and was about to answer it when Superintendent Hodge burst out of her igloo and marched across the floor, her face a mask of fury.

*Shit.* He let the call go to voicemail.

Will hunched over his computer in an attempt to make himself invisible. Jenny scuttled to the photocopier. Only Rob stood his ground, mentally preparing for the bollocking that was coming his way.

"I told you not to follow up on Raza Ashraf," she yelled.

Heads turned in surprise.

"And what do you do? You go to interview his work colleagues and blatantly disregard my orders."

"We weren't investigating Ashraf," explained Rob. "We were interviewing Noah Palmer's colleagues."

"Who were also Raza Ashraf's colleagues!"

"That's true, but we didn't ask about Ashraf."

Hodge's eyes narrowed. "Then why did I just get a call from his solicitor threatening to take legal action against the department?"

"What?" Rob gawked at her.

"Exactly. You must have said something to piss him off."

"Honestly, we didn't even speak to him," confirmed Will.

Rob sighed. *Heather.* It must have been. Not one to gossip, eh? She must have been on the phone to Ashraf the minute they'd left the building.

He stood up. "Noah Palmer and Raza Ashraf had a fight in the weeks leading up to Noah's death." He hoped the information would take some of the wind out of Hodge's sales. "Palmer hit him across the floor at the office summer party. There was no love lost between them."

"That doesn't mean Raza murdered him," she ranted. "I don't like most of the people I work with. It doesn't mean I'm going to crack them over the head and carve weird symbols into their bodies."

Rob stifled a grin. "Good to know."

There were a few sniggers.

"Don't be flippant. I've had enough of this nonsense," she said. "I'm shutting down your investigation."

"You can't do that!" Will was staring in shock.

"Not ours, I hope," cut in Galbraith, surging forward. "Whitaker's on the run, but we'll get him. He's guilty as sin. No doubt about it."

"Not the pentagon case," she huffed. "The Palmer case."

No one bothered to correct her.

"Noah Palmer and Raza Ashraf had history," Rob pleaded. "There might be a motive there."

"Might be?" She sighed. "That's all we've got, DCI Miller. A bunch of 'might bes'. I've had enough of this. Consider this investigation closed. I'm going to reassure the Deputy Commissioner that we've dropped the case. I don't want to hear another word about it, is that clear?"

Rob clenched his jaw. "Yes, ma'am."

She was right about one thing. There was no definite proof. Even if Ashraf did leave work early on the day of the murder, even if he did have a beef against Noah Palmer, even if he did want to keep him quiet about the money laundering, there was no way any of it would stand up in court. It was all circumstantial.

Superintendent Hodge strode back to her desk, her hands curled into tight fists at her sides.

Rob raked a hand through his hair.

Will shook his head. "I can't believe she did that."

"I'm sorry, guv," said Jenny. "I know you wanted to solve this one for Lawrence."

Rob turned around. "I'm going to take a walk." And he marched out of the office before he said something he'd regret.

* * *

"Fancy a commiseration drink?" Will placed his laptop into the foam compartment in his rucksack. He took it home with him every night in case he needed to work. "Jenny, Jeff, Harry and I are going down the pub."

Rob looked at the pile of paperwork on his desk.

*Fuck it.* "Why not?"

The Coat & Badge was relatively empty, but then it was a Tuesday night. Rob bought the first round of drinks and they got a table where they could see the sport on the mounted screen. France was thumping Italy in a replay of a Six Nations rugby match.

"I heard Hodge was a personal friend of Ashraf's," said Harry, with a sly smile. Ridiculously good-looking, Harry was well connected socially and while he wasn't a gossip, he did keep his ears and eyes open. His intel often came in handy during police investigations. "Vikram in IT saw them having lunch at the Ivy the other day."

Will rolled his eyes. "No wonder she created such a fuss."

"I was aware they knew each other, but I didn't realise they were that close," said Rob, frowning. "It explains a lot. If Ashraf were any other suspect, we'd have had him in the interrogation room days ago."

"It's not right," said Jenny, who was the only one drinking wine.

"You can say that again," muttered Rob.

The bigwigs had closed ranks and now they'd never get a chance to find out where Ashraf had gone the day of Noah Palmer's death.

"Do you really think he's capable of mutilating a body like that?" asked Jeff. He'd returned to the investigation after his stint on the domestic homicide. "I mean, you'd have to hate someone an awful lot to whack them over the head and carve a pentagram into their chest. Especially since they used to be friends."

Rob grunted. He was beginning to regret coming out. He wasn't in the best mood for socialising. "I guess you never really know what's going on in people's heads."

"Scary if he did do it," said Jenny. "Particularly since he could be mayor of London one day."

"In the not-too-distant future," muttered Will.

"The guy's obviously motivated by greed and self-interest," said Jeff. "I'm guessing there were various kickbacks involved in the money laundering?"

Jenny nodded. "Well, the bank gets the business, so they're smiling. In addition, the bankers who process the funds are usually paid off-book. A little holiday in St Tropez here, a fortnight on a luxury yacht there. There could have been financial pay-outs too. Consultancy fees and the like."

"That's a nice way of putting it," mused Jeff. "Sounds better than 'bribe' on a financial statement."

While Jeff got another round, Rob rang Jo to ask if she wanted to join them.

"I'll come over on Friday," she said. "It's a bit late now."

"That sounds great," he replied, suddenly missing her. "I'll look forward to it."

Even though they'd been together for six months and were having a baby together, they were still overly polite to each other on the phone. The baby had forced them to dive head first into a relationship that they would have taken at a much slower pace. It wasn't a bad thing, Rob reflected as he walked back inside, but it had made him think about what he wanted out of life. He knew he wanted to spend his with Jo and their baby, but things were moving so fast, it both terrified and excited him.

When he got back to the table, Will was talking to a willowy blonde in tight jeans and knee-high boots.

Rob smiled as he brushed past to get into his seat.

"Tasha this is DCI Rob Miller, my boss. Rob, this is Tasha. We just met, but she's a West Ham fan like me. What are the chances?"

Rob glanced at the big West Ham sticker on the back of Will's rucksack. "What are the chances, indeed?"

Tasha shot him a sultry smile. "It must be fate."

Rob shifted up so Will and Tasha could sit on the end.

"Are you all policemen?" She glanced around the table.

Rob nodded. "Yeah, disappointed?"

"Intrigued," she replied.

That was a first.

Will commented on the last game and they were off. Rob didn't speak to his sergeant again that evening. He didn't really feel like talking anyway. After he'd finished his second beer, he bid the rest of the team goodnight and headed home.

There was an emptiness inside him, a frustration that wouldn't go away. Bloody Hodge. He hated leaving a homicide unsolved. But what could he do? His hands were tied.

# CHAPTER 26

The call about the burglary–homicide came in the middle of a briefing Galbraith was giving on the missing Alfred Whitaker.

"Still haven't found the fucker," was the main takeaway.

Rob's team was on call and so Jenny, Jeff and Mike, who'd just returned from leave, were dispatched to contain the scene and assess what had happened.

Female. Late thirties. Found dead on the living room floor.

Rob followed, Will driving. The victim lived in the Raynes Park area, between Wimbledon and New Malden. Her terraced house was situated in a winding cul-de-sac off Grand Drive. At first, the satnav had taken them around the back to a recreational ground. Rob had to call Jenny for directions.

The little street was crowded with law enforcement vehicles when they arrived. Rob immediately spotted his team's specialist police vehicle. Behind that were two other police vehicles, an ambulance and the forensic van.

"Morning, Liz," called Rob. The Home Office pathologist had her white coat and glasses on, ready for action.

"Rob, fancy seeing you here."

She was waiting for the CSI technicians to put down plastic steps so they could enter the crime scene without compromising any evidence.

"There you go, ma'am," said an officer, placing the last step on the ground.

"Thank you." She walked into the house carrying her metal suitcase. A crime scene photographer followed her, eager to get to work. He stopped halfway up the path and took some shots of the front door, the lock and the entrance to the house.

"Was it tampered with?" Rob asked a uniformed policeman standing guard.

"Yes, sir. It looks like the door was jimmied. We're still assessing the damage."

As Rob pulled on a forensic overall and shoe covers, he checked the street for CCTV, but didn't see any.

"Nearest camera is on Grand Drive." Will zipped himself up. "I'll get hold of it when we get back."

They walked into the house. Rob whistled under his breath. The living room was a mess — chairs overturned, papers strewn across the parquet floor, a vase shattered in its own puddle of water. It was clear someone had been looking for something.

Dr Kramer was leaning over the body of the victim, a woman in her late forties wearing jeans and a shirt tucked in at the waist. She lay face down on the tiled floor, her head to the side, eyes shut. She could have been asleep, if it hadn't been for the pool of dark blood beneath her matted brown hair.

"The victim's name is Judith Walker." Jenny came up to him, iPad in hand. "According to the neighbour, she was a psychologist."

"Did she live alone?" Rob surveyed the room. He picked up a framed photograph with his gloved hand and studied it. The victim was standing in front of a Christmas tree with two young girls, their happy smiles filled with festive cheer and a smudge of chocolate. Nieces, perhaps.

"Yes, divorced a couple of years back," said Jenny. "No kids."

"Definitely a struggle." Will walked slowly around the room, gazing at the mess. "She must have backed into the cabinet, knocked over the vase and the frames, then fallen to the floor."

Rob angled himself so he could better see the body. "Why is she on her stomach?" he asked. "If she'd confronted her attacker head on, you'd expect the blows to have come from the front, not the back. Does she have any defensive wounds on her hands?"

Liz shot him an exasperated look. "I've only just got here, Rob. Give me a chance to do a preliminary once-over before you start quizzing me."

"Sorry," he muttered. Liz had her process and wouldn't be rushed. She'd answer his questions when she was good and ready, and not a moment before.

He walked around, careful not to tread on anything. It was a large room, stretching from the front of the house, right through to the back, where French doors looked out onto a neat garden. She'd obviously done some extensive renovations.

"There's severe trauma to the back of the head." Liz gently tilted the head to the side. "Hence the blood."

"Is that the cause of death?" Rob asked.

"Looks like it." She moved on to the neck and shoulders. "I can't see any other cause. No strangulation, no stab wounds."

"Murder weapon?" asked Rob.

"A blunt object, possibly a hammer judging by those indents."

Rob leaned forward but all he could see was a matted, sticky mess. "Jesus," he murmured.

"She's been hit several times. I'll know more when I get her back to the lab."

"The killer made sure she wasn't going anywhere." Will peered over his shoulder.

"You don't often see this level of violence at burglaries." Liz glanced up at them over the rim of her spectacles. "Usually, the person is only attacked if they try to intervene, and then the blow is enough to render them unconscious, not to kill them. This looks intentional to me."

Rob remembered Tony saying that a burglar's mentality is different from that of a violent offender. Burglars are concerned with material gain. Burglary is non-confrontational in nature, which is why thieves break in when the homeowner is out or away. A typical burglar will not resort to violence unless provoked, and even then, their aim is not to murder, it's simply to stun or render inactive for long enough to get away with the loot.

"So, we're looking for a burglar who kills," he said.

"Or a killer who burgles," suggested Liz.

Rob stared at her. "Perhaps this wasn't a burglary."

Will's eyes widened. "You mean whoever broke in wanted to kill the victim, then made it look like a burglary?"

Rob shrugged. "It's possible." He turned to Jenny, who along with Jeff and Mike, was doing a systematic search of the house. "Anything taken?"

"Well, her laptop's gone," she said. "We've searched the study and the charger is there, but no device. It looks like it's been pulled out in a hurry."

"What about a mobile phone?" asked Rob.

"I didn't see one." Jenny glanced at her colleagues. "You guys?"

Jeff and Mike both shook their heads.

"Not on the body either," confirmed Liz, who'd patted her down.

"There must be a handbag or purse somewhere?" Rob looked around the room.

"It's in the kitchen," Jenny confirmed. "Hanging over the back of a chair. It's untouched. Her purse is still inside containing a fifty-quid note and some change. I don't think the robber was after that. No phone."

"They just took the electronics?" Rob frowned.

"Looks that way, guv." Jenny nodded towards the staircase. "We haven't been upstairs yet."

"Get Forensics to dust her office for prints," Rob ordered.

"They're already on it." She gave him a thumbs up.

"I can't see anything beneath her fingernails." Liz was carefully lifting each hand to inspect them. "No defensive wounds either."

Rob grimaced. *Bugger.* "Considering the mess, I would have expected there to be some trace of DNA on the body," he said.

"The ransacking could have been done afterwards," remarked Will. "If the killer wanted to make it look like a robbery."

The mess did look staged, like someone had swept an arm over the sideboard, sending everything flying onto the floor. One chair had been tipped over, but the rest were standing.

"She must have had her back turned to the attacker when the blows struck," Rob surmised.

"Or been running away," added Will.

"But why turn your back on a burglar? If someone had jimmied the door, she'd have heard them break in."

"Maybe she was reaching for her phone to dial the emergency services," Will suggested. "That might be why her back was to the killer?"

Rob grunted. "It's possible. Dust everywhere for prints," he told a hovering forensic investigator. "We need to piece together what happened."

"That's standard procedure with a burglary, sir."

Jenny, Jeff and Mike came back downstairs.

"Neat as a button up there," said Jenny.

"Nothing out of place," added Mike. "All her jewellery is still in the dresser drawer. Doesn't look like anything's been taken."

Rob stood in the centre of the room and pictured the sequence of events. "The perpetrator gained entrance to the property via the front door and then killed her shortly after. Once she was dead, the murderer trashed the room, stole her laptop and phone but left everything else."

"That sounds about right," agreed Will.

Rob scrunched up his forehead. "Why the laptop and phone? Was that the sole reason for the break-in and she just got in the way, or was she the target and the laptop and phone were taken in case they had incriminating evidence on them?"

"If it's the latter, it would suggest that she knew her attacker," said Jenny. "A client, maybe? Someone she worked with?"

"What was her name again?" said Rob.

"Judith Walker."

Rob knelt down and peered at the papers lying on the floor. Some were wet with spilled water from the vase, the writing blurry, but others he could read.

"Dr Judith Walker," he read slowly. "Did you say she was a psychologist?"

"The neighbour did," Jenny replied. "She does have stacks of books on the subject in her study."

"Let's confirm that, shall we?" asked Rob.

Jenny went back into the kitchen and returned with the purse. She riffled through it. "Aha."

Rob looked up.

"She's a registered criminal psychologist." She held up a laminated ID card. "There's also a civilian police pass for Kingston Police Station."

"That puts a whole different spin on it," said Rob.

"She's a shrink for criminals," mused Will. "Any one of them could have done this to her."

"Bag everything in her office," barked Rob. "We're going to have to go through it all and when we get back to the station, contact Kingston and ask for a list of her clients. Jenny, organise a door-to-door. Someone might have seen something. Tell the officers to double-check for footage from CCTV or residents' private security."

"Will do, guv."

"And let's find out everything we can about Dr Walker. What was she like, where did she hang out, what did she do for fun? Did she have a significant other? Is there a new Mr Walker? You know the drill."

"Yes, sir." Jenny, Jeff and Mike hurried outside and began to organise the house calls.

"Anything else, Liz?" Rob asked, before he left the crime scene.

"Nothing at this point," she confirmed. "I'll let you know when the post-mortem is. I've got a bit of a backlog, so don't expect anything until Friday, earliest."

He sighed. "Okay, if that's the best you can do."

Rob stopped to speak to a uniformed officer on his way out. "Please check the bins at the front and back of the house for the murder weapon, probably a blunt object like a hammer. It will be covered in blood. Also check up and down the road. It's possible the murderer ditched it in someone else's bin when they left."

"Yes, sir."

They got into the car. Rob stared out of the window as Will drove, thinking. Why force the door if they knew the victim? Why not just knock? Would Dr Walker have refused to let them in? Were they a client? An ex-con? Someone with a grudge against her? But then why take the laptop and phone? Was there incriminating evidence on them? Something to do with her work that they didn't want the police to find?

He checked his phone — a voicemail from Hodge. She was probably demanding an update.

He saw there was a second message. "Shit."

"What?" Will glanced across.

"Nothing, I forgot about an earlier message, that's all."

He pressed play, then his blood went cold.

# CHAPTER 27

*Hello. You don't know me, but my name is Dr Judith Walker. I read about Noah Palmer's illegitimate daughter in the newspaper and that you've reopened the case. I have some information that might be of use. I can't go into detail on the phone, but if you call me back, we can arrange to meet. I think it might have a bearing on the case. Thank you.*

"Holy shit." Will was battling to keep his eyes on the road.

Rob closed his eyes and pictured Judith Walker's dead body. Her pale face, the hair matted with blood.

He slammed his fist down on the dashboard. "If only I'd checked my bloody messages earlier, there might have been something we could have done."

Will gnawed on his lower lip. "You weren't to know, guv."

"No, but I should have checked." He shook his head. *Shit.*

"I wonder what she wanted to tell us," muttered Will.

"It was obviously important enough to get her killed." Rob scowled out of the steamed-up window. "What I don't understand is how the killer knew she was going to talk to us. After all these years?"

"The case has been dormant for over a decade," said Will. "There was no reason to bump off the doctor before now. The article must have made them nervous."

"What about after Noah Palmer's murder?" Rob couldn't get his head around this one. "Why not kill her then? If she knew something, she must have been a threat."

"Perhaps she didn't know it then. Perhaps she only found out recently."

It was possible. There could be any number of reasons. "I guess we'll never know."

Will indicated and changed lanes to come off the motorway. "Whatever the reason, it proves the killer knew the doctor."

"I agree. Let's get all the items from her study, every last file and folder. I want to find out who her clients were, who her friends were, and who she was in regular contact with. Also, any people she hadn't spoken to for a while."

"Are we going to tell the Super?" Will's eyes widened as he realised the implications.

"And have this case shut down too?" said Rob. "I don't think so. Let's keep the connection to ourselves for now and treat this like any other homicide."

"Hodge will go apeshit when she finds out," warned Will.

Rob ground his jaw. "We'll cross that bridge when we come to it. With a bit of luck, we can use this case to solve Noah Palmer's murder as well. Two cases closed will look good on her target sheet."

"You do realise there is a chance they're not related?" cautioned Will.

Rob gave him a sidelong glance. "A possible witness leaves a voicemail on my phone and is killed the next day? Come on."

"Okay, I admit it's a hell of a coincidence, but it's not impossible."

"No, it's not, which is why we just treat this like a normal homicide. Not a word to anyone."

"What about the rest of the team?" Will looked worried. Rob understood how he felt. He didn't like the thought of leaving the others in the dark.

"Don't say anything yet," he said. "I'll tell them when we have something more definite to go on."

"You're the boss."

* * *

Rob called a briefing in Incident Room Three, where Will had pinned up photographs of Dr Judith Walker on the whiteboard. A 'before' picture of her smiling on a tropical beach. Jenny had found it on a social media profile. Tranquil waters, cloudless blue sky and in the distance, little cocktail umbrellas dotted on the sugary white sand. Indonesia perhaps? Far away from the horror in the next photograph, taken at the crime scene.

This was not the same incident room Galbraith was using for the pentagram killings. That was next door, and through the glass panels, they could see his crowded whiteboards containing the macabre photographs of the three victims.

Noah Palmer's had been removed. He had his own room now. His own whiteboard. Except the door remained firmly shut. Off limits.

The sun had dipped below the surrounding buildings, casting long shadows across the floor. Will switched on the light and it buzzed before flooding the room. Jenny, Jeff and Mike had just got back from Raynes Park, all looking a little worse for wear. Tired eyes, wan faces, stubble and shadows. It had been a long day. It always was at crime scenes. They walked in munching sandwiches and holding takeaway coffees. Their day wasn't over yet. Celeste joined them.

"This is what we know," began Rob. "Dr Judith Walker was a criminal psychologist. She had her own practice but worked for Kingston Police Department, as well as the Prison and Probation Service. I spoke to DI Stanley at Kingston, who confirmed she performed offender assessments for their custody cases. Apparently, she was very good at her job."

"A perp could have held a grudge against her," suggested Jenny.

"Stanley gave us a list of recent offenders she'd worked with. She didn't have any contact with them after her initial assessment, so it's unlikely one of them had it in for her, but you never know. We'll look into that."

Jenny nodded and put down her coffee to make a note on her iPad.

"She worked for the Prison and Probation Service in an independent capacity, performing prisoner and parole risk assessments," continued Rob. "Jenny, we need a list of her private clients. Celeste can help you. Speak to the Parole Board and the Prison Service and ask them if anyone had reason to be angry or upset with her."

Jenny added it to her to-do list and Celeste nodded eagerly. She'd come on a lot in the last few years and Rob was confident she'd make a decent sergeant in the not-too-distant future.

"Do you think it was a revenge killing?" asked Jenny.

"Could have been." Rob was trying to keep an open mind, even though he was almost a hundred per cent convinced that Dr Walker's killer was someone connected to Noah Palmer. Still, in order to prevent confirmation bias, it was best they treat this as an independent inquiry.

"We'll look into the released prisoners." Jeff gestured to himself and Mike. They'd joined at the same time and were good mates, even though Jeff was from up north and Mike was a diehard south Londoner.

"Good," said Rob. He turned back to Jenny. "What did the neighbours say?"

"Mrs Woodbridge at number twenty-one said Judith seemed nice but kept to herself for the most part. They didn't know her very well, although they didn't think she was married. They did mention an incident a few days ago, though. There was an outburst outside in the street. A man was shouting obscenities through the window."

Rob raised his eyebrows. "What kind of obscenities?"

"Bad language, cursing. He called her the C-word and said she was going to pay for what she'd done."

Rob perked up. "Did she describe him?"

"Yep, I've got the details here. 'Short, stocky build, dark hair, unshaven, covered in tattoos and dodgy-looking.'" Jenny winced. "Not sure I can put that in the report."

"Sounds like an ex-con," said Will.

Rob nodded in agreement. "Let's get ID photos of everyone she was seeing in a professional capacity. See if anyone fits that description."

Could the murderer really be an ex-con and it was just a coincidence that Judith had left that message on his phone? Even before he'd finished thinking about it, his brain was screaming *No*. What were the chances?

"The young couple living at number twenty-five confirmed the outburst," added Jenny. "They were having a drinks party at the time. One of their guests witnessed the commotion on their way in."

"Excellent. It's great we've got it double-sourced. Speak to them and see if the description matches. Show them photographs of the shrink's clients. I want to find this guy." Rob flashed her a grin. "Great work, Jenny."

Superintendent Hodge came in as everybody was filing out. She looked distracted and her dark hair, usually slicked back in a tight bun, was loose.

"What do we have, DCI Miller?"

*She might have made an effort to come to the briefing,* Rob thought, but he updated her anyway. He told her about the burglary, the missing laptop and phone, and the possible lead. "We're tracking down the man involved in the incident outside her house. We're confident he's an ex-con, someone she recently assessed."

"Okay, keep me posted." Her phone buzzed as she walked away. "Finally," she hissed into it. "I've been calling all bloody day."

Rob didn't hear the rest as she stalked into her igloo and closed the door.

"What's that all about?" murmured Will.

"She's pissed off about something," he said, not wanting to spread rumours about Hodge and her partner. "But for once, it isn't me."

Will grinned. "That makes a change. She has been acting a bit weirdly lately, though. I mean, look at her." Through the open blinds, they could see her pacing up and down.

"No weirder than usual," Rob replied. "Right, let's get to work. I want to find the guy yelling obscenities at Dr Walker and have him brought in for questioning. That's our number one priority."

On his way back to his desk, he passed Jenny looking boot-faced. "Everything's shut until tomorrow," she said. "Celeste and I can't get through to the Prison Service or the Parole Board."

"That's okay," Rob said. "Let's make a start on the items in her study. You can try again tomorrow."

Jenny nodded. The contents had been delivered and placed on the boardroom table in the incident room. There were five or six large cardboard boxes.

It was going to be a long night.

# CHAPTER 28

Mrs Winterbottom was more than happy to keep Trigger overnight, although her bad back meant she wasn't able to walk him. Rob would make it up to the Labrador when he got home.

He had a brief chat to Jo, who'd put together an interesting profile on Raza Ashraf. "He's not as squeaky clean as he'd like people to think he is," she divulged.

Rob smiled. She'd been busy. Even on leave, she hadn't been able to resist helping him with the investigation. How she was going to give it up to stay home with the baby full-time, he didn't know. Perhaps she'd feel differently when the little guy — or girl — was born.

"After he left Global Standard, he got a job at the Co-operative Bank and shortly after that, became a councillor for Wandsworth."

"His first step into local politics," Rob mused.

"Yes, he kept his nose clean. Left the bank somewhat abruptly in 2012 but managed to retain his Wandsworth seat, becoming one of a handful of ethnic minority MPs elected that year."

"Do we know why he left?" asked Rob.

"To 'focus on his political career', is the official line. Shortly after that, he announced he was seeking the London nomination for mayor. He'd already been tipped as a possible contender, but shrewdly, he had refused to be drawn on the subject until he'd sounded out MPs and councillors in private to see if he had enough support."

"Which clearly, he does," grumbled Rob.

"Yes. I'll email you my report," said Jo. "Call me if you have any questions?"

"Thanks, Jo. I mean it. You didn't have to do this."

"I wanted to."

He smiled. "I'm going to be sifting through boxes of documents tonight, but I'll look at it tomorrow. Chat soon."

Rob went back to the incident room, where the team were hard at work sorting through the boxes. Every time they found a possible client, they wrote the name on the whiteboard.

Rob took a box and began going through the contents. It was full of invoices dating back several years. He flicked through all of them. She'd done a lot of work for Kingston, Hounslow and Esher Police over the years, although none of her invoices specified the suspect's name. The same went for the invoices she'd issued to Her Majesty's Prison and Probation Service.

Celeste, who was going through Dr Walker's work diaries and calendars, hadn't had any more luck. "No names," she said. "Just appointments at the various police stations, prisons or parole offices."

"Nothing here either." Jenny sighed. She had divided her box into two piles of papers. "I've got the deed for the house, various utility bills, some travel brochures, but no client names."

"They must have been on her laptop." Will rubbed his eyes. His phone buzzed and he glanced down and chuckled.

"It's pretty late for a text," said Rob. It had gone midnight.

"It's from Tasha, that girl I met at the pub the other night."

"Perhaps you could tell her you're busy and you'll sext her back when you get home?" suggested Jenny with a wink.

"We're not sexting," said Will, but he'd gone bright red.

They ploughed on. It was Mike who hit pay dirt when he pulled out a paper folder with *CLIENT NOTES* written on the front. "Got something!" he called.

They all looked up. Inside were handwritten notes by Dr Walker on selected clients. "These look to be from the Parole Board," he said, paging through the A4 papers.

"Write the names on the board," barked Rob.

Finally, they were getting somewhere.

"Are they recent?" asked Jenny.

"Yep, all in the last year," Mike said.

"Excellent."

"I wonder why she wrote these down when she had a computer," mused Will.

"Maybe she transcribed her notes," suggested Jenny. "She could have typed them up when she got home."

Rob nodded. "It's possible. It's a pity we can't get our hands on that laptop."

"Most of her stuff must be computerised. I'm not seeing a lot of handwritten material," said Celeste.

"Me neither," put in Jeff.

"Yet she wrote those few down." Rob nodded at the folder in front of Mike.

Jenny stifled a yawn. It was time to go home. "Once you've gone through your box, you can bugger off," said Rob. "Get some shut-eye. We'll chase up these clients tomorrow."

"Yes, boss," came the collective murmur and one by one they left to go home.

Rob was the last to leave. It was nearly two a.m. when he fell into bed.

\* \* \*

"Ugh," he groaned as the alarm sounded. It couldn't be morning already, could it? He felt like he'd just this minute shut his eyes.

Sadly, it was true. His phone flashed unapologetically. Six o'clock.

Yawning, he got up and zombie-walked into the shower. Five minutes of standing under the steaming jets and he began to feel normal again.

He put on the coffee machine and got dressed. It had snowed overnight. Not a lot, but enough for a fine smattering to have accumulated on the pavements. The roads were still clear.

Rob drank his cappuccino — he still hadn't read the damn instruction manual — and then left for work. He wanted to get a head start on the day's tasks and read Jo's report on Ashraf. Once the team got in, he wouldn't get a chance.

\* \* \*

Ashraf had been in charge of investment accounts at the Co-operative Bank. He'd headed up a team of eight savings and investment account managers. There had been no rumours of money laundering, and his boss only had good things to say about him.

It was while he was at the bank that a young boy in his neighbourhood was stabbed. Ashraf had happened to be one of the first people on the scene. He'd called the emergency services and held the boy as he died. According to all the interviews he'd given since, that experience had changed him, and he'd decided then and there that something had to change.

He'd become a councillor for Wandsworth and had worked hard tackling localised crime. He had started youth clubs aimed at helping young people get out of gangs. He had also helped improve relations between police and the communities they served. His ideas had got a lot of traction from the diverse local population and he'd had no trouble being voted in as a member of parliament for the borough.

Now Ashraf had decided to make the move to the mainstream and had been nominated by a fellow MP as a candidate for mayor of London. It was a hotly contested race, but the polls showed he was in the lead.

Londoners had had enough of knife crime and senseless deaths and wanted someone with a hard stance against that sort of thing. The incumbent mayor had been all talk and no action and crime in the capital had skyrocketed over the past few years. It was now higher than it had ever been. Enough was enough.

Rob studied a brochure Jo had attached to the file.

*RAZA'S PLAN TO GIVE LONDON A FRESH START*, screamed the lettering above a photo of Raza Ashraf flanked by smiling kids in football kit.

Rob raised his eyebrows. It was a good campaign. He came across as humble, genuine and determined to clean up the city. Had he really changed his ways, or was this about something else? Power, maybe? Knife crime was one thing, but Ashraf had had no qualms about blurring the lines when it came to laundering dirty money.

At eight thirty, he rang Jo.

"Interesting read," he told her. "Thanks for that. How did you get the information?"

"I have my sources," she said, and he pictured her smiling into the phone. Jo had always been a thorough detective. No stone unturned.

"Do you want me to chase up a couple of things?" she asked, somewhat hesitantly. "I could question Ashraf's colleagues at the Co-operative Bank. Get their take on it."

Rob hesitated. "It's tempting, but I can't afford to make waves right now. Not with Ashraf. Hodge is already out for my blood."

"Okay. Well, let me know if I can help."

"Will do. Thanks, Jo."

She was bored, he could tell. She missed the excitement of a case, the adrenalin when the pieces fell into place, and the final hunt to apprehend the suspect. She wouldn't be able to give that up any more than he would.

Rob hung up as Will walked in, carrying two coffees. "Here you go, guv."

"Thanks." Rob took it gladly. God only knew what would happen if he decided to give up caffeine. His body would probably go into shock.

Jenny came in next, followed by the rest of the team.

"Hodge not in?" Jeff nodded to the igloo.

"Not yet," said Rob. It was strange that she was late. She was usually one of the first to arrive. Not as early as Sam Lawrence had been. Somehow, their old Chief Superintendent had managed to beat everyone into the office no matter how early they came in.

Hodge arrived half an hour later in crumpled clothes, no make-up and with her hair sticking up in all directions.

"Jesus," muttered Will.

"She looks awful," whispered Jenny. "Do you think something's wrong?"

"Must be," murmured Rob. They watched as she strode across the floor and into her office without saying a word to anyone.

"Why don't you go and ask, Jen?" Jeff grinned. "Woman to woman."

"And get my head bitten off? No thanks. Besides, I've got work to do."

They all did. The clients they'd identified the night before needed confirmation and identity photographs had to be found. The best source for that was the DVLA website. Hodge was forgotten as the team got stuck in.

Just before lunch, Rob called for a progress report.

"I followed up with the Prison Service," said Jeff, tapping his pen against a sheet of A4 paper. "I've got a list of prisoners Dr Walker was working with. Several are up for parole."

"What about those that are out already?" asked Rob.

"Yep, got a list of those," cut in Mike. "Got their mug shots too, although they're not very pretty."

"As long as we can see their faces," said Rob.

"Celeste and I have been working through the Kingston suspect list." Jenny nodded to the young DC. "It's quite substantial. However, Dr Walker didn't have any contact with them after the initial assessment."

"Okay, fine. We'll leave those till last." He turned to Mike. "Let's print out the ID photos of the parolees and take them to the neighbour and the party guests. We need to pinpoint this guy who was hurling abuse at our murder victim."

Twenty minutes later, Jenny was holding the pile of mug shots. She showed them to Rob. "Handsome lot, aren't they?"

They were a right motley crew. "You okay to go out to Raynes Park and talk to the neighbours?" he asked her.

"Yes, I'll take Celeste with me."

If the neighbour or one of the guests who had attended the dinner party could identify the suspect, they'd be able to bring him in and question him. Maybe he was responsible for the burglary and Dr Walker's death, but maybe not. The way the case was going, Rob was betting on the latter.

# CHAPTER 29

"Suspect's name is Rudy Shaw," said Jenny triumphantly when she and Celeste got back from Raynes Park. "He's a construction worker, or rather he was, before he was done for armed robbery with aggravated assault."

"Really?"

"Sounds like he could be our guy, sir." Celeste was standing beside Jenny, her cheeks flushed.

Will shot a meaningful glance across the room at Rob.

"Let's get him in here," he said. "We need to talk to him and see whether he has an alibi for the afternoon Dr Walker was killed."

Liz Kramer had put the time of death at roughly three thirty in the afternoon. It was a weird time for a burglary. Even more reason to suspect the killer had known Dr Walker would be working from home and had broken in with the express purpose of murdering her.

Rudy Shaw was a short, stocky man with tough eyes and a tattoo of a spider's web on the side of his neck. He looked dangerous, but Rob had learned not to take anyone at face value. In his experience, it was the quiet, unassuming ones who harboured the darkest secrets, and were not necessarily the most obvious of suspects. Besides, Shaw was here voluntarily, at the request of the police. As such, he wasn't cautioned and didn't need a solicitor present.

"Mr Shaw," began Rob. "We wanted to ask you about your altercation with Mrs Walker on the evening of the twelfth of February."

He stared at them through hooded black eyes. "What altercation? I ain't been in no fight."

"I'm referring to the incident outside Dr Walker's house in Raynes Park."

Still no reaction.

"Apparently, you were seen shouting obscenities at her."

"Oh, that."

"Yes, that. Could you tell us about it?"

"The bitch told social services that I wasn't fit to see my little boy," he spat. "It's because of her my boy ain't seen his father."

"So you thought hurling abuse at her outside her property was the best thing to do, did you?"

He frowned. "I can do what I like. It's a free country. I was letting her know how I felt."

"In no uncertain terms," said Rob.

"Because of her, my wife won't let me see our kid. He's seven years old and he needs his father. What kind of woman does that?"

"Did she give a reason?" asked Rob. He'd read the case notes and knew why Dr Walker had come to the conclusion she had. Rudy Shaw was a live wire, even worse when under the influence of drugs or alcohol, and his report stipulated he was fond of both. She'd felt that it wasn't safe for the seven-year-old to be left unsupervised with his father.

"She said I was unfit to be a dad."

"I see she granted supervised visits." Rob glanced down at the file.

He snorted. "How am I supposed to talk to him with a social worker present? They watch you like a hawk. I want to take my boy out, spend some quality time with him. She stopped all that." He swore under his breath.

Rob could imagine Rudy Shaw appearing quite menacing to Dr Walker and her neighbours.

"Why are you asking me this?" he asked. "Has something happened to her?"

"What makes you think that?" Rob asked.

The ex-con grunted. "Why else would I be here? If someone's done her in, she probably deserved it."

Rob studied him. Short, crew-cut hair, angular face, nose that had seen a few knocks. This guy wasn't used to playing nice. He had no doubt Dr Walker's judgement was sound.

He slid a photograph of Dr Walker lying in a pool of her own blood across the table. "Dr Walker was murdered at her home on Wednesday."

Rudy's eyes dropped to the crime scene photograph and widened slightly, then he scoffed. "Like I said, she probably deserved it." But there was a flicker of uneasiness.

"Where were you on Wednesday afternoon between two and four p.m.?"

"Oh, now you think I must have done it? Because we had words?" He snorted. "That's fucking typical. Go for the ex-con. The easy target."

"I asked you a question," said Rob, his face expressionless. Will sat beside him, unmoving.

"I don't have to tell you nothing."

"No, you're here of your own free will to assist us with our investigation. We can make it official if you refuse to cooperate. My sergeant here will arrest you, you can get yourself a solicitor, and then we'll go through the questioning again. Won't look good on your parole record."

Rudy stared at the photograph, a sulky expression on his face. "I was at the pub on Wednesday afternoon."

"Which pub was that?"

"The Star and Garter in Wandsworth. My neck of the woods. I was nowhere near her fancy neighbourhood."

"Can anyone vouch for you?" asked Rob.

"Yeah, the barman and a couple of my mates."

Rob nodded. "Names, please? We'll have to check up."

Will slid a piece of paper and a pen over to him.

The ex-con sighed but wrote down a couple of names in an untidy scrawl. "Don't ask me for their phone numbers, 'cos I don't have 'em. They're drinking buddies, you know?"

"Who's the barman?"

"Pete."

"Pete who?"

A shrug. "No idea."

"Okay, Mr Shaw. Thank you for coming in. We'll let you know if we have any more questions."

Will escorted the ex-con out, while Rob made his way back upstairs. Jenny had been watching the interview on her computer via the office network and looked up as he walked in. "I'm looking up the address of the Star and Garter now. I thought Mike and Jeff could check out Mr Shaw's alibi."

"Good."

"Also, there's one name that appears regularly in Dr Walker's diary — Adele Simpson. I think it's a friend. They have lunch once a month. I've spoken to her and she's agreed to come in and talk to us."

"Great work," said Rob. "If they're close, Dr Walker may have confided in her."

"That's what I thought."

Mike and Jeff were dispatched to Rudy Shaw's local pub. Stationed in the incident room, Jenny and Celeste were still methodically following up on Dr Walker's current client list and anyone else whose name had popped up in any of the documents found in her study.

Rob got himself a coffee and surveyed the crime scene photos pinned on the whiteboard. Pictures of the upturned lounge and office, papers everywhere, files pulled out of the bookshelf and scattered all over the floor.

"The killer searched her study too," Rob said to Jenny, who glanced up. "They must have been looking for something in particular. See how there are spaces in the bookshelf where files have been removed?"

"We took everything that was in there," she said. "But now you mention it, there are gaps in the shelves, even if you take into account the files on the floor."

"What were they looking for?" muttered Rob.

Jenny shook her head. "It's impossible to know. Without her laptop or the missing files, we're in the dark."

"Jenny," Rob said slowly, "you haven't found anything that connects Dr Walker to Noah Palmer, have you?"

Jenny gaped at him. "Noah Palmer? No. Why would you ask that?"

He pulled out his phone. "I'd like you to listen to something."

## CHAPTER 30

"No, it can't be."

Rob gave a terse nod. "Judith Walker left that message the day before she died."

"What does it mean?" Jenny swept a hand through her hair. She usually wore it back in an efficient ponytail, but today it was loose around her shoulders.

"She obviously knew Noah Palmer," said Rob. "Or she had some information about his death."

"But how?" Jenny was still gaping like a goldfish. "I–I don't understand."

Rob shook his head. "That's what we need to find out. You're sure you haven't come across anything in the items in the study?"

"No, but then, I wasn't looking for a connection between the two. I'll have to go over everything to be sure." She hesitated. "Do the others know?"

"No, only you and Will. I didn't want to risk it getting back to the Super."

"We'll have to tell them," she whispered, staring at the board. "It changes everything."

"I know. Let's see what they come back with. Rudy Shaw is still our primary suspect until we can prove otherwise."

"Okay." She turned to face him. "If Dr Walker knew something, why wait all these years before coming forward?"

"That's what I thought. She mentioned the article, so perhaps that triggered something. Who knows?"

"That piece about Rachel Norton?"

He nodded.

"I'd like to see it," she said.

"There's nothing in it that rings any bells," said Rob, who had a copy at home. "But by all means, take a look. You might find something I missed."

Jenny pursed her lips. "Maybe Adele Simpson can shed some light."

"Let's hope so."

* * *

Adele Simpson was a stylish, well-kept woman in her fifties, slightly older than Judith Walker. She had a blonde bob streaked with grey and an endearing smile. Rob liked her immediately.

"Thanks for coming in," he told her.

She nodded. "Anything for Judy. She was a good friend. I still can't believe she's gone."

Jenny sat beside him, since she'd been the one to make contact. "Do you mind if we record this conversation, Mrs Simpson?"

"No, I don't mind."

"Great, thank you."

Rob nodded to Jenny to begin the interview. She was taking the lead on this one. He was there as an observer.

Jenny had a sincerity about her that made people open up to her, especially other women. He'd noticed it several times over the years they'd been working together. She made a great interrogator, and it wasn't surprising that she was thinking of specialising in the field.

Jenny started with a reassuring smile. "How long have you known Judith Walker?"

"Oh, nearly twenty years." A self-deprecating smile, a quick flicker into the past. "It seems like eons ago now."

"Were you close?"

"Yes, I'd say so. We met regularly for lunch and talked about things that were going on in our lives."

"What sort of things?" asked Jenny.

"You know, work issues, relationship problems, that sort of thing. We both got divorced around the same time, so we commiserated over that. It was a few years ago now."

"Was she seeing anyone?"

"Actually, now that you mention it, she had met someone recently." Adele scrunched up her forehead. "A man called Richard, I think."

Rob glanced up.

"You think?"

She bit her lip. "Yes, I'm sure that's what his name was."

"You didn't catch his surname?"

"No, she didn't say. I'm sorry." Adele gasped. "You don't think he did this to her, do you?"

"I don't know," Jenny said honestly. "But we have to consider all options."

The woman nodded, clearly disturbed.

Jenny tried a different tack. "Did she say where she met him?"

Adele perked up. "I believe it was in the coffee shop across the road from Kingston Police Station. I remember because she said he was there almost every lunchtime. They struck up a conversation and one day he asked her out."

"Do you know where he worked or what he did?"

"She didn't talk about him much. It was very new, and she wasn't sure where it was going, if anywhere."

Jenny nodded. "I understand."

"Her husband, Dean, left her for a younger woman, you see. He hurt her badly. She couldn't have kids, but he wanted a large family." She shrugged. "Now he's got what he wanted."

Rob grimaced. That had to sting. He suddenly felt extremely grateful that Jo had been able to conceive so easily.

"What were these work dramas you mentioned?" asked Jenny. Rob nodded in approval.

"Oh, nothing in particular. Just hassles with clients. I'm an estate agent. I run my own agency, which comes with its own set of problems. Although her clients could be a lot more difficult than mine."

"Ex-cons, you mean?"

"Yes. I couldn't work with criminals day in and day out. It would get to me. But Judy enjoyed her job — she was fascinated by the way the criminal mind worked and what drove people to commit offences. It's all a bit macabre for me. But that was Judy." She gave a sad smile.

"Did Judy mention a particular client who was giving her a hard time?" Jenny adopted Adele's familiar version of the name.

"Actually, last time we spoke, she mentioned this one guy who was harassing her. Something to do with the custody of his child, I think. I can't remember the details."

"Rudy Shaw?" asked Jenny.

Adele's brows shot up. "That's him. I got the impression it was a child safety issue."

"Yes, we know about him."

There was a short pause as Adele gazed at them, waiting for the next question.

Jenny glanced at Rob, who gave a brief nod. "Does the name Noah Palmer mean anything to you?"

Rob found he was holding his breath.

Adele crinkled her forehead. "No, I don't think so. Why? Who is he? Is he involved?"

"No, he's been dead for twelve years," said Jenny. "We think that Judy used to know him, though."

"I've never heard her mention that name. Of course, it could have been from before, when she worked for the London Met."

"The Metropolitan Police?" blurted out Rob, unable to help himself.

"Yes." She gave them a funny look. "Didn't I say? That's how we met. We were both family liaison officers. We did our training together at Hendon Police College."

## CHAPTER 31

There was a pause as both Rob and Jenny assimilated this information.

"When was this?" whispered Jenny.

"Oh, about eighteen years ago now. I knew straight away it wasn't for me. Too much angst. Too many grieving people. I did a year, but that was enough. I couldn't stop thinking about them, about their misery. It gets to you, that sort of thing. So I retrained as an estate agent. Judy stuck it out for longer than me, but her interest was in criminology, really."

"She must have retrained as a psychologist," said Rob.

"Yes, that's right. She was always very bright. She studied psychology through correspondence, the Open University, I think, or one of those online organisations. Then she did a work placement with the council and started her own business after that." Her face fell. "She did extremely well for herself."

She certainly did, if her house in Raynes Park was anything to go by.

"I'm sorry for your loss," said Jenny.

Adele nodded. "Thank you. I'll miss her."

* * *

"She was a FLO? Do you think that's the connection?" asked Will.

"Could be," said Rob. If that was the case, it opened up a whole host of possibilities. "We need to check. There'll be records somewhere."

Jenny stood. "I'll get on it."

"Should we ask Suzie Palmer to come in? She might remember Judith Walker," suggested Will.

"No, not yet," said Rob. "We're off the case, remember? Let's confirm that link between Dr Walker and the Palmer family before we risk Hodge's wrath."

Will snorted. "I just saw her outside. She was yelling at somebody on her phone. I've never seen her that mad, not even at you." He smirked.

"Thanks." Something was going on with her, but it was none of his business. At least if she was distracted, she wasn't delving into their investigation.

"If there is a link between Dr Walker and the Palmers, it's going to be hard to keep that quiet. I'll have to put it in my report," said Jenny.

"Let's cross that bridge when we come to it." Rob got to his feet. That was the last thing they should do. As soon as Hodge realised the cases were related, she'd shut this one down too. "I don't want to jump to conclusions."

"Okay, guv."

Rob went outside to clear his head. Putney high street was buzzing with traffic, pedestrians and the after-school crowd. He walked down to the river, grabbed a coffee and a sandwich and sat on the low wall that ran along the tow path.

What was it Judith Walker had wanted to tell him?

He thought back to the voice on his phone. Warm, urgent, to the point. He had a feeling he would have liked Judith Walker.

His chest constricted. Guilt. If only he'd listened to that message sooner.

He gritted his teeth. He ought to know better than to play that game. The only place 'if only' led to was despair.

Right now, he had to find out who had killed the woman who'd left that message. He owed her that much.

His phone rang.

"Miller."

"Guv, Judith Walker *was* the Palmers' family liaison officer. She was assigned after Noah's murder."

Rob's heart skipped a beat. They had confirmation. That was the link.

"They also have copies of Walker's report on the family, although they've been archived. We're going to need permission to access them."

Rob stood up. "Okay, leave it with me. I'm on my way back to the station now."

"There's one other thing, guv. Mike and Jeff just called. Rudy Shaw's alibi doesn't check out. The barman said he was in on Wednesday night, from around six, but not any earlier. His whereabouts for the time of Dr Walker's murder are unknown."

Rob picked up the pace. "Shit, really?"

"Yeah, shall I get him picked up?"

They couldn't ignore their prime suspect. There was no doubt the man had a grudge against Judith Walker, and it would serve his purposes if she were taken out. Shaw would now be assigned a new assessor, who might look more favourably on his situation.

"Yes, we'd better bring him in." He sighed. The coincidences were piling up. If Shaw had broken in and threatened Walker, why take her laptop and riffle through her study? It didn't make sense. But the ex-con was looking guiltier by the second and they couldn't ignore that.

* * *

"Boss, can I have a word?" Evan, from Galbraith's team, approached Rob in the lobby.

"Sure, what's up?"

"It's about the Superintendent," he began.

191

Rob arched an eyebrow. "Oh, yeah?"

"She asked me to pull the phone records for a particular number. Made out like it was connected to an active case, but there's no case number attached."

"So? Did you ask her about it?"

"No, but I pulled the call logs. It's her husband's phone."

Rob let this sink in. Hodge was spying on her husband's call records. What the hell was going on?

"Did you give them to her?" Rob asked.

Evan nodded. "Yeah, she asked for them. I didn't let on that I knew, and she didn't mention it."

"Okay, thanks for letting me know. Have you told Galbraith?"

"I would have done, but he's out chasing a lead on Whitaker. He won't be back until later. I thought I'd better let you know."

Rob nodded. "Thanks."

\* \* \*

"Maybe she suspects her husband of having an affair," said Will, once they'd assembled in the incident room to discuss next steps. "That would explain the erratic behaviour of late."

"Her personal life is none of our business," Rob said.

"Except she's using police resources to keep tabs on him," pointed out Will.

"True. Perhaps now's a good time to ask her for permission to pull those old FLO files."

Jenny gasped. "You can't tell her about the Palmers."

"I won't. For all she knows, it's background information on Judith Walker." He strode across to Hodge's office and knocked on the door.

There was a pause. "Come in."

He pushed open the door. Hodge was behind her desk, her eyes red-rimmed and glassy. Papers were scattered everywhere, and while she appeared to be working, the chaos around her said she wasn't.

Rob was shocked. It wasn't like her to be so unprofessional.

"Everything okay?" He wondered if he should even go there.

"Everything's fine," she snapped. "What can I do for you, DCI Miller?"

"It's about the Judith Walker investigation. We need to access some old case files on her, mostly background stuff, but it might be relevant to the case. It's archived material."

She frowned. "That must be going back a bit."

"Yes, but since her study was ransacked and her laptop taken, we have to access the files some other way. It could give us a lead."

She nodded. "Okay, do it."

He grinned. "Thanks, ma'am."

She didn't respond, merely went back to staring at her computer screen.

Rob winked at Jenny. She immediately picked up the phone. Even though the records were all computerised, it would take some time for the request to be logged and for the operator to retrieve the files and send them over.

She hung up. "Twenty-four hours."

*Shit.* "I'll give Lawrence a ring and see if he remembers Walker. He was close to the family, he might have met her."

Sam remembered her straight away. "Yes, of course. Nice girl. Friendly smile. I met her once or twice after Noah's death. Why do you ask?"

Rob hesitated. "Because she was found dead in her house two days ago. Murdered. The perp made it look like a burglary gone wrong."

"Jesus." There was a pause as the retired Chief Superintendent digested this information. "Are you saying it's related to the Pentagram Killer?" His voice was breathy.

Rob sighed. "I don't know. It's possible."

"Christ."

Rob wrestled with his conscience. Lawrence was his old boss and he trusted him, but he couldn't discuss an ongoing investigation. Nobody outside the department knew Noah Palmer's case was no longer linked to the ritualistic murders.

"We're still trying to get to the bottom of it," he said. "I just wondered if you had any information on the FLO."

"I'll have a little think," he said.

"Okay, thanks, Chief."

Lawrence made a tsking sound, but he wasn't displeased by the title.

Rob called it a day after that and sent his team home. After last night's late one, they could all do with some extra shut-eye.

He collected a thoroughly overexcited Trigger from the neighbour's and fed him, and then put a steak in a pan for himself. While he was cooking, he gave Jo a ring.

"I was just about to call you," she said, right after she picked up. He could hear the excitement in her voice.

He smiled. "What's up?"

"I went to speak to Ashraf's old colleagues today."

"You did what?" Rob stared at the sizzling steak.

"Don't worry. I said I was a journalist doing a piece on the future mayor of London."

He exhaled. "Shit, Jo. I didn't ask you to do that."

"I know, but I couldn't leave it alone. Anyway, don't you want to know what happened?"

"Did they buy it?" he asked.

"Of course. I was seamless."

The room began to fill up with smoke. He switched on the extractor fan and waved the spatula in the air. "What did you find out?"

"It turns out that Raza Ashraf wasn't well liked by his colleagues. In fact, one of them went so far as to say he was a selfish prat and he wouldn't vote for him in a million years."

Rob laughed. "That's not quite the image he's going for."

"Apparently, he had an overinflated sense of his own importance and wouldn't take advice from anybody."

"That doesn't make him a murderer." Rob flipped the steak.

"No, but there's something else. One of his colleagues remembers him meeting a woman at a nearby bar after work. They all used to go there, apparently. At the time, no one knew he was married. My source said they were all shocked when they found out he had a wife at home."

"Who was the woman?"

"Suzie Palmer," said Jo with a flourish. "When I showed him Suzie's photograph, he recognised her instantly."

"They were an item?"

"It seems so."

Rob whistled. "Do you realise what this means?"

"Yep," she said. "It means Raza Ashraf had even more of a motive to want Noah Palmer dead."

# CHAPTER 32

Rob had come clean and brought the rest of his team up to speed on Judith Walker's voicemail message. Celeste, dumb-struck, hadn't said a word since she'd listened to it, while Jeff and Mike were trying to remember if they'd read anything in her documents that might link back to Noah Palmer. Rob had also filled them in on what Jo had discovered about Ashraf.

"We can't bring him in," said Will. "Hodge will go berserk."

Rob paced across the narrow space at the front of the incident room. "I know, but what if he's guilty? He's got no alibi for the time of the murder, he was sleeping with the victim's wife, and Noah Palmer had information about him that Ashraf wouldn't have wanted to get out."

"Still, it's all circumstantial." Jenny flicked a pen against the table. "No court is going to convict him because he can't remember where he was on the fifth of August twelve years ago."

She was right, unfortunately. It was just too long ago.

"And given his standing in parliament and his relation-ship with the Deputy Commissioner . . ." She didn't need to go on. They all knew what it meant. He was off limits.

For now. "We need hard evidence," growled Rob.

"I don't see how we're going to get it." Will glanced down as his phone beeped.

"Hot date tonight?" teased Jenny, puncturing the tension.

Will flushed. "Yeah, I'm meeting Tasha for a drink."

Rob wasn't listening. His mind was still focused on Ashraf. "Unless . . . he was also responsible for Dr Walker's murder."

Everybody turned back to him.

"Hear me out. What if Suzie Palmer told her family liaison officer about her affair with him? Or if Judith Walker had found out some other way? It would have put her in danger. Ashraf is vulnerable right now. He can't afford any bad press."

Jenny had frozen, her pen in the air.

"So you think he silenced her to keep the affair from coming out?" Will asked.

"He might have. Noah Palmer's love child was in the papers recently. There's renewed interest in the story. If a journalist were to uncover the affair, it would make Ashraf a person of interest."

"Shit," murmured Jenny, her eyes huge. "What are we going to do? If we can't question him, how are we going to find out where he was on the afternoon Dr Walker was killed?"

Nobody had an answer.

\* \* \*

"Guv, I've got the DNA results back from the crime scene," said Mike, later that morning. "You'll never believe it."

"What's that?"

"Rudy Shaw's prints were found all over the front door."

Rob's jaw dropped. *No way.* "Rudy Shaw was the one who broke into Judith Walker's house?"

"I thought it was connected to the Noah Palmer case," whispered Celeste.

"We all did." Jenny glanced at Rob.

He pulled himself together and cleared his throat. "Yes, well, we have to keep an open mind. If it isn't related, it's a hell of a coincidence, her leaving that message the day before her death."

"What do we do, boss?" asked Jeff.

"We've got to find him and bring him in," said Rob, his mind whirling. "Any news on his whereabouts?"

"No, uniform are still out looking. He hasn't come home yet."

"Okay, as soon as he's picked up, let me know."

"Will do," said Jeff.

"There were also several unidentified fingerprints found at the crime scene," Mike added. "I've run them through the database. Nothing so far."

"Would Ashraf's fingerprints be on the system?" enquired Will.

"Not unless he has a previous conviction." Rob felt strangely deflated. He'd been so convinced, so sure the two cases were connected.

"One of those sets could be his." Jenny jumped up.

"Not if Shaw was responsible," muttered Rob.

"But what if Shaw wasn't responsible?" Jenny said. "There's always a chance he didn't murder Dr Walker."

Rob perked up. "He may have inspected the lock on the door. Found her dead and got spooked, maybe?"

Jenny shrugged. "You never know. Like you said, let's keep an open mind. If we can prove Raza Ashraf was at the crime scene, that ought to be enough to pick him up."

"But how do we get his fingerprints?" asked Will.

Rob took a deep breath. "I have an idea."

* * *

"Are you sure?" Jo asked that night over dinner. "I mean, I'm happy to do it, but it won't be admissible in court."

"All I need is a reason to bring him in," explained Rob. "Once he's in custody, we can fingerprint him officially."

Jo looked doubtful. "Even if the unidentified prints belong to him, will your superintendent agree to an arrest? You'll have to tell her how you got them, and she won't be happy."

"No, she won't, but she won't be able to deny he was there. It's not the way I wanted to do it, but unfortunately, she hasn't left me with much of a choice."

Jo nodded. "I've got a contact at the *Argus*. I'll get him to arrange an interview. He owes me a favour."

"Great, thanks, Jo. One thing Ashraf loves is publicity. He won't be able to refuse."

Jo grinned. "I'd do it myself, but his security team are bound to check my credentials."

"I owe you," he said.

She squeezed his hand. "You can make it up to me later."

After supper, they took Trigger for a walk. It was bitterly cold, not that the Labrador minded. He raced across the fields in near-pitch darkness, ferreting out his favourite trees to pee on and getting rid of his excess energy.

"Watch out for the icy patches." Rob took Jo's arm.

She smiled at him. "You'll make a great dad."

He met her gaze. "I'd like to try." His heart beat in his throat. "Jo, can we at least try to make it work? Living together, I mean. I really want to be a part of this. It's important to me."

She gripped him a little tighter. "I'd like that too," she whispered.

He walked home feeling lighter than he had in weeks.

\* \* \*

"You know, there is another possibility," said Jo, emerging from the shower the next morning, a towel wrapped around her and her gently swelling belly. Pregnancy suited her. She looked even more beautiful than before.

"What's that?"

"We could corner Ashraf's wife."

Rob started. "What do you mean?"

"It's not strictly ethical," she said with a wry grin. "But what if we were to have an informal chat? Confront her with Ashraf's betrayal, ask her about the affair or threaten to go public? She might be willing to divulge his whereabouts the afternoon of your psychologist's murder."

Rob thought about this for a moment. Intimidating witnesses was against the law. There were heavy penalties for that sort of behaviour. Charges could be brought.

"It's too risky," he said. "She might run to her husband and tell him everything, then all manner of hail and fury will rain down on me and my team."

Jo spread her arms. "I'm just playing devil's advocate here. You might find she'll do anything to protect her husband's reputation."

Rob shook his head. "I can't, Jo. I agree, it might work, but it's just not worth the risk."

"I could do it," she offered. "I'd go in my guise as a journalist. She'll never know. She'll think I'm from the press and even if she does tell Ashraf, he won't be able to trace me. He'll never know it was the cops."

Rob exhaled. It was tempting. Very tempting.

"Let's get his fingerprints first and if that doesn't give us anything to work with, perhaps we can talk about taking it further."

She nodded. "Sure. The offer's there if you need it."

Rob kissed her. "Thank you. Now, what do you say we wander into Richmond and grab a couple of croissants for breakfast and talk about how we're going to convert the spare room into a nursery?"

Her clear blue eyes met his. "You're enjoying this, aren't you?"

He nodded. "Shouldn't I be? I'm going to be a father."

She touched his cheek. "Of course you should. It's just a big step, that's all. What if it doesn't . . ."

"Shh . . . It will work out. I promise. We'll make it work."

She nodded and kissed him, but her eyes were wary. He'd just have to keep convincing her it was the right decision. For them and the baby.

# CHAPTER 33

Rob was in the process of dismantling the double bed in the spare room when he got a call from Galbraith. On a Sunday, that was never a good sign.

He set down the screwdriver. "Yeah, mate?"

"We've found the fucker," boomed the voice down the line. "He's been hiding out at one of the houses on his old postal route. The armed unit have surrounded the building and I'm heading over there now. Thought you might like to know."

He'd been wrong — it was bloody great news. "Text me the address. I can be there in twenty minutes."

"You might miss the action, but sure. See you there."

Jo wasn't about to be left behind, so together they jumped in the car and raced out to the address they'd been given.

"Shouldn't we tell Lawrence?" she asked. "This was his case, after all."

"I'll tell him once we know we've got him," said Rob. "Don't want to jinx it."

Jo smiled and squeezed his thigh.

They flew through Kingston and down the A309 towards Esher. They got there just as the Specialist Firearms

Command was bringing out a bedraggled Whitaker, hands wrenched behind his back. He looked defeated. Limp, greasy hair, pallid complexion, dead eyes. The battle was over. He'd lost. Finally, after twelve years, he'd been caught.

Galbraith arrested him on the spot for the murder of Kyle McKenzie, Nathan Langton, Paul Sutton and Mabel Henderson, the old lady whose house he'd appropriated. Her decomposing body was found in the shed at the bottom of the garden.

"She used to be friendly with him when he did his rounds," Galbraith told them, his face grim. "So much for kindness, eh?"

Jo shook her head. "That's terrible."

They watched as the paramedics took her away on a stretcher, in a black body bag. Her only crime, being chatty with the postman.

"How'd you find him?" asked Rob.

"A neighbour called it in," he said with a tight smile. "He noticed Mabel hadn't been around lately and when he peeked through the windows, he saw a strange man sitting in her favourite chair watching television."

"Thank goodness for snooping neighbours." Jo gave a sad grin.

"It's a good thing he called the cops and didn't knock on the door," said Rob. "Or else things could have ended very differently."

"Aye." Galbraith nodded. "We'd have had another murder on our hands." He glanced at the police car in which Whitaker was sitting, his pale face peering out from the gloomy interior. "That fucker deserves everything coming to him."

Jo nodded.

Rob patted him on the shoulder. "Good work, Gav. You finally got him."

Galbraith gave a watery smile. "I'd better get back to the station to interrogate this scumbag. He's got a lot to answer for."

"Good luck," called Jo.

They watched as Galbraith jumped into his car, Evan at the wheel, and sped off back in the direction of Putney, their work only beginning.

* * *

There was jubilation at major crime's headquarters on Monday morning. The infamous Pentagram Killer had been apprehended and had given a full confession. He hadn't even bothered to deny it.

"It was almost as if he wanted to tell us all about it," said Evan tiredly. He had dark shadows beneath his eyes and twenty-four-hour stubble. It was clear he hadn't slept a wink. "Like he was proud of what he'd done."

Harry shook his head. "It was fucking mental. He explained in detail how he'd abducted his victims, hit them over the head until they were dead, then strung them out, painted that weird circle around them and carved the pentagram into their chests. Said he got the idea from that batty old witch in the woods. She was mad about pentagrams, had them everywhere."

"Mrs Knowles," said Rob. "She must have been on his postal route too."

"Yep, that's what he said. He used to stop by there for a cuppa at the end of his round. He thought he was smart, pinning it on her. He knew that was the first place the police would look."

"Luckily he didn't decide to move in there." Jenny shuddered.

"It's very isolated. I'm surprised he didn't," said Rob.

"Mrs Henderson was closer and more convenient," supplied Evan. "He didn't have a lot of time and the police were looking for him."

"That poor, poor woman," mused Jenny, her soft side showing.

It was tragic. A spin of the dice and her number came up.

"Whitaker's on suicide watch." Evan grimaced. "Death is too good for what he did, for the lives he ruined."

"How did Lawrence take it?" asked Rob.

"Galbraith's gone to tell him now," Evan said. "He'll be ecstatic. It's closure for them. Twelve years." He shook his head.

Rob grinned. "Congratulations, you guys did great. Hodge must be over the moon."

Evan lowered his voice. "She's not even in yet. No one's been able to get hold of her."

"Shit, really?" This was a career bust, and the Superintendent wasn't around to take credit for it. Things must be really bad.

* * *

Once things had quietened down and Galbraith's team had gone home to catch a few hours' sleep, Rob called his team together.

"Jo has a contact at the *Argus*. He's going to interview Raza Ashraf and get his fingerprints. This is strictly on the QT. If it gets out, we're in the shit."

Nods all round. Everybody understood the need for discretion.

"It's purely so we can place him at Judith Walker's house," explained Rob.

"Or not," pointed out Jenny.

"Indeed. Either way, we've got to know."

The interview was arranged for two o'clock that afternoon. Ashraf, true to form, had jumped at the chance of a profile piece and an opportunity to "get his message out there."

In the meantime, more forensic data had come back on Judith Walker's death. The post-mortem confirmed that the cause of death was blunt force trauma to the head. No surprises there. The murder weapon was said to resemble a hammer, judging by the shape and depth of the markings, but because there were multiple blows, it was hard to tell exactly which model.

A search of the bins and tips in the neighbourhood hadn't turned up anything. Rob was debating requesting a search of the bins in Ashraf's street, but thought it might attract too much attention. Besides, four days had passed since the murder. In all likelihood, the refuse had been collected and taken to the dump already. They'd missed their opportunity.

Superintendent Hodge eventually made an appearance. She also looked like she hadn't slept — her blouse was crumpled, her hair wild — and she kept darting out of the office on undisclosed errands.

"She even missed a meeting with the Deputy Commissioner," Rob told them, after she'd left for the third time that morning without explanation. "He called me to find out if she was ill."

"What's she playing at?" hissed Will. "She's all over the show."

"I think her husband's having an affair," whispered Jenny. "Evan told me there was a number that showed up repeatedly on her husband's phone records with some saucy text messages. They weren't to her."

Celeste gasped. "That's awful." The young constable had recently got married. The entire team had attended the wedding.

"Still, she shouldn't be falling apart like this," remarked Jeff. "It's not professional."

Rob reserved judgement. He could imagine himself in a similar state if things broke down between him and Jo, particularly now with a child on the way. "Does she have kids?" he asked.

"Yeah, a teenage son, I think," said Jenny. When all eyes turned to her, she said, "What? There's a photograph of him on her desk." She shook her head. "Call yourselves detectives."

Rob snorted. "I don't think I've been around that side of her desk before. She usually starts yelling at me the moment I walk through the door."

Everyone chuckled.

"Guv, uniform have arrested Rudy Shaw," Mike told him. "He smells like a brewery but is sober enough to be interviewed. He's downstairs in a holding cell whenever you're ready."

"Thanks, Mike. I'm going to let him sweat a bit. Sounds like he needs it."

It had taken some time to locate the evasive Mr Shaw. He'd gone on a bender and had spent the night at an unknown woman's house. The uniformed officers had waited outside his residence until he'd staggered home at ten this morning.

Rob's phone buzzed. Sam Lawrence. He took it outside.

"Hi, Chief. Great news about Whitaker, eh?"

"Incredible. I can't believe they finally got him. But that's not why I'm calling."

"It's not?"

"No. Suzie Palmer just rang me. She's received a letter from Isabella Norton's lawyer informing her that Rachel is claiming a portion of Noah's inheritance left to his biological children."

"Yeah." This wasn't news to Rob.

"Did you know about this?"

Rob cleared his throat. "I knew she was looking into it."

"Does it hold water?"

"Well, Rachel is his biological child too. As far as I understand it, it depends on the wording in the will, but I'm no expert."

There was a pause. "It's hit Suzie rather badly. She was in tears when she rang me."

"Rachel is entitled to a portion of her father's legacy," Rob reminded him. "She's had a hard life and she's a bright kid. It's only fair."

"I guess so." Lawrence hesitated. "What's the status of the case?"

"We've been taken off it," Rob grumbled. "As soon as Ashraf became our prime suspect, the Superintendent shut us down. Apparently, Ashraf is a close friend of the Deputy Commissioner."

"Fucking politics," muttered Lawrence, who had hated it as much as Rob although he had been much better at hiding it. During his years as Chief Superintendent, he'd managed to schmooze with the best of them.

Rob didn't mention the lengths to which they were going to prove — or disprove — Ashraf had been at Dr Walker's house. There was something he wanted to talk to the retired Chief Superintendent about, though. "Sir, there's something I've been meaning to ask you."

"Yeah?"

Rob didn't miss the wary tone in his ex-boss's voice. He knew Rob too well. "Is it possible Suzie Palmer was having an affair?"

"Heavens, no," came the expected response. "At least, not when I knew them. They were always so . . . together."

Appearances could be deceiving. Rob had been married for nearly a year and it had been the most miserable time of his life. Even before he'd married Yvette, he'd had doubts, but she'd walked around smiling, flashing her engagement ring, acting like they were the happiest couple on the planet when nothing could have been further than the truth.

"It's just that we've heard two reports now that there may have been something between Suzie and Raza Ashraf when he was Noah's partner at Global Standard."

"I thought Noah was the one being unfaithful?" Lawrence said.

"It looks like Suzie might have been too."

"Well, if she was, I never knew about it. Noah certainly didn't confide in me, and Suzie always seemed dedicated to her family. The kids were very young then. I'd be surprised if she'd found the time."

"Still, it happens. Maybe she was trying to get back at her husband."

"Hmm . . ." Lawrence didn't sound convinced.

"I'd appreciate it if you didn't mention this to Mrs Palmer," Rob said, after a moment's hesitation. "There's nothing conclusive, just rumours."

"I wouldn't dare," Lawrence said. "She'd soon put me in my place."

They said goodbye shortly after that and Rob made his way to the holding cells. It was time to collect Rudy Shaw and find out why he'd lied about where he was on the afternoon of Dr Walker's death and why his fingerprints were on her front door.

He called Will, who met him outside the designated interrogation room where Shaw was waiting.

"Ready?" his sergeant asked.

Rob nodded. "Let's do this."

Rudy Shaw looked rougher than he had the last time, if that was possible. Deep purple rings underlined his hooded eyes, his complexion was blotchy, and he had two days' worth of stubble on his jaw. He gazed warily at them through bloodshot eyes, then ran a hand through his greasy hair. The entire room smelled strongly of stale alcohol.

"Why am I here?" he demanded.

"You've been arrested because you lied to us during our last little chat. This time we're doing it properly." Rob nodded at Will to turn on the recording. "Now, when you were last interviewed, you told us that you were at the Star and Garter pub on the afternoon of the seventeenth of February. Isn't that right?"

Shaw nodded over hunched shoulders, as if wishing the hard, wooden chair would swallow him whole.

"We checked, like we said we would, and it turns out that you came in after six o'clock that evening, not early afternoon as you had led us to believe."

Shaw fidgeted in his seat. He looked guilty as hell.

Rob didn't know what to think. Sure, the evidence was stacking up against him, but was it really that simple? Had the ex-con lost his temper and beat Dr Walker to death the day after she'd left that urgent message on his voicemail?

"What do you have to say about that?"

"Someone's lying," Rudy muttered. "I was there. My mates will vouch for me."

"Your drinking buddies?" clarified Rob.

Rudy Shaw nodded.

"The men whose names you wrote down were either too drunk to talk to my officers, or couldn't remember what time you got to the pub. I'm afraid they couldn't substantiate your alibi."

Shaw fell silent. He crossed his arms over his chest and rocked back and forth ever so slightly.

His solicitor looked on with sharp eyes. "That doesn't mean he wasn't there when he said he was," he pointed out.

"Please don't interrupt," snapped Rob. He was there for advice, not to offer his opinion.

"I may have got the time wrong," admitted Shaw sullenly.

"Right, so would you like to amend your previous statement?"

"I don't know what time I got there. It was in the afternoon, that's all I know."

"Do you drive a metallic blue Ford Focus with the registration number LR55 XJH?" Rob asked.

"Yes, but—"

"Your vehicle was picked up on the ANPR database on the A3 towards Raynes Park on Wednesday afternoon, around the time you said you were at the pub." He opened the folder Will had brought down and pushed a photograph across the table. "Is that you? It certainly looks like you behind the wheel."

Shaw shuffled in his seat and avoided Rob's gaze. His solicitor looked concerned.

"Where were you going, Mr Shaw?"

The ex-con glanced at his solicitor.

"You don't have to answer," he advised.

Shaw jammed his mouth shut.

*Fuck.* "Do you know where I think you were going?" said Rob.

Rudy glanced up. There was real fear in his gaze. Rob's pulse skipped a beat. Surely not?

He pushed on. It was time to find out. "I think you were going to Judith Walker's house. You were going to threaten her into letting you see your son, weren't you? You felt like you'd been treated unfairly, and you were going to pressurise her into changing the custody order."

"I wasn't," he yelped.

His solicitor put a warning hand on his sleeve and gave a little shake of his head.

"But when you got there, she wouldn't answer the door. So, you jimmied the lock, and went inside and confronted her. There was a fight, and you lost your temper. You hit her repeatedly on the head with a hammer or something similar, killing her instantly."

Shaw's lips were moving but no words came out.

"Am I right?" demanded Rob.

Shaw shook his head. He'd gone very pale and seemed to have lost the ability to speak.

Rob waited a moment. "Rudy, can you explain why your fingerprints were found on the broken lock on Judith Walker's front door?"

Shaw's gaze flickered to his solicitor. "No comment," he croaked.

Rob was losing his patience. He needed to know. Needed to know whether he was wasting his time with Shaw or if the ex-con had indeed bludgeoned Dr Walker to death.

"Let me explain something to you." Rob leaned forward. "Murder carries a heavy sentence, as I'm sure you know. So if you are innocent, and you were there for some other reason, say to talk to her about your son, then you should come clean. Keeping quiet is not going to help you, and your solicitor knows that. At the moment, it's not looking good. There is a lot of evidence against you. I could charge you right now with Judith Walker's murder."

The bloodshot eyes widened. They reminded Rob of a deer in headlights. He continued, "Keeping quiet could see you charged with burglary and murder. You're looking at twenty years, minimum."

"I didn't kill her," he burst out.

His solicitor pressed his lips together.

Rob breathed a sigh of relief. Shaw was about to shit himself, he was that scared of going back inside.

"Why don't you tell us what happened? Why were you at Judith Walker's house the afternoon she was killed?"

Shaw stared at his hands. "It wasn't like that." He gulped and looked up. "I went to see her to talk about Mikey. I wanted to explain how much he means to me, and that I can't cope with supervised visits. I was going to beg her to let me see him."

Rob nodded. Finally, they were getting somewhere. "Go on."

"I knocked on the door, but she didn't answer. I thought she was ignoring me, so I got mad and forced the lock."

"You mean you broke in," clarified Rob.

Shaw glanced down again and nodded. "That's when I saw the mess."

Rob frowned. "What exactly did you see?"

"It was like the place had been burgled — stuff everywhere. I know you don't believe me, but it's true. Someone had done a number on the place. I got scared and bolted. I didn't want anyone to think it was me."

"Except you forgot to wipe your fingerprints off the front door," said Rob.

"I panicked," he grumbled. "I'm not a thief. I don't rob people for a living."

"You were convicted of armed robbery and aggravated assault," pointed out Rob. "Or have you forgotten already?"

"That was an off-licence," Shaw said. "And I was desperate. I couldn't make my rent. I don't rob people's houses."

"Well, that's good to know," said Rob. He'd read Shaw's file. There was only the one charge for armed robbery. Other than that, he'd received an order for antisocial behaviour and there'd been a call-out for a domestic dispute, but no charges had been brought. "What happened next?"

"Nothing. I fuckin' legged it, didn't I? Drove straight back to Wandsworth and parked at my flat, then walked to the pub."

They'd checked the CCTV near the pub and knew exactly what time he'd got there. It tallied with what the barman had said.

"Did you see Judith Walker's body in the living room?" asked Rob.

"No, I didn't even go into the living room. I could see the place had been turned upside down from the entrance hall. That was enough for me."

"You do realise we've only got your word that you didn't kill her?"

"I swear." He was panicking now. "Check my car, check my house, I didn't take anything."

"We are," said Rob. "There's a search team at your house right now, and your car has been taken in for analysis. We're going to hold you until we get the results. We're also comparing your fingerprints to those found inside the house. You'd better hope they aren't a match."

Shaw turned his panicked eyes to his solicitor. "Can't you do something? I didn't kill her."

"Detective, I must advise my client not to say anything further."

"That's okay," said Rob. "We already have him for breaking and entering. He admitted as much."

"No . . . no . . ." Shaw muttered. "I can't go back. I can't."

"You should have thought of that before you forced your way into Dr Walker's house," said Rob.

But he wasn't a complete bastard. He studied Shaw, who was now quite agitated. He was biting his nails and Rob noticed how inflamed his fingertips were. He doubted they'd find any items from Judith Walker's study in the suspect's car or house, but they had to check. He also doubted they'd find Shaw's fingerprints anywhere else but on the door.

"Rudy, there's something you can do to help us. Something the magistrate will look favourably on."

"Yeah?" His eyes were desperate.

"I want you to think very carefully. While you were outside Dr Walker's house, did you notice anything unusual?"

Hope flashed across Shaw's face. He was being offered a lifeline, and he knew it. His brow furrowed. "I didn't see anyone else if that's what you mean."

"You didn't hear anything inside the house?"

"No, nothing."

"What about when you were leaving? Any cars in the street, anyone hurrying away from the house?"

"No, nothing like that." He looked disappointed. Then his face lit up. "Hang on."

Rob raised his eyebrows. Will leaned forward.

"There was that car that nearly drove into me at the end of her street."

Rob's pulse quickened. "What car?"

"A big four-wheel drive. BMW X5, I think. It shot past the stop sign. I only just braked in time."

"BMW? Are you sure?"

"Yeah, I'm sure. It wasn't coming out of the shrink's street, though. It was coming from the street behind, like."

"Could be nothing," murmured Will, but he made a note anyway.

Rob wasn't so sure. It wouldn't stand up in court, that was for sure, but it might not be nothing. Also, he knew someone who had a car like that.

Raza Ashraf.

## CHAPTER 34

"It's his wife's BMW." Jenny looked up from her computer. "She drives an X5, just like the one Shaw saw."

"There are bound to be loads of X5s around that neighbourhood." Will was always the voice of reason.

He had a point. Raynes Park was an upmarket neighbourhood thanks to its proximity to Wimbledon, abundant green spaces and the recent developments there.

"Still, we can't rule it out. Ashraf could have taken his wife's car, driven to Raynes Park, silenced Judith Walker and then escaped via the back garden," Rob said. "There's a recreation ground behind the property. Remember, we got lost the first time we tried to find it. He could have left the car next to that. It would have made sense not to park in front of the house anyway. Too obvious."

Jenny was nodding, but Will still looked doubtful.

Rob paced up and down the incident room. "Now we know Shaw didn't kill her, Ashraf is our main suspect. If only we could get a search warrant for the BMW," he fumed. "We might find some fibre or DNA from Dr Walker's house."

"You know the Super will never allow it," Will cautioned. "There's still no hard evidence. The word of a crook isn't going to stand up in court."

"This is ridiculous." Rob stretched his arms back, suddenly claustrophobic. He'd never felt so frustrated during an investigation in his life.

"It's nearly two o'clock." Jenny glanced at the oversized digital clock on the wall.

All thoughts turned to Jo's contact, and what they were about to do.

\* \* \*

Jo took a steadying breath and entered the restaurant in Covent Garden. It was a ten-minute walk from the *Argus*'s office, and she'd chosen it so her contact, Paul, could dash out and meet her.

He was a wily creature, as most investigative journalists were, with an eye for detail and nerves of steel. They'd met a few years earlier when he'd tried to lowball her into giving away details about the county lines drug investigation the National Crime Agency had been working on in conjunction with the police.

He'd had sources she'd wanted to tap, and so they'd struck a deal. He'd passed on information to her, and she'd let him tag along on the notorious dawn raids that had resulted in the police bringing down an entire network.

Considering the accolades he'd won for that feature, he owed her big time.

Paul glanced up and lifted a hand in a wave. She made her way to his table. It was in a dark corner at the back, out of sight of the windows.

"Still lurking in the dark, I see." She took off her coat and sat down.

"Still investigating when off duty," he retorted.

She grinned. "Guilty as charged. So, how'd it go?"

The waiter approached. "Can I get you anything, madam?"

"Mineral water, please."

"Nothing for me," said Paul, who was nursing a beer.

When he'd disappeared back to the till to enter the order, Paul leaned over and placed a brown paper packet on the table.

"I believe this is what you wanted."

Jo smiled, immediately sliding the package off the table and into her bag. She didn't need to ask what was in it. "Thanks, Paul. You're a star. Was it difficult?"

"No, although I had to endure forty minutes of Ashraf rattling on about himself and his position on everything from knife crime to racial inequality."

"Anything you can use?"

"I'll pass it on to the political correspondent. Why don't you tell me what this is all about?"

"I can't." Jo gave a helpless shrug. "It's not my case. I'm helping out a friend."

"That friend wouldn't happen to be your partner, the intrepid DCI Rob Miller, would it?"

"Can't say."

The waiter placed the bottle of Evian on the table. Jo reached for it and poured herself a glass.

"I'll take that as a yes."

Paul was too damn intuitive for words.

"I smell a story, Jo." He watched her take a sip. "What is Ashraf up to? What's he done? Why does Miller need his fingerprints?"

She ought to have known he wouldn't give over the goods that easily.

"It's an elimination thing," she said, not meeting his gaze. "I don't know more than that. Because of who he is, my friend couldn't use the usual channels, so this was the next best thing."

"Jo, what aren't you telling me?" the journalist persisted.

She sighed. "Shut up, Paul. I can't tell you anything else now, but since you've been so helpful, I'll ask my friend if you can have an exclusive if and when an arrest is made."

Paul's eyes lit up. "If Ashraf's in the firing line, I'm in! Thanks, Jo. I knew you'd come through for me."

Jo huffed. "Don't thank me yet. Ashraf may have nothing to do with this."

* * *

Rob blatantly lied on the evidence sheet used to send the glass in for fingerprint analysis. He put it through as a rush job, stating it was a piece of evidence found at Dr Walker's house.

As he sealed the evidence bag, he felt a tinge of guilt, then shoved it aside. Needs must. It wasn't his fault they'd been taken off the Palmer case. If he'd had his way, Ashraf would have been brought in for questioning according to proper police procedure. If anyone had acted out of turn, it was Hodge and the Deputy Commissioner, not him.

He got Jeff to drop the new evidence off at the lab, then went back to his desk. The phone rang and he picked it up. "DCI Miller."

"Detective Chief Inspector Miller, this is Commander Peterson from Scotland Yard. I need the budget forms for the last quarter, and I can't get hold of Superintendent Hodge. Any idea where I might find her?"

"I think she had an urgent appointment, sir," Rob said. It was the same thing he'd said to the Deputy Assistant Commissioner when he'd rung earlier. It seemed everyone was looking for Hodge. "I'll tell her you called."

She'd left earlier that morning without a word and hadn't come back. It had been much the same last week. He'd been fielding her calls, but he couldn't cover for her much longer.

"I need those forms," the Commander said. "Otherwise, her department won't have any funds allocated."

"I'll check her office, sir," he said. "She might have left them on her desk."

"Okay, go ahead. Call me back ASAP."

Rob walked over to the igloo and knocked, even though he knew there'd be no answer. He opened the door and switched on the light.

The mound of documents on her desk was getting higher. Rob took a closer look. Scattered to the side were itemised phone bills. The name on the top left was Marcus Hodge.

Shit, she was still keeping tabs on her husband.

He picked them up and saw she'd circled several instances of the same number in biro. There were loads of circles, all down the page. Marcus had been a very naughty boy. Still, it was none of his business.

Rob put the call logs aside and looked around for the budget folder. It was bright red and hard to miss. He used to go through the reports and allocations with Lawrence.

It wasn't there.

What he did find, however, was another stack of telephone records. This time, they were text messages. He scanned the first page. Saucy didn't even begin to describe it.

*Phew.* He pursed his lips. Whoever the sender was, she was into some kinky shit. No wonder Hodge was distracted. There was no name. Marcus always referred to her as 'Babe', 'Gorgeous' or 'Sexy'.

His phone buzzed, but before he had time to look at it, the door swung open behind him.

"What do you think you're doing?"

*Fuck.* Rob turned around. "Commander Peterson from Scotland Yard asked me to look for the budget forms. He said it was urgent. I thought they might be on your desk."

She came over. Her eyes were worse than Rudy Shaw's and she smelled of alcohol. He thought she was stumbling a bit.

"It's not. I haven't done it yet."

He put the phone records down. "If you like, I could—"

"This office is off limits." Her words were more clipped than usual, as if she was trying not to slur.

"I know, I'm sorry, ma'am. It's just Peterson needs that report ASAP. He's waiting for me to call him back."

"For fuck's sake."

Rob stifled a snort. He'd never heard her swear before. She was usually so composed.

"I've done them before, ma'am," he said. "If you want to give me the file, I can do it."

She swayed to a filing cabinet behind her desk and opened it. The red folder lay on top of another pile in a plastic tray.

She threw it down on the desk. "Sort it. I couldn't give a shit." Then she collapsed into her chair with a groan.

Will poked his head around the door but Hodge didn't notice. Rob waved him away. Nobody ought to see the Superintendent in this state.

"Ma'am, I don't mean to intrude," he said, "but it's obvious you're having some personal problems. It might be best if you took some time off." Rather than coming into work drunk. That could get her fired.

She glanced up at him, her eyes glassy. "That is none of your business."

"I know, ma'am. It's just—"

"Get out!" she yelled, making him jump. "Mind your own fucking business and don't tell me what to do."

"Yes, ma'am." He backtracked to the door, taking the red folder with him. If he didn't do it, it sure as hell wasn't going to get done today.

"I wouldn't go in there for a while," he muttered to the detectives sitting closest to her office. "She's not in a good mood."

They nodded grimly.

"Tell me you didn't piss her off again." Will was waiting when he got back to his desk.

"She was pissed." Rob met his gaze. "Like, completely out of it."

"Bloody hell," whispered Will.

"I tried to tell her to take some personal time, but she lashed out." He grimaced. "Think I'll mind my own business from now on."

An hour later, Hodge emerged from her office and ricocheted off the desks to the door. The entire department tried not to notice.

* * *

"They're not his." Will rushed up to Rob's desk. Rob, who'd just finished the budget reports, was momentarily confused.

"What's not?"

"None of the prints inside the house are Rudy Shaw's. His were only outside the front door. It looks like he was telling the truth."

Rob exhaled. "I thought as much. What about the search on his house and vehicle?"

"Same. They didn't find anything belonging to Judith Walker. No laptop, no phone, no DNA. His Ford Focus registered on an ANPR camera on the way back to Wandsworth too. Timestamp is twenty minutes after the first one."

"Not a lot of time to commit murder and trash the house," muttered Rob, although strictly speaking, it was possible, if he'd been quick. But then it would have been more of a rush job and the crime scene hadn't looked hurried to him.

"Exactly."

"Okay, let's release him with a warning. He got lucky this time."

Will grinned and marched out to give Shaw and his solicitor the good news.

# CHAPTER 35

"Where's Hodge?" asked Rob when he arrived at work the next morning.

"Not in yet." Will shrugged. "Probably nursing a hangover."

"Is she expecting visitors today, do we know?"

"Eh?"

Rob nodded to the door. "Who's she?"

Everybody looked up as a predatory redhead in four-inch stilettos stalked in, flanked by Sir Charlton, the Deputy Commissioner.

"Can I have your attention, everyone?" Charlton bellowed in a voice used to ushering commands.

The squad room stilled. In the background, a telephone went unanswered.

The Deputy Commissioner waited for it to ring off. "Denise Hodge has been removed from duty pending an official inquiry," he announced. "I'd like to introduce you to Acting Superintendent Felicity Mayhew who will be taking over her role until a new superintendent can be appointed."

The redhead stepped forward. She had pale skin dotted with freckles and piercing blue eyes. Her angular cheekbones and arched eyebrows made her face appear hard and uncompromising, as did the bright red slash of lipstick across her mouth.

Why did he think things were about to go from bad to worse?

"Thank you, Sir Charlton," she said. To his surprise she had a soft Irish accent, although it made sense, given the hair. "Hello, everyone. I'm sorry to be brought in under these circumstances, but I'm sure you'll appreciate the need for strong management with so many important cases on the go."

Her laser eyes roamed over the detectives present and finally settled on Rob. "I've heard great things about this department and it's my wish that we continue to operate at your usual high standard and at full capacity. I'll be meeting with each of you in due course, but right now, I want to get to grips with your most pressing cases. To do that, I'm going to need your help." She smiled. "I believe congratulations are in order. Well done on your successful apprehension of the Pentagram Killer. Yet another serial offender brought down on your watch. Where is DCI Galbraith?"

The burly Scot got to his feet. "Here, ma'am."

"Excellent work. And where is DCI Miller?" Her eyes turned back to him. She knew exactly who he was.

"Here, ma'am." He got to his feet.

She nodded coolly in his direction. "I'd like to see both of you in my office as soon as possible."

"I'm sure you'll give Acting Superintendent Mayhew your full support," cut in Charlton.

"Thank you for the introduction, Deputy Commissioner," she said, offering her hand. "I won't waste any more of your time."

Charlton beamed and shook it. "Good day to you all." He strode out without a backwards glance.

* * *

Felicity Mayhew approached Celeste's desk. She prowled rather than walked. Smelling weakness, she'd homed in on the youngest detective in the room. "Hello, you are?"

"D–DC Parker, ma'am," stuttered Celeste. Usually cool-headed, she was clearly thrown by the sudden changing of the guard, as they all were.

"DC Parker, could you show me to your ex-boss's office and then get me a cup of coffee? Black, one sugar. I want to get straight to work."

"Yes, ma'am." Celeste leaped up and led her towards the igloo. Moments later, she was back, scurrying around to find a clean mug.

"Here, use this one." Jenny handed her one from her desk drawer. "It was a present and I've never used it." It had a picture of a ladybird on it and a quote in a swirly font. *Don't bug me. I haven't had my coffee yet.*

"Appropriate," said Rob.

"This should be fun," Will muttered under his breath.

Everybody else looked shell-shocked. Hodge's departure had been rather sudden. News of her erratic behaviour must have made it back to the higher-ups. Rob wondered who it had been. Not him — he'd tried to cover for her until she'd got her shit together.

But someone had.

He cast his eye around the room. Most people were whispering quietly to one another or getting on with their work. Nobody looked particularly smug.

"Guv, more bad news, I'm afraid."

Rob looked up. Jenny stood in front of his desk, a piece of paper in her hand.

"Let me guess, Ashraf's prints weren't a match either?"

She grimaced. "Sorry. I really thought they would be. We all did."

"Perhaps it wasn't his car speeding away from the vicinity?" said Will. "I checked all the cameras in the area and couldn't find it anywhere. It's like it disappeared."

"Or he knew which roads to avoid," muttered Rob.

Damn it. Another dead end. They were back to square one.

Mike slid his chair over. "I've just spoken to a Tanya Barkova. She's Judith Walker's cleaner. Her prints are a match to those found in the house."

"How did you trace her?" Rob asked, perking up. Perhaps all was not lost.

"Through the victim's bank account," said Mike. "She had a monthly standing order made out to Miss Barkova for three hundred pounds."

"Very good." Rob gave him an approving nod. "Can we bring her in for questioning? She might know something."

"Yep, will do." Mike slid back to his desk and picked up the phone.

Rob had just turned back to his paperwork when Acting Superintendent Mayhew's Irish lilt floated across the room. "DCI Miller, if you have a moment?"

He walked towards the igloo feeling like he had been summoned to the gallows. Why did she give him such a bad vibe? She wasn't unattractive or unpleasant. In fact, she was smiling at him, showing off a set of very white teeth.

"Ma'am."

He walked past her into the office, and she closed the door behind them. Already, she'd stamped her mark. The blinds were up, displaying a clear view of the squad room. No one was invisible. The air conditioning unit had been turned off and the window was open. There was an exotic scent in the air that he hadn't smelled before. Woody with a hint of citrus. Her perfume, no doubt.

"I prefer fresh air," she said, following his gaze.

He nodded.

"Please, sit down, DCI Miller."

He did so. She probably wanted an update on the Judith Walker case and he had nothing definitive to give her.

"Your reputation precedes you." She gave a calculated smile. Genuine, but not entirely free.

"Thank you, ma'am."

"Although, I have heard reports that you're a law unto yourself. I hope that's not true?"

"I think my team can vouch for my effectiveness as an SIO, ma'am." He kept his gaze steady, not surprised when she did the same.

"That's not in dispute." She broke eye contact with a casual flick of her fiery hair. "It's procedure I'm worried about. As a department, we have to be above board and the way we do that is to make sure there is complete transparency. That means thorough police work, unbreakable chains of evidence, up-to-date reporting. Are we clear?"

"Yes, ma'am."

"Good." Another metered smile. She looked friendly but she could bite. "Now, talk me through the Judith Walker investigation. I believe this one is hot off the press?"

"Yes, we got the call-out last Wednesday and since then, we've been working around the clock to find a suspect."

"I thought you already had one," she said.

Rob blinked. "Er, no. We're going through her client list but—"

"What about the ex-convict, Rudy Shaw?"

She'd already read the file. "He's a person of interest, not a suspect. We interviewed him and—"

"You arrested him," she corrected.

"Yes, we arrested him so we could question him, but we are satisfied he had nothing to do with Judith Walker's death."

"Now that is fascinating," Mayhew said, her voice a deep purr. "Because on paper, I'd say it was a slam dunk."

Rob frowned. "Far from it, ma'am. Rudy Shaw was a parolee who'd been assessed by Dr Walker upon his release. She'd determined he was unfit to have custody of his son and proposed supervised visits every other weekend. Shaw was unhappy with the arrangement and went to speak to her to see if he could persuade her otherwise."

"I believe he yelled obscenities outside her house less than forty-eight hours before she was murdered," Mayhew said without looking at the folder on her desk.

She'd more than read up on the case. She knew it backwards. "He did, yes. He was drunk and lost his temper."

"Is that what happened when he broke into her house and bludgeoned her to death?"

There was a pause.

"We don't know that, ma'am. In fact, it's our belief that Shaw didn't have anything to do with her death." Rob found he was clenching his fists.

"His fingerprints were on the door. He admitted to breaking in. What more do you want, Detective? A signed confession?"

"It's not as simple as that." Rob felt his blood pressure rise. He could see the way this was going. Mayhew wanted to close the case, tick another one off the list. That way, she'd meet her targets and get promoted. It was clear she already had the ear of the Deputy Commissioner. Now she wanted to make an impression.

"Neither Shaw's fingerprints nor his DNA were found inside the house. His vehicle was caught on camera leaving the area precisely twenty minutes after he got there, which is hardly enough time to have killed Dr Walker and ransacked the place. Plus, none of her belongings were found in his house or vehicle. There was no blood-spattered clothing — multiple hammer blows would have left quite a mess — no blood on his shoes or any other items. No transference. His statement makes sense. He broke in to confront her, saw the state of the place and legged it." Rob sat back, breathing hard.

Mayhew studied him for a long moment. "I can see you're very thorough. But in my mind, the fact that Mr Shaw was there at the time of the murder and that he admitted to breaking into the house is enough for a conviction. We should let the defence prove that he's innocent. We have enough to charge him with murder."

"I'm sorry, ma'am. I disagree."

A slight flush appeared in her cheeks. "Do you have any other suspects?"

He hesitated.

Yes. Raza Ashraf. Would she take the same stance as Hodge, along with the Deputy Commissioner? He didn't know her well enough to judge, but from what he'd seen so far, he wasn't going to take the chance.

"Not exactly, ma'am. We've got a sighting of a black SUV speeding out of the area, but we're still trying to locate the driver. We've also identified Dr Walker's cleaner, who's coming in for questioning. She might know something."

Mayhew closed the folder. "Right, before you leave tonight, I want you to run this past the Crown Prosecutor. If he gives you the go-ahead, you arrest Rudy Shaw and charge him. Is that clear?"

Rob got to his feet. "Perfectly, ma'am."

CHAPTER 36

The Crown Prosecutor agreed and so exactly one week after the murder, Rudy Shaw was arrested and charged.

Rob filled in the charge form with a heavy heart. He was arresting an innocent man. He only hoped Shaw's solicitor was good enough to get him off. Rob would make sure his team drafted fully documented notes and reports and that they were made available to the defence. It was the least he could do.

Mayhew was happy, though. She stopped by his desk to congratulate him. He didn't respond.

Tanya Barkova came in that afternoon for her interview. Rob met her in the downstairs lobby. She was a willowy young woman of Eastern European origin with high cheekbones and wide, expressive eyes.

"Thank you for coming in," Rob said as he met her. Will was busy preparing Rudy Shaw's trial documents, so Rob was interviewing her alone. It was an informal chat. Barkova was only a person of interest at this stage.

"I can't believe that Judith is dead," she said in heavily accented English.

"Would you like something to drink?" Rob asked. He preferred to stick to neutral topics until they got to the interview suite.

"No, I'm okay."

He opened the door, and they entered the coldly formal room. She glanced around, taking in the sparse furniture, the mounted cameras, the one-way mirror. She pulled her jacket more tightly around her slender frame and sat down.

"Right, well, like I said, thanks for coming in. I'm Detective Chief Inspector Miller and I'm the lead investigator on Judith's case."

She nodded, hanging on to his every word. Perhaps it was because English was her second language or maybe she was just an avid listener, but her attentiveness was refreshing. Usually witnesses slouched in the chair with a total disregard for their interviewer. She was young, probably just into her twenties, fresh-faced and eager to please. He liked her.

"How long have you worked for Dr Walker?"

"Three years," she said without any hesitation.

"That's quite a while," remarked Rob. "Did you get on with her?"

"Yes, she was a lovely person. She helped me improve my English." Tanya smiled sadly. "She was nice to me."

"How often did you clean for her?"

"Two mornings a week. On Monday and Thursday." She stifled a sob. "I don't know what I'm going to do now. I have to find a new job."

That wasn't his problem, but he felt sorry for her. "Where do you live?" he asked.

"Hammersmith," she replied. "But I can travel anywhere. I have a train pass. Do you have a cleaner?"

She thought he was enquiring for himself. "No, I don't. I'm just asking for the record, Miss Barkova."

"Ah, okay." She dropped her shoulders.

To be fair, he could use a cleaner. The entire three-bedroom house was a lot to keep tidy and he fell short in so many areas. He tried to give it a quick once-over on a Friday or Saturday morning before Jo arrived, so that she wouldn't be too disgusted with him, but with his work hours, it left a lot to be desired. He gazed thoughtfully at Tanya. "How old are you?" he asked, aware he'd veered off-topic.

"Twenty-three," she replied.

"And how long have you been in the UK?"

"Three years. I came when I was twenty."

"Did Judith Walker employ you as soon as you arrived?"

"Yes, we met outside the police station in Hammersmith. My bag was stolen, and I reported it. She helped me explain what happened. Then she offered me a job." Tanya broke into a wide grin. "She was a very kind person."

It seemed like it, thought Rob, although Rudy Shaw would disagree.

"Did you ever see anyone arguing or fighting with Judith?"

She looked startled. "No, she was nice to everyone."

"Did you meet any of her clients?"

Tanya shook her head. "No, she didn't see clients at her house. She told me it was because some of them were dangerous. She only saw them at the police station or the prison. Never at home."

"She told you this?"

"Yes, we spoke a lot. She asked me about my town in Poland and about my family." Her eyes filled with tears. "I can't understand why anyone would want to kill her."

Sometimes there was no understanding. Bad things happened. End of story. It was up to him to find out the details.

"When last did you see Judith?" he asked.

"On Monday."

"And how did she seem to you? Was she normal?"

"Yes, she was the same as always. Happy, I think because she had a new boyfriend, an architect. Is that the word? He designs houses."

"Yes, architect is right."

Now they were getting somewhere. Richard the architect.

"Did you meet him?" Rob asked.

She nodded shyly. "He was still there on Monday morning when I arrived. I get there at eight to miss the traffic and he was leaving."

So, he stayed over on Sunday night. Things must have been hotting up between them.

"Can you describe him?"

"Average height. Grey hair. A nice face. Friendly, you know?" She shrugged.

"How old was he?"

"About fifty." She smiled. "Much older than you."

He snorted.

"Did you see what kind of car he was driving?"

"Mercedes. Silver. I don't know what model or anything."

"That's okay. You're doing great." She'd given them a lot more than they'd had before. "Is there anything else you can tell me about him? Where he works, what his surname is? Anything?"

She thought for a moment. "When he left, he said, 'See you when I get back.'" She gasped. "What if he doesn't know Judith is dead?"

"We are trying to trace him," said Rob. "But it's proving challenging. We don't know much about him. Do you know where he was going?"

"No, but his number will be on her phone," she said earnestly.

"Her phone is missing."

Tanya gulped. "Oh."

"Tanya, did Judith mention a client or an acquaintance that she'd had an argument with? Someone who'd made her angry?"

The girl shut her eyes, then shook her head. "I don't remember. I'm really sorry. I want to help, but I don't know."

"You've already been extremely helpful," said Rob, and he meant it. He asked a few more questions but it was clear the girl didn't know anything else. Still, her information about Richard's vocation would help them narrow down their search.

"If you need cleaner, you can call me." She fished inside her back pocket and pulled out a business card. It was very simple, just her name, occupation, email and telephone number.

"Thanks." He took it and put it in his pocket.

\* \* \*

"Richard, the missing boyfriend, is an architect," Rob told Will when he got back upstairs, but Will was gazing worriedly at Mayhew's office from which loud voices were emanating. "What's going on?"

Jenny rushed over, thrusting a newspaper at him. "It's bad, Rob." Her face was ashen.

He glanced down.

*ASHRAF QUESTIONED IN POLICE PROBE*

*Hell no.* He read on.

*Mayoral candidate Raza Ashraf was secretly investigated for the police by a journalist in connection with the death of criminal psychologist Judith Walker. It's unclear at this point what Mr Ashraf's connection to the dead woman was. We do know that the journalist sought Mr Ashraf for an interview on behalf of the police in order to obtain his fingerprints. Mr Ashraf has refused to comment.*

Rob threw the newspaper onto his desk. "This is fucking marvellous."

Jenny grimaced. "The Superintendent's mad as hell. Ashraf phoned the Deputy Commissioner, who's been calling around trying to find out which department is responsible. Nobody admitted to knowing anything about it, although I think Will was about to come clean about the reporter."

"Don't," barked Rob.

Will looked like he was about to throw up.

"They can't trace this back to us," Rob hissed. "Jo didn't tell the journalist who we were."

"Here she comes," warned Jenny as the Superintendent's door swung open.

Mayhew strode directly towards his desk. "Is this your doing?"

He stared at her blankly. "I don't know what you mean."

"Don't play games with me, DCI Miller. This is exactly the sort of thing I meant when I said 'law unto yourself.' Did you ask a journalist to interview Ashraf to get his fingerprints?"

"We're not on that case anymore, ma'am," he said. "Your predecessor took us off it because our main suspect was pally with the Deputy Commissioner." He met her furious gaze with his cool one.

"You didn't answer my question," she hissed. "Was this you?"

"No, ma'am."

She shot him a long, hard look, but there was uncertainty there. "It had better bloody not be. I won't tolerate these types of underhand tactics. I'm going to review the Noah Palmer case and I expect a full briefing in my office at four o'clock. The Deputy Commissioner is convinced it's our department because of your previous investigation."

"Yes, ma'am."

His heart sank. If she was reviewing the case, she'd know how desperately they wanted to question Ashraf. What she wouldn't know, however, was the link to Judith Walker's murder. They needed to keep that under wraps until they found hard evidence that placed Ashraf at the crime scene. They still hadn't got his alibi for the afternoon in question, but there was no way of doing that now.

Rob remembered Jo's offer to talk to the wife. It could be that was their only option. Any attempt to contact Ashraf himself would lead to heads rolling. Rob's in particular.

Needing some space to think, Rob went for a walk to Putney Bridge. He stood on the stone arch and looked down. The river was flowing fast, pushing great volumes of water upriver, threatening to burst its banks. High tide often saw the Thames lap the edges of the towpath.

He called Jo. "Have you seen the article in the paper?"

"No, what's happened?" Her voice was wary.

"Our plan to get Ashraf's fingerprints is all over page three."

She gasped. "No way. They can't be. Paul would never—"

"He must have done," replied Rob. "He was the only one who knew about it other than you and my team."

"Was it in the *Argus*?" she enquired.

"No, the *Mail*."

"Paul writes exclusively for the *Argus*. He wouldn't publish in the *Mail*."

"Perhaps he submitted it as a freelancer," said Rob, rubbing his head. "It can't be anyone else. It has to be him."

"Hang on, I'm looking online now." There was the sound of fingers on the keyboard. "Got it. The byline is 'Staff Investigative Reporter.' No name."

There was silence as she read. It didn't take long for her to scan the article. "It's definitely not Paul," she said firmly. "It's not his style, and he'd never drop me in it like this."

"Then who?"

"You said your team knew."

"Yes, but they wouldn't leak it to the press."

"Someone did," she said.

*Bugger*. He took a steadying breath. He didn't want to think anyone in his squad could have done something like that.

"They know how sensitive this issue is," he said. "I can't see any of them leaking it."

"I'll give Paul a ring. He's probably already seen it. I'll see what he thinks, then call you back."

"Okay, appreciate it. Thanks, Jo."

He hung up.

While he'd been talking, he'd wandered down to the water's edge and now it was licking at his boots, getting higher and higher with each ripple.

*Damn it*. This was bad.

He walked a short way along the towpath, watching branches and other debris bob along, swept up by the current. That was how he felt — out of control.

No way anyone in his team would have leaked it. Not willingly.

His phone buzzed. It was Jo, calling back.

"Rob, I've just spoken to Paul. He's as livid as you are. I promised you'd give him an exclusive when the story broke, now he's playing second fiddle to this Natasha Carson woman."

"Who?"

"The staff reporter for the *Mail* who wrote the article. Paul called them this morning and a contact on the travel desk gave him the information."

Rob frowned. Why did that name sound familiar?

"Jo, I've figured it out. I've got to go. I'll call you later."

He turned around to find Will standing on the grassy verge behind him.

"I'm sorry, guv," He was crestfallen. "I didn't know she was a reporter."

Rob put a hand on his shoulder. "I just clocked it. Tasha, that was her name, wasn't it?"

Will nodded. He looked like he was about to cry. "I thought she was into me," he said. "I was completely taken in. She fooled me."

"Did you tell her about the fingerprints?"

He nodded miserably. "Yeah, sort of. We were talking and she asked what I was working on, so I told her bits and pieces, you know. Nothing serious. Then, later that night, she asked if I'd ever done anything sneaky. I told her how we'd sent a journalist in to get a suspect's fingerprints." He hung his head. "It was stupid, I know. I didn't for a minute think she'd write about it. I didn't know she was a journalist, I thought she worked at H&M in the high street."

Rob shook his head. "Rule number one. *Never* talk about a case to a civilian, not even your wife or girlfriend. Ever."

"I guess I've learned that the hard way," he said.

Rob sighed. "You weren't to know. Besides, it was my idea to do it in the first place. If I hadn't gone off-book, this wouldn't have happened." Frustration at Hodge and the Deputy Commissioner resurfaced. If they'd just been allowed to do their jobs in the first place . . .

"I'll come clean," said Will.

"You'll do nothing of the kind."

Will stared at him. "But—"

Rob held up his hand. "No, don't say a word. At the moment, they don't know which department was responsible. Mayhew is reviewing the Noah Palmer case files. Once she's done, she'll probably guess it was us, but unless we say anything, she won't be able to prove it. Keep your trap shut, okay? This isn't the time to take one for the team."

He nodded uncertainly. "If you're sure, guv?"

"I'm sure."

CHAPTER 37

Rob watched as Mrs Ashraf went into the pharmacy. She was alone.

"Let's confront her when she comes out." Jo was standing beside him at the bus stop across the road.

The BMW X5 was registered to Mrs Ashraf, not her husband. That was a stroke of luck. If they questioned her about the car itself, it would disguise the fact it was Ashraf's location they were after.

After a few moments, the woman reappeared carrying a brown paper packet in her hand.

"Mrs Ashraf?" Rob showed her his warrant card. "I'm DCI Miller and this is DCI Maguire. Can we ask you some questions?" He didn't say which department they were from.

She hesitated. "What's this about?"

"Are you the registered owner of a BMW 5 Series, licence plate LR67 YTZ?"

"Yes." She frowned. "What's happened? Has it been stolen?"

"No, nothing like that. Your car was picked up on a camera last Wednesday afternoon in the vicinity of Raynes Park. We think it might have been involved in a burglary in the area. Could you tell us if you were anywhere near there on the day in question?"

She seemed stunned. "A burglary? No, there must be some mistake."

"There's no mistake, ma'am. This is your car, isn't it?"

He showed her a picture of her BMW that he'd taken from a different ANPR camera. There was no timestamp on it, so she wouldn't know it wasn't the one he was referring to.

She squinted, trying to make out the number plate. "Oh, yes, that is my car, but I was nowhere near Raynes Park last Wednesday."

"Would anyone else have taken your car?" Jo asked. "Another family member perhaps? Your husband?"

"I don't think so."

"Please think. This is important. If we know why your car was in the area, we can rule you out of our investigation," Rob explained.

She wrinkled her forehead. "Last Wednesday, you say? Well, it definitely wasn't me. I haven't been out that way in years. It can't have been my husband, either. He gets picked up by his driver and taken to work. He rarely uses my car and never during the week."

"Are you sure he didn't use it last Wednesday?" pressed Rob. "Perhaps he came home from work and took it to run an errand or something?"

"Impossible." She shook her head. "I have a book club on a Wednesday and I used the car to go to my friend's house in Wembley. I don't know where you got that photograph, but it couldn't have been my car in that robbery."

Rob sighed and put away the photo.

"Okay, thanks for clarifying, Mrs Ashraf," said Jo. "We're sorry to have ambushed you like this. Rest assured, we can now eradicate your vehicle from our inquiries."

"Is that it?" She seemed surprised. "But the photograph?"

"It must be another BMW," Rob said with a tight smile. "Sorry for wasting your time. And thanks again for being so accommodating."

"Oh, okay." She frowned, confused.

They left as quickly as they could.

"Not him," gritted Rob, once they were back in his car. "Damn! Without the car, we can't connect him to Judith Walker's murder."

Jo touched his leg. "Sorry it didn't pan out. I know he was your prime suspect."

"I was so sure it was him. He had reason enough to want Noah dead, and if Suzie Palmer had told her family liaison officer about their affair, he had a motive to kill Judith too." He shook his head. "Except, it can't be him."

"You don't know that for sure," said Jo. "Just because he didn't take his wife's car, doesn't mean he wasn't there."

"True, but according to his wife, Ashraf was at work last Wednesday. He couldn't have done it." The black SUV was obviously just a red herring. Or perhaps Shaw had made the sighting up to point suspicion away from himself.

Rob gripped the steering wheel. "I know Shaw didn't do it, and now he's sitting in a prison cell awaiting trial just so Acting Superintendent Mayhew can carve another notch in her belt. They're all as bad as one another," he ranted. "Give me Lawrence back any day."

"The Chief was one of a kind," agreed Jo. "We should go out for supper with him and his wife sometime. They've got the time now the kids have all flown the nest."

Sam had been fond of Jo. Rob forced himself to calm down. "Good idea. As soon as this case is over, we'll do that."

She gave his leg a squeeze.

At least he had her. No matter how bad things got, she was always there for him. His partner in crime.

It was late afternoon when Jo dropped him back at the station. The sunset was non-existent, blocked out by an ominous grey cloud. It matched his mood.

"How are things?" he asked Jenny, when he walked in. The light was on in Mayhew's office and he could see her bent over her desk, working. He still hadn't briefed her about the Noah Palmer case.

"All quiet on the western front," she murmured.

Will was also working diligently, keeping his head down. There was a surreal hush in the office as if nobody wanted to make a noise. The printer hummed as it spat out pages and he could hear members of the team talking in low voices on the telephones. There was no camaraderie or boisterousness, like there usually was. Their new boss had succeeded in dampening everybody's spirits.

"I'd best go in." Rob took his coat off. "I'm already late for the Noah Palmer briefing."

"I got a call from Mrs Jenkins's care home this afternoon," said Jenny, before he left. "She's back home after her hip op. I thought I'd drive over this evening and see her."

Rob clicked his fingers. "The neighbour. Yes, good idea. Why don't you knock off early? Go now, before the old girl gets too tired."

"Righty-ho." Jenny nodded towards the office. "You going to be okay?"

"Yeah, should be fine. I'll catch up with you in the morning."

She flashed him a sympathetic smile and went back to her workstation to log off and pack up.

"Ah, DCI Miller. I was worried you'd forgotten about me," Mayhew said as Rob pushed open the door and entered the office. They couldn't call it an igloo anymore. Like Lawrence, she preferred the blinds up and the door open. The retired Chief Super had liked to feel like he was in the thick of things, while Mayhew wanted to hear what was going on. Same result, different agendas.

"If you've read the case file, I'm not sure what else I can add."

He sat down opposite her. He noticed she'd cleared Hodge's things into a cardboard box, which sat at the side of the room. The photograph of her son lay on the top, frame facing upwards.

Mayhew didn't have any personal effects. No family snaps, no pot plants, the only mug was the one Celeste had brought her coffee in earlier this morning, and that wasn't even hers. Christ, had it only been this morning that she'd waltzed in and taken over?

Perhaps she wasn't planning on staying long. For some, being superintendent was just a stepping stone to greater things. Rob got the feeling Mayhew had her sights set somewhat higher than the Putney Major Investigation Team.

"You can start with why you reopened the case."

"New evidence came to light, ma'am," he told her. "It started with a young girl, Rachel Norton, who was thought to have been involved in a moped robbery in the West End. She was cleared, but her DNA flagged up as a familial match to an unknown DNA sample that was found on the body of Noah Palmer."

"Whose mutilated body was found in the woods on Box Hill twelve years ago? Part of the pentagram killings?"

"That's what we thought at the time."

"Except you since discovered that wasn't the case?"

"Noah Palmer was killed by a copycat. There were discrepancies in the way the body was staged, along with some other things that didn't add up. We've since learned that Alfred Whitaker committed the first three murders, which he has confessed to, but not Noah Palmer's. He was in hospital at the time."

Mayhew nodded. "Noah Palmer's case remains unsolved."

"Yes, ma'am. Like I explained before, we were taken off the case due to the primary suspect—"

"Raza Ashraf," she cut in.

"Due to his political connections, ma'am."

She held up a hand. "Take me back to the DNA, DCI Miller. I see you interviewed the girl's mother."

"Isabella Norton, yes. She was Noah Palmer's lover and they share a child."

"The same girl whose DNA was flagged."

"Yes, ma'am."

"Why is Ms Norton not in custody?"

"She had nothing to do with his death. Noah was paying her maintenance. He was worth much more to her alive than dead. She was considerably worse off after he died."

"Hence the lawsuit to claim her daughter's inheritance."

Mayhew didn't miss a trick. "They could do with the financial assistance."

"What made you suspect Raza Ashraf?" she asked.

If she'd read the report, she'd know what. "He used to work with the victim," Rob said. "And we've since discovered that he was also having an affair with the victim's wife."

That wasn't in the file.

Mayhew stared at him. "How do you know that?"

"It was insinuated by several of their colleagues."

"So it's not confirmed?"

He gave her a hard look. "No, we weren't allowed to question Ashraf further and since we're off the case, we couldn't ask Suzie Palmer about it either."

"Hmm . . ." She tapped her lip. "Pity."

Rob thought he'd heard her incorrectly. "Pardon?"

"I agree, Ashraf looks suspicious."

That was a turn-up for the books. "We could ask Suzie Palmer to verify it," he said. "With your permission, of course."

She fixed her arctic eyes on him. "Let's put that on ice for now. I don't want to rock the boat unnecessarily. What I do want to know is why you needed Ashraf's fingerprints."

Rob went very still. "We didn't."

She sighed. "There isn't another department working on a case involving Raza Ashraf. It had to have come from here."

"Neither myself nor my team have any reason to analyse Ashraf's fingerprints. Noah Palmer has been dead for twelve years."

She pursed her lip, unconvinced. "Okay, Rob. May I call you Rob?"

He nodded.

"I'll give you the benefit of the doubt, for now. But if I find out you're lying to me, there will be consequences. Is that clear?"

"Yes, ma'am."

"Right, thank you. That's all. You can leave the door open when you go out."

* * *

Rob's phone buzzed. It was Lawrence.

"Hi, Chief. What can I do for you?" He was inordinately pleased to hear from his previous boss. Dealing with Hodge and now Mayhew had made him long for Lawrence's terse but effective leadership.

"Rob, do you have a minute?"

"Sure, what's up?"

"I couldn't stop thinking about that FLO, Judith Walker. Something was niggling at me, and then I remembered."

"Remembered what?"

"She sent me an email, off the books. I'd completely forgotten about it. She called me after she'd been reassigned and told me she'd sent me something. A few observations about Suzie Palmer. It didn't seem important, and to be honest, I didn't even open it."

"What kind of observations?" Rob's pulse kicked into overdrive.

"I've forwarded it to you," Lawrence said. "I don't know if it's important, but it makes for interesting reading."

Was that regret in Lawrence's voice?

"I don't know what to make of it. Have a read and let me know what you think."

"Sure. I'll call you back."

Rob strode back to his desk, sat down and searched his emails for the one from Lawrence. He opened it and began to read.

"You staying late, guv?" Will's voice interrupted him some time later.

Rob glanced up. The open-plan office had emptied out. Mayhew was still illuminated at her desk, her hair a fiery red under the glow of her desk lamp, but everyone else had gone home for the day.

Rob blinked. He'd read the email three times. "Will, take a look at this."

Will bent over his desk to look at his screen. "What is it?"

"It's an unofficial report on Suzie Palmer, written by Judith Walker back in 2009."

Will gaped. "How did you get that?"

"Lawrence sent it over. He had it in his personal emails. It was an informal report by Judith after she'd been dismissed as the Palmers' FLO. She felt it important enough to put in writing, even though she was no longer assigned to the family."

Will started reading.

"This is where it gets interesting." Rob pointed to a paragraph three-quarters of the way down the page, towards the end.

*Mrs Palmer showed a marked lack of empathy towards her husband's horrific death. At no time did I see her cry or display any emotion. At first, I thought this might be due to the trauma associated with his murder (people process grief in different ways), but as time passed, I suspected she wasn't suppressing the trauma, but that she was devoid of emotion.*

*When I asked her about her feelings, she got angry and told me to leave. Shortly after that, I was reassigned. Having watched Mrs Palmer interact with her family and deal with the situation surrounding her husband's death, I suspect that she is suffering from a form of alexithymia or psychopathy.*

*I am unable to make a definite diagnosis as I am not a clinical psychologist and am no longer seeing Mrs Palmer, but I thought I'd let you know in case it had any bearing on the case. This is not an official report, merely my own opinion.*

Will looked up. "What does that mean for our case?"

Rob exhaled slowly. "It puts Suzie Palmer in the frame as Noah's murderer."

## CHAPTER 38

Rob could tell it was bad by the looks on the faces of his colleagues when he walked in the next morning.

"She knows it was us," whispered a white-faced Jenny.

*Crap.* The shit was about to hit the fan.

Will watched him with wide eyes. Rob shot him what he hoped was a reassuring smile and sat down. This was on him. It had been his idea to use Jo's contact to obtain the finger-prints, no one else's. His team shouldn't suffer because of it.

Jeff came over. "Guv, I know this probably isn't the right time, but I managed to track down Judith's boyfriend, Richard."

Rob looked up. "The architect?"

"Yes. He's been in Berlin for the last week, consulting on a project there. He got back yesterday and was horrified to find out Judith had been killed. He was expecting to see her tonight. They had a date lined up."

"When did he leave?"

"Last Tuesday, the day before she was murdered."

"That rules him out, then."

Rob's desk phone rang. It was like a death knell. He picked it up. "Miller."

"My office. Now."

He pushed himself up and glanced grimly at the others. This was it.

He walked towards Mayhew's office, feeling the heat from their gazes penetrate his back. The door was open. He knocked anyway.

"Come in."

Mayhew's blue eyes lasered into him. "Take a seat, Rob."

He did so, mentally preparing for the onslaught that was about to follow.

She regarded him without saying anything. He could see her trying to formulate the words in her head. She was angry, no doubt about it. Her angular bone structure was even more pronounced, her neck taut, shoulders strained. But she wanted to be diplomatic, to do this in the right way. She wasn't sure how to handle him. He saw it all in her face, clear as day.

"It's the fingerprint analysis, isn't it?" he asked. There was no point in denying it. A typed A4 piece of paper lay on the desk in front of her with a breakdown from the lab. He'd told Forensics it was an item from Dr Walker's house, but it wouldn't take a genius to figure out he'd lied. The glass had been added to the inventory days after the murder. No one had been back to the crime scene. His name was on the form.

She nodded. "Did you really think you could get away with it?"

He shrugged. "I didn't think anyone would care enough to check. If that article hadn't been in the newspaper, no one would have been the wiser. We could have quietly ruled Raza Ashraf out of our inquiries and moved on."

"Instead, I have him bellowing down the line to me as well as the Deputy Commissioner. That article has got people talking. Journalists are sniffing around looking for a story. He's running for mayor, for Christ's sake."

"Perhaps he shouldn't be," muttered Rob.

She narrowed her eyes. "Why'd you say that?"

"He's as crooked as they come. Money laundering, insider trading, you name it. He might not have been

247

complicit in Noah Palmer's or Judith Walker's murders, but he's hardly squeaky clean."

"Nothing was ever proven," she stated.

He gave her a look. "Come on . . ."

She frowned and leaned back in her chair. "Be that as it may, there is no evidence linking him to either crime. Your fingerprint analysis came up empty, I see."

"Yes, ma'am. His prints weren't at the crime scene."

"What on earth made you think they would be? I hope this is more than a gut feeling, Rob."

"It was, ma'am." He took out his phone and pulled up the voice message left by Dr Walker. "Listen to this."

He placed his phone on the desk. Judith Walker's voice resonated from beyond the grave.

He looked at Mayhew. "She left this on my phone the day before she died."

"Christ." Mayhew stared at the phone, then up at him. "Why didn't you say anything? I didn't read about this in any report."

"I knew Superintendent Hodge would take us off the case. She'd made it perfectly clear that we were to stop investigating Noah Palmer's murder, and since this one is connected . . ." He petered off.

"We can't be sure it's connected."

He narrowly avoided rolling his eyes. "What are the chances? She leaves a message saying she's got information on a cold case and the next day she's murdered?"

"It was a burglary gone wrong."

"No, it was made to *look like* a burglary gone wrong," Rob corrected. "Only her laptop and mobile phone were taken, along with a select number of files from her study. The other valuables in her house were untouched. She even had money in her wallet." He shook his head. "The burglar was looking for something in particular, something he or she didn't want found."

"Like what?"

"Like files dating back to Noah Palmer's murder. Judith Walker was a family liaison officer for the London Met back then. She was assigned to the Palmer family after Noah's death."

Mayhew frowned. "How do you know this?"

"We spoke to a friend of the victim. They trained together." He didn't mention the unofficial report that was sent to Sam Lawrence's personal email account.

"Something else you neglected to put in the report?"

He didn't respond.

"What did the files have in them that was so important?" Her shoulders were still tense, and he could see her barely suppressed anger, but also the knowledge that if she came down hard on him, he'd clam up and she'd get nothing out of him. She was right.

"It's purely supposition at this point, but I think they were Judith's notes on her sessions with Suzie Palmer, Noah's wife."

Mayhew's eyes widened. "You suspect his wife had something to do with Dr Walker's death?"

He shrugged. "I don't know. I'd like the chance to find out, but I don't think I'm going to get it."

She shook her head. "I've read the file. The wife had a watertight alibi."

That reminded Rob he hadn't spoken to Jenny about Mrs Jenkins's statement yet. "It would seem so," he replied. "But she was also having an affair with Raza Ashraf, who at the time worked with her husband at Global Standard. In addition, Noah Palmer was paying maintenance to an escort for a secret child. Suzie Palmer had more than enough reasons to want him dead."

Mayhew studied him for a long moment. He could sense her brain ticking over.

"The Deputy Commissioner wants you suspended," she said eventually. "And I can't say I blame him. You've dragged a high-profile member of society through the mud, resorted to subterfuge, withheld information, leaked information, and all without a shred of finite evidence. The whole thing's chaotic."

"He wants me out because if Ashraf becomes mayor, he'll be the one doing the hiring and firing and the Deputy Commissioner is worried about his job," said Rob. "We may as well say it how it is."

Her face reddened. "Watch what you say in this office," she hissed.

He threw his hands in the air. "I don't believe the truth should play second fiddle to politics. It's not right. The victims deserve better than that."

"I agree with you," she said stiffly. "But you've ruffled more than a few feathers in this investigation — and we still don't know if there is a connection. Judith Walker may well have been murdered by Rudy Shaw. All the evidence points to him."

He couldn't dispute that, even though he knew it wasn't true.

She sighed. "I'm bringing in an impartial DCI to do a review of the case. Please make sure your reports are up-to-date, and that includes everything you've just told me. And if I were you, Rob, I'd take whatever leave you have owing and keep your head down until this blows over. If you want to keep your job, that is."

"Just so we're clear, my team had nothing to do with it." Rob leaned forward. "It was *my* decision to get Ashraf's fingerprints, *my* decision to withhold the voice message from the reports. They didn't even know about it."

She hesitated. "What about the leak to the *Mail*? I know that wasn't you."

"No, but that wasn't my team's fault either. One of them was tricked into divulging the information. Again, if I hadn't gone off-book, there wouldn't have been anything to leak."

She tucked an errant strand of hair behind her ear. "Okay, Rob. Have it your way. I should warn you, though, that shouldering the entire blame will make it worse for you. Sir Charlton wants your head."

Rob shrugged. "I'll take leave, get out of the way."

She gave a terse nod. "It's for the best."

He got up. *Fucking marvellous.* Well, he wasn't about to leave without having his say. He got as far as the door, then turned around. "You know, if we hadn't been sidelined because of who Ashraf was, we'd have been able to do our jobs properly and none of this would have happened. All it would have taken was a simple interview and voluntary fingerprint. Nobody would have known. Yes, I went outside the usual protocols, but my hands were tied. This shambles is the Deputy Commissioner's fault, not mine or my team's. You might want to remind him of that."

He stormed out, leaving her staring after him.

# CHAPTER 39

Rob called Jo on the way home and told her what had happened.

"Come round and we'll talk it through," she said, but she sounded worried. He was too. With his career up in the air and her on leave, things were uncertain. One of them, at least, had to have a secure job, and that someone had to be him.

He'd taken copies of the case files home with him. Mayhew would go berserk if she found out, but he'd always preferred working on paper and had most of them printed and ready to go anyway. Jenny had hastily made copies of the reports he was missing and caught him up as he left the building.

"Guv, there's something I have to tell you." She caught her breath as she walked with him to his car. "It's about Mrs Jenkins, the Palmers' neighbour."

He unlocked the car and threw his rucksack on the back-seat. "Did she confirm Suzie Palmer's alibi?"

"Oh, yes." Jenny nodded. "She confirmed that she'd spoken to Suzie Palmer around five o'clock, after her husband left for his cycle. She'd also seen her in her kitchen a short time later when she took the bins out. Suzie was cooking supper for the kids. That was at about six thirty."

Rob's shoulders slumped. He didn't know what he'd expected. Perhaps that the old lady had been confused or got the times wrong, but she'd reiterated exactly what was in the original police report. "That's pretty definite, then."

"Except—" Jenny frowned — "She never actually saw Noah Palmer leave."

Rob tilted his head. "Hang on? You mean she didn't see him ride off?"

"No. I don't know if that's relevant since she confirmed Suzie's alibi, but the only reason she knew he'd gone was because Suzie had said she'd just waved him off."

"Hmm . . ." Was it relevant? He didn't know either. It was interesting, though.

"Okay, thanks, Jenny. I'll dwell on that for a while. Keep in touch."

"I will. Er, guv?"

"Yeah?"

"Are we going to keep going with the investigation?" She glanced over her shoulder as if worried someone had heard her.

He managed a smile. "I can't stop now. I have to talk to Suzie Palmer and find out why she lied about her affair with Ashraf, and also where she was the night of Judith Walker's murder."

Jenny inhaled sharply. "Do you think it was her?"

He shrugged. "I honestly don't know, Jen. Maybe, but even if she did murder Judith, I don't see how she could have killed Noah. Her alibi stands."

"Perhaps her and Ashraf were in it together?" Jenny suggested.

It was a theory he'd been working on too. "It's possible. Unfortunately, we don't have anything substantial to back it up." He opened the driver's door.

"You'll find something, guv," she said. "You always do."

Her faith touched him. Jenny had been with him from the beginning, loyal and supportive. She was an invaluable member of the team.

"Thanks, Jenny. Listen, don't hesitate to put yourself forward as Acting DCI in my absence."

She looked shocked. "Oh, I could never . . ."

"The team needs someone competent in charge. If they don't bring in an independent DCI, it'll be you or Will who'll have to step up. Considering Will's last error in judgement, you should go for it."

She hesitated. "I'm sure they'll bring someone else in."

He nodded. "Probably, but I just wanted you to know how I felt. You can handle it."

"Thank you, sir."

He nodded and got into the car. She was still standing there watching as he accelerated away.

* * *

Rob drove home via Lonsdale Road so he could see the river. Its presence was comforting, like an old friend who was always there. It sliced silver through the landscape, mirroring the steely grey clouds above, flowing thickly like mercury around the bends.

He cruised, taking his time. It felt like the world had slowed down. His sudden enforced leave had put the brakes on the case. He needed time to regroup, to think about what had happened and to formulate a plan.

No way was he giving up, but he had to be careful. He couldn't afford to lose his job over this.

He'd underestimated Acting Superintendent Mayhew. She'd known from the start it was their department who'd conned Ashraf into giving his fingerprints and leaked that article to the press. With that certainty, it had only been a short skip and a jump to tracking down the glass. He should have covered his tracks better, but then subterfuge wasn't really his thing. He was more of a straight-talking, 'let's get this done' kinda guy.

Trigger was ecstatic he was home early. He ran circles around him, wagging his tail and barking a warm welcome.

"This is a special treat," his neighbour, Mrs Winterbottom said. "Why are you home so early?"

"I'm taking some time off," he replied vaguely.

She gave a knowing nod. "I can imagine being a policeman must be very stressful. Trigger will be delighted to have you home for a while." She smiled fondly at the overexcited dog.

Since it wasn't even lunchtime yet, Rob took Trigger for a long walk along the river, through Petersham and into Richmond Park, where he let him run free. They were both muddy and exhausted by the time they got back.

"Let's go see Jo," he said once Trigger had drunk two bowlfuls of water and he'd hosed off his paws. The Lab gave an excited bark in response.

* * *

Jo had a spacious one-bedroom apartment above a leather goods manufacturer in Southwark. It was more of a converted warehouse than a traditional apartment, but she'd done it up so it was modern and comfortable.

Trigger loved it. He even had a paw-patterned bed in the corner along with his own water bowl. Jo was busy in the open-plan kitchen when they arrived.

"I've made some coffee and there's some fresh sourdough bread from the market if you're hungry."

He was ravenous. He sat down at the breakfast bar that separated the kitchen from the rest of the apartment and dug in. The food levelled out his blood sugar and made him feel much better.

"I was thinking," he said, wiping crumbs off the table and onto his plate, "that the only way out of this mess is to solve the bloody case. Both of them. Not only would I get justice for Noah and Judith, but I'd also get my job back."

"Hero of the hour again."

He grinned. "Something like that."

Jo perched on the stool beside him. "Why don't you give Sam a ring? I'm sure he'd help you."

"Even off the book?"

"Yeah, why not. He's a bit of a maverick, in his own way."

She was right. Lawrence may have been Chief Superintendent, but he'd given Rob and his team a lot of leeway. More so than other Supers would have — or did. He wasn't against using unconventional methods to get results, and now that he was retired, he didn't have to conform to so many rules and regulations.

"You never know," said Jo. "He might relish the opportunity to get stuck into one last investigation — especially one he'd started so many years ago."

\* \* \*

Jo was right. Lawrence didn't take much convincing.

"You do realise that none of what we find will be admissible in court?" he told Rob over the phone. "And we have no real jurisdiction. If someone doesn't want to talk to us, they don't have to."

"I know. I'm in regular contact with my team and they'll do all the heavy lifting."

"What about this new DCI?" Lawrence asked. "Won't they put a spanner in the works?"

"Possibly, but it will take them a day or two to get up to speed, and then they'll be looking for a definitive connection between the cases. Without one, poor old Rudy Shaw will take the blame."

"Not if we can help it," murmured Lawrence. "How do you want to play this?"

"I'm staying at Jo's, but I've got the case files with me," said Rob. "If you can't make it here, I'll come to you."

Lawrence lived in a Georgian townhouse on Richmond Hill, but Rob had his car and it was only a half-hour drive, if that.

"No problem," Lawrence replied. "Diana's gone to her sister's for a few days. I can be there in an hour."

"Perfect." Rob gave Jo a thumbs up. "See you then."

# CHAPTER 40

Lawrence entered the converted warehouse apartment. "Nice place you got here, Jo."

"I like it." She gave him a warm hug hello.

Lawrence had known Jo for as long as Rob had, ever since she'd been sent to assist with their first serial killer case, deemed too complex for Putney Major Investigation Team to handle on their own. Three serial killer cases later and Rob's murder squad were getting the calls when any new serial cases cropped up.

Jo brewed them a fresh pot of coffee and they sat at the breakfast bar.

"These are the original pentagram case files." Lawrence dumped a plastic bag full of folders onto the table.

"You kept copies?" Jo raised her eyebrows.

"Couldn't let it go," he admitted. "The bloody case stuck with me for years, even after I had admitted defeat. I always knew there was something we were missing, but I couldn't put my finger on it. Turns out it was the darn postie's connection to the victims. The first three victims. We just didn't see it." He shook his head.

"We got him in the end," said Rob.

Lawrence grinned, his eyes crinkling at the sides. "Yes, indeed. Justice was served, as they say, albeit twelve years later."

"Whitaker will spend the rest of his life in prison," said Rob. "He's going down for four counts of murder."

"Deservedly so," muttered Jo.

Lawrence put his hand on the bag. "I brought them with me because firstly, I don't need them anymore and secondly, there is quite a bit of research into Noah Palmer in here. You probably know it all already, but it won't hurt going over it. Something might pop up."

Rob nodded. "Thanks, I'll do that, although right now I really need to speak to Suzie Palmer and find out her alibi for the afternoon of Judith's murder."

"You can't really suspect her?" said Lawrence.

Rob shrugged. "It's hard to say. That report was pretty damning. Devoid of empathy? Possibly psychopathic? It puts a different spin on things."

"It doesn't mean she killed her husband," said Lawrence. "And I'm not sure how seriously we should take that report. Judith Walker was a junior liaison officer at the time, not a trained psychologist."

"She seemed pretty convinced," remarked Jo, frowning.

Lawrence shook his head. "I spent a lot of time with Suzie in the aftermath and I've never seen someone so upset. She completely withdrew, hardly ate, couldn't stop crying. I find it hard to believe what Judith wrote."

"Two very different accounts," said Jo.

"Well, if it was an act, she sure as hell fooled me," said Lawrence.

"There's only one way to find out," Rob said. "We've got to pay her a visit. She won't object if you're there, Chief."

He nodded. "Right, let's do it. I won't ring her. It'll be better if we arrive unannounced. She won't be expecting that."

Rob grinned. It was good to see Lawrence back in action. The retired Chief Superintendent had a spring in his step as they left the apartment.

"Let's take my car," Lawrence said, once they got outside. "I'll drop you at the station afterwards."

It was mid-afternoon by the time they got to Chiswick.

"She's home," confirmed Rob. Suzie Palmer's white Mercedes was parked in the driveway.

She opened the door in an apron, with flour on her hands.

"Oh, Sam. It's good to see you. Come in." She nodded to Rob, but that was as far as her warmth extended.

"Doing some baking?" Lawrence asked.

"Yes, Becca is having a party tomorrow. We've got a gaggle of teenagers coming round."

Rob was glad to hear that the newspaper article about their father's indiscretions hadn't dampened the teen's spirits.

"Suzie, do you mind if we have a chat? I'm sorry to interrupt, but it's important. It's about Noah."

Her gaze flickered from Lawrence to Rob and back again. She sighed. "Okay, if we must. But you'll have to let me pop this in the oven first. I'm nearly done. Why don't you take a seat in the living room?"

Rebecca sauntered in, phone in hand. She glanced up in surprise as she saw the detectives. "Hello, I didn't know we had company."

"No, because you've always got those things glued to your ears," said Suzie. "Rebecca, show Sam and—" she frowned — "DCI Miller, was it?"

He nodded.

"Show Sam and DCI Miller into the living room and offer them a beverage, there's a good girl. I'll be there in a sec."

Rebecca pulled the earphones out of her ears. They followed her into the lounge.

"Tea or coffee?" she said.

They both declined. It wasn't that kind of visit.

She hovered after they'd sat down. Flushing, she turned to Rob. "Is it true I have a half-sister?"

He nodded. "Yes, her name's Rachel. She's sixteen, like you."

Rebecca smiled. "What's she like?"

"She's very nice," he said, glossing over the brick-throwing episode. "She's bright and ambitious. I believe she's studying for her GCSEs like you."

"Yes." Rebecca shuffled her feet. "We've just had our mock exams. Our GCSEs are this summer."

"Good luck," said Lawrence.

"Thanks." She hesitated, then glanced around to make sure her mother wasn't about to come into the room. "Do you think I could meet her?"

Rob's eyebrows shot up. What would Suzie say to that? "I'm sure you can," he said. "But it's not up to me."

"Mother will never allow it." Her mouth turned down in a sulk. "She doesn't even like me mentioning her name. I know she was here, I saw her. And I was here when the bricks came through the windows." She flashed them a cheeky grin. "I think she's very brave."

"Perhaps one day I'll introduce you," Rob said, smiling.

Lawrence shot him a look that said, *That'll be the day*.

"Right, I'm here. Sorry to have kept you waiting." Suzie strode in, clean hands and no apron, but she still had a smudge of flour on her cheek. "Did Becca offer you a drink?"

"She did, but we really can't stay long," said Lawrence. "We just have a few questions for you."

Suzie sat down, and Becca waved and darted out of the room.

Rob glanced at Lawrence. They'd agreed he'd ask the questions as she was more likely to respond to him. Rob would observe and only interrupt if necessary.

"I want to ask you about Raza Ashraf," Lawrence began.

Suzie's smile drifted into a hard line. "What about him?"

"I apologise for the bluntness of my question, Suzie, but — as I'm sure you can appreciate — it's important you tell us the truth. We don't want any misunderstandings that could lead to complications later."

She looked worried. "What's this about, Sam?"

"Did you have an affair with Raza Ashraf?" Lawrence asked.

Suzie blushed, then gazed at the bowl of roses on the coffee table. They were much lower than the lilies and didn't block the view.

"Suzie?"

"Yes," she whispered. She raised her gaze to Lawrence. "It was just the once and we both regretted it immediately afterwards. We made a pact not to tell Noah. Raza was worried about their working relationship and I . . . Well, I was worried about my marriage."

"Did you know about Isabella Norton?" asked Lawrence. Rob had filled him in on everyone's name on the way there. His memory was still as good as ever, honed over years of reading case files.

She shook her head. "No, I had no idea. All I knew was he'd become distant and erratic. He was going out more with his friends and colleagues and leaving me with the children. Noah was always a free spirit. I thought the pressure of a young family had got to him. I didn't for a moment think he was seeing someone else, let alone that he'd had a child with them."

Rob studied her. Her eyes were shiny with unshed tears and her face was pale. The earlier blush had faded, and she now looked drawn and tired. It was hard to believe she was lying.

"When did you find out?" Lawrence asked.

"I didn't. Not until DCI Miller told me a week or so ago. I was shocked, hurt. I couldn't believe that all this time . . ." She shook her head, unable to go on.

Rob saw Lawrence grit his teeth and hoped he wasn't going to cave. She was a family friend, after all. He was about to step in when his former boss said, "I was sorry to hear about the lawsuit."

Suzie's eyes narrowed. "If that woman thinks she's getting a penny of Noah's money, she can think again," she snarled. "Opening her legs and getting knocked up does not entitle one to someone's hard-earned trust fund."

"I believe her daughter could use the money," he said.

She shot him an icy look. "So could a lot of people, but that doesn't mean they're entitled to it. Did you see what that girl did to my windows? She could have injured us. Clearly, the child is as uncouth as the mother."

Sam wisely changed the subject, but Rob had seen a glimpse of what he suspected was the real Suzie. The one hidden behind the polite, stylish exterior. Not so much the grieving widow as the spurned spouse.

"Do you remember a woman called Judith Walker?" Lawrence asked.

Her brow wrinkled in confusion. "Who?"

Rob stared at her. Did she really not remember?

"Judith, the family liaison officer assigned to you after Noah's murder. I remember meeting her here a few times."

Her forehead cleared and she inhaled. "Oh, yes. Vaguely. Dark-haired, pushy woman. Why do you ask?"

Lawrence smiled. "That's the one. It's just that she was murdered last week."

Suzie gasped. "Murdered? How?"

"Could have been a burglary gone wrong," said Rob, cutting in. "We aren't sure yet. We're still following up on several different leads."

"Of which you're one," added Lawrence.

She shook her head. "Excuse me?"

"I'm sorry about this, Suzie, but we need to know where you were on Wednesday the seventeenth of February."

"What? I'm a suspect now? I didn't even know the woman."

Lawrence didn't relent. "There might be a connection with Noah's death, so we have to ask everybody involved in the original investigation."

"Noah's death? What could it possibly have to do with that? He died over a decade ago. A monster killed him."

"I'm afraid I can't divulge that information," Lawrence said automatically. Years in the force had made him react without thinking. Rob would have said the same thing. "Please, Suzie. Give us your alibi so we can exclude you from the inquiry."

She exhaled noisily. "The seventeenth? I can't remember offhand. I'll have to look it up."

"Go ahead," said Lawrence.

She pulled her phone out of her pocket and stared at it for a moment, her thumbs working the screen. "Ah, yes. I didn't have anything on that day. I remember now. I had one of my migraines and stayed home. I think I popped to the chemist for some co-codamol, but that was it."

"Which chemist did you go to?" asked Rob.

"Lloyds, it's the closest one."

He nodded. He'd get his team to check the pharmacy security cameras and any CCTV.

"Was anyone here with you?" Lawrence asked.

"No," she replied. "The children were at school."

"What about the neighbours, a delivery driver, anyone who might have popped round during the day?"

She widened her eyes. "Oh, actually, a supplier dropped off some fabrics for me last week. I wonder if it was Wednesday?" She glanced up. "I'll have to ring them and check. I can't recall."

"Okay, will you do that and let me know?" said Lawrence.

"Of course."

"Thanks, Suzie, and apologies for disturbing you." He smiled awkwardly. "I know it's upsetting, dragging all this up. We'll get out of your hair now."

* * *

"What did you think?" asked Rob. Lawrence was driving him to Putney station. He was going to catch a train to Waterloo and walk to Jo's apartment from there.

"Hard to tell," said Lawrence. "At first I was convinced we'd got it wrong, then I saw her reaction to my question about the lawsuit."

"She turned in an instant," agreed Rob.

"Still," Lawrence mused, "it's obvious she's very upset about it. I mean, who wouldn't be?"

"True. I'll get my team to look into her alibi. We might be able to verify when she was at the chemist."

They pulled into the station car park. "Keep me posted, Rob."

"Will do."

\* \* \*

"How'd it go?" asked Jo when he got back.

He filled her in on their conversation with Suzie. "You know, she really didn't appear to know about her husband's affair. It is plausible that she only found out about Bella and Rachel when I told her."

"What about Noah's friend's statement?" pointed out Jo. "Greg Fairchild said that Suzie went round to his house looking for Noah and when he wasn't there, she went berserk."

"Yes, but he didn't tell her where Noah was. He kept to their agreed story, that he was still at the bar. Suzie said Noah was back home when she got there. They would have had an almighty row, but that doesn't mean she found out about the affair."

"How do you know she's not lying?" Jo narrowed her eyes. For all her cool-headed logic, Jo was more suspicious than he was. While he wasn't gullible, he did like to give people the benefit of the doubt, whereas Jo never would. She questioned everything.

"I don't know. She seemed sincere. If she's lying, she's a damn good actress."

"But that's just it," said Jo. "She was an actress."

Rob frowned. "What are you talking about?"

"Suzie *is* a trained actress. She studied at the Royal Academy of Dramatic Art. She was even in a few sitcoms when she was younger, before she got married. She gave it up when she married Noah."

Rob vaguely remembered her saying something about being in the film industry. "How do you know all this?"

She shrugged. "I googled her. If anyone can put it on, it's her."

# CHAPTER 41

Rob woke up to his buzzing phone. He frowned when he saw the screen. *Will.* Why was his sergeant calling on a Sunday morning?

"Will, what's up?" he said, his voice groggy.

Jo stirred beside him.

"I'm sending you a link to Rachel Norton's Instagram account," he said. "There's something you should see."

The phone buzzed again. It showed a photograph of Rachel giving the camera the finger. Behind her was the neat facade of Suzie Palmer's Georgian house.

"Whoa! What's she doing there?"

"Check the date she posted it."

Rob glanced down below the likes to the date.

"She was at Suzie Palmer's house the day of Walker's murder?"

"It looks that way. There's no timestamp, so we don't know what time she was there, but there's no Merc in the driveway."

"Which means Suzie Palmer wasn't at home when she said she was," concluded Rob.

Jo had woken up and was peering over his shoulder at the screen.

"We have to find Rachel." Rob pulled back the covers and climbed out of bed. "She'll be able to verify the time, although what the hell she was doing outside Suzie Palmer's house, God only knows."

"Making a statement." Jo nodded at the photograph. "She's acting out. It probably comes from a place of hurt because Suzie rejected her."

At Rob's raised eyebrow, Jo smiled. "Psychology major, remember?"

"Right." Jo had studied psychology before she'd dropped out to pursue a career in the police force. "Still, it was asking for trouble going there."

"She's not breaking any laws," said Jo, also getting up and wrapping a dressing gown around herself. It emphasised the bump. Rob put his hand on her stomach.

"No, she's not — but she may have disproven Suzie's alibi."

"What do you want us to do, guv?" asked Will, still on the line.

"I'll give Rachel a ring now and call you back. Are you at home?"

"Yeah."

This week wasn't their on-call week, which meant his team had the weekend off.

Rob hung up and dialled Rachel's number. While it was ringing, he walked into the open-plan kitchen and switched on the coffee machine. Jo had gone into the bathroom.

After several rings it went to voicemail.

"Shit," he muttered.

He tried Bella's number and thought that was going to ring off too, when she answered. "Hello?"

"Bella, it's DCI Rob Miller speaking. Is Rachel with you?"

"No, she's out. Have you tried her mobile?"

"Yeah, she's not answering."

"Oh, well, I can give her a message for you when she gets home."

"Do you know where she is?" he asked.

"She went to meet a friend. I'm not sure where they were going."

"Do you have the friend's number?" he asked. "It's imperative I get hold of her."

"Why? Has something happened?"

"Nothing to worry about," he said quickly. "I just need to ask her some questions."

"I'm afraid I don't have Cherry's number, no," she said. "But I know where she lives?"

"That'll do," Rob said.

"It's Hanworth Towers, Block C, Flat 46. It's the next estate over."

He wrote it on Jo's shopping list notepad lying on the countertop. "Right, thanks. If she comes back, tell her to give me a ring. It's urgent."

He said goodbye and hung up.

Jo wandered into the kitchen and poured herself a cup of coffee. She only had one a day, now she was pregnant. The rest of the time she drank herbal teas, which Rob thought were disgusting.

"Hmm . . ." She took a sip and closed her eyes. "It tastes so much better now that it's rationed."

"I'm sorry, I'm going to have to leave. I need to track down Rachel Norton."

"Want some company?" asked Jo.

He hesitated. *What the hell.* He was on leave anyway. "Sure, if you want to."

Her eyes lit up. "Give me five minutes."

Soon they were speeding across west London in Rob's SUV. He'd bought it the previous year, after he'd been promoted to DCI. It was a great car and he loved driving it.

It took nearly an hour to get to Hanworth Towers in Hounslow. Bella hadn't rung back, so he was assuming Rachel was still out. Jo tried her mobile again, but she didn't pick up.

"Why isn't she answering?" muttered Rob.

He manoeuvred into a parking spot and together they walked up to the high-rise that said Block C on it.

Tall, brown and uninviting, the tower blocks were typical of countless council estates all over London. Downstairs was dingy and unwelcoming. A single elevator blinked annoyingly at them as they waited for it to reach the ground floor.

"What number was she?" asked Jo.

"Forty-six," Rob replied.

It was excruciatingly slow, but eventually they emerged on the twelfth floor. The four on the door was lopsided, hanging on by a single screw. Rob knocked. The door was opened by a short, overweight woman in a bright-green jumper. She looked like an apple.

"Can I help you?" she wheezed.

"We're looking for Rachel Norton," he said. "Her mother thought she might be here."

"No, Rachel's not here. She went to meet someone."

"Really?" Rob frowned. "Who?"

"I don't know. Hang on. Cherry!" she yelled behind her into the apartment, then spent a good minute coughing.

A skinny teenager the same age as Rachel appeared. "Yeah?"

"Where did Rachel go? These coppers want to know."

Rob grimaced. He hadn't said who they were. Was it that obvious?

Jo smiled. "We're worried about her. Anything you can tell us would help."

"She got a message from that woman who was married to her dad, you know, the rich bitch."

"Suzie Palmer?" Rob glanced at Jo.

"Yeah, that's her. Rachel was mouthing off about her all week, and then out of the blue she gets this message asking if they can meet up."

"Do you know where Rachel met her?"

"At the station, I think. The woman said she'd pick her up. I think Rachel wanted to find out about her dad."

Rob exhaled. She was with Suzie Palmer. That didn't bode well.

They left the building.

"Do you think Suzie saw the photograph and realised her alibi was at stake?" Jo asked.

"I don't know, but I'm concerned. Suzie may have murdered Judith Walker and now she has Rachel, who she hates even more. She might try to get rid of her to protect her own children's inheritance."

"Do you have her number?"

"Yeah, I'll give her a ring."

They sat in the car as he dialled Suzie Palmer's mobile. Not surprisingly, it diverted to voicemail.

"It's switched off. I'm going to call Will to see if he can trace it."

Will answered immediately. "What's the news, boss?"

"Not good, I'm afraid," said Rob, and proceeded to tell him what had happened. "I need you to trace Rachel's mobile. It's ringing, but she's not picking up. Suzie's is going straight to voicemail, so she's probably switched it off."

"I can't do it from here," said Will. "I'll go into work."

"Okay, as soon as you can. Suzie might do something to Rachel."

There was rustling in the background as Will scrambled to get ready. "Call Jenny," came his muffled voice. "She mentioned going in today. She may already be there."

"Right, thanks."

Jenny picked up straight away. "Hi, guv."

"Jenny, are you in the office?"

"Yes, how did you know?"

"Listen, I need to find Rachel Norton. Suzie Palmer has kidnapped her."

To her credit, Jenny didn't waste any time asking questions. "I'll see if I can ping either of their phones."

"Suzie's seems to be switched off. Start with Rachel's. And see if you can pick Suzie's SLK up on the ANPR database."

"Okay. I'll call you back as soon as I have something." She hung up.

"What now?" asked Jo.

"I'm not sure. Suzie would have picked Rachel up at Hounslow station, but I've no idea where she would have taken her after that."

"There are several industrial and waste sites out that way," said Jo. "Lots of places to dump a body."

Rob grimaced. "Let's hope it doesn't come to that."

"If Suzie killed her husband and Judith, it's not a stretch to believe she'd kill Rachel too."

Rob drummed his fingers on the steering wheel.

The phone rang.

"Hello?" He picked it up before the first ring had ended.

"Guv, I've got Suzie Palmer's car heading towards Heathrow on Staines Road. It's the A315."

*Yes!*

Jo exhaled.

Rob put the car into gear. "If Suzie's driving, there's a chance Rachel is still alive." He pulled out of the parking area and accelerated down the road.

"I'm still trying to pick up Rachel's phone signal," said Jenny. "She might be in an area with dodgy reception."

Rob turned a corner and weaved through dense traffic until he got to Nelson Road, then turned onto Staines Road. They were retracing Suzie's route.

"I won't be able to tell if she's turned off until she passes through another camera," Jenny said.

"I'm nearly at the junction with the Great South West Road." He passed the phone to Jo, who put it on speaker and attached it to the dashboard holder.

He didn't have a blue light on his SUV, so he settled for the hazards and gunned it down the arterial road. Jo, firmly buckled up, sitting grimly beside him. She didn't once tell him to slow down.

Rob changed lanes to undercut a lorry plodding along in the outside lane. Conscious of his precious cargo, he didn't take too many chances.

"There's another ANPR camera three miles ahead at the Terminal Four junction," said Jenny. "I'll let you know when they go through it."

"Anything?" Rob asked a few moments later, when Jenny hadn't responded.

"No, guv. She must have turned off."

*Fuck.*

Jo opened Google Maps on her phone. "There are three major junctions between their last known location and the Terminal 4 camera," she said. "She must have taken one of them. There's no other way off the motorway."

"I'm approaching Heathrow now," said Rob. He kept driving. The first junction was coming up on his left.

"It doesn't look like it leads anywhere," said Jo. "Mostly industrial areas. A dead end. She'd have to come back this way to get out."

Rob ignored the turn-off. "What about the next one?"

"It winds down to a reservoir of some sort." Jo zoomed in on her phone. "I can't make it out. There doesn't appear to be a name."

Rob hesitated. The slip road was coming up ahead. The bars on the side of the road began counting down the yards. Should he take a chance? A reservoir was likely, but what if he was wrong? What if she'd taken the next one?

"What about the third?"

"It leads to a residential area," said Jo.

Will's voice could be heard in the background. "Suzie Palmer's phone is definitely off. Probably so we can't track her. Rachel's pinged the cell tower near Heathrow five minutes ago."

"It looks like a longer than five-minute drive between the second and third junction," said Jo. "Definitely turn here."

Rob indicated and moved into the left-hand lane. "Now what?" he said.

"Got it," yelled Will in the background. "Rachel's phone pinged briefly. She's down by the lake."

Thank fuck for that.

Rob took the road heading down to the reservoir. It wound through scrubland and the occasional concrete out-building before petering out into a dead end. In front of them was a raised grassy bank, beyond which was the reservoir.

"We can't get through," Rob said. "Is there another access road? Where was that last signal?"

"Near the south bank of the reservoir," said Will, his voice clearer now. "But it's gone off. I can't locate the signal anymore."

Rob glanced at Jo. "That's not a good sign."

"I saw another small dirt track on the approach road," Jo said. "Let's try that."

Rob turned around and they drove back less than a hundred metres. "There! Is that how we get down to the water?" Jo leaned forward in her seat, straining against the seat belt.

"Yeah, looks like it." Rob drove along the bumpy dirt track into a makeshift gravel car park. "That's Suzie's car," he breathed.

He drove up behind the SLK and cut the engine. They both climbed out. Suzie's car was empty, both the front doors open.

Rob felt the bonnet. Still warm. He could hear the engine ticking over. Both he and Jo peered up and down the water's edge, but there was nobody in sight. It was as if the occupants of the car had vanished.

# CHAPTER 42

The text message had been a surprise, but Rachel had jumped at the chance.

*I'm sorry about before. Let's meet and talk about Noah. Hounslow station? 11am?*

Rachel had hastily said goodbye to Cherry and left the housing estate, catching the bus into Hounslow. It was a sombre, windy day. Not many people about. It was only her and a geriatric man with a walking stick on the bus.

Even the Tube station was quiet. Only a few travellers milling about. Mostly youngsters in groups laughing and jostling. Rachel didn't know any of them. She pulled her coat around her thin body and waited. Mrs Palmer drove a fancy white Mercedes — she'd seen it in the driveway the first time she'd been to her house. When the bitch had kicked her out.

What had brought on this change of heart? Had her daughter said something? Had Mrs Palmer finally decided to do the right thing? Or had she just taken pity on the girl from the council estate?

Whatever it was, Rachel didn't care. All she wanted was to learn more about Noah. Her Dad.

Now, driving into this deserted car park, Rachel wasn't so sure what she was doing here.

"Where are we?" She looked at the grassy bank and the cold, deep body of water. It seemed to stretch for ever in all directions.

"I thought we could take a walk," Mrs Palmer said, smiling. Her teeth were so white and even they looked fake. "Get to know each other."

"Here?"

"Why not? It's pretty enough. There's a walkway around the reservoir."

Rachel stared at the grassy verge in front of her and the fenced concrete walkway around it.

"You want to find out about Noah, don't you?" Suzie was dangling the carrot.

"Can't we talk in the car?" Rachel shivered. "It looks cold out there. I think it's going to rain."

"No, don't be silly. It's nice and refreshing."

"I'd really rather talk here." Something didn't feel right, although she didn't know what it was.

"There's a little café on the way back to the motorway," Mrs Palmer said. "We can stop there for a hot chocolate after our walk."

Rachel didn't remember seeing any café.

"Come on. Let's go." Mrs Palmer climbed out of the car.

Rachel hesitated, then she slowly opened the door and got out. The wind knocked into her, lifting her hair and whirling it about. It was stronger than she'd thought. Stronger than back at the estate. "I can't swim," she said nervously. "I'm not sure I want to walk around the reservoir."

"It's perfectly safe," Mrs Palmer insisted. "Look, there's a fence around it. Now what do you want to know about Noah? What kind of man he was? What he did for a living? What kind of father he was to the children?"

She nodded. She wanted to know all those things, and more. Did he like ginger beer, like she did? Did he have hazel eyes, like her? What was his sense of humour like? Did he make bad dad jokes?

"Well, he was a good man. A hard worker. He worked in a bank. Did you know that?"

She shook her head and tentatively joined Suzie on the open path. There was a fence on the reservoir side, but it wasn't very high. The water spat up against the sides, grey and foreboding.

"He used to leave early and come home late. Always working."

"Was he good at his job?" she asked.

"Yes, he was very bright. That's one of the things that attracted me to him in the first place. His intelligence."

Rachel smiled. They had that in common then. "I'm good with numbers too," she said. "I want to go into finance when I finish school."

"A worthy career choice." Mrs Palmer smiled, but it didn't reach her eyes.

"What does your daughter want to do?" Rachel asked. "Rebecca, isn't it?"

"She wants to be an actress." The smile had disappeared, replaced by an icy glare.

"Oh, how lov—" Rachel stopped. Mrs Palmer was looking at her with such hatred that it took her breath away. "I–Is something wrong?" she stammered.

"Don't you mention my daughter again," she hissed, coming closer. "She's nothing like you."

Rachel gasped as Mrs Palmer's hands grabbed her shoulders. "What are you doing? Let me go!"

"I've had just about enough of you," Mrs Palmer said. "It's time you disappeared for good. Little troublemaker."

She pushed Rachel towards the edge of the reservoir.

"No! Please don't! I can't swim."

"Good." Mrs Palmer gave a hard shove and Rachel lost her balance. She wobbled precariously, swiping at the fence for something to hold on to, but it was too flimsy and bent backwards, tumbling into the water with a metallic screech.

Rachel screamed. She reached out and grabbed Mrs Palmer's jacket. If she was going to die, she was taking the bitch with her.

"Get off me," yelled Mrs Palmer, trying to pry her fingers loose. Rachel held on for dear life. A gust of wind blew her hair across her face and suddenly they were both toppling over.

Mrs Palmer cried out as they went over the edge.

A moment later, they hit the water.

# CHAPTER 43

Rob and Jo climbed the grassy verge to the path at the top. It wound around the reservoir and would have been quite pleasant if it hadn't been so windy.

"I can't see anyone." Rob gazed in both directions. The cold wind made his eyes water.

"Oh my God, Rob. They're in the water!" Jo took off along the path at a run.

*Jesus.* Rob called Will. "Get me some backup at the reservoir," he yelled. "And an ambulance. Actually, make that two ambulances."

Then he hung up and sprinted after Jo.

"Don't do anything stupid," he yelled, pumping his legs as hard as he could. His heart was in his throat.

*Please don't fall in*, he prayed. She was six months pregnant, for Christ's sake.

Two people could be seen splashing in the water. One frantically waving her arms about, the other swimming for the side.

Rob heard a garbled scream. It was Rachel. She was going under.

"I'll get Rachel," shouted Rob, taking off his jacket as he ran. "Suzie can swim."

He kicked off his shoes and dived into the water.

*Fuck.* It was freezing. He came up spluttering, the cold sucking the air out from inside him.

He looked around. Rachel had disappeared.

He swam to where he'd last seen her and dived down. It was murky below the surface and he couldn't see further than a few feet in front of him.

"I can't find her," he gasped as he came up for air.

"Over there!" screamed Jo, pointing to a spot behind him. He turned and dived again.

Where the hell was she?

He kicked downwards as hard as he could, peering into the gloom. A dark shape floated some distance below him. Was it her?

He swam closer, ignoring his throbbing head and burning lungs. Reaching out, he grabbed a fistful of hair.

*Rachel.*

He pulled her towards him, her body floppy and unmoving like a ragdoll.

*Please let her be alive.*

He circled his arm around her neck and kicked as hard as he could, propelling them upwards. Time slowed down. He fought the urge to inhale. Finally, they broke the surface.

Rob gasped at the air, filling his lungs, trying not to splutter. Rachel was limp in his arms. He swam to where a steep metal ladder led up the side of the reservoir.

"Suzie's making a run for it!" Jo was about to go after her.

"Leave her," barked Rob. "Help me get Rachel out."

Jo leaned over the ladder and helped haul the unconscious girl out of the water. It took a lot of pulling and pushing but eventually they got her onto the path. Jo immediately began CPR.

"I'm going after Suzie," Rob called.

Jo didn't look up. She was concentrating on the chest compressions.

He left her to it and dashed off after the drenched fleeing figure. Suzie ran into the scrubland behind the reservoir.

Rob followed, his feet sinking into the squelchy mud. It was hard going, the ground saturated by the rain and the underground water. He fell a couple of times. Suzie was having the same problem.

Slowly, he gained on her.

"It's over, Suzie." He grabbed at her sodden blouse. She writhed out of his grasp and kept going, stumbling further into the marshland.

"You can't get away." He rugby tackled her legs and she went flying. He pounced on her and wrestled her arms behind her back.

"Suzie Palmer, you're under arrest," he panted. He'd have to wait until he got her back to the car to put cuffs on her. "You do not have to say anything, but it may harm your defence if you do not mention when questioned something which you later rely on in court. Anything you do say may be given in evidence."

He was so cold he could barely get the words out. She wriggled, but he held her firm.

"The little bitch deserved it," she spat, eyes blazing.

"Get up." Rob hauled her to her feet. She was shivering violently, her lips turning blue. His were probably doing the same.

They stumbled back towards the hard ground. Jo was holding a vomiting Rachel in her arms, stroking her hair.

"I think she's going to be okay," said Jo. She looked exhausted. Rob felt a protective pang but pushed it aside. Rachel was the one needing attention right now.

He smiled at her. "Well done."

Jo had spread his jacket out over Rachel to keep her warm, but the air was frigid and they were both trembling with cold.

Rob heard sirens approaching. Thank God. Warmth was coming.

A police car screeched to a halt next to theirs and three uniformed officers clambered up the grassy bank and ran towards them.

Rob handed Suzie over. "This woman is under arrest for kidnapping," he told the coppers. "She's also wanted by the Putney Major Investigation Team in connection with two homicides."

Suzie Palmer tried to shake off the uniformed arm that held her. "You've got nothing on me."

Rob didn't comment. He nodded to the officer to take her away.

An ambulance arrived and two paramedics lifted Rachel onto a stretcher.

"We'll take her in for observation," the one said. "But it looks like you saved her life, ma'am."

Jo smiled wearily and patted Rachel on the hand. "You'll be okay," she said.

# CHAPTER 44

Rob decided to interview Suzie Palmer straight away while the events of the last few hours were still fresh in his mind. He was charging her with the attempted murder of Rachel Norton.

He would have loved to have charged her with Judith Walker's and Noah Palmer's murders, but she'd been right when she'd said they had nothing on her. They didn't. It all boiled down to a bunch of circumstantial evidence and a gut feeling.

Rob had no doubt she'd done it. She'd killed her husband twelve years ago and she'd murdered Dr Walker last week. He just had to find a way to prove it.

"You could get her to confess," suggested Jenny, as they stood in the viewing room and studied Suzie Palmer through the one-way glass. Bedraggled, exhausted, but strangely composed. Her head bobbed up every now and then as she looked at the mirror. Was she seeing herself or picturing those beyond?

A confession would be ideal, but he didn't think it likely. Suzie would deny she had anything to do with the murders. *I'm Noah's grieving widow. I was left to raise three small children on my own. A victim myself.*

With Judith Walker it would be, *I barely knew her. It was so long ago. I have no idea why anyone would want to kill her.*

Deny. Deny. Deny.

He'd heard it all before.

At least Mayhew wasn't here. Away for the weekend, apparently. With Rob on leave, she could relax, he imagined. Recover from the most recent scandal to befall the department. Raza Ashraf's outrage. The Deputy Commissioner's scramble to smooth things over. Assurances given, promises made, egos soothed.

It was a relief not to have to explain his actions to her. Not yet, anyway. That would come later. Right now, his focus was on Suzie Palmer.

"How'd you want to play it, guv?" asked Will, who was sitting in with him. Rob felt Suzie might respond better to two men than to him and Jenny, who was soft-spoken and sympathetic. If a suspect needed coaxing, there was no one better than Jenny, but Suzie required a harsher approach.

The suspect had lawyered up. A middle-aged man with a shock of white hair and decades of experience sat beside her. He tapped his notepad with a gold pen, impatient to start. Time was money. They'd be lucky to get anything past him.

"Let's confront her with what we've got and take it from there," he said.

The atmosphere in the interrogation room was heavy with denial. Rob sensed it the moment he walked through the door. It was in Suzie's erect stance and the defiant expression on her solicitor's face.

He sat down. Will introduced everyone for the purposes of the recording and when the digital light flashed red, they began.

"Suzie Palmer, you're under arrest for the kidnapping and attempted murder of Rachel Norton. Do you have anything to say about that?"

Suzie glanced at her solicitor, who gave a small nod.

"I didn't kidnap Rachel, nor did I attempt to murder her," she said.

Rob's eyebrows shot up. "Can you explain what you were doing at the reservoir?"

She nodded, gave a rueful smile. The consummate actress. "We were taking a walk. She wanted to talk about her father."

"I see, except when DCI Maguire and I arrived, you were both in the water. Rachel claims that you pushed her in."

"She's mistaken." Suzie's jaw stiffened.

"I don't think so," said Rob. "According to her statement, you lured her out to the reservoir under the pretence of talking about her father, your late husband, Noah Palmer. When you got there, you suggested a walk along the reservoir path. Rachel grew uneasy and when she tried to go back, you pushed her into the water."

"That's not what happened," Suzie said. "We went for a walk along the path, and *she* became aggressive. *She* tried to push me into the water. I resisted, but then we both toppled over. That's when you saw us."

An earnest expression, a half-smile. It was her word against Rachel's.

"That's not what Rachel says," countered Rob.

"Are you going to believe the word of a juvenile delinquent over mine?" asked Suzie. "Don't forget that girl threw two bricks through my window last week. I was reaching out to her, trying to be nice, and this is how she repays me."

Rob ground his jaw. He should have known she'd bring that up.

"Rachel Norton couldn't swim." Rob kept his voice steady. "She would never have risked falling into the water."

"I don't think she meant to go in," Suzie said. "After all, she pushed me. It was only because I grabbed her coat that she fell in with me."

"Mrs Palmer," said Rob, "*you* sent Rachel those text messages inviting her to talk. *You* picked her up at Hounslow station. *You* drove her out to the reservoir, an isolated and deserted place. I find it hard to believe your actions were not premeditated."

"It's not for you to believe," cut in her solicitor. "It's for you to prove."

Rob glared at him. He wasn't wrong there, but he didn't need reminding.

"What did you mean when you said, and I quote, 'The little bitch deserved it?'" he asked.

Suzie remained composed. "I meant she deserved falling into the reservoir since she tried to push me in. Why? What did you think I meant?"

Rob ground his teeth. This wasn't going well. She had an answer for everything. To be fair, neither Jo nor himself had actually seen Suzie push Rachel into the water. After reading Rachel's testimony, it was clear that was what had happened, but proving it was another story. It truly was Rachel's word against Suzie's — and despite the text messages, Suzie was the better actress and the one without the shoplifting record.

"I think you meant to punish her for bringing shame on your family."

Suzie's gaze hardened.

"It was Rachel who came to your home and threw bricks through your window. It was because of her that article appeared in the newspaper about your late husband's love child, and it's because of her that your children are likely to lose a substantial portion of their inheritance."

"She won't get a penny," snapped Suzie.

Rob's pulse quickened. He was on the right track. Her solicitor put a warning hand on his client's arm.

"Like it or not, Rachel Norton is Noah Palmer's biological daughter," he said. "That means she is entitled to her inheritance. I'm sure your solicitor will tell you the same thing."

Her legal representative didn't respond, merely glared at Rob.

"Is that why you tried to kill her?" Rob asked casually. "To protect your children's inheritance?"

"My client has already said she did not try to murder Miss Norton," the solicitor said.

"I was asking Mrs Palmer, not you."

"I didn't try to kill her," came the sulky response.

Not so much the actress now.

"You must have harboured a great deal of resentment towards her," Rob continued. "Didn't you get kicked off the PTA because of the negative publicity about your late husband?"

Suzie went bright red.

"Image is important to you, isn't it? You can't stand the thought of the other parents gossiping behind your back."

She was breathing heavily now.

Rob pushed on. "And to top it all, your husband had an illegitimate child with a prostitute." He shook his head. "That must have stung."

"The stupid whore," hissed Suzie. "Why did she have to go and get pregnant?"

Rob studied her. "So, you did know about Noah's affair?"

"Of course I knew." Her lips curled back in a snarl. "I'm not blind. I could tell things had changed between us."

"Suzie," warned her solicitor, but she was barely listening.

"Why do you think I slept with Raza? I was trying to get back at him, to make him sit up and notice me again."

"Did it work?" asked Rob.

She shook her head. "He didn't care. He said he was going to divorce me. Me?" She laughed bitterly. "I was the perfect wife. I gave up my film career to have his children and keep his house and that's how he was going to repay me. A divorce."

"Is that why you killed him?" Rob asked.

She balked, suddenly aware of where she was and what she was saying.

Her solicitor cleared his throat. "I suggest you stop talking now, Suzie."

She gathered herself together. "I didn't kill him," she said. "It was that crazy person, that religious nut."

"You're referring to the Pentagram Killer?"

"Yes, him. You saw the photos of how my husband died. A ritualistic murder, DCI Lawrence called it."

"Alfred Whitaker swears he didn't kill Noah Palmer. Why would he admit to the other three murders, but not that one?"

"I don't know. Because he's insane?"

Rob nodded. "Let's talk about Judith Walker."

Suzie flopped back in her chair. "Not her again."

"Yes, I'm afraid so. You've stated that you were at home on the afternoon of the seventeenth of February when Dr Walker was bludgeoned to death."

"Yes, I was."

"Except Rachel Norton posted a photograph online taken in front of your house on that exact same afternoon."

Jenny had gone to the hospital and taken Rachel's statement. According to the teenager, she'd taken the photograph shortly after two o'clock in the afternoon. A quick CCTV check at a bus stop in Hounslow confirmed she'd got on a bus heading for Chiswick at thirteen minutes past one. They were still waiting for the camera on the bus to verify when and where she got off.

They could never verify the actual time of the photograph, since Rachel's phone had ended up in the reservoir along with the rest of her. The forensic team were trying to dry it out and retrieve whatever data they could from it, but the chances were slim.

Except Suzie didn't know that.

"Your car wasn't in the driveway."

"That little shit," Suzie said. "I want to lay a charge of harassment."

"Where were you between two and four last Wednesday afternoon?" asked Rob. "And I'd advise you to think very carefully about lying again. It's not looked on favourably by the jury."

"That must have been when I popped to the shops," she said.

"You said that was in the morning. We viewed the camera footage at the chemist, by the way, and you didn't step foot inside the place all day. You were lying about that too."

She looked sullen.

Her solicitor cut in. "Just because my client wasn't home when she said she was, doesn't mean she was committing murder."

"No, it doesn't," Rob had to admit. "But it does raise suspicions. And we have a witness who saw her fleeing the scene."

"What witness?" demanded Suzie.

Rob kept a straight face. "A parolee was on his way to Dr Walker's house. As you know, she was a criminal psychologist. He saw you driving away in your vehicle."

"He can't have," she snapped. "I wasn't—"

"Suzie," barked her solicitor. "Can we have a word?"

"I'm afraid you've already had a word with your client, Mr Johnson. You can speak to her afterwards, if you want, but not in the middle of an interview."

He turned back to the suspect. "You weren't what, Suzie?"

She took a deep breath. "I wasn't anywhere near there. I did go to the shops, just not in the high street."

Rob pursed his lips. "If you say so."

"You can check," she said, a bit too haughtily.

Rob knew what she was up to. He leaned forward. "Suzie Palmer, I'm charging you with the abduction and attempted murder of Rachel Norton. This interview is suspended, but we're going to keep you in custody for the full duration permitted to us. We'll be interviewing you again regarding the murder of Judith Walker and Noah Palmer."

He stood up. Will terminated the session.

"I'd like to have that word with my client," specified the solicitor.

Rob gave a curt nod. "Be my guest. You can use this room. An officer will take Mrs Palmer into custody when you're done."

They left the room. Will glanced at Rob. "What's going on? I thought you were getting to her."

"It was taking too long," said Rob. "Besides, I think I know how we can nail her, but there's something I need to check first."

Will's eyebrows shot up. "You mean hard evidence?"

Rob nodded. "A novelty, I know. But bear with me. I think I know how she did it."

## CHAPTER 45

"Guys, I need your help," Rob said once he got back to the squad room. Despite it being Sunday, the whole team was in.

Mike looked even bigger than usual in a tracksuit, Jeff was wearing jeans and a sweatshirt, while Celeste was in a fluffy jumper and leggings. They'd all given up their day to be here.

"Check Suzie Palmer's alibi. All of the supermarkets have security cameras or CCTV. Find out where she went on Wednesday afternoon."

It took some time, but they eventually located her car at the Westfield Shopping Centre in Shepherd's Bush.

"Just popped out for some paracetamol," muttered Will.

Rob smirked. "Exactly, but I think I know why she went there."

"Why?" asked Jenny.

"Because she wanted to hire a car and she couldn't do that in Chiswick high street."

"She hired a car . . . to drive to Judith Walker's house in Raynes Park," said Will, his eyes widening in understanding.

"What made you think of that, guv?" asked Jenny.

"It was what she nearly said," Rob explained. "When I told her we had a witness, she started to say we couldn't have because 'she wasn't . . .' And then she stopped."

"You think she was going to say because she wasn't driving her car?" said Will.

Rob nodded.

"If you check, I'll bet you'll find she hired a car on the afternoon of Dr Walker's murder and she hired it from somewhere in Shepherd's Bush."

"We're on it," said Jeff.

A short time later, he'd printed out a sheet of car hire companies with branches in Shepherd's Bush. There were twenty-eight of them.

"That's a lot of companies," breathed Jenny.

"Start with the more obscure ones," Rob advised.

They each took seven and got calling. It was Mike who hit the jackpot. "Found it!" He slapped his thigh.

They all spun around.

"Galaxy Car Hire leased her a blue Toyota Yaris at 2.23 p.m. on Wednesday the seventeenth of February. I've got the reg number."

"Excellent. Good work." Rob grinned. "Now we have to find her on the ANPR cameras in the vicinity of Judith Walker's house."

"On it," said Jenny.

They got back to work, fingers flying over keypads, eyes glued to their screens.

Rob went into the incident room and stared at the whiteboard covered in the original crime scene photos of Noah Palmer's bizarre murder.

How had she managed it? How had she staged it to look like it was the work of the Pentagram Killer? The painted circle. The carved pentagram. The candles. Her attention to detail was spot on. She would have ascertained a certain amount from the newspapers, but not the paint. Never the paint.

And how the hell had she done it when she hadn't left the house?

He decided to give Liz Kramer another call.

"Liz, it's Rob."

"It's also a Sunday night," came her taut reply.

Shit, he'd forgotten. "Sorry," he said. "It's just I have Suzie Palmer in custody, and I know she killed her husband twelve years ago, I just can't figure out how. Do you have a minute to talk it through with me? I thought it might help."

She sighed. "I was relaxing in front of the television. Go on, shoot."

"Do you remember the post-mortem report I asked you to look at?" he said.

"How could I forget?"

"A witness puts Suzie Palmer outside her house shortly after five o'clock. They talked. The same witness also saw her an hour later making supper for the kids through the kitchen window. That's not up for dispute. She was there."

"So? What can I do then?" asked Liz.

"The neighbour didn't actually see Noah Palmer cycle off," said Rob. "She went outside to chat to Suzie, who said she'd just waved him off. Now two things don't make sense. Firstly, Suzie and Noah were hardly talking at that stage. They were both having affairs and in fact, Noah had asked Suzie for a divorce. It's unlikely she'd waved him off, as she said."

"Unless they'd made up," said Liz.

"They hadn't. Suzie confirmed things were tense between them at the time of his death. She would have said if they'd reconciled."

Liz grunted. "What's the other thing?"

"I can't help thinking it's relevant that the neighbour didn't see Noah leave the house. I guess I'm just wondering if she could have killed him earlier and staged the body. I know she said she was home with the kids, but what if she took them with her? What if she found a way to kill him and make it home to speak to the neighbour and give herself an alibi?"

"The time of death was pretty precise," Liz said, her mind sharp as ever. "If I remember correctly, it was between five and six that evening, which ties in with him going for a cycle and being ambushed by the killer. If he'd died earlier, or later for that matter, it wouldn't correlate with the pathologist's report."

"How accurate are those time of death assumptions, really?" asked Rob.

"Very," she snapped. "They are based on precise calculations taking into account the victim's body temperature, the ambient temperature, and any other conditions that might have affected the body."

"Okay, okay," he said. "I'm just wondering if there wasn't a way around it?"

"Not unless she killed him between five and six and dumped the body later that night," said Liz.

Rob froze.

"It's possible," he whispered. Was that what she'd done? His brain went into overdrive. "What if she killed Noah at home, hid his body from the kids, then went out to talk to the neighbour and pretended she'd just waved him goodbye."

"That could work," said Liz. "But the cause of death was a rock found at the scene. There was blood all over it. According to the report, the rock was endemic to the area. The stabbings and mutilation were post-mortem."

"Which adds up," said Rob, his pulse racing now. "She could have fetched that rock earlier in the day then used it to kill him. Once she'd driven his body out to Box Hill, she tossed the rock and staged the body."

There was a heavy pause.

"That might work," said Liz. "Although I don't know how you're going to prove it. Any forensic evidence will be long gone."

Rob's mind was spinning. "Okay, thanks, Liz. I've got to go, but I'll let you know what happens."

"You'd better," she said.

He hurriedly rang off. Next, he dialled Sam Lawrence. "Chief, it's Rob."

"Working late?"

"Yeah. Listen, did anyone search Suzie Palmer's vehicle after her husband was murdered?"

"Her car? No, of course not. She was never a suspect. Why do you ask?"

"Forensics didn't go over it?" Rob hadn't seen anything to that effect in any of the old case files, but he had to check.

"No. Have you found something?"

"I think she did it, Chief. I think Suzie killed Noah because he was going to divorce her."

"Jesus."

"But since she was never a suspect, her house and car were never analysed."

"At the time, we thought it was the Pentagram Killer. The MO was identical, right down to the same brand of paint." Lawrence was silent. Eventually, he said, "You're telling me she staged the body to make it look like the Pentagram Killer? That little woman? She's only five foot four. How did she kill her husband? How could she have carried his body out to Box Hill? He was found half a mile from the nearest track. How did she know about the paint?"

"I don't know," said Rob. "But I'm going to find out."

## CHAPTER 46

"You were right, boss." Jenny's cheeks flushed with excitement. "We picked up the Toyota Yaris on the A3 southbound towards the Wimbledon turn-off."

*Yes!* "What time was that?"

"2.37 p.m."

"Perfect timing. Is that all we've got? Anything closer to Judith Walker's house?"

"Nothing on the ANPR. Jeff's checking the speed cams and Mike's looking at possible CCTV footage along the route she would have taken."

"Okay. Let me know if you find anything else."

The evidence was stacking up. There was still nothing definite, but they had enough to convince the Crown Prosecutor to charge her for Dr Walker's murder.

Noah Palmer's was a bit trickier. Rob had worked out how she'd done it, but there was no way of proving it.

"Jenny, what vehicle did Suzie Palmer have twelve years ago?"

She frowned. "I'll check with the DVLA. Give me a minute."

He got himself a much-needed coffee and rang Jo to give her an update. "It's a pity you can't get her to confess," she said, echoing Jenny's sentiment. "That's the only way you're going to be able to charge her for Noah's murder."

Rob knew she was right. Too much time had passed to gather any new evidence. The leads had gone cold. Jenny confirmed this when she got back to him about the make of the car. In 2009, she was driving a VW Tuareg, but she had traded it in for a brand-new Land Rover Evoque a month after Noah's death."

"Like that isn't suspicious?" muttered Rob. She'd got rid of the car in which she'd transported Noah's dead body to the crime scene as soon as possible, without arousing suspicion. It had all gone according to plan and she'd got away with it.

*I plan everything. It's just the way I am.*

Even the tenacious DCI Sam Lawrence had believed her.

He walked back into the incident room and stared at the whiteboard, going through the sequence of events. The only time he'd seen Suzie truly rattled was when that newspaper article had appeared in the press. Even now, in the interrogation, she'd angered when he'd brought it up.

An idea flickered at the edges of his brain, but he couldn't quite grasp it. He sat down to ponder it.

His phone buzzed. Acting Superintendent Mayhew.

*Shit.* "DCI Miller," he said, dreading the barrage of abuse that was about to fly down the line at him.

She didn't bother with hellos. "What's going on there? I heard you've got Suzie Palmer in custody."

"Yes, ma'am. She abducted Rachel Norton earlier today with the intention of killing her. We caught her in the act. I had no choice but to make the arrest."

"You were off duty," she hissed. "You're supposed to be on leave. Why are you still investigating? There are officers on duty to handle circumstances like this."

"I was able to act much faster, ma'am," said Rob. "I know Rachel Norton. I have her phone number. We were able to trace her mobile to the reservoir where Suzie Palmer was attempting to drown her. If we'd left it to another team, they would have been too late. As it was, my partner had to resuscitate her."

Mayhew paused. Rob could hear her breathing down the line.

"If I wasn't in the bloody Lake District I'd come in and reprimand you in person," she fumed.

"Congratulate, don't you mean, ma'am? We managed to apprehend the suspect and save a life in the process."

There was a stony silence.

"Oh, and while I've got you on the phone, ma'am, I may as well tell you I'm planning to question the suspect in connection with the murders of Judith Walker and Noah Palmer."

"You can't be serious, Miller. On what grounds?"

"We have ample evidence, ma'am," he said. "Most of it is circumstantial, but we're hoping she'll crack."

"You do realise this is going to piss off the Deputy Commissioner," she said.

"That can't be helped. If she's guilty, then we have to charge her with the murders." He paused as the flicker of an idea he'd had before finally took shape. "Of course, if she's prosecuted, Raza Ashraf will be dragged into it by association."

More breathing.

Rob continued. "Suzie Palmer admitted to having an affair with Ashraf at the time of her husband's murder. At first, we thought they might have been in it together. In fact, we're still not convinced they weren't."

"For fuck's sake," she muttered. "Charlton's going to go ballistic."

Rob took a deep breath. "We could request a closed trial. The public doesn't need to know about Ashraf's involvement. If Suzie Palmer confesses, then he's off the hook. A closed trial would ensure his name wasn't mentioned in the press. In fact, we could put a gag order on the whole thing. No one need be any the wiser."

He could almost hear Mayhew's brain ticking over.

She sighed. "If you get a confession out of her, I'll speak to the Deputy Commissioner about a closed trial. I agree, we need to keep this from the press. I have no doubt that is what Ashraf would want."

"Very good, ma'am."

"I hope you know what you're doing, Miller," she said.

*So do I*, he thought, before he said goodbye. *So do I.*

\* \* \*

The second round of interviews took place close to midnight. Rob was conscious that the detainee was entitled to eight hours of uninterrupted sleep, and he wanted to have another crack at her while she was exhausted from the day's events.

This time he took Jenny with him. Suzie might need a bit of persuading.

The red light flashed to say the recording was on.

"Interview commencing at five past twelve," said Jenny. "Present are DCI Miller, DS Bird, Suzie Palmer and her solicitor, James Johnson."

"Right," said Rob, getting straight to it. "Mrs Palmer, I'd like you to explain why you hired a car on the afternoon of Wednesday the seventeenth of February."

She blinked. The long day had taken its toll. Pale skin, dark rings, bloodshot eyes. Her normally glossy dark hair was dull and matted from the reservoir water. The dark blue standard-issue tracksuit emphasised her pallor and swallowed her hands and ankles. It was like she was disappearing. A shadow of her former self.

"I didn't . . ."

He pushed a document across the table to her. "This is the rental agreement sent to us by Galaxy Car Hire in Shepherd's Bush on the day in question. You hired a blue Toyota Yaris, leaving your car in the Westfield Shopping Centre car park." He pushed a photograph over to her. "Here's your car, in the undercover car park."

There was no denying it was her car in the photograph.

Rob repeated the question. "Why did you hire the car?"

She glanced at her solicitor, who shook his head.

"No comment."

Rob sighed internally. They were going down this path, were they?

He pushed another photograph across the table. "This is the same blue Toyota Yaris on the A3 at 2.37 p.m. that day. Twenty minutes after you rented it. What were you doing on the A3 motorway, Mrs Palmer?"

"No comment."

In one respect, a no comment was good. It meant he was getting to her — and she had no rational explanation.

"Here you are again, driving up Grand Drive, in Raynes Park." He pushed two more photographs across to her. "These were taken on two separate CCTV cameras. See, the time is stamped on the top right corner. 14.43 and 14.45."

Suzie stared sulkily at the pictures.

"This only confirms she was in the area," the solicitor said, dabbing his brow.

"True, the area in which Judith Walker lived."

"I told you, I had nothing to do with that," Suzie snapped.

"Except your car was spotted less than a kilometre from her house on the afternoon of her murder. How do you explain that?"

"No comment."

"If you weren't there to kill her, what were you doing there?"

"No comment."

Rob leaned forward so he had Suzie's full attention. "There's something you don't know, Suzie. Judith Walker left a voice message on my phone the day before she was killed. She said she had something important to discuss regarding Noah Palmer's murder."

Suzie's blue eyes flickered to his face.

"When we investigated, we discovered Judith Walker was the family liaison officer assigned to you after your husband's death."

"So?"

"So here's what I think happened." Rob crossed his arms over his chest and fixed his gaze on her. "I think that Judith Walker found out something about you twelve years ago. Something you didn't want anyone to know. When the case was reopened, you went to her house to get rid of any notes or records she may have kept," said Rob.

"That's preposterous," exclaimed the solicitor. "Pure supposition."

"Maybe," admitted Rob. "Except only Dr Walker's laptop and mobile phone were stolen, along with some files from the cabinet in her study. Nothing else."

Her gaze flickered.

"That got us thinking . . . Why would someone be so concerned with destroying that evidence?" mused Rob. "And then we found our answer."

Suzie narrowed her eyes.

"In a stroke of luck, Judith Walker had sent DCI Sam Lawrence an unofficial email voicing her concerns. In this email, she said you lacked empathy, and that after observing you for some time, she came to the conclusion that you were incapable of that emotion. That you were suffering from some form of . . . How did she put it? Alexithymia. Psychopathy."

"That's nonsense," Suzie blurted out. "I was in shock, that's all."

"Dr Walker didn't think so," said Rob. "And she was trained to notice these things."

The solicitor turned to his client. "Suzie, if you had anything to do with this, I would strongly advise practising your right to silence."

She shut her mouth.

"I know none of this is hard evidence, although a team of forensic experts are searching your house as we speak."

She didn't react. Not even a flicker.

Rob's hopes sank. The electronics and files she'd stolen from Dr Walker's house weren't there.

"But I do think a jury will be very interested to hear about it. Don't you?" He asked the solicitor, who sat in stony silence.

Suzie refused to meet his gaze.

"Can you imagine what the press are going to make of all this at the trial?" he said. "They'll rake up Noah's love child again, bring your kids into it, make their lives a living hell."

Suzie went as white as a sheet.

*Bingo.* Rob knew how he was going to break her.

He sighed dramatically. "Oh well, it can't be helped. Even if you are proven innocent, the damage will be done. Nobody will want to associate with you or your family again. Your business will be ruined, your kids' friends will turn away from them. It'll be carnage."

"No, please . . ." She gripped the table in front of her. "You can't do that. It's not fair on the children."

Rob's phone buzzed. Perfect timing.

He glanced at Jenny, who gave a little nod. Time for her to take over.

"Excuse me." Rob pushed his chair back. "That's the search team at your house. I have to take this. I won't be a moment."

"DCI Rob Miller has left the room," Jenny stated for the tape. Then she turned to Suzie, who was holding herself and swaying back and forth in her chair.

"You know," Jenny said gently, "we could keep this out of the papers if you're willing to make a deal."

The solicitor jerked his head sharply towards DS Bird.

"No. Absolutely not. Suzie, don't even consider—"

Suzie held up a shaky hand. "What kind of deal?" she whispered.

Jenny pretended to think for a moment. "Well, we could request a closed trial. That means the press aren't allowed in. Nothing you or any witnesses say will get out. Your anonymity would be protected."

"What about my children?"

"They'll be safe," Jenny said. "Their peers will never know about your conviction. They'll be able to finish school without anyone knowing their mother was a murderer."

"This is utter rubbish." Johnson stomped his foot under the table. "Suzie, I hope you're not seriously considering this."

"Please, James," she said.

"It would mean you confessing to the murder of Noah Palmer and Judith Walker," continued Jenny. "We might even be able to issue a gag order on any information regarding Noah Palmer, including the lawsuit that Rachel Norton is filing." She leaned forward. "Under the circumstances, Mrs Palmer, I think that's the best you can hope for. We have your hired car on camera, we have you in the vicinity of Judith's house, we have her email from twelve years ago. DCI Miller was right, even if you're exonerated, the damage this will cause your family will be severe."

Suzie's lips began to tremble.

"Think of your children," Jenny urged. "Don't ruin their lives too."

Suzie's knuckles turned white, then she gave a little nod.

"Is that a yes?" said Jenny. "Could you speak up for the tape?"

"Yes," murmured Suzie. "I want to make a deal."

Her solicitor groaned and dropped his head back.

"You've made the right decision," said Jenny. "Please wait here while I get DCI Miller."

"We want it in writing first," the solicitor snapped. "Signed by the Deputy Commissioner. Without a signed document, my client says nothing."

Jenny smiled. "I'm sure we can arrange that."

When she walked into the squad room a short time later, the rest of the team burst into applause.

They'd done it. They'd got her.

## CHAPTER 47

Rob wanted to act fast, before her solicitor had a chance to talk her out of it. He rang Acting Superintendent Mayhew and told her Suzie Palmer wanted to confess.

She was astounded. "You mean she actually did it? She killed them both?"

"Yes, ma'am."

"Bloody hell."

A male voice in the background said, "What's going on, darling? Come back to bed."

Rob froze. He knew that voice. He'd heard it before, outside the police station.

*Fucking hell.* Was that why Hodge's marriage had fallen apart? Is that why *she'd* fallen apart?

A chill ran down his spine. Had Mayhew purposely seduced Hodge's husband to send the Super over the edge so she could take over her position at the major crime squad? Was she that cold and calculating?

"It's work," came her reply.

Rob told her about the deal he'd made with Suzie Walker and asked her to speak to the Crown Prosecutor about a closed trial and press injunction. Since it was in everybody's best interests that a gagging order be put in place, she agreed and said she'd call him back.

The wait was excruciating. If, for some reason, the injunction was rejected, the deal would fall through and they'd be back to square one.

"Ashraf will insist on it." Jenny tried to calm everybody's nerves. "He's a public figure. This would damage his career."

"The Deputy Commissioner will go along with anything Ashraf wants," added Mike, screwing up his nose. "He knows which side his bread is buttered."

Jeff agreed. "If he doesn't, he's likely to lose his job when Ashraf becomes mayor."

"Can you believe he's ahead in the polls?" murmured Jenny.

Rob shook his head.

They all jumped when the telephone rang.

Rob snatched it up on the first ring. "Miller."

He listened, then fist-pumped the air. The team gave a collective sigh of relief.

"Thank you, ma'am. That's great. I'll look out for it."

He grinned. "The Deputy Commissioner is going to email us a signed agreement in the next ten minutes."

As soon as it came through, Rob printed it out and took it down to Suzie Palmer's solicitor to look through. Tight-lipped, he read it over and gave a stiff nod. "All seems to be in order."

Suzie visibly relaxed. Her shoulders slumped and the pinched look at the bridge of her nose disappeared.

The interview recommenced.

"Let's start with Noah Palmer," Rob began after Jenny had restarted the recording. Will, Celeste, Mike and Jeff had crowded into the viewing room to watch the final showdown. No one wanted to miss a thing.

"Do you admit to killing your husband on the fifth of August 2009?"

"Yes." She gave a faint nod.

The solicitor's jaw tightened, and he shifted uncomfortably in his chair. This was one battle he hadn't won. A guilty client. A confession. The best he could do now was to make sure both parties stuck to their side of the deal.

"Will you talk us through it?" he asked.

Her expression remained neutral. Rob saw what Judith Walker meant when she'd said the woman was devoid of empathy. There wasn't an iota of remorse on her face.

"Things had been tense between us ever since our eldest was born. Noah shirked his responsibilities, preferring to go partying with his mates or out cycling. He couldn't admit his carefree life was over."

Rob could see how that might create tension.

"He became more and more distant, and I began to suspect he was having an affair. It was little things like spending more time at work, having to go in on weekends, secret text messages. It carried on for months. I didn't know with whom, but I knew it was serious. He used to tell me he was staying at his friend Greg's house, but I knew he was with her." Bitterness dripped from her tongue.

"One day I followed him to that council estate." She shuddered. "I saw him park and go inside. It was a dreadful place. Run-down and bare. I couldn't believe he'd rather be there than with us."

Clearly money wasn't everything to Noah.

"When he got home, I confronted him. We had a terrible fight. He said he wanted a divorce, that he was leaving me and the kids — for her!" She shook her head as if she still couldn't believe it. "That's when I decided to kill him."

Silence settled over the interrogation room. Even her solicitor was staring at her with dread.

"I couldn't let him leave us destitute," she said, by way of explanation. "I had the children to think about. Noah had money, he had powerful friends, there was no way he was going to award us a decent settlement."

"You would probably have got fifty per cent," said Jenny.

She scoffed. "Fifty per cent of what? Most of his accounts were offshore. He was a banker, remember. He knew how to hide money. No, I had no choice. He had to die."

"So you formulated a plan," Rob whispered.

She gave a tiny nod. "I knew I had to be careful. It couldn't be linked back to me, which meant it either had to be an accident or someone else had to take the blame."

"The Pentagram Killer," said Rob.

"Yes."

Her eyes glittered and Rob caught a glimpse at how unhinged she really was.

"I'd been following the murders in the papers. I mean, who hadn't? Wealthy, influential men brought to their knees. It was perfect." She almost smiled.

Jenny inhaled softly and met Rob's gaze. He held it for a second, then turned back to Suzie. She seemed to want to talk now, to get it off her chest after all these years. She'd been carrying the secret long enough.

"I picked the day. I knew he would come home early to go cycling. He was always on that bloody bike and there was a race that weekend. Earlier in the day, I drove the route of the race and picked an isolated spot. I took a rock from the area and brought it home with me in the boot of my car. I wore gloves, of course."

Rob nodded. No fingerprints had been discovered on the blood-soaked rock.

"I hid it in the garage and when he went downstairs to fetch his bike, I hit him with it."

"He collapsed straight away, but I hit him a few times to make sure." She looked surprised. "It was easier than I thought. I bundled him into the boot of the car and left him there."

"How did you know he was dead?" asked Rob.

"I felt for a pulse." She shook her head. "Nothing. I knew he was dead."

"What happened next?"

"I went outside and saw Mrs Jenkins, our nosy neighbour. I told her I'd just seen Noah off and we had a chat. Later, when I was making the children's tea, I saw her again. She was always peering through our windows. I purposely left the light on, so she'd see me."

All that time, Noah's body was in the boot of her car.

"When did you drive out to Box Hill?" asked Rob.

"Much later that night," she said. "I waited until the children were asleep, then I snuck out. I took a wheelbarrow with me, I'd even put it on the back seat of the car the day before, saying it needed to be fixed. Noah had no idea it was to transport his body from the car to the so-called crime scene."

Her solicitor stared at her, horrified.

Beside Rob, Jenny shuddered.

"Once I got him there, I laid him out like the pictures I'd seen in the paper. It wasn't hard. I even painted a circle around his body."

"How did you know which paint to use?" Rob asked. "That detail hadn't been released to the public."

She did smile then. Fondly. "I overheard Sam, I mean, DCI Lawrence mention it on the phone once. We had him and his wife over for dinner when he got a call. They'd identified the brand of paint." She shrugged. "It was a lucky coincidence."

She'd been smart to use that nugget of information. It was what had convinced everybody that Noah Palmer had been murdered by the serial killer terrorising the area and not somebody else.

He shook his head. "What then?"

She tilted her head. "I drove home and cleaned the car as best I could. I put the wheelbarrow back in the garden shed, then I rang Sam and told him Noah hadn't come home."

"You left your children by themselves?" gasped Jenny.

"They were asleep," she said, as if it were the most natural thing in the world to go out and dump a body, leaving three young children alone in the house. "I made sure of it. I gave them a little Piriton before bed. It knocked them out like a light."

Rob exhaled. Judith Walker had been right. This woman had no conscience. He thought of her sixteen-year-old daughter, Rebecca. Becca. The shy smile, the natural curiosity. *Do you think I could meet her?* She seemed normal and well-adjusted. It was a miracle the kids had turned out all right. "That's when DCI Lawrence came over?"

"Yes, he was a real sweetheart, and so concerned. He was the one who reported Noah missing and sent out the search team. He was there when they discovered Noah's body the next morning. He came round himself to tell me the news."

What would Lawrence say if he could hear Suzie now? See how easily he'd been taken in?

Suzie Palmer had fooled them all. Hadn't Will said it would have to have been an Oscar-winning performance? And it was.

Rob pushed on. "After you got the pay-out, you decided to get rid of your car, the one you'd used to transport Noah's body, and buy a new one."

She nodded. "I thought I'd better get rid of the evidence."

She'd thought of everything. Or maybe not.

"What did you do with the wheelbarrow?"

A pause. A glimmer of a smile. "It's in the garden. I upcycled it. Turned it into a wheelbarrow planter. It's barren now, of course, but it always looks fabulous in the summer when the petunias and lobelia come out."

There was a shocked pause.

He glanced at the mirror and gave a little nod. Will or Celeste would be on the phone to Forensics, requesting they bring in the wheelbarrow for analysis. Noah Palmer's DNA might still be on it. A blood stain, a stray hair, some skin particles. Damning evidence that would back up their case, should they need it.

"Let's move on to Judith Walker," Rob said.

Suzie bristled. "That woman was nothing but trouble. I didn't even want a family liaison, or whatever you call them. I just wanted to grieve in peace."

*Grieve, my arse*, thought Rob. According to Dr Walker, she hadn't spilled a tear. "She was assigned to you after Noah's death. Is that right?"

"Yes. It was awful. Constantly asking me if I was all right, probing into my business, confusing the children. They didn't know who this stranger was in our house or when their daddy was coming back."

"Did that upset you?" asked Rob.

"Yes, she was constantly in my face. I had no breathing space."

"I meant, weren't you upset the kids were asking when their daddy was coming back?"

"Oh. No, they were young. I knew they'd get over it. I lost my parents when I was five. I don't remember a thing about it."

That explained a lot. "How did your parents die?"

"Murder-suicide," she said. "My father caught my mother having an affair and killed her, then he shot himself."

*Jesus.* Rob stared at her for a long moment, as did Jenny. Neither knew what to say. Her solicitor was shaking his head.

Suzie sat calmly, unmoved by the story she'd just told. How had they missed this? How had Lawrence missed this?

"Was it you who found their bodies?" Rob whispered.

She nodded. "But like I said, I don't remember it."

"Where were you living at the time?" he asked.

"Norfolk," she replied. "After that, I was sent to my grandparents in Surrey. They raised me until I went to university."

"Did Judith Walker know this?"

"No, how could she have? I certainly didn't tell her. It was none of her business. It's nobody's business but my own."

It had clearly had a huge effect on her. It had effectively killed her ability to feel. Rob didn't know what made a person a psychopath, but losing one's parents so violently at such a young age couldn't have helped.

He was so stunned, he'd lost his train of thought. It was Jenny who got him back on track. "What made you decide to murder Judith Walker all these years later?" she asked.

"Now that I didn't plan," she admitted. "I bumped into her in Kingston town centre a week or so ago and she mentioned she'd read the article in the paper about Noah and his . . . whore. She asked if I was okay. I mean, why the hell should she care?"

"Because that's the type of woman she was," said Rob quietly.

Suzie shrugged it off. "Anyway, I knew then I was in trouble. With your lot prying into the case, I thought I'd better take precautions. Turns out I was right, eh? She called you and left that message on your phone. Sneaky bitch. She always had it in for me."

*Rightly so*, thought Rob. He felt a surge of anger towards Suzie for taking Dr Walker's life. By all accounts she had been a decent person. She didn't deserve to die like that.

"You tried to make it look like a burglary." He managed to keep his voice steady, even though he was simmering inside.

"Yes, although I didn't have to break in. I knocked and she answered. Stupid woman. She even invited me in. As soon as her back was turned, I hit her over the head."

"What did you use?" asked Rob.

"A hammer. I figured it would do the most damage."

Jenny cringed.

Her solicitor had his head in his hands.

Rob glared at her. "You hit her more than once."

"I wanted to be sure. Then I searched the office and took the file containing her sessions with me. They were all marked by year, it took no time at all to find them."

"And the laptop and phone?"

"Those were just a precaution. I didn't know if she'd made digital copies."

"Where are they now?" asked Rob.

"In my daughter's locker at her gym. I would have moved them before she went back, but she's been studying for exams, so I knew they would be safe there for a while."

"Name?" asked Rob.

"The Virgin Active in Chiswick."

Another glance at the mirror. Another silent message to his team. Her daughter's gym was not somewhere they would have thought to look.

"Then you ransacked the house."

"Yes, I thought if I made it look like a robbery, no one would think it was me."

"Except for the message on my phone," said Rob.

She sighed. "Yes, except for that."

It seemed Judith Walker had had the last laugh, so to speak. If it wasn't for the message, they might not have considered Suzie Palmer at all. They'd still be looking at Rudy Shaw or one of Dr Walker's other clients for the murder.

Too bad Suzie had got to her before he could, or he might have saved her.

## CHAPTER 48

Rob smiled at his team. They were all squished into the inci-dent room for an update. There was a jubilant atmosphere, a sense of accomplishment that always went with solving a case, particularly one as complicated as this one. Not even Acting Superintendent Mayhew's presence could dampen their mood.

To everyone's amusement, the new DCI had turned up, only to find both cases solved.

"Sorry to have wasted your time," said Rob, shaking his hand. DCI Linden was a stocky, salt-and-pepper-haired man in his mid-forties with lines of experience on his face. Probably not a bad cop, just not needed right now.

He shrugged. "Glad you got it sorted."

Rob was impressed he didn't moan more. He'd have spent most of the weekend reading up on the case files. All for nothing.

"Right." Rob faced the group. Even though they'd got a confession, the case didn't end here. They would have to ensure they had all the correct information, write, sign and document reports and prepare the case for trial, whenever that might be.

Suzie Palmer had been charged with both murders, in addition to the kidnapping and attempted murder of Rachel

Norton and would be moved to a women's prison until her trial.

"Thank you, everyone, for your hard work. I know most of you have been here during the weekend and overnight."

They nodded. Mayhew, who'd just got back from her romantic minibreak, didn't comment. DCI Linden hovered at the back. Having digested all the material, he was probably interested in the outcome.

"Will, tell us what you found?"

Will cleared his throat. "Judith Walker's laptop, phone and missing files were in Suzie Palmer's daughter's locker at the Virgin Active in Chiswick, just as she said. The technical team are taking a look at the electronics but so far, they haven't found any mention of Suzie or Noah Palmer on it. We've been given the files, but we'll have to look at them under sterile conditions so as not to damage any possible fingerprints or DNA."

Rob nodded. They had time to prepare. Suzie's confession meant she wasn't going anywhere.

"As per the deal we made with the offender," said Rob, "the court has issued a press injunction on the whole thing and agreed to a closed trial. This is mainly to protect Raza Ashraf, but it played nicely into our hands."

"Very clever to dangle that in front of her," remarked Mayhew from the back.

There were a few murmurs of agreement.

"Thank you, ma'am." Rob forced a smile. He still couldn't get over how she'd used Hodge's husband to get this position. He hadn't told anyone about it, and he wasn't sure he was going to. That knowledge might come in handy one day.

"Might I remind you all that the injunction includes us. Not a word to anyone about the case, not even your spouses." Mayhew fixed her eyes on Will, whose face flushed. He'd learned his lesson.

"A family liaison officer has been sent to Suzie Palmer's house to inform her children about what's happened," said Rob. "This is going to be tough for them."

"What will happen to them now?" asked Jenny.

"The eldest son is on his way back from university, but I believe Noah Palmer's parents are still alive and have offered to take care of the two youngest, Rebecca and Joey. They live in Sussex, which isn't too far away. I don't think they spent much time with their paternal grandparents, so it'll be good for them to get reacquainted."

"Probably better off than having a crazy psychopath for a mother," muttered Jeff.

Nobody disagreed there. To be fair, Suzie Palmer had done the best thing for her kids in the end. She'd given them anonymity and secured their future. At least they wouldn't have to live with the stigma of being known for having a convicted murderer for a parent.

"Rachel Norton has been discharged from hospital," Rob told them. "She's coming in later to give an official statement. Once again, I want to thank Will, Celeste, Jenny, Mike and Jeff who came in on Sunday and helped Jo and me track her down. She's alive because of us."

Rob ended the briefing shortly after that.

DCI Linden wanted a word, so they went down to the canteen and grabbed a cuppa while Rob brought him up to speed.

"Great detective work," Linden told him after he'd heard the full story. "I'm not sure why I was brought in when you had it all under control."

"It was a political decision," Rob told him, and explained about Ashraf and why the Deputy Commissioner had forced Hodge to drop the case.

"You've had a few leadership changes here recently, haven't you?" Linden remarked.

"Yeah. Chief Superintendent Lawrence left a hell of a gap. It's been hard filling his shoes. Superintendent Hodge couldn't crack it." *Thanks to Mayhew.* "And the jury's still out on this one."

"Changes can be unsettling."

"Are you sticking around?" Rob asked. He had a good feeling about this guy.

Linden shrugged. "Not sure there's space for another DCI, but I'll go wherever they send me."

Rob nodded.

Linden's phone beeped.

"I've been summoned. Got to get back to base." He shook Rob's hand. "Pleasure to meet you."

"Likewise. See you around."

Linden shrugged, as he headed for his car. "You never know."

# CHAPTER 49

*One month later*

Rachel sat in the police car outside the Palmers' house, her heart pounding.

"Are you sure about this?" Rob asked her.

She nodded. Ever since she'd found out about her half-siblings, she'd been desperate to meet them. They had the same father, after all.

When Rob had called and told her Rebecca Palmer had asked to see her, she couldn't believe it. She'd expected the rest of the family to have the same attitude towards her as their mother, but it seemed that wasn't true.

"Come on then." Rob got out of the car and opened the passenger door for her. She hesitated, then climbed out.

They walked up the path, but before they got to the front door, it swung open, and a fresh-faced young girl stood there. She had dark hair hanging down her back, a grungy look to her that Rachel liked and black nail polish.

"You're Rachel," she said. "I remember you."

Rachel nodded.

"I'm Rebecca. Come in. We've been expecting you."

Rachel glanced at Rob, who nodded encouragingly, so she followed her half-sister into the house. They went into the lounge, where Rachel skidded to a halt so suddenly Rob bumped into her.

So many people! And they were all staring at her.

She gulped, glad she'd worn her best jeans and put make-up on.

"Let me introduce you to the family," said Rebecca. Rachel was relieved to hear the tremor in her voice. She was nervous too.

"This is Nanna and Pops — Veronica and Peter — our grandparents on our father's side. They're going to be looking after me and Joey now that mum's—" Her face fell. "Well, you know?"

Rachel nodded.

"It's good to meet you, Rachel," said Veronica smiling. She had a kind face and crinkly eyes. Peter nodded a welcome. They were her grandparents, too.

"Hi, I'm Matt," said a deeper voice from behind her. She turned to see a handsome boy with ash-blonde hair and eyes the same hazel as her holding out his hand. She shook it, a tinge of excitement ran down her spine. This was her older half-brother.

"Rachel," she replied.

He nodded. "I know. It's good to finally meet you."

"This is Joey." Rebecca ruffled the younger boy's hair, also ash-blonde but with the watery-blue eyes of his mother.

Joey jerked away from her. "Becca, no." Then he grimaced at Rachel. "I hate it when she does that."

Rachel grinned. He reminded her of some of the younger boys who hung out around the estate. Sweet, but filled with testosterone and pent-up energy.

"Hi, Joey," she said.

"Would you like something to drink?" Rebecca asked. "Sure."

Veronica patted the seat next to her on the three-seater couch, so Rachel went over and sat. Rob remained by the door.

"Shall we call you Rachel, dear?" Veronica asked. "Or do you have a nickname you prefer?"

"Rachel's fine."

Veronica smiled. "Now, I believe you wanted to know about your father?"

Rachel nodded eagerly. More than anything. She could scarcely believe they were being so nice to her. Maybe they felt sorry for her, the poor relative. But when she studied their faces, their expressions seemed genuine. It was hard to believe that the horrible woman who'd tried to drown her was from the same family.

"Well, let's start at the beginning," Veronica said. "Noah was born . . ."

As she talked, Rachel listened with growing amazement. Her father seemed bright and fun-loving, just like her.

"I believe you're also good with numbers," Veronica said.

Rachel nodded. "Yes, I wondered where I'd got it from."

"Your father always wanted to go into finance," Veronica told her. "Do you know what it is you want to do when you grow up?"

"I want to be rich," she said. "I know that much."

They laughed politely. "With your brain, I'm sure you will be," said Veronica.

"I wish I was cleverer at maths." Rebecca handed her a can of Coke. "But I'm better at the arty subjects." She plonked herself down on the floor near Rachel's feet.

"I could help you, if you like," Rachel said.

Rebecca grinned. "That would be cool."

The detective's phone rang, and he went outside to answer it. Rachel stayed where she was. They talked some more, and as she relaxed, she realised that she felt complete. This was the other half of her family, her father's half. This was what she'd been missing her whole life.

Sadly, she'd never get to meet him, but at least with his family, she felt closer to him.

Tears welled up in her eyes.

"Are you all right, dear?" asked Veronica.

"Yes." She smiled, blinking them away. "I'm fine."

And she really was.

\* \* \*

Rob got home to find Jo in the spare room with a paint roller in her hand and a smudge of baby-blue paint on her cheek. He'd cleared out the furniture the previous weekend and put it in storage. When he'd left to fetch Rachel and take her to the Palmers' house, Jo had been going to the DIY store to buy paint.

"Still set on a boy?" he said.

She chuckled. "I just liked the colour." She put down the roller. "How'd it go?"

"Fine. I think she was a bit overwhelmed at first, but they welcomed her into the family. I'm not sure how often she'll see them since they're moving to Sussex, but at least they've got over that first hurdle."

Jo nodded. "It'll be easier now. I'm so pleased for Rachel."

"Me too. Bella hasn't plucked up the courage to meet them yet, but that'll come in time."

"I love a happy ending." Jo put her arms around his neck.

Rob held her close. "Me too, which is why I'm so glad you decided to move in."

"I'm keeping the apartment," she said. "We can rent it out for extra income."

"From what I've heard, we're going to need it," he said.

She arched an eyebrow. "I'm still toying with the idea of not going back to work."

"You risk losing your job if you don't," he said.

"I know, but somehow this feels more important."

He put a hand on her bump. "You know I'm behind you a hundred per cent," he whispered. "If you don't want to go back, then don't."

She gazed up at him. "I did have this other idea . . ."

He raised an eyebrow. "Oh, yes?"

"I thought I might consult for a while, you know, after the baby is old enough to go to nursery."

"Consult? A consulting detective? That sounds very swanky."

"Doesn't it?" she grinned. "I meant for law enforcement. There are lots of agencies who'd hire me."

"You're not wrong there." Her skills were in demand and she had a terrific track record. Catching the serial killer who'd murdered her sister had brought her national acclaim, even if her boss at the National Crime Agency hadn't liked the way she'd gone about it.

"Private companies would probably use you too."

"You mean I could be a private investigator?"

"Yeah, or a corporate investigator? Corporate espionage is a hot topic, and some companies don't like to go to the police."

"Very true." She pursed her lips.

He took advantage and kissed her. "I think your rebel spirit is well suited to consulting." He smoothed a hair behind her ear.

She smiled. "I agree. I'm quite excited about it." She patted her bump. "But that's in the future. Right now, we have to get this room painted. Oh, and the carpet's filthy, by the way. When did you last give the place a good vacuum?"

"I meant to," he said sheepishly, "but then this case exploded."

"You could use a cleaner," she said. "I'll be damned if I'm cleaning this whole house all the time just because I'm at home."

Rob grinned and pulled a card out of his wallet. "Actually, funny you should mention that . . ." He handed it over.

"Tanya Barkova," she read. "Who is she?"

"She was Judith Walker's cleaner," Rob explained. "Seems like a nice woman. Needs the work. We could give her a try."

Jo nodded. "Okay, I'll call her tomorrow."

Rob picked up the roller brush. "Come on, let me do the rest. It's time you took a break."

She eased herself into a wooden chair. Rob rolled up his sleeves and got to work.

"You know," she said watching him roll baby-blue paint onto the wall. "I think we're going to be just fine."

He grinned. "I know we are."

## THE END

# ACKNOWLEDGEMENTS

The list of people to thank gets longer the further into the Rob Miller series I get. There are so many people who have contributed to this series and its success.

My family, as always, for their patience, advice and inspiration. It's wonderful to have such a creative clan to turn to in moments of confusion. Scott, for his genius plot suggestions — some I incorporate, others I can't because they're just too out there. Tammy for her creative insights, Robyn for her understanding of human nature, Mum for tirelessly looking for typos and consistency errors, and Jack for his moments of brilliance, one of which was particularly relevant to this book.

I also need to thank the team at Joffe Books for their hard work and dedication. Jasper Joffe and Emma Grundy Haigh for their ongoing enthusiasm and encouragement, Cat Phipps for her incredible eye for detail, and without whom the book wouldn't be nearly as good, and Matthew Grundy Haigh for proofreading it. Laura Coulman for taking good care of me, Nina Kicul and Annie Rose for their tireless marketing and promotion, and Nebojsa Zorić for his brilliant, vibrant cover designs.

As always, my police advisor, Graham Bartlett, was instrumental in helping me sort out the intricacies of police procedure and making sure I didn't overstep the boundaries of what is possible.

Finally, I'd like to thank my dedicated readers who have followed me from the very beginning and may have waited longer than expected for this book. Thanks for your ongoing loyalty and support. Without you, I wouldn't be able to do this for a living.

**Thank you for reading this book.**

If you enjoyed it please leave feedback on Amazon or Goodreads, and if there is anything we missed or you have a question about, then please get in touch. We appreciate you choosing our book.

Founded in 2014 in Shoreditch, London, we at Joffe Books pride ourselves on our history of innovative publishing. We were thrilled to be shortlisted for Independent Publisher of the Year at the British Book Awards.
www.joffebooks.com

We're very grateful to eagle-eyed readers who take the time to contact us. Please send any errors you find to corrections@joffebooks.com. We'll get them fixed ASAP.